BETTER OFF DEAD

A Casey Jones Mystery

BY KATY MUNGER

ISBN-13: 978-1477572320
ISBN-10: 1477572325

DEDICATION

This book is dedicated with love
to Helen Berkey.

.

BOOKS BY KATY MUNGER

LEGWORK
OUT OF TIME
MONEY TO BURN
BAD TO THE BONE
BETTER OFF DEAD
BAD MOON ON THE RISE

ANGEL OF DARKNESS
ANGEL AMONG US

WRITING AS GALLAGHER GRAY

PARTNERS IN CRIME
A CAST OF KILLERS
DEATH OF A DREAM MAKER
A MOTIVE FOR MURDER

WRITING AS CHAZ MCGEE

DESOLATE ANGEL
ANGEL INTERRUPTED

Visit http://www.katymunger.com for more
information on the author and her books.

CHAPTER ONE

It was a dark day in Durham. Duke had just lost its sixth straight football game—the worst season opening anyone could remember. Worse yet, the disgrace had played out on regional television as the featured evening game.

My boyfriend Burly was jubilant.

"Yankee bastards!" he screamed at the television set, bouncing a crumpled beer can off the blue-painted face of a Duke fan in mourning.

"Watch it, Buster," I warned him. "That's my appliance you're abusing."

Burly ignored me. He was too busy wheeling toward the bedroom window. He liked to come in from the country and watch the Duke home games at my downtown Durham apartment, then sit by a window and shout anonymous insults at the students filing past, fresh from another defeat at Wallace Wade Stadium.

"Yankee college bastards," Burly yelled, his arms pumping like pistons as he raced toward the window. He didn't want to waste a moment of gloating.

"May I remind you that it was a 'Yankee college bastard' who built the ramp outside that lets you get your ass up and over the new steps?" I said.

"That guy is from Vermont," Burly replied. "He doesn't count."

Maybe he had a point. Vermont really was like a whole other country.

"Burly, you are going to get us shot one night." I spotted students heading our way and pulled the curtains shut.

"Are you kidding me?" he crowed. "Those Duke pansies don't carry guns. What are they going to do? Squirt me with ink from their fountain pens?" He bellowed out the window with all the subtlety of Ralph Kramden: "Suck my ass, Duke University!"

Burly is not really the Neanderthal he appears to be after a six-pack of Bud and a Duke defeat. He just hates anyone who has the money to attend a college that has ivy either on its campus or as part of its reputation. Duke had both. Its pretensions were evident in its self-proclaimed status as the "Ivy League of the South." This did not sit well with the many other Southern colleges nearby. Was Duke not content with being a mere university? Did it have to go around claiming to be an entire league? Jeepers. Most Southerners felt that bragging about your pedigree was a sure sign you were hanging by your fingertips from the wrong branch of the family tree.

"Eat dookie, you Duke Blue Goobers," Burly screamed in a burst of maturity. He laughed as shouts broke out from a group of Duke students across the street.

"Who said that?" a male voice yelled back.

"Your mother!" Burly screamed out the window, laughing hysterically.

Maybe if I'd had fourteen more beers, I would have laughed along.

Instead I turned off the bedroom lights, just in case.

Burly began to howl like a wolf—a reference to the victors who were returning in glory to nearby N.C. State University.

I shook my head and went back into the living room to pick up the crumpled beer cans left in Burly's wake. For a guy in a wheelchair, he sure can cover a lot of ground when it comes to littering.

The doorbell rang.

Crap. I was not in the mood for a rumble. Burly never hesitated to jump into the fray, paralyzed legs or not. And most people in a similar state of non-sobriety did not hesitate to beat the shit out of him in return, one having gone so far as to ask his buddy to prop Burly up so he could have a better shot at his face. Once that testosterone starts pumping, I've found it's every man for himself.

The doorbell rang again.

"Burly," I warned him. "I'm gonna be real pissed off if—"

"Maybe they'll refund your forty thousand!" he screamed out the window, ignoring me. "You can use it to go to mechanic's school."

The doorbell rang again, insistently. I answered it, fully prepared to lead with my right.

It was not what I expected. At all.

A tallish woman stood in the hallway, swathed from head to toe in the veils and flowing robes of a practicing Muslim. Only her dark eyes and the upper half of her nose showed above the pale orange scarf masking her face.

"Are you Missus Jones?" she asked in an accent I was pretty sure was Turkish. It was not the first time I had heard one. North Carolina was becoming a regular United Nations. As a devotee of restaurants that serve something beyond barbecue, I applauded the change.

"Yes?" I said warily.

"You must help my friend," she said. Her dark eyes filled with tears. "She is a prisoner and needs your help."

It took a moment for the words to sink in. Miss Turkey stared at me, waiting, a bit dumbstruck, I suppose, by my size— which is large for a woman—and my attire, which is not. I was wearing my traditional home-at-night-with-Burly fare: a sheer black teddy and matching see-through robe. I wore pink marabou mules on my feet. Hey, what was I supposed to be wearing? A cheerleading outfit? Hmmm... maybe next time.

"Want to come in and tell me about it?" I finally said to the woman. Would you have turned her away? It's not every night Scheherazade shows up on your doorstep. Besides, my job is helping people. And curiosity keeps me doing my job.

"How did you know where I live?" I asked as she sat tentatively on the edge of my worn pink sofa. I had rescued it from a curbside dump just minutes before the garbage truck arrived. With pastel satin pillows, it looked pretty good—in a Miami whorehouse sort of way.

"Your employer tell me where you live," she explained slowly. "He very big and very wet."

"I'll say," I agreed, though what she had probably meant was a more literal interpretation of "wet" than what I had in mind. Our office roof had recently sprung a bigger leak than the West Wing of the White House. With the heaviest rainfall on record for an autumn in North Carolina ever, our carpet had been soaked for a solid month with no sign yet of the landlord. Bilge water had started to collect and we now had the beginnings of a baby pool at our feet. Bobby D. had taken to wearing hip-high waders to work and storing his ever-present Little Debbie cakes in the tops of them. I could only imagine what this poor woman had thought when he had reached inside his rubber britches and fished around for a snack.

"You met Bobby D.?" I asked, studying her eyes.

To my surprise, they sparkled. "Oh, yes. Very big heart," she said.

"Very big everything," I added.

"He say you will help me. He say it right up your street."

"Alley," I corrected her. "Bobby said that, did he?"

She nodded vigorously. "He give me your address and say you work out of home because of the water."

That was one of the reasons I worked from home, I thought. After too many years in partnership with him, Bobby was starting to get on my nerves. His innate inertia, always annoying, had grown even worse in recent months, thanks to his doctor's warnings to take it easy on his overloaded heart. Plus, he had found true bliss with a woman just his size, oops, I mean type, and kept harping on me to do the same. Is there anything on this planet more annoying than a person who has discovered domestic bliss and wants the rest of the world to imitate their decision to settle? I think not. Well, maybe natural blonds.

"Could you excuse me just a moment?" I asked as yet another obscene bellow from Burly was followed by the unmistakable sound of a beer bottle crashing against my building's brick facade.

The woman nodded, eyes wide, as I marched into the bedroom to issue my traditional post-Duke defeat ultimatum. "Open your mouth again and I'll break both your legs."

"Go ahead," Burly invited me. "I won't feel a thing."

"Okay then, try this: open your mouth again and I'll puncture every tire on your brand new customized Voyager," I threatened.

That shut him up.

"I have a client in the other room. It would help my credibility if my apartment did not sound like an insane asylum."

"I'm just trying to have some fun." He pouted.

I pointed toward the bed. "Get in there and wait for me. Then you'll have your fun."

He let out a war whoop and did a wheelie as he turned from the window. Do I know how to handle my guy, or what?

I called Bobby D. on the way back to the living room. He answered with his usual idiocy: "Acme Investigations. Robert Dodd, owner and proprietor, speaking."

"What is this woman doing at my home?" I asked without preamble.

"Talk to her," he ordered me. "You'll thank me next time we speak." He hung up without another word. Probably in the middle of a meal or something.

"Okay," I told my guest as I sat down beside her on the sofa. "Tell me about your friend."

Her English was rusty, but her compassion was certainly up to speed. From what I could glean, the Turkish babe in front of me was about to quit her job cleaning house for some woman who was afraid to leave her home. "My neighbor tell me she must be angoraphobic," the girl explained.

I doubted the prisoner-in-her-own-home was allergic to sweaters, and decided she meant "agoraphobic," as in a fear of open spaces. "Why does she want my help?" I asked. "I'm not a shrink. I'm a private investigator."

The woman's eyes looked puzzled.

5

"You know?" I prompted her. "Like Columbo on TV." Only I had a better-looking raincoat, of course.

Her dark eyes blazed. "I know what you are. That's why I am here. She is in danger. In the mail. On telephone. Ugly voices." She leaned forward and I caught a glimpse of a slender nose beneath the veil. "Man on the telephone say he kill her again and again." She made a slashing gesture with one hand. Her robes fluttered like prayer flags in the wind. "I hear his voice and I believe him."

"Is that why you're quitting your job?"

She told me she was leaving her job at her husband's urging, but felt guilty at abandoning her employer. "I leave also because the old lady make me cuckoo-cuckoo," the woman explained, smoothing her robe over her knees. "She is evil."

"How old is this woman?" I asked. Why would someone threaten to murder a little old lady? Little old ladies were supposed to solve crimes, not be victims of them.

"No, no, my employer is young," my visitor explained. "She your age. My age. Is her evil mother driving me cuckoo-cuckoo."

Oh, god. The poor woman really was a prisoner in her own home. Trapped, living with her mother at my age?

"Okay," I agreed. "I'll go see her. I'll see if she wants my help."

"Good person!" the woman cried, leaping to her feet. She pressed my right hand between her own far more slender palms. She'd left a piece of paper in my hand: a name and address.

"You're the good person, not me," I corrected her as I tucked the paper into a corner of my hallway mirror. "You cared enough to come here in the first place."

We were interrupted in our "I'm Okay, You're Okay" congratulatory session by frantic honking outside my apartment house.

"My husband," the woman cried, just as Burly shouted a warning from the bedroom.

"Trouble!" he called in gleeful triumph.

"Stay here," I warned as I threw my raincoat over my negligee and raced outside. The Turkish woman made mewing sounds of distress right behind me.

A group of drunken Duke students had surrounded a battered Chevy parked at the curb in front of my building. The driver was a small man with a heavy black mustache. He was crouched low behind the steering wheel, his eyes darting from one student to the next.

"Break it up," I ordered, grabbing a shoulder and shoving one student out of the way.

"This guy started it," another kid complained in a New York whine. "He's been shouting shit at us." The others nodded their agreement.

"Are you out of your mind?" I asked him. The ringleader was gangly with dark hair. He was staring open-mouthed at the wide gap that had opened in my raincoat. I guess he had never witnessed the glory of a Southern belle in full bloom before.

"This guy can hardly speak English," I said, gesturing toward the driver. "He's not the one screaming at you. Use your freakin' head."

Burly, always helpful, chose that moment to prove I was telling the truth. "Duke sucks!" he bellowed out my bedroom window. His voice cut through the crowd's outrage like a bullhorn. "Duke sucks my Southern ass!"

The pack of students stampeded toward my bedroom window, crushing the pansies my poor landlady had planted in an attempt to wring more rent from my yuppie neighbors.

"Go now," I urged the Turkish couple. "I'll visit your friend in the morning, I promise."

The woman scrambled into the front seat as her husband gunned the engine nervously.

"Crazy Americans!" he shouted out the window, shooting the crowd an enthusiastic middle finger. How nice. Already he was picking up quaint American customs. He'd be a road rage enthusiast soon.

"It's just football... fever," I explained into the cloud of exhaust that the Chevy left behind as it screeched from the curb.

I have bars on my ground-floor bedroom windows to discourage unwanted intruders. And it's a good thing, too. Within seconds Duke students were clinging from them like drunken Spidermen, banging their bodies futilely against the metal while Burly taunted them with insults from inside the safety of my apartment.

Sirens approached from a few blocks away—I was within spitting distance of police headquarters and some neighbor had finally had enough.

My only consolation in the entire debacle that ensued was that one of the responding officers turned out to be a good-looking Hispanic guy dressed in a very nice suit. I had never seen him before. He was cuter than a June bug, in a Mormon-missionary-meets-Andy-Garcia sort of way. "Are you going to frisk me?" I asked hopefully.

"Take a hike, Casey," his cop buddy answered for him. "Go pick on someone your own speed. Angel here is taken."

"Thanks for the warning, Charlie," I said. "But you know what they say about angels—when you're up that high, there's always room to fall."

The Angel in question hid a very nice smile as I buttoned up and shivered my way back inside. I'd let the Duke students sort out their own mess: Burly had grown as quiet as a church mouse once the cops arrived, and no one was believing a word the pack of inebriated students said. Especially since Burly had long ago perfected the art of looking pitiful. He'd loll his head back, stick his tongue out a little and tremble. It worked every time. How could that poor, afflicted man in a wheelchair have done anything wrong?

"Are you behind this mess?" Charlie the cop called after me. He threw a student over the hood of his patrol car so he could pat the kid's pockets down.

"You're just mad because I wouldn't go out with you," I yelled as I slammed the front door shut securely between me and the law.

I didn't add that Charlie was about the only single male on the Durham police force I'd never dated. Not having the opportunity

to see me out of my black teddy and pink marabou mules
seemed punishment enough.

Burly was contrite the next morning—aren't they always?—
and I managed to leverage his guilt into homemade waffles for
breakfast before I set out to meet my possible new client. Her
name was Helen Pugh, and she lived way out on Turkey Run
Road where the subdivisions that border the outskirts of
Durham and Chapel Hill finally run out, leaving a stretch of
small farms and older clapboard houses. It was a beautiful,
rolling patch of countryside, especially in early autumn. The
hardwoods had barely started to turn, feed corn still swayed in
the fields and the grass was even greener than it had been in the
wilting heat of August. I rolled my car windows down and
savored the clean air, letting the wind blow my hair back as I
thought about where I was headed.

For all I knew, Helen Pugh wanted nothing to do with me.
But I'd made a promise to her cleaning lady, and I would keep
that promise.

Besides, there might be a good fee in it. The Pugh farm was
definitely old money. It had to be. You never saw that kind of
sprawling wooden structure anymore. A large, two-story main
house branched out into three different one-story wings that
meandered leisurely over a landscaped yard, while the outer
buildings nestled into the nearby hills as if shelter and wilderness
had coexisted there forever. Huge apple, oak and pecan trees
shadowed the main house. A small forest obscured the land on
either side of the sloping front lawn, but a dirt road wound
through the thick trees back into the darkness. From the curve of
the sloping hills, I was pretty sure a pond waited at the end of the
road.

I stopped the car to stare. I'd grown up in a ramshackle hovel
on the edges of a tough piece of land that was more leather than
soil. In my dreams as a child, a place like this had been paradise.
God, how my grandpa would love it.

I parked next to a blue Volvo with a front windshield so
coated by pollen that it was obvious the car had not been driven

in months. Paradise, it seemed, was little more than a rustic-looking prison for Helen Pugh.

I rang the front doorbell and waited on the porch, wondering who took care of the grounds if the owner was housebound. Someone did. That was obvious. The apples and pecans had been neatly harvested and the grass was meticulously cut. Strategically placed plumes of sawgrass alternated with crescent-shaped marigold patches for nearly half an acre on either side of the house.

No one answered the door. I rang again and waited.

Someone was on the other side, I finally realized, waiting as I was waiting. It had to be Helen Pugh. I could hear her breathing on the other side of the door. "Hello?" I asked, conscious that my breathing had adapted to hers. We inhaled and exhaled together. Her fear seemed to seep through the keyhole, leaking from the darkened exterior of the house into the bright, sun-filled October day, as tainted as an obscene gesture in church.

"Your friend sent me," I said, reading the unfamiliar name off the piece of paper I held. "Fadime Yarar-something." I stumbled over the syllables. "She said that you were being threatened. I'm here to help."

"Fadime sent you?" the woman asked.

"Yes. She's very concerned."

There was a short silence. "I didn't know she cared that much," the woman finally said. "Will she come back to work for me?"

"That I don't know. But, look, I'm not here to help you get your cleaning lady back. There's a limit to what even the best P.I. can do. I'm here to ask you about the man on the phone who seems to want to kill you. Again and again, according to Fadime."

"Fadime is a good person." Her voice was soft.

"Yes. But that guy on the phone? Well, he sounds like trouble. Why don't you let me in and we can talk about it."

The bolt was drawn back slowly, the metal cylinder rasping as it slid open. This process was repeated twice more. There were more bolts on that door than on Frankenstein's forehead. Finally the door opened maybe an inch. I could not see inside.

"Here." I held my P.I. license to the crack and waited. It looked real enough to have fooled everyone else in North Carolina for the past twelve years. I figured it would hold up for another day.

After a moment, the door finally opened, still with no one in sight, as if it operated under its own power.

I stepped inside, instincts on edge, eyes fighting to adjust to the sudden darkness. How much did I really know about what I was getting into?

When the door slammed shut behind me, my reflexes went into overdrive. I whirled around and damn near pulled my gun on a slender woman standing behind me in the space between the doorway and wall. She was literally cowering in the shadows. One hand rested at the base of her throat, the other clutched a sweater tightly around her middle.

As my eyes adjusted to the darkness, I could see that she was wearing a blouse and slacks. She was tall and gaunt, with shoulder-length brown hair that framed a sharp, unhappy face. I wondered who cut her hair if she never went outside. Because if hairdressers were doing house calls these days...

"I'm Helen Pugh," the woman said in a soft, Southern, well-educated voice. Fear trembled beneath each syllable. "Fadime sent you?" she asked again.

"Yes." I looked at her more closely. "Are you okay? You look pale."

"I need water." She brushed past me. I followed without being invited. She led me into a spacious kitchen with a black-and-white tile floor. Sunlight streamed through huge windows lining two of the walls. It was a beautiful room, one that should have been filled with shrieking children and the clatter of noisy dinners. Instead, every surface was scrubbed free of life. Hardly an item marred the endless counters stretching from corner to corner. It was as impersonal as a mental ward rec room.

Helen Pugh walked to a cabinet, removed an old-fashioned crystal jelly glass and filled it with water from the tap. She kept her back turned as she sipped the water steadily until half the glass was gone. Then she stood, staring at the sink, as if she had forgotten me completely. Her shoulders moved up and down in a careful rhythm. Breathing exercises, I thought, to help her over a panic attack.

"Miss Pugh," I asked softly, "is this a good time for you?" Jesus, what an idiotic question. This woman obviously never had a good time. I waited by a huge kitchen table, wondering whether to sit down or not.

She finally turned to me and stared. The sun streaming in the huge windows caught the highlights in her hair, causing each strand to shimmer. She was actually quite beautiful, I realized, and only in her early thirties, though she had seemed much older at first. Her fearful demeanor had diminished her to a frailer, far older woman.

"Please sit down," she said. "If you're here, we may as well talk." She glanced at me furtively. "I don't want to be this way, you know."

She removed her hand from her throat to pull a chair out from the kitchen table and her sweater fell open. A red welt encircled the base of her throat. It was a band of pink scar tissue that gleamed with that rubbery glow new skin gets. Whatever had happened to this woman, it had extended well beyond threats.

Outside, the sound of a lawn mower buzzed in the distance. Every now and then, a car whooshed past on the road. These were the only signs of the outside world in Helen Pugh's life, I realized. She waited silently, gathering her courage to begin, a prisoner inside this sunny, sterile kitchen.

"Where should I start?" she asked, clutching her sweater once again to hide her scars.

"How about at the beginning?" I suggested. "Start with what happened to your throat."

She fixed her eyes on an antique milk jug perched atop the refrigerator. "You don't know, then," she said.

"Know what?" I asked.

"My married name was Helen McInnes."

"Jesus," I said. "You're her."

"That's me." She paused. "My marriage didn't last out the... trial. I've gone back to my maiden name."

Everyone in Durham knew who Helen McInnes was. She had accused a Duke University professor of rape a couple years ago. The details of the attack were horrific and recounted in loving detail by the press as the trial unfolded: Helen McInnes was attacked while walking alone in a remote part of Duke Gardens one July evening, she claimed, by a man who had overpowered her from behind, taping her eyes shut with duct tape and rendering her unconscious with an aerosol drug. When she came to, she was bound and gagged. He had apparently dragged her into an empty patch of woods and blinded her further with a black hood tied over her head. Then he had twisted a scarf around her neck and repeatedly raped her for the next two hours. She had been alternately strangled to near-death and penetrated by a man strong enough to prop her up against a tree, sling her across a boulder and arrange her in other postures until he was satisfied. She swore she had heard a series of clicks and whirrs made by a Polaroid camera throughout the attack. No photos had ever been found. Which meant that these photos were floating around out there somewhere, a fact that would have kept me inside my house for the rest of my life without any further encouragement.

When he was done with her, the rapist had dumped her facedown in a holding pond in the Gardens, sure she would quickly drown. Instead, a med student returning home late from the nearby medical library had heard a loud splash and been bored enough to investigate. He discovered Helen McInnes thrashing around in two feet of muddy water, still bound and gagged. He was able to drag her from the pond in time to save her.

The student became a hero. Helen McInnes became a pariah.

Especially after she accused a professor specializing in aberrant psychology of having committed the crime. David Brookhouse was acquitted in a rapid and highly publicized trial. But the story didn't end there. Not content with having been found innocent, he had recently filed a multimillion-dollar civil suit against his accuser, claiming Helen McInnes had falsely implicated him in retaliation for his having ended an affair between the two of them. It had yet to come to trial, but I knew it was scheduled to soon.

Revenge for an ended affair was the same defense Brookhouse had used successfully during the criminal trial. Only then Helen's name had been kept out of the papers as a victim of rape. The same courtesy did not extend once she was named plaintiff in the civil suit. Over the last six months, she had become an unseen lightning rod for the town, with women's rights advocates raising hell over her predicament and many ardent Duke supporters accusing her of trying to tear down an honorable man.

What had been forgotten in the ensuing months-long media debate was that Helen McInnes had been undeniably raped by someone. She had disappeared from sight, ceased to give statements, and was never in court when her lawyer appeared to answer preliminary motions pertaining to the civil trial.

No one had missed her. Including me. Until I sat down across from her and stared at the welt around her throat.

"A lot of people think you got a raw deal," I told her, remembering the flamboyant lawyer that David Brookhouse had brought in from Atlanta to defend him against the rape charges. The whole experience had turned into the proverbial media circus, and as much as I hated to admit it, the down-home trial judge had not been prepared for the maneuverings of a media-savvy defense attorney. A lot of things had gone wrong at Helen McInnes's trial, most of them unnoticed until David Brookhouse walked out a free man, outraged at having had his reputation smeared. The district attorney had chosen not to appeal: she had been slaughtered by a worthier opponent and was anxious to put the experience behind her, before the defeat infected all of her pending acquaintance rape cases.

The prosecutor was probably not the only person anxious to put the experience behind her. Only now it appeared, from the threatening letters and phone calls, that someone was not willing to let Helen McInnes forgive and forget.

"I remember a lot about that trial," I told her, when she did not respond. "A lot of women around here do. At first he claimed you had staged the whole thing, didn't he?"

She nodded, then spoke so softly I could hardly hear her words. "Until someone pointed out how unlikely it was I'd been able to duct tape my eyes and mouth and then tie my own hands tightly behind my back. Not to mention how lucky I was someone walked past to save me." She stared down at the table top, as if it were the surface of a pond and held some mystery beneath its surface.

"Then he conceded you had been raped," I said, "Right? But claimed it had not been him. He said you were angry because you'd had an affair and he had dumped you and that's why you were blaming him."

She nodded. "That's right." I could barely hear her words. "I had to testify. I didn't want to." She looked around the room. "Already I was having trouble going to new places. Appearing in public. But there was no DNA. I had no choice."

I remembered that, too: the lack of DNA had hurt the prosecutor's case severely. With DNA-typing relatively new, it was still perceived as a magic bullet in the mind of juries. The fact that a rapist might wear a condom—and that pond water might wash away external evidence—did not occur to the twelve good people who were accustomed to one-hour episodes of intrigue that ended with the discovery of a crucial dab of DNA.

No one seriously disputed that Helen McInnes had been raped—two broken ribs, severe contusions, the damage done to her throat plus internal injuries that required reconstructive surgery tended to put a damper on those doubts. But enough people disagreed that David Brookhouse had done it to her to send him packing, a free man now free to sue.

"It was the cross-examination that did it," I remembered.

She nodded. Her voice fell to a whisper. "I told the prosecutor what would happen, that we'd had an affair. But she said that I was being ridiculous, that courts weren't like that anymore, that this was a new decade and women were protected from becoming the accused."

"Except women with the bad luck to have slept with their rapists before the rape," I said. "I guess she forgot that part."

Helen was struggling to finish her story. She wanted to get it over with. "I wasn't going to lie. We'd had an affair. But I had been the one to end it, not him. And I had ended it months before the attack. He seemed fine with it. That's why I was so... shocked when I recognized his voice during the attack and realized it was him."

"Is that why your marriage broke up?" I asked.

She nodded. "I had to tell my husband in advance what was going to happen if I got on the stand. So I warned him the day before. He didn't know about the affair until then." For the first time she looked me in the eye. "He went out later that night to buy a pack of cigarettes and I haven't seen him since."

And people wonder why I've never remarried.

"That Atlanta lawyer got pretty rough with you during the cross-examination," I said. I remembered what a Durham detective had told me: "shredded her," was how he put it. "Annihilated her, destroyed her, made her sound like a vindictive slut. Let's hope this shyster lawyer goes back to Atlanta soon." My detective friend, like quite a few people on the force, was inclined to believe that David Brookhouse had been guilty.

"How long was the affair with Brookhouse?" I asked, curious to know what she had paid so heavy a price for.

"It only lasted a few months. But it was long enough for me to..." She hesitated. "... to know that he was the one who attacked me."

"What do you mean?"

She looked away. "It sounds crazy now, but I was positive at the time."

"He did something while he was raping you that made you think it was him? Something besides his voice?"

She nodded. "It was the way he... moved me around." She flushed a deep red, still ashamed. "The way he would roughly turn me over. He had... done that to me before." She exhaled. "It was one reason I broke it off with him. He wanted to try a lot of stuff I just wasn't into. That... and my husband. My husband at the time."

"Did the rapist speak much?" I asked.

She nodded. "Yes. To call me... names. Horrible things. I don't really want to repeat what he said."

"Fair enough. I don't really want to hear them. But you did recognize his voice?"

She nodded. "He was trying to disguise it, but I could tell it was him. And when he laughed, I knew it was him. He has this sort of high-pitched laugh." She gnawed at her lip. "It's hideous, really. The first time I heard it was when we went to the movies and he laughed at this scene where a dog jumps out the window. It was funny, but the way he laughed was horrible. People turned to stare. It was so... cruel. And strange. It sounds silly now. It's not silly, though. It's an awful sound. And the man who raped me made the same sound."

"And you said all this in court?"

She nodded, "It didn't do any good. His lawyer made me sound insane on cross-examination, like I was hearing things all the time, like the rape had destroyed my mind." She ran a hand through her hair. "Maybe it has."

I stared out the window at the beautifully landscaped yard. "How long since you've been outside the house?"

"Thirteen months and three days," she answered promptly.

"And you've tried?"

She nodded. "When I go out onto the porch, I can't breathe. It's not imaginary. It's real. I could barely get back into the house last time I tried."

"When was that?"

"Monday morning." She stared at her trembling hands. "I try every Monday morning. Hoping, I guess, that the feeling has gone away."

I was impressed. She had courage. To have withstood the trial and, now, to face her demons every week like that, not to give up on trying to beat them—it took guts. I wanted to help her. Maybe all she needed was a little help.

"What did your cleaning lady mean when she talked about terrible phone calls and letters?"

She winced.

"You didn't save them?"

"No, I have them. I even kept some of the phone messages on tape. It's just that... I can't."

"You don't have to look at the letters or listen to the tapes," I told her. "But let me take a look. I want to know if you're in any real danger."

Without a word she rose and led me into the living room. It was furnished with a floral-patterned couch and matching armchairs. A thick area rug and large pillows scattered around the hearth added to the welcoming air. Yet the whole room looked brand-new, as if no one ever sat in it.

There was a desk in one corner of the room. Helen unlocked a side drawer filled with stuffed white envelopes, the cheap kind sold in every 7-Eleven from here to Alaska. The postmarks were all local and ranged in date from just after the rape trial had ended to a few days ago. An old cigar box in the bottom of the drawer held a collection of microcassettes as well as a small tape recorder. I sat down and began to go through the letters, opening up each one and reading the contents.

They looked so innocuous. No cut-out letters pasted together. No torn magazine photos or psychopathic scrawls. No weird symbols or satanic drawings. Each letter consisted of nothing more than one simple paragraph, computer-printed in the center of the page, using a universal typeface.

The first letter read: "Nothing will ever erase the fact that you liked it. I felt you responding beneath me. I could feel your excitement. I am counting the days until we can do it again."

The second one read: "I saw you today on Ninth Street buying a book. I never knew you liked art history. Your hair was up and you wore a white sweater buttoned to the neck. Why are you hiding your scar? That scar is a symbol of our love."

The next one was worse: "Your days of hoping are over. Soon I will visit you again. Maybe at your home this time. I followed you there. Apple trees are lovely, aren't they? I would like to take you beneath the apple tree, maybe tie you to the trunk first for old time's sake. Prop you up the way you like it. Give you what you want once again. Before I take what is mine."

The rest of the letters grew progressively more threatening. He was watching her, that much was clear. No wonder she never left her house.

"Helen," I called out into the quiet. No one answered.

I found her perched on a counter in the kitchen, a cup of coffee in hand. She was staring out the window, watching two squirrels chase each other up the trunk of a beech tree.

"Helen?" I said again. She turned to me. "Did you tell the police about these letters?"

Her eyes flickered. "Why would I?" she asked. I couldn't blame her. It hadn't done much good the last time she went to the cops.

I returned to the living room and listened to a few of the tapes. They were worse than the letters. The voice was muffled, sometimes altered with a whisper or phony accent, even, at times, disguised by an electronic device. He kept the messages short but sweet: "That pink nightgown looks delicious on you." "Would you like wrist scars to match your neck?" "Thinking of you. And the rock." Oh, yes—the rock. The rock where she had been repeatedly raped.

I'd heard and read enough. Whoever was sending these threats knew Helen and knew what would frighten her. He was fucking with her head big time—and that's what made me think it was David Brookhouse. I would need help protecting her.

"Where's the telephone?" I asked Helen when I found her in a small interior room, staring at a painting of spring flowers.

"By the door," she whispered.

"Which door?" I asked, then stopped as I spotted a wall telephone mounted near the door that led to the hallway. An odd place to have a phone, I thought.

I walked into the next room for privacy and saw another telephone, this one also mounted near the hall door. I continued on my search, the realization hitting me. She had a telephone in the kitchen, the drawing room, near the front door and in both downstairs bedrooms. There was even a telephone mounted in the bathroom, next to the toilet.

That struck me as saddest of all.

So many telephones for a woman unable to ask for help. Yet it was her only stand against evil, her only attempt to protect herself. Unable to bring herself to do anything else, she had invited the outside in for one day to install useless telephones everywhere. Just in case of what? I wondered who she was planning to call to save her if she no longer trusted the police.

I used the phone in the bathroom to call Bobby D.

"What's shaking?" I asked him.

"Nothing's shaking," he answered sourly. "We're all too busy swimming." I heard a sloshing in the background.

"What was that?" I asked.

"My leg. The office is going under. I feel like I'm on the Titanic."

"Still can't find Rosy?" I said, asking after the landlord.

"We're never gonna find that dame again. It's women and children first." He stopped to take a bite of something, I knew, as food was never far from Bobby's reach. "What's up?" he asked, mouth full.

"Clear the decks," I told him. "I need you."

"Oh, baby. Your place or mine?" He said this halfheartedly, his auto-pilot lascivious instincts kicking in. In truth, Bobby was too scared to ever really proposition me. He liked his women older—and a lot more grateful than I was likely to be.

"Neither. I'll let you know where to meet me later today."

I hung up and went to find the woman who, whether she liked it or not, was my newest client. "Helen?" I called out loudly. She was still in front of the painting. "Why don't you call the police now? Before something happens? What will all these telephones do for you if he..." I hesitated. "... if he gets inside?"

She was silent.

"Are you afraid the cops would want you to come downtown?" I asked. She glanced at me briefly and nodded. "And that they wouldn't believe you?" She nodded again.

Abruptly, she walked to the base of the steps that led to the second floor. "David Brookhouse has filed a two-million-dollar civil suit against me," she said. "That's a lot of motives to make up these letters and threats, don't you think?"

"I believe it's him," I told her. "I always have."

Without warning, she yelled up the steps in a voice so loud I was astonished: "Mother," she bellowed. "It's almost twelve o'clock. How long do you plan to stay in bed?"

An answering crash told us that, while Mother was out of bed, she was still clearly in the throes of waking up.

"Your mother lives with you?" I asked, remembering what Helen's cleaning lady had told me when she visited my apartment. She'd called the old lady "evil."

"Yes." Helen turned abruptly and marched back into the kitchen. I got the feeling she spent a lot of her time pacing from room to room. Who wouldn't? I'd implode if I had to stay in one place all day, all night, never going outdoors, no fresh air, no... god, I was getting claustrophobic just thinking about it. I stared out the window in longing.

Helen was drinking more water at the kitchen sink.

"I'll find out who's doing this," I told her. "And a friend of mine is going to stay with you while I'm gone."

She looked up at me, surprised.

"Helen," I said firmly. "You can't go on living like this. This is not living at all."

She put her head down on the sterile counter and began to weep.

CHAPTER TWO

"I gotta bodyguard who?" Bobby asked. His feet were propped up on a trash can filled with bilge water from a leak in the ceiling above. Each time a new drop landed in the bucket, it splashed between his legs with a satisfying plop.

"Helen McInnes. Remember? The Durham rape trial?"

"That's who that Turkish dame was working for? I should never have sent her to your apartment." A wilted leaf of lettuce trailed from Bobby's mouth like a mouse tail, bobbing when he spoke. He had recently taken to eating BLTs by the truckload, the catch being that he was in Raleigh and would only eat BLTs made by American Hero in Durham—which made me the delivery boy. This obsession with bacon, lettuce and tomato sandwiches was proving handy, however. I suddenly had a very effective hold on him when it came to cooperation.

"Give me another section," he mumbled, wiping his mouth on the sleeve of his blue leisure suit and reaching for the other half of the sandwich.

"Uh, uh, uh, uh." I held the BLT just out of his reach. He growled, like a disgruntled lion who wants his meat.

"I will only continue to waste half my life ordering and delivering these babies to you if you agree to guard Helen McInnes while I find out who is harassing her."

"Why can't you guard her?" he whined.

"I need to take a closer look at the professor she suspects of having raped her. I can't be at her house the whole time. But I'll be spending the night there."

"It's in the middle of nowhere," Bobby complained, drumming his sausage fingers on the desk as he eyed the sandwich half. I moved it to the right; his head swiveled toward it. I held it up; he turned his nose to the ceiling, following the scent. Amazing, he was just like a dog drooling over a dried liver treat.

"You can stay there overnight, too," I told him. "Move in for a while. She's agreed. There are plenty of bedrooms. The place is an old farmhouse that was converted into a rest home at one time."

"You're kidding."

"Nope. She inherited it from her father."

"You want me to go to a rest home?" Bobby asked incredulously.

"No, you moron." I tossed the sandwich on his desk, defeated. Unless Bobby was eating, his brain cells clearly did not work. "It's a private home now. Will you or won't you?"

"Fanny's coming to visit," he complained. "What am I supposed to do with her?" Fanny was Bobby's rotund girlfriend, a jolly, gray-haired woman whose heart was as big as her considerable bank account, though only half as large as her legendary bosom. The two of them together were like a horny version of Tweedledee and Tweedledum. They cooed over each other even more than they oohed and aahed over the meals they loved to share. But Fanny did keep Bobby in line. It was not such a bad idea to invite her along.

"Bring her with you," I suggested. "She'll enjoy the excitement."

As he was thinking it over, an acoustic tile in the ceiling ripped from the weight of the water backed up above it. A cascade of brownish liquid showered Bobby's desk, soaking his sandwich.

We stared at the soggy mess.

"Unless, of course, you want to stay here," I said.

"Give me the address," he decided, opening a desk drawer and examining his gun collection. He selected several for their stopping power and caught me staring. "If I'm going to do this, Case," he told me, "I'm going to do it right."

With Bobby on his way to hold down the fort, I could concentrate on business. I hadn't discussed a fee with Helen McInnes yet, but I wasn't worried. We could settle up later. It was about time someone cut the lady some slack. Besides, we sure as hell weren't paying rent for the office until the roof was fixed, and for the first time in years, Bobby and I had extra money in the bank, courtesy of a few months' worth of corporate security work we'd done for a software firm in the Research Triangle Park. Or, rather, work I'd done. Bobby had mailed the bill.

I considered where to begin. If I was going to protect Helen McInnes, I had to find out who was sending her the letters. And if the letters were connected to the rape, as they almost certainly were, that meant I had to look into her rape. And looking into the rape meant finding out more about the man who many thought had gotten away with it: David Brookhouse. If he was guilty after all, the letters could be coming from him. If he was innocent, the letters could still be coming from him in retaliation—or from one of his close supporters.

It was like following a long and winding maze and discovering a rat cornered at the end of it. Only this rat was a big one, a respected Duke University professor who had been hired with a great deal of fanfare, thanks to his groundbreaking work in a new field, and had then had his reputation besmirched, thanks to an unstable scorned female—at least according to some people. I was not going to get much cooperation from strangers on this one. I'd have to do most of it alone, I realized, and much of it undercover.

And I'd have to do it well. A lot was riding on this case, more than I was used to. Finding out the identity of her harasser might, quite literally, set Helen McInnes free and allow her to step outside her home again, while proving that David Brookhouse had, in fact, been the rapist would pretty much torpedo the civil suit he had filed against Helen.

I wasn't exactly in over my head, but I was in it up to my thunder thighs.

The phone at my office wouldn't work. Must not have been waterproof. I tried to call my contact in the Durham Police

Department, a clerk named Marcus Dupree, but got nothing but static. The flood waters in my office, which were beginning to soak my high-tops, were taking a toll. When the overhead lights flickered, it occurred to me that we were being idiots to mix electricity and water. I'm all for tingles, but only when they are one hundred percent manmade. I decided to abandon ship. I flipped all the circuits, unplugged the phones, locked the door and walked away. It was time to take this show on the road.

Contrary to popular belief in some quarters, I do not make a habit of hanging out in men's rooms. But when I need to get in touch with Marcus Dupree, without being seen, I have no other choice. Which I hope explains why I was sitting on the can in the third-floor bathroom of the Durham Police Department headquarters, stall door firmly locked, blue slacks around my ankles and heavy boots on my feet. I was pretending to be a patrolman in gastric distress. For the sake of authenticity, I had a magazine which I paged through loudly whenever the door opened and someone clomped into the room. Unlike a ladies' room, not a lot of socializing was done in the men's bathroom. Men walked in, did their business, shook it off, and walked out. I waited, confident Marcus would be arriving soon. He cannot get through an hour without an illicit cigarette, and this was the only room in the entire building without a smoke alarm, an oversight Marcus treasured. He'd show up sooner or later.

Just when I was actually bored enough to start reading an article on Jell-0 molds, Marcus arrived. I knew him at once because he is so willowy that his step is much lighter than the heavy thuds of the doughnut-stuffed, barrel-shaped men in blue. I climbed up on the toilet seat so my feet were hidden from view and waited while Marcus checked the room for occupants. He then slipped into the stall next to mine. I heard the click of his lighter. The pungent smell of burning tobacco soon followed.

"You're under arrest," I shouted, popping my head above the stall and smiling down at him. He was crouched over in shock, hiding his cigarette behind his back, desperately fanning the air around him.

"Smoking in a public building is a misdemeanor in the state of North Carolina," I reminded him. "Up against the wall and spread 'em."

"Casey," he gasped in his precise voice. "Please don't go shouting things like 'up against the wall and spread 'em' within hearing distance of the men I have to work with. I have enough problems as it is."

Poor Marcus did. His effeminate nature was nothing out of the ordinary for most Southerners. Almost every big family had its flamers, but the macho-crotcho guys of the Durham PD were less accepting than your average elderly Southern aunt. Marcus took a lot of crap from the men he worked with, and I admired him for never letting them beat him down. He made a good salary and wasn't about to give it up, not with a handful of brothers and sisters still depending on him for college tuition, never mind the seven he'd already bankrolled through school.

"We've got to stop meeting like this," I said cheerfully.

"Why didn't you call first?" Marcus demanded, casting a nervous glance toward his stall door. He relit the cigarette and inhaled deeply.

"No phone. We've been flooded out."

"So? You never heard of pay phones? Or why can't you buy a cellular phone like the rest of the world?"

"They give you brain cancer. Besides, it's more fun this way," I admitted.

He blew a smoke ring, then poked the tip of his cigarette through it. "What do you want from old Marcus this time?"

"Why do I have to want something?" I asked innocently.

"So you just dropped by to chat?" He raised a nicely shaped eyebrow at me and rolled his eyes.

"Not exactly." I glanced toward the front door. "Can we lock it?"

"No." He ground out his cigarette. "Is it that important?"

"Maybe the most important thing I've ever done."

"Then meet me outside in half an hour," he said. Marcus always took me at my word. It was why I loved him. "By the stadium. I'll take a late lunch."

26

I was about to thank him when the front door of the bathroom opened. Panicked, we plopped back down on our toilet seats and held our breath. A man entered singing a slow mamba song. I peered out the crack in the stall door—it was the plainclothes Hispanic detective I'd seen the night before outside my apartment. He looked even cuter in the daytime. His dark hair was brushed back and he wore a nicely tailored blue suit.

Cute or not, I'd have a lot of explaining to do if he went for the stalls. And so would Marcus. I held my breath as he walked past the mirrors—he got two points for not glancing at himself—then headed for the urinals. I briefly considered the skank quotient of what I was about to do, then stared out the crack of the stall door. I had a perfect view of the detective. Nice technique. When he turned to go, he got two more points from me for washing his hands before he strode from the bathroom, still singing.

Marcus was hyperventilating next door. I popped my head back over the partition like a demented gopher and grinned. "Who was that?" I asked innocently.

"Keep your hands off him, Casey," Marcus ordered me. "That's Detective Ferrar. He's some new guy, moved up from Florida. He's been riding shotgun, touring the different departments, getting the lay of the land for the past couple of weeks. He's headed for a permanent spot in Homicide. Supposedly he was a big deal down in Florida solving drug murders. Which means we sure as hell could use him here."

"What's his first name?" I asked, though I already knew it.

"Angel. So don't go getting any ideas."

I grinned wickedly. "I had a good view," I admitted.

"No!" Marcus sounded shocked, but quickly dropped the pretense. "What's the verdict?"

"Detective Ferrar walks softly and carries a big stick."

Marcus nodded sagely. "Still, he's a married man and has pictures of his wife and kids all over his desk, so don't you be messing with his head. Promise me."

This time I pretended to be shocked. *"Moi?* Would I risk the bad karma involved in seducing a married man. Never." I might, however, let one seduce me.

Marcus began rearranging his perfectly curled hair in preparation for his return to the squad room. "Casey, you and I both know that there are three kinds of people in the world. Those that loved Ashley Wilkes and his nobility, those that thought he was the biggest pussy who ever set foot in Georgia, and those people—like you—who couldn't wait to rip his clothes off and corrupt him. Say what you will. I know the truth. You, my dear, would have screwed Ashley Wilkes six ways to Sunday."

I thought it over. "Okay, so maybe I would have. Does that make me a home wrecker?"

Marcus stared me in the eye. "Well, I admired Ashley Wilkes for his honor, so don't you go messing with my Detective Angel Ferrar."

"Your detective?" I grinned in satisfaction. "You have a crush on him, too."

"Bulls Stadium. Half an hour," he reminded me, slamming the stall door shut behind him.

I scurried after Marcus, making it out of the bathroom seconds before a determined-looking sergeant rounded the corner and pushed into the men's room with a frantic look on his face. Thank god we'd made our escape. There are some mysteries only a wife should be privy to.

"This is ridiculous," I complained. We were crouched inside a large plastic tunnel that wound through a playground next to the Durham Bulls baseball stadium complex. "We look like we're doing a drug deal."

"No one can see us from the road and that's what counts." Marcus was eating a carton of lime yogurt like he had to make it last the rest of his life. It had taken him five minutes just to skim an inch off the top, a process he stretched out while we caught up on our personal lives. Now he was ready to get down to business. "What is so important?" he asked me. "You're not usually this serious."

I told him about Helen McInnes and what I needed. His reaction was immediate. "I can't do it," he said. "It's too risky."

"I just need to see her file, and the files on any other rapes near the Duke campus in the past couple of years," I explained. "Don't give me the date rapes, just the violent, possible stranger rapes. I need a starting point and I need to know more about what the cops got on this professor. I can't trust what Helen tells me, she's too out of it, too confused. And it was too long ago. She's been blocking it out."

Marcus shook his head. "You don't understand. There was another rape a few days ago, a brutal attack. On the campus itself. The parents are coming in later this afternoon to talk to the investigating officers." He checked his watch. "I have to be back by three. I'm the only one who ever thinks to offer these poor people coffee or tea." He shivered. "I hate it when the parents come in."

"Another one? Where's the girl?"

"Dead," Marcus said flatly. "She died this morning."

"Why haven't I read about it in the newspapers?"

Marcus took a leisurely lick of yogurt, then stared at me. "It happened on the Duke campus. Do you really think they're anxious to publicize it? It will be in all the papers by tomorrow. Believe me."

"No shit." I thought it over. "Same M.O. as Helen McInnes?"

Marcus shook his head again. "Not even close. That's the problem." Marcus, who had six sisters and a very big heart, was not immune to the magnitude of the horror we were discussing. But he wouldn't budge. "I wish I could help you. But those files are hot right now. The pressure is on. They may name a task force. The girl who got raped and killed was only eighteen, and her parents are good, solid North Carolina folk."

"How many rapes are we talking here?" I pressed. "Take a guess."

Marcus shrugged. "This is a college town, Casey." He sighed. "Rape reports come in every week, sometimes through the campus police, sometimes from the girls or their friends. There are days when I think rape is our number two sport. After basketball, of course." He carefully scraped the bottom of his yogurt container, mining another half spoonful. God, but he was a healthy eater. I could never survive on shit like that. A girl like me needs to keep her protein levels up.

"Okay," I conceded. "Take a guess on the violent stranger rapes only."

"I don't have to guess," he said primly. "It's my job to know. There have been five attacks on women in the vicinity of the campus over the past two and a half years. Not counting this last girl. She was the first to die. Though I am sure the others considered it. Helen McInnes is only the most famous victim. Some of the other women got it worse than her. None went to trial. No suspects to arrest."

"Five? Is that a lot?"

"I'm sure it's a lot for the five women who were raped," he answered primly.

"There must be a connection."

He shrugged. "They looked into connections every time it happened again. There aren't any. It's not the same man."

"That's impossible," I said. "I want to see those files."

He shook his head resolutely.

"Please, Marcus," I begged him. "Think of that poor woman, trapped in her house. You should see her. She's like a ghost already. Half-hearing what the world says, half- seeing the things around her. She's disappearing, shrinking. She's going to roll up into a ball and die if someone doesn't help her soon."

"Stop it." Marcus pressed his hands on his ears. "None of that is my fault."

"Please, Marcus," I pleaded. "Be a human being. Someone has to help this woman. I'll give you money. Lots of it."

"It's not about the money. Those files are being tracked. If I pull them up on the computer, someone will know it. I'll lose my job."

"Just let me peek at the paper files, then," I said. "Just for one night. I promise. Just one night."

Marcus stared out across the stadium's pristine infield. It gleamed under the autumn sun, immaculate, untouched, in suspended animation until next year's season began. I didn't know what Marcus was thinking about, but I didn't push him. I could tell I'd gotten to him.

"All right," he finally agreed, with a long martyr's sigh. "But I'm not doing it for the money. I'll drop the files by your apartment tonight, and I am going to wait while you go through them. I am not leaving until I take them back with me."

"Marcus, I swear to god, you are such a good person."

"I know that already," he said. "Now you stay here and give me a five-minute head start so no one sees us together." Some people might have been offended, but I was used to that reaction from people. He slid from the crawlspace.

"I owe you one," I called after him.

He walked away with exaggerated dignity.

Marcus would kill me if he saw me, but I didn't care. I had to see the parents of the girl who had died that morning. I was compelled by some lurid wish to look on a sorrow I would never know. I sat in my bathtub Porsche—conspicuous everywhere but in a hot rod-heavy police department parking lot—and waited until they arrived. Just before three o'clock, a sedan pulled up to a side door and the driver hopped out. He helped a man from the car. It had to be the father of the dead girl. He was beefy, but in a muscular way, as if he had labored hard all his life. Despite the father's apparent physical strength, the driver hovered around him, steadying him, guiding him around an azalea bush. After a moment, the father gained his balance, shook off the driver and turned back toward the car.

He leaned into the backseat and stayed there, frozen, for at least a minute. His shoulders moved as if he were speaking to someone inside. Finally, he helped a woman from the car with infinite care. She was small but stocky, her compact body dressed in a lavender suit that was neither stylish nor attractive. Her short brown hair was going gray and it did not look as if she had spent any time staring at it in the mirror lately. Her face was what startled me the most: before she could take her sunglasses from her purse and cover her eyes, I caught a glimpse of her expression. A hopeless, uncaring, unseeing gaze emanated from two red-rimmed eyes. Heavy wrinkles ran from her nearly bloodless lips to her chin in deep furrows, proving she had slept little in recent days.

It was as if her face had collapsed inward, like a rotting jack-o'-lantern. As if she were shrinking from the gaze of a world she did not want to be in. She fumbled with the sunglasses, masked her face and gripped her husband's arm. He held her up as she took a few tentative steps. The driver hesitated, unsure of whether to take her other arm. When the father stumbled, the driver hurried to his side, steadying him instead. Together, the trio moved slowly toward the door of the station, where photos of their dead child awaited them.

Jesus, I thought. If they look like this now, what in god's name were they going to look like when they left, the image of their dead and violated daughter burned forever in their memories?

Sitting around my apartment, waiting for Marcus to show up, was not going to shake the image of those two now-old people from my mind. I decided to drive out to Helen Pugh's to see how Bobby was doing with his bodyguarding duties.

I had worried he would sit around on his considerable ass.

I should have worried he wouldn't.

I spotted him in the side yard the second I drove up. Bobby had trapped a Mexican kid against one side of a toolshed and was pressing him against the structure with his massive belly. He'd twisted one of the boy's arms behind his back and was holding a .40 caliber Glock to his head. The Mexican looked like he was about to faint from fear. Above this scenario, Helen Pugh stood framed in a picture window of her house, face contorted as she yelled, unheard, behind the glass.

Why did I have a feeling that things were off to a bad start?

"Bobby!" I shouted, leaping from my car the second it stopped rolling. "What the hell are you doing?"

"I found this guy sneaking around the back of the house," he said, kicking the kid's feet apart. The guy's head smacked against the side of the shed with a thud. "Look at this—the little shit is armed." Bobby pulled up the boy's checkered work shirt. The grip of an old-timey pistol stuck out of the back of his jeans. It looked like something Pecos Pete would wave around.

I stared at the gun, then up at Helen. She was jumping up and down now, waving her hands frantically, pointing to the lawn and the trees.

"Uh, Bobby," I said slowly. "I think you have just apprehended the gardener."

"What?" Bobby lowered his gun and stared at me.

"That's the guy that works on the lawn. Who else do you think does it?" I gestured toward the rolling acres of green. "Helen Pugh won't even step outside."

"The gardener?" Bobby backed up in disgust. The Mexican scurried to the edge of the shed and took shelter behind a corner. He looked to be in his late teens, or maybe early twenties. For someone who'd had a gun at his head, he was being pretty cool about it now that he was safe. Hell, maybe he was used to it. Out here in the country, traffic stops on Mexicans can be mighty thorough.

"Why the hell didn't the dame say something about it?" Bobby groused.

"I think she was trying to." I pointed to the window, where Helen still stood, her forehead pressed against the glass in relief.

"Why the hell is he armed?" Bobby demanded. "Don't tell me he's shooting gophers with that damn thing." But Bobby slipped his Glock back into his shoulder holster as he spoke, then hitched his pants up in a gesture of surrender. He was willing to step down.

"I use my gun to protect Miss Pugh," the kid spit out angrily. He glared at us and rubbed his arm where Bobby had gripped it.

"I can't take you anywhere," I complained to Bobby. "This poor guy is probably the only thing that has been standing between my client and disaster for the past six months, and now you've gone and pissed him off."

"How was I supposed to know?" Bobby whined. He ran his fingers through his greased-back hair and looked defiant. Bobby wouldn't apologize if his next meal depended on it, which was saying a lot, so this admission was as close to a confession as the gardener was going to get.

The Mexican kid surprised me. He let it go. So much for machismo. Thank god. He gave Bobby a final glare, then shifted his attention to me. "You are here to protect Miss Pugh?" he asked in a heavily accented voice. But he spoke rapidly, as if he had been around the English language for a while.

"That's right. I'm looking into the situation for her. You know about it?"

He nodded and stepped out into the sunlight. He was a good-looking guy, with broad shoulders and a small waist. He had one of those wide Mexican faces that looks like Aztec blood is bubbling just below the surface. His cheekbones were high and chiseled, his eyes dark above a broad nose. His chin jutted out prominently beneath thin lips, but his strong features were balanced by thick dark hair that fell over his ears and forehead. He caught me looking at him and stood a little straighter, then made a big show out of pulling his pistol from his pants and checking to see that it was loaded.

"Have you had to use that yet?" I asked.

He shook his head. "But I chased someone from the yard a week ago. At night."

"You live here then?"

He cocked a thumb toward an outer building. "I have water and a bed in there. I listen carefully at night."

"Did you get a look at him?" I asked.

He shook his head. "It was a man. That was all I see. Tall. Very fast. Once he saw me, he didn't stay. He run down the road and a car engine started."

"I'm glad to know you're here. What's your name?"

"Hugo." He looked down at his feet, embarrassed.

"Okay," I decided. "Let's all go inside and make nice. If we work together, maybe no one will get his balls blown off." At least not by me, I thought.

"Speak for yourself," Bobby grumbled, hitching his pants up again. "All the guy had to do was say something."

"I try to speak," Hugo protested, indignant. "You be too busy bumping me with that gordo belly of yours."

"Watch it, buster," Bobby answered sharply. "I speak Spanish." Yeah, right, so long as the word appeared on a Taco Bell menu.

"You speak my language?" Hugo retorted. "Then maybe you understand this: *chupar mi chulupa.*" He grabbed his crotch.

"Stop it," I warned as we approached the front porch. "Save it for later. This lady has enough troubles as it is."

Helen was hovering inside the front door, frantic.

"Are you all right?" she asked Hugo, brushing off his shoulders and checking his arms. For bullet holes, I guess. "I was scared to death." She started to say something else then stopped, ashamed, I figured, at her inability to come to his rescue.

Hugo had seemed to grow progressively taller as we neared the house. Now that we were inside, his whole body appeared to swell. He went from being a timid kid crouched against the shed to a full-grown man, confident and protective of his woman. Having a dirty mind and all, I started to wonder how far his relationship with Helen went. Was he plowing more than the north forty around here?

"Why didn't you tell me who this dude was?" Bobby complained to Helen. He had made himself right at home. He plopped down on the couch and helped himself to a bag of potato chips that he'd thrown on the coffee table earlier.

"I tried to tell you," Helen protested. "But you ran outside too fast."

As improbable as it sounded, she was likely telling the truth. Despite his girth, Bobby moved like Nijinsky when he had to.

We stood in an accusatory line, glaring at each other.

"Why don't we start over?" I suggested. "Everyone sit down."

They obeyed, surprisingly enough, each claiming a chair in the cheerful living room. We made a rough circle. I was about to stand up and confess to being a sex and drug addict when Helen spoke up.

"I'm not sure this is a good idea," she said. "Maybe if I just ignore the—"

"Trust me," I interrupted. I was not letting her back out now. "It's going to take us a while to get a good system set up. Until we do, things like this may happen. I didn't know Hugo was... armed."

"Armed?" Helen looked alarmed. Hugo looked away.

"We're all armed," I explained grimly. "Because you never know what might happen next."

As if to prove my point, a terrible crashing echoed in the outer hall. It sounded as if a dozen cardboard boxes full of silverware had just tumbled down the stairs. Everyone but Helen jumped. She just glanced toward the hallway.

"What the hell?" I said.

"Mother?" Helen asked loudly.

Bobby started to get up, but Helen gestured for him to sit back down. "Mother," she shouted calmly, "if you don't stop moving those boxes of stupid props around, I'm going to tell Hugo to throw them into the pond." Her tone was edged with a steel I had not heard in her voice before.

"Go ahead," someone croaked from the hallway. "Go ahead and destroy five decades of an illustrious acting career. Go ahead and destroy what little remains of the greatest actress ever to eschew Hollywood."

Oh, god, I thought, suddenly remembering the mother whose unseen presence had so oddly colored my earlier visit. Who the hell ever actually used the word "eschew"? Without people replying, "Bless you," that is.

Hugo, who had clearly met the mother many times before, tried to disappear into the overstuffed chair. Bobby, who'd had no inkling of her existence until that moment, was trying to catch my eye. I was avoiding his. So I had left out a few details about this gig. Sue me. There was no way he would have accepted the assignment if he'd known about the mother living there.

"A mother?" Bobby asked into the silence. "Whose mother?"

"Is there a man in the house?" a throaty voice called out. "Do we have gentlemen callers? I would have thrown on something more suitable had I known."

As the husky, drama-filled voice grew closer, a strange tension filled the room. Helen and Hugo exchanged a glance I could not interpret. The footsteps grew louder, accompanied by a shuffling sound.

Just when I could not stand the suspense any longer and was about to make a bad joke, Yoda wearing a Carol Channing wig tottered into view.

My god. I had never in my entire life seen an old lady who looked like Helen Pugh's mother. It was all I could do to keep from running out the front door.

She had a wide, taut face that was tanned a deep brown and seemed mashed down on either side, giving her the appearance of a leathery frog. Her skin had been surgically stretched across her cheekbones, pulling her mouth out at the edges and bestowing her eyes with a vaguely Asian tilt. Her lips were wide and glistened with ruby red lipstick as she cast a beaming, professional smile around the room, her chin tilting upward as if the flashbulbs might start popping at any second. Her nose had been bobbed and reshaped so often, there was little more than two nostrils linked by a flesh bump left. Worse, this scapel-sculpted parody of a face was topped with an improbably blond wig that featured thick bangs and shoulder-length hair that curled under at the ends.

Her outfit matched the disjointed bizarreness of her face. She wore a loose gray cardigan over a multicolored caftan that flowed in neon folds to the floor, nearly obscuring bare feet. Her toenails had been painted to match her lips—as had the fake nails protruding from each finger like talons on a hawk. She was gripping a three-sided walker on wheels as she tottered forward and barged into the living room with an expectant "Well? Who the hell are these people?"

Bobby D. was so astonished that his mouth dropped open and a potato chip plopped out on the carpet.

Helen Pugh looked bored. "You know damn well who these people are," she said, sounding as if she simply did not have the energy to play her mother's games.

I closed my eyes and wondered what had made me accept this assignment without meeting the old lady first.

"This is my mother," Helen Pugh said grimly, a statement made entirely redundant by the realization of everyone in the room that no one would live with such a creature unless there was a damn good reason. Like you had to.

The old dame fixed a piercing glare on Bobby. "Stand up, you brute," she ordered him. "Have you no manners?"

I thought she might spit on him. So did Bobby, apparently. He stood hastily, looking like a little boy who's been caught shoplifting *Playboy* magazines.

"Much better," the old woman purred, her voice a trained instrument that could clearly run the gamut of overacting from outrage to delight—in three seconds flat. "I am Miranda Reynolds de Plessé." Before anyone could say anything, she held up a hand to protest. "Yes, yes—the very one. I am still alive and kicking, though producers and directors fail to grasp that concept. Any woman over thirty is over the hill so far as they are concerned. I am afraid my romantic lead days are over."

Over thirty? Who was she kidding? She looked closer to three hundred. Over the hill did not begin to describe this woman. She was over the moon and probably out of her head to boot. They'd have to start digging to unearth a suitably-aged actor to play opposite her.

"Oh, Mother, put a cork in it." Helen sighed and put her feet up on the coffee table. I suddenly liked her very much. "Your name is Martha Crumpler. So cut out that phony French name. That guy was your husband for what, ten minutes? Five decades ago? And the 'Reynolds' part doesn't impress anyone, either. Half the people in this state tack 'Reynolds' onto their name and it doesn't mean a damn thing. You could call yourself 'Miranda Reynolds Haynes Gray Roberts de Plessé, Queen of the World and Ruler on High,' and it wouldn't make the slightest bit of difference. You're still Martha Crumpler from Boylan Heights. And your father was still a barber."

"You watch your mouth. My mother was a Lanier," the old lady retorted. In another abrupt change of mood, she rolled her walker into the center of the room and smiled at Bobby in what I am sure she thought was a flirtatious manner. Unfortunately, the effect was more like a gorilla in the zoo peeling its lips back to grimace at the watching audience just before it flings something nasty at the glass. I started to laugh. I couldn't help it. Bobby looked so alarmed, it was comical. I clamped my hands over my mouth, but it didn't help much, just made it sound like I was having an asthma attack.

The old lady's reaction was remarkable. She suddenly clutched her right side, grunted and slumped over her walker. I jumped to my feet as she began to wheeze and moan: "Help me, help me." She slid to the ground, grasping the edges of the walker for support as she slowly crumpled to the floor. She lay at our feet, moaning even louder, thrashing from side to side.

No one moved.

"She's having a heart attack," I yelled. Bobby and I exchanged a glance that clearly told the other: "You're the one doing the mouth-to-mouth."

Oddly enough, Helen Pugh still did not move. She acted as if she did not notice what was happening to her mother.

"Someone do something," I demanded as her groans grew louder.

Hugo only hid his face behind his hands. His shoulders started to shake. I was in a loony bin.

"Someone do something," I repeated.

"Get up off that floor!" Helen Pugh snapped.

The old lady stopped moaning and began to laugh in great whooping gulps. I backed away, appalled.

"Fooled you, didn't I?" she said, still laughing as she scrambled to her feet with the agility of a younger woman. "I'm going to be famous again, I'm telling you. I'm going to get the right part one day soon and become the next 'Help me, I've fallen and I can't get up,' lady."

"Oh, do shut up and sit down," Helen Pugh ordered. "Mother is a re-enactor now," she snapped at me. "She appears in all those cheesy shows that restage unsolved crimes and stupid mysteries."

"I bring dignity to those roles," her mother interrupted. "They are lucky to have someone of my caliber and they know it. That's why they hire me."

Helen Pugh rolled her eyes. "She's been mugged, she's been murdered, she's been afflicted with every disease known to man. But what she really suffers from is terminal overacting."

I was still staring at the old lady, my mouth open.

"Close your mouth, dear," the old bat said. "You look indescribably stupid with it hanging open like that."

I closed it, determined not to retaliate. Helen Pugh could not be held responsible for her mother, nor should she have to pay a price any greater than the one she had no doubt already paid.

Miranda abandoned her walker and marched over to confront Bobby again. "Stand up again, young man. There's a lady in the room who wants to get a good look at you."

Oh yeah, I thought. A lady in the room? Where?

Bobby lumbered sheepishly to his feet once more. The old lady inspected him from his fat head to toe, as if she were evaluating a slave on the block.

"I like a husky man," she finally declared. I laughed. Calling Bobby "husky" was a little like claiming the Grand Canyon was a big rock quarry. She glared at me, then sat down on the sofa, arranging her robes. She patted the cushions beside her. "Sit, sit. Let's get acquainted. Tell me all about yourself. Are you married? Helen, dear, we need refreshments. I'll take a Sea Breeze."

Helen, dear, ignored the command.

Bobby sat beside the old lady, his poundage cowed by her imperious manner. His sudden weight on the sofa caused her to roll toward him. She had planned it all along, I was sure. She tumbled against him, then pushed off his chest with playful hands, giggling in a ghastly parody of a Southern belle several centuries younger than she was.

Helen Pugh's eyes had a glazed look, as if she were many, many miles away. Perhaps this was how she tolerated being confined to her home so well. She had years of experience tuning out the present and finding another dimension as haven. With a mother like that, who wouldn't?

Bobby's face had slowly turned from pale tan to pink to red to purple, like a pot being brought to boil. He looked like he was having trouble breathing, and no wonder. The old lady's hand was crawling like a disembodied claw up his thigh as she attempted to engage him in inane conversation about the dangers of being a big, strong man who carried a gun and walked into perilous situations.

I bit my lip. Any danger Bobby might accidentally stumble into was nothing compared to this dame.

Just when I thought it could not get any worse, the doorbell rang.

Bobby's reaction was immediate. He looked at his watch, flushed even deeper, jumped to his feet and dashed to the door—blatantly cutting off anyone else's attempts to answer it.

I heard a flurry of muttering punctuated by a familiar burst of cooing. Of course—Fanny, Bobby's girlfriend, had arrived. He had called her after all.

Fanny could save the day if anyone could. As the epitome of a Southern-bred woman, she could converse with a fence post and be civil to a pedophile, if the situation called for it. She'd be the perfect one to handle Helen's mother.

I joined Bobby at the door, before he could warn her away. He tried to block me by shifting a massive hip in my way, but I wiggled around it and stuck my head out the door.

"Casey," Fanny chirped. "Why, you're here, too. This must be a most exciting assignment."

"You have no idea," I told her. I grabbed one of her plump arms and dragged her inside. "Do come in. We were just about to have a drink."

"Oh," Fanny squealed in delight. "I wouldn't mind a stiff one myself."

Well, who among us wouldn't? I thought. "After you." I waved her inside.

"A little drinkie-poo never hurt anyone," she added as she trundled past. There you have it: breeding shows. Fanny was hardly in the door and already she grasped the essential component of surviving the unfolding scene: get drunk quick.

Fanny scurried after me as I dragged her by the arm toward the living room. She held a massive pocketbook in her free hand. As Hugo seized his chance to escape, she inadvertently whacked the poor guy in the head with it when he dashed past her and slipped out the front door.

"Oh, my," Fanny cried, thoroughly confused. She turned to see who had just blown past her. "Did I just hit someone in the head?" She was mystified. Hugo had disappeared. No one answered.

Bobby was furious with me. He muttered threats in my ear. I ignored him.

"Oh." Fanny stopped short in the doorway. "I didn't realize so many people were here."

Helen Pugh looked up blankly. Her mother was busy fishing a pack of cigarettes out of a pocket and didn't even bother to acknowledge Fanny's presence.

"This is Helen Pugh," I said loudly. My client took the hint. She stood, extending a hand, smiling thinly. "And this is Bobby's girlfriend, Fanny Whitehurst." I gave Helen's mother a rather triumphant glance. She acknowledged my salvo with a discreet sneer.

"Delighted to meet you," Fanny cried with an enthusiasm that was already tainted with desperation. Not a good sign.

There was a silence in the room, broken only by the sharp click of Miranda's cigarette lighter.

Helen remembered her manners. "This is my mother, Miranda de Plessé," she said mechanically. "But if you grew up in the area, you may have known her as Martha Crumpler. She's from Raleigh, actually. Quite nearby."

It was the automatic family-history introduction any decent hostess might give, but the effect on Fanny was unexpected.

"Martha Crumpler!" Fanny cried. She took a step forward and eyed the old lady's bowed head, getting a face full of rising cigarette smoke for her trouble.

"It's me, Martha," Fanny said. "The former Fanny Byrd. Don't you remember? We went to Peace College together. I was president of our junior class?"

Miranda looked up for the first time. Fanny flinched when she caught sight of the old lady's scalpel-ravaged face. But she was too polite to react beyond that. Fanny lived in a less self-centered world and probably assumed her old friend had been in a catastrophic car wreck. Who would voluntarily choose a face that looked like that?

Miranda had no such scruples. "I have no idea who you are," she said in her best Bette Davis voice. "I'm sure you have mistaken me for someone else."

"We took drama class together, remember?" Fanny insisted. "Of course, that was a long time ago. Not that you look it or anything," she added hastily. Fanny patted her own gray curls nervously and smoothed her dress over her plump figure. Her face fell slightly. She had been a triumph at her girls' college and delighted in remembering those heady times. "Don't you remember me?" she finally asked outright.

Helen's mother blew smoke out of her nostrils, a lady dragon in full flame. "I can't be expected to remember everyone I meet," she snapped. "I've met thousands of admirers over the course of my dramatic career."

That was more than enough for Fanny. She was well-bred, but no one's doormat. "Well, I certainly remember you," Fanny retorted in a sweet voice. "If I recall, you were expelled for having sex with the gardener. Or was it the art teacher? No, wait, it was the German teacher, a funny little man with a stiff mustache like Hitler. Or perhaps it was all three? Yes, that was the scandal, wasn't it? You were sleeping with all of them. Rather amusing to have made such a fuss about it. Promiscuity is so much more acceptable these days."

Fanny smiled beatifically at her foe. Martha stared back at her, frozen in mid-puff, her carefully studied mannerisms thrown off by Fanny's unexpected volley.

Touché.

As the two older women eyed one another, Bobby cleared his throat and looked to me for help. We both knew what had happened: the gauntlet had been thrown—just when we thought it couldn't get any worse.

I fled to the sanity of my apartment in downtown Durham as soon as I could, leaving behind an incipient soap opera. There was no way Fanny was leaving Bobby to the sole attentions of Miranda, and so she had insisted on bringing her suitcases inside the house for "a little visit" as well. Helen Pugh's home—once a silent prison—was fast approaching bawdy whorehouse status.

Marcus and the case files arrived at my place promptly at seven o'clock. He clutched a large shopping bag in his arms.

"I knew you'd keep your word," I told him, dragging him inside before his fidgeting made one of my neighbors suspicious. "Will you relax? You're making me nervous."

"I can't relax. The task force is a go." He collapsed on my sofa and fanned his face with a file folder from the shopping bag. "By tomorrow, these files will be hotter than two foxes fornicating in a forest fire. I only hope they don't form the task force tonight and throw me in the hoosegaw." He sounded mildly hopeful about the possibility.

"Relax," I told him again. "I am sure the powers that be are way too busy making phone calls and covering their asses over that girl's murder."

I unpacked the shopping bag. There were over a dozen files inside. Marcus watched me with proprietary disapproval.

"If you're hungry, order pizza," I told him. "I'll pay." I knew Marcus had not been kidding when he had sworn to stay beside those files. He took his responsibilities seriously, an annoying habit in a snitch. I was stuck with him for the night.

While Marcus went about making himself at home—which, for him, meant checking out my lingerie, rifling through my video collection and inspecting my medicine chest for new prescriptions—I organized the case files. As requested, Marcus had culled out any rapes involving known acquaintances.

"You know those date rape cases?" I asked him, just to make sure I'd covered all the bases. "Were any of them exceptionally violent?"

"All rape is violent," Marcus chided me primly. He was holding up a see-through black body suit. "May I?"

"No, you may not," I said emphatically. "You may not try on anything of mine that has a crotch. Sharing has its limits."

"Spoilsport." He hung it back up in the closet and kept browsing.

"Would you answer my question about the date rapes?" I complained. "I'm not interested in being politically correct."

"Well, I think we all know that already," he answered, one eyebrow raised.

"What I mean is, did any of the date rapes seem related to these?" I tapped the stack of folders in front of me. "Maybe the guy started with someone he knew?"

Marcus shook his head. "You have all the worst ones in front of you. If the woman was beaten, tortured, attacked, ritualized in some way, I included it. I think I flagged them all. I have been doing this for fifteen years, my dear."

"And these are all unsolved?"

"Unfortunately, yes. Except for the ones you helped solve," he said, flashing a satisfied smile.

Sure enough, I was able to cull out six rape case files that I had previously helped the Durham Police Department solve. It was nice to know my work had made a difference. Of course, the files were still open since the rapist was currently whooping it up in Paris, but I'd get him one day. I always—but always—get my man. One way or another. I put those folders aside and concentrated on the remaining incidents.

Before long, I was lost in the details of life-shattering events, the horror of what the women must have felt sanitized in a series of observations by people who had seen it all too many times before. Helen Pugh's file was the thickest. Her statement was also the most thorough. But she had not claimed to have recognized the rapist's voice as belonging to David Brookhouse until more than a week after the incident. That had probably hurt her in court.

I made careful notes of the victims' names, workplaces and addresses. I wondered how many of the women still lived the same lives they had led before their rapes. I know I would have started over somewhere else. I noted the details of each attack, searching for similarities. Because three of the violent rapes had taken place near a shopping center in North Durham, far from the campus, and had stopped abruptly when the main suspect was jailed on an unrelated charge, I set those aside to concentrate on the rapes that had occurred on or near the Duke campus.

Marcus had been right. There were no similarities between the campus attacks whatsoever. Besides being amazed at the creative brutality of man, I was dismayed that there were no apparent connections. Helen had been bound and gagged while walking. Another woman had been carjacked and raped in a parking lot, still another knocked out while reading on a bench in broad daylight, and a fourth had been overpowered in a hospital elevator at the Duke Medical Center in the middle of the night, then dragged outside for the finale. The next victim had apparently been drugged while attending a campus reception. She could remember nothing of leaving the event or what happened afterward. Only severe bruising, a few murky flashbacks and internal injuries bore witness to the reality of her experience. Jesus, I thought, these women had all done everything right from a personal safety standpoint, yet all had been brutally attacked. Was it really as random as it seemed?

For a moment, I thought I had found a connection: three of the women, including Helen, either worked in the building that housed the psychopathology department's offices and labs, or they took classes in the department. But two of the women did not fit that profile. They were taking classes nearby the same building, but that was little help. Of course they would all link to classes in the area; they had apparently been stalked precisely because of that.

"They do any decoying?" I asked Marcus.

He nodded. "Nothing happened except some of our lady officers got hit on by some hunky college men."

"Really?" I asked hopefully. "They need any more volunteers?"

Marcus looked at me from over a tabloid he had discovered under my couch. I didn't have the heart to tell him it was over a year old. It wouldn't have mattered anyway. The stories were all the same.

"What?" I asked defensively.

"The men of Duke campus are not ready for you, my dear," he said cryptically, then went back to gathering gossip.

Smug bastard. I kept reading, hoping for enlightenment. It didn't look good. None of the women could describe their attacker physically, other than three of them being sure he was white and taller than average. Two believed their rapist had been of average height and indeterminate race. The lack of detail was not surprising given the premeditated, ritualistic nature of the attacks. Some of the women had lost consciousness, others claimed the man wore a mask or other disguise. One woman believed there had been a second man present, though she had seen or heard nothing to back up this feeling. Still another insisted during her initial hospital interview that she had been raped by Ronald Reagan. Later, a rubber Halloween mask with the former President's face on it had been found in a campus trash can, proving she had not been as out of it as was first thought.

Still, nothing substantive among the cases matched. I spent over three hours searching and came up with zippo.

"I just don't get it," I mumbled. "There's not a single distinguishing factor to link these." I thought of something. "What about the professor, David Brookhouse?" I asked Marcus. "Did they look into his whereabouts during the times of all the rapes, or just the one of Helen McInnes?"

Marcus sounded offended. "Of course they did. He's not considered a suspect. There was no evidence to suggest he was involved. And with the details of the other rapes being so different compared to the McInnes attack, he was cleared."

"How convenient," I muttered. "Do you think he was guilty of raping Helen McInnes?" I valued Marcus's opinions; he had been working in the police department for a long time.

He shrugged. "All I know for sure right now is that I am mighty glad that I am a man." He paused, trying to decide how much to tell me. Our friendship won out over departmental discretion. "I do have one teensy observation to make," Marcus admitted. By then, he was lounging on my sofa sipping Diet Pepsi and nibbling the edge of a pizza crust. It typically took Marcus two hours to eat two slices of pizza. I could eat a whole pie in a quarter of that time.

"What?"

"Nothing concrete. But consider this: there really are no elements in common between the attacks," he explained. "Trust me on this one, I ran the computer program that tried to match them and produced the report."

"The report you wouldn't let me see, so I had to duplicate it all by hand?" I complained.

He arched his eyebrows at me. "When I say it is too dangerous for me to access a computer file, I mean it. They're tracking every hit on those files, no matter what."

"Why?" I asked.

He looked away, refusing to answer.

"Marcus," I warned him. When he still wouldn't answer, I continued. "What's so odd about none of the crime elements matching? Except for the elements you'd expect to find in just about any violent, stalking rape of course."

"Well, do you notice anything odd about all of the differences between them?" he asked seriously. "Think about it." This was a new Marcus to me, the Marcus-on-the-job, a clerk so competent that even the most homophobic of redneck cops on the force asked to have him assigned to their cases.

I stared at the files, searching for the answer, comparing my columns of carefully noted details. It took me a moment, but I finally got it. "They're too different," I said. "It is impossible that this many violent rapists would be working in the same area over the course of two years, and that every single one of the five would have a completely different M.O."

"Exactly." Marcus took an actual bite of pizza in celebration. "They are too different and each one is just a tad too distinctive for my tastes."

"They're staged," I realized. "That's why the department is tracking computer access to the files. You guys are afraid it's one of your own, someone who has access to rape profile information."

"Detective Ferrar was the one to point out that possibility," Marcus admitted. "So it wasn't my idea. We had a meeting late this afternoon. It looks like he'll head up the task force." Marcus coughed modestly. "I was, of course, the one who originally suggested we run the M.O. of each attack through the national crime system. It was the first thing Detective Ferrar asked us about, and I was able to give him a thorough answer. That's what led to his theory."

"Good for you," I said, knowing Marcus's department victories were few and far between. "What happened when you ran the searches? Any matches?"

Marcus nodded. "Absolutely. Perfect matches in every case."

"So, you had a main suspect in each case?" I said, knowing the purpose of the exercise had been to identify known rapists whose typical crime elements matched those of each Duke incident. Coming up with a name was the entire point of the computer search.

But Marcus shook his head. "Actually, no. Not really. The system came up with names right away, but in each case the main suspect was behind bars and had been behind bars for something like a minimum of twelve years."

"Damn," I said. "Someone is messing with our heads."

I kept reading, then thought of the file I didn't have: the newly murdered girl's. "Detective Ferrar is Homicide, right?" I asked Marcus.

He nodded.

"So is this task force being formed to investigate the girl's killing or the rapes?"

"Both. And Detective Ferrar has experience in both areas, let me tell you. The man is sort of a super cop, from what I hear tell." Marcus sighed. "He is certainly super in my book. But he thinks the rapes have to be related to the murder. Like you, he doesn't believe it's possible for five or six different monsters to be preying on Duke co-eds in a two-year period."

"Fraternities notwithstanding?" I asked.

Marcus wagged a finger at me. "These women were sober when they were raped. It doesn't point to any frat boys."

I thought it over some more. "So what about unsolved murders? Have you looked into those? Maybe some of the murder victims were raped first?"

Marcus shook his head. "Until this week, there hadn't been a random, stranger murder in Durham for nearly a year. When the good people of Durham kill, it appears they kill those they know best. Their drug dealers, their drug customers or their families."

"The beauty of small-town life," I muttered. I stared at the files. "When do I get the dead girl's file?"

"Never," Marcus said abruptly. "No way. It's active. No way."

I knew he was right. "Assuming the same man is committing all these rapes, why would he kill this last girl and not the others?"

"He didn't mean to?" Marcus suggested. "Perhaps it got out of hand? Or she got a good look at him?"

I nodded, agreeing. "Maybe a better question is why he didn't murder the other rape victims," I said, "especially since he tortured them. It's not like he's afraid of violence."

Marcus shook his head. "That I cannot tell you."

"I think I know," I decided. "It's because he believes he is better than a common murderer. More in control. I think you're right. This last attack, the one where the girl died, it was a mistake."

"Of course, that's assuming that we're talking about the same man," Marcus pointed out, stifling a yawn.

"True." I yawned with him. It was well past midnight. "But if it's not the same guy, god help us all."

CHAPTER THREE

I slept late the next day, telling myself that since I had no need to drive the thirty miles to my office in Raleigh, I might as well enjoy the extra time. As this theory was the only silver lining in the flooding fiasco, I planned to use it often in the weeks ahead. When I finally dragged my sorry ass from bed, another perfect October day was streaming in my kitchen windows, spotlighting the dust bunnies and counter stains. I contemplated doing some very belated spring cleaning, then decided a breakfast at Elmo's Diner was a much better idea.

The moment I walked in the door, the headlines on the newspapers scattered around the waiting benches told me that the murder of the young Duke coed had been made public with a vengeance. I grabbed a couple of sections and headed for an empty table, scanning the news while I fueled up on coffee and waited for my favorite waitress, Francine, to bring me my order.

I could not find a connection between the dead girl and Duke's psychopathology department, but the information on her background was still sketchy at best. The details they did have on the girl's life—as well as her violent death— depressed me. Seeing her parents had made her real. The thought of her sprawled across a stone wall in a remote corner of the campus, neck broken and body battered, enraged me. Who had discarded her as carelessly as an unwanted rag doll? If, as I suspected, it was the same man who had attacked Helen Pugh, I wanted to do more than bring him down.

Before I lost my appetite thinking about it, I tossed the papers aside and concentrated on a big plate of cheese grits with sausage bits crumbled on top. I savored every calorie, not giving a shit if it landed on my thighs the next day or not. Some mornings you just have to gorge. As I ate, I wondered how I should approach the other rape victims.

I could not do it directly. Chances were too great that people would trace my inquiries back to Helen. She had suffered enough intrusions into her life as it was. Plus, the victims' names were technically confidential. If I went right to them, Marcus would be busted as my informant for sure.

I decided that the best strategy was to print up an anonymous flyer saying I had been sexually harassed by a Duke professor and wanted to hear from any students who'd had similar experiences to discuss possible legal action. Then I would distribute the flyers around the neighborhoods where the rape victims lived and hope that they called me. I might as well target women who had been in David Brookhouse's classes while I was at it. That way, I would not be pointing the finger directly at Brookhouse, but I would be leaving the door open to anyone who'd had problems with him. If he'd had an affair with Helen, a graduate student at the time, he had probably crossed that line before and since. Maybe some of his jilted honeys could give more insight into his character—or lack of it.

It would be easy enough to track down his class lists and the current addresses of the rape victims. At least it would be if I had a computer. Unfortunately, mine was bobbing along in the flood waters over in Raleigh, so I was technologically unarmed. And this was not the sort of search that could be conducted safely at Kinko's, as it was a stone's throw from the campus and likely filled with dozens of people who knew David Brookhouse in one way or another.

I stopped by my apartment and called Burly to see if he'd be willing to let me use his special edition iMac for the job. Burly liked spending his money on high-tech toys and had been taking a few computer classes over at Durham Tech to justify his continual lust to upgrade. It was better than sitting in front of the television set, drinking beer and provoking Duke students, so I encouraged his hobby. Besides, I was not without insight when it came to Burly: the Internet was a world where he could move instantly from place to place, exploring with a speed that the real world no longer offered him.

I reached Burly just as he and Weasel Walters were about to take apart Weasel's Harley in search of the cause of chronic sputtering. Weasel was a friend of Burly's from the old, pre-wheelchair days—one of the few I actually liked. He had a face like a rat and a heart like a lion. But he kept Burly relatively sober with his own AA devotion, and there were times when I felt I would not be able to handle my boyfriend's occasional journeys into darkness without Weasel's help.

"How is good old Weasel?" I asked Burly when I got him on the phone.

"Pootin' in tall cotton," Burly said. "He's got a new girlfriend."

"Another one?" I hoped this one lasted longer than the previous five. Fat chance, as Weasel seemed to pick them up at the exit door of the mental ward.

"Who knows?" Burly answered cryptically, which told me that already they were having problems.

When I asked him about using his computer, Burly sprung a trap on me so quickly that I suspected he'd been planning it for months.

"Sure," he agreed. "But let me do the searching for you. I'm just sitting around on my ass."

Who could argue with that when it was a paraplegic talking?

"I don't know, Burly. I don't like mixing business with pleasure." The exception being good-looking police detectives, of course.

"Babe," he said in his wheedling voice, the one that usually ended up with my being naked and him being busy. "You're wasting my talents. I could be your greatest resource. Think of all the stuff you could do while I'm at the computer, doing all that boring shit for you. I am starting to know the Web like the inside of your thighs. I know places you have never dreamed of. I can find out where those women live now, along with everything from the balance of their bank accounts to their favorite stores."

"That's really reassuring," I said. "God knows what's on there about me."

"Come on, it makes sense to let me help."

I thought about it. "You live too far away for me to check in every day," I complained. "I'd waste a couple of hours a day driving to and from your place."

"I can set my system up at your place. Weasel will help me."

Now, I love my boyfriend. But there's a reason why I live alone—and that's so I can be by myself whenever I damn well feel like it. Besides, I wasn't even going to be home for the foreseeable future, and there was no way I was leaving Burly alone in my apartment to poke through my private life. I had an entire drawer of objects with uses so specific that there was no way I could come up with a cover story for why I had them, no matter how far ahead I tried to think of one.

I confessed to Burly that I was staying at my client's house, along with Bobby D, Fanny and the scariest mother since Joan Crawford picked up a coat hanger.

"Cool," Burly said. "I want in on it. We'll make it Crime Central."

"We will?"

"Sure. I'll get Weasel to help me bring my stuff over and we can work on the case twenty-four hours a day. I'll dig up stuff on that professor you would not believe. I'm telling you—it's scary what you can find if you know where to look."

I wondered briefly if Helen Pugh had envisioned this when she gave me the go-ahead to "do what I had to do" to get the job done.

I agreed dubiously, then remembered the front steps. "You're not going to be able to get inside the house."

"I'll crawl up the steps if I have to," he proclaimed confidently. "And once I get there, I'm not going anywhere."

Weasel, who was eavesdropping in the background, interjected loudly to point out that he had carried his pal many a time when Burly was too drunk to wheel himself to his van. I knew then that I was outnumbered, so I gave them Helen's address and hung up.

It wasn't a bad idea, just a half-bad idea. If Burly could do even a fraction of the things he claimed, he'd be able to cut down on my computer time considerably, leaving me free to get out there and do some old-fashioned dogging of the professor. By the time I drove out to Helen Pugh's house, I had a plan in mind.

It would all hinge on Fanny.

Whatever worries I'd had about so many people descending on Helen Pugh's house evaporated when I saw my client. She was sitting at a table playing cards with Fanny and Bobby, her face more animated than I had seen yet. After greeting me happily, she resumed concentrating on her game.

"What are you guys playing?" I asked.

"Hearts," Helen explained, dropping a six of hearts onto the top of the pile and laughing as Bobby grumbled and raked in the hand.

I had never heard Helen laugh before. It was a contagious trip up and down the scale so unlike anything I had heard from her before that I stopped short in surprise. If this was what the rape had robbed her of, she had paid a high price indeed.

This good mood was apparently contagious—though it was late morning, Helen's mother was lounging on the sofa in the room next door, dressed in a floor-length silk gown. She was watching an old Deborah Kerr movie and muttering at the television screen. Smoke filled the air and cigarette butts filled the ashtray, their scarlet-stained tips explaining why Miranda's lipstick had worn off in the middle, leaving a small O of withered lip to anchor the center of her overstretched face.

I did not bother to bid her good morning since she did not bother to acknowledge my presence. I simply opened a window to let fresh air into the house before we all asphyxiated.

Helen's gardener, Hugo, was in the side yard, spreading peanuts on a slab of wood near a sycamore. If I didn't know any better, I'd think he was actually feeding the squirrels. This suspicion was confirmed when a bushy tail twitched into view on the far side of the tree trunk. A small gray head popped out on the opposite side, then the squirrel lifted its nose, sniffing at the air. It scampered down the bark and crept toward Hugo, standing on its hind legs to accept an offering. It held the peanut between two paws and regarded Hugo with dark eyes as it munched.

Now, there are some people in the South who would have followed this touching scene by whipping out a frying pan, conking the squirrel over the head, then skinning and eating the creature. I am thankful to say Hugo was not one of them. He crouched down a few feet from the squirrel and solemnly handed the little fellow a new peanut every time he finished his old one.

What a softie. I tapped on the window and Hugo looked up, waving when he saw me. I waved back, laughed and shook a finger at him. He looked away, embarrassed at being caught.

When a commercial blared loudly, interrupting the television movie, Miranda deigned to glance my way.

"Darling," she croaked. "Would you have that precious Fanny make me another one of her special drinky-poos? That woman can make a sensational Mai Tai. I've never tasted anything like them. They pack a terrific punch."

"Fanny makes a sensational Mai Tai?" I asked skeptically.

"Who would have thought it?" Miranda held out her empty glass in an imperious, yet curiously laconic, gesture. She seemed to be moving in slow motion. I took the glass obediently and returned to the sitting room to find Fanny. If the old dame wanted to get soused to the gills, who was I to stop her? With any luck, she'd pass out by noon.

Helen and Bobby were arguing over a recent hand, while Fanny beamed at them in approval.

"Uh, Fanny?" I asked.

"Yes, dear?" She tossed an opening card out with great élan.

"The dragon lady in the other room claims you make a sensational Mai Tai. She wants another one."

"Does she now?" Fanny had a peculiar smile on her face. "I must make her another one, then. At once." She saw my look and smiled beatifically. "All in the interest of harmony, my dear."

Fanny excused herself from the table and swept into the kitchen. I scurried after her like a duckling in search of its mom.

Something peculiar was going on. There was a smirk in the air, as if everyone were in on the joke but me.

Fanny opened the refrigerator and took out a pitcher filled with a virulently pink liquid.

"That's not antifreeze, is it?" I asked.

Fanny laughed. "God, no. I sent that lovely Hugo out to the grocery store this morning for some very special ingredients. It's cherry and pineapple juice, some lemonade, grenadine and fresh fruit soaked in Everclear. Plus two kinds of rum. That we did not need at the store. I do believe Miranda is determined to pickle herself as her next unsuccessful anti-aging strategy."

"Fanny," I said, shocked. She had never said anything remotely nasty about another person in my presence, at least not until Miranda. I can't say as I blamed her.

I watched as Fanny refilled the tumbler with fresh ice from the freezer. Then she turned her back to me and fumbled with something in her dress pocket.

"What are you doing?" I demanded. I was at her side in an instant. She was unscrewing the top of a prescription pill bottle. A yellow, round pill with a V-shaped notch in the center fell out: Valium, a ten-milligram dose. I ought to know. It's been one of my favorite recreational drugs for going on twenty years now. Other drugs may come and go, but Valium will always have a special place in my muscular system.

Fanny cut the pill precisely in half with a steak knife, then carefully crushed one section with the back of a spoon. She scraped the powder into a Mason jar, added some of the red punch mixture, then screwed the top on it and began to shake it vigorously.

"What the hell are you doing?" I asked. She had a faraway smile on her lips and seemed to take no notice of me.

"Fanny?" I asked in a low voice.

"Damage control," Fanny answered calmly. She unscrewed the top, dipped a finger in to taste it and smiled. "Perfect. The touch of pineapple juice disguises the bitterness quite nicely." She poured the concoction over the ice in the glass and added a handful of fresh fruit cut into cubes on the top.

"Are you crazy?" I said. "You could kill her."

"Nonsense. I estimate her weight at one hundred and thirty-five pounds. I have checked her medicine chest and bedroom drawers carefully, and she is on no conflicting medications. And I am limiting her dose to five milligrams every two hours." She looked up at me proudly. "I know what I am doing."

"Fanny," I protested. "You can't drug a person without their knowledge."

"Of course you can, dear. I've been doing it since eight o'clock this morning. She got up early simply to annoy me. It's working quite well, I assure you."

"I can't believe you would do that."

"My dear," Fanny said, patting my hand. "When you have lived as long as I have, you come to recognize a desperate situation quickly. That poor girl, Helen. It's bad enough what happened to her, but to be trapped in this house with that creature." She shivered. "I could not abide to see her suffer so. Not to mention the pitiful flirting she tried to trick Robert into. The simple truth is, she had to be stopped or we would have all gone insane. You weren't here. It was either distribute Valium to everyone else—or give that raging harridan the dosing she deserves. I simply do not have a big enough supply to shower my pills willy-nilly on a household full of shell-shocked people. Believe me, what I am doing is the best idea I've had since I divorced my husband."

I was too dumbfounded to say anything else. Not that it mattered to Fanny. She wrapped a gaily printed napkin around the tumbler and headed for the television room. Miranda's eyes lit up when she saw the glass topped with fruit.

"Yummy," she purred. "You're such a dear. I can't think of why we weren't better friends in school." She gulped greedily. "Heavenly," she pronounced.

"Enjoy," Fanny said with a cheerful wave. "I really must get back to my card game." Without a shred of conscience, she marched back into the sitting room. I followed hard on her heels, not sure of what to do.

When Fanny sat back in her chair, Bobby began shuffling a new hand. Helen was happily checking the math on a long line of match scores.

"Fanny," I began, pulling a chair up to her elbow.

"Trust me on this one," she interrupted firmly.

"Trust you on what?" Bobby asked.

"Nothing, darling," Fanny said. "Now deal, would you? You are going to eat the queen of spades this time around. I plan to make you beg for mercy."

Burly arrived a little over an hour later. By then, the card players had switched into high gear. Miranda was still in the other room, snoring on the couch, her honking-loud rasps a dramatic touch more in line with a foghorn than a diva.

Before I could greet Burly, Hugo appeared from behind the house. He took in the special van and electric side lift with quick eyes. After greeting Burly at the window, he began talking rapidly and gesturing toward the front steps. Burly answered back, his hands waving. I detected testosterone trouble and hurried outside.

I was wrong. I saw Burly shrug just as Weasel hopped out of the van and accompanied Hugo toward a large garage. An overweight basset hound sort of plopped to the ground, trying to follow Weasel. Killer—the dog I share with Burly—had come along for the ride. He lay in the grass for a moment, resting his fat, then rolled to his feet and trundled after Weasel.

"What's up?" I asked Burly, giving him a kiss that let him know I was happy he was there to help, even if I had balked at first. It took me a moment to make my point. One thing about Burly: since kissing is the bulk of his repertoire, he takes it very seriously and never rushes a single one. By the time we came up for air, the boys and Killer were back, dragging their tails behind them. Or, more specifically, dragging a long wooden ramp behind them.

"This fellow says the place used to be a rest home," Burly explained. "They had a ramp in storage."

"Karmic," I said, wondering at how perfectly the invasion of Helen's home had come together. And wondering what it would all mean.

Within minutes, Burly was inside the house and Weasel and I were toting in his computer equipment. Finding a phone line was no problem, the place was more wired than a sorority house. We finally set him up in one of the extra back bedrooms, where the whoops and hollers from the card game would not disturb his concentration.

"I thought you told me she was depressed," Burly said as he checked a connection and examined a compact disc to see if it had been scratched in transit.

"She was," I said, "but it seems she is a card freak. They're going nuts in there playing hearts."

"Hearts?" Burly's head jerked to attention. "No shit? I love hearts." He started to wheel toward the door.

"Hey," I complained. "Work first. Then play."

"I'll play a couple hands for you," Weasel offered. "Just to set them up for the sucker punch. You can take over my spot tomorrow."

Before we could stop him, Weasel was on his way to play cards and I was left to help Burly network fifteen thousand dollars' worth of equipment. It didn't take long. He was off and searching before mid-afternoon arrived. He promised me class lists and schedules, new addresses and background information by midnight.

After a while, the card game quieted down and I wandered in to see why. They were eating, or stuffing themselves, to be more specific. Hugo had apparently been sent out to fetch a carload of submarine sandwiches from American Hero. Killer lay at Helen's feet, gazing at her lunch with mournful eyes. That dog was one opportunistic little bastard. He was always on the lookout for a new sucker to con.

"One of those sandwiches better be mine," I warned them.

Helen nodded and shoved a foot worth of food my way. I was glad to see her eating. Already, the gauntness of her face had softened around the edges and she seemed unaware of the scar around her neck. Weasel was being very attentive to her, sliding her napkins across the table, handing her fresh ice tea. He caught me watching, blushed and glanced away. That Weasel. He'd have made a hell of a nurse. He ought to be working with people instead of computers.

I brought Burly food, then returned to the sitting room, determined to get my plan under way. Over a late lunch, I explained what I wanted to do. Fanny, mindful that she owed me one for my silence, was quick to agree.

"I am sure it can be done, my dear," she said. "I give quite a bit to their alumni fund and I know a lovely young woman in the registrar's office. She helped me out with a teensy problem when my youngest was an undergraduate there." Teensy problem probably being that her megabucks ex-husband had failed to pay said child's tuition.

"Can she swing it so it looks like I've been enrolled all along?" I asked.

Fanny nodded. "Probably. But you'd better pick a large class, so it isn't so obvious."

"Good point." I left to pester Burly for David Brookhouse's class schedule. He already had it printed and waiting for me on the dresser.

"I'm impressed," I admitted, nibbling on his ear. He did not even look up from his computer screen, which was filled with a long list of names and addresses. He had cracked the psychopathology graduate school registration rolls and was searching for the name of one of the rape victims.

"You are an amazing man," I said. "Please strip naked so I can prove it."

Burly didn't blink.

"Four dozen naked women are on the front porch and there's a gang of methamphetamine freaks on their bikes outside who wish to kick your ass."

He still did not look up. I left him to his superhuman powers of concentration and took the class list back to the sitting room.

"Abnormal Psychology 152," I decided, passing it over to Fanny for a quick look. "It must be a huge lecture class, there are nearly one hundred students. It meets in early afternoon three times a week."

"Perfect," Fanny agreed.

Bobby was too busy eating to butt in. He nodded his approval, wiped his mouth with the back of his hand and reached for another sandwich.

"When are you going to get tired of those?" I asked. He was eating BLTs again.

"Tonight," Fanny promised, "when I make chicken and pastry."

We all perked up at that one.

The card game was put on hold for a far more entertaining exercise: deciding just how I could disguise my thirty-six-year-old face and body so I could pass as a student. This was not as easy as it sounded. Not only was I unfashionably sturdy for today's waifish coed look, I regret to say that my face clearly showed signs of various hard knocks that ranged from a disastrous first marriage to occasional fistfights and too many years baking under the Florida sun.

"When my oldest girl attended Duke," Fanny said helpfully, "the girls always wore those nice Laura Ashley dresses."

Weasel started laughing so hard he choked on his lunch. I kicked him in the shins viciously enough to dislodge the chunk of ham blocking his traitorous throat, then explained to Fanny that I did not believe an eighties-era sorority look would work for me.

"What about that add-a-bead shit?" Bobby suggested. "You could fix those roots of yours and flip your hair out and wear a tight sweater with them."

"You wish." I gave him a withering look. Bobby and his tight sweaters. "The straight approach is out," I said firmly. "I'd look like Madonna searching for yet another new look."

"A lot of girls were into grunge a few years ago," Helen suggested, getting into the swing of things. "Blue jeans low on their hips, straight hair to their shoulders, ugly flannel shirts."

"I can't pull that off," I said regretfully. "When I wear a flannel shirt and blue jeans, I look like Elly May Clampett on a bad day."

"I know!" Fanny said triumphantly. "You can be a jock! My son once had a girlfriend who was as big as a house. She was a field hockey player. Wore these mannish shorts and football jerseys. I saw her toss my son over the couch as easily as I pick up a potato chip." She demonstrated this by reclaiming a bag of chips from Bobby and eating a few.

Fanny ate Lay's as if she were tasting *foie gras* on crackers: she held each chip between two fingers and extended her pinkie straight up in the air, then nibbled the edges down daintily before popping the rest into her mouth. This was vastly different than Bobby's technique, which was to cram as many chips in at one time as possible. But damn if she didn't somehow manage to match him chip for chip anyway.

Her comment about manhandling had piqued Bobby's interest. "No shit," he said. "Your son liked that rough stuff?"

Fanny gave him a look that ended the discussion. I thought her suggestion over. "I don't think so," I finally said. "I'd stick out too much. The Duke dyke look is too conspicuous and I don't want to have to deal with moronic guys giving me shit about how they could change my mind in a heartbeat."

"Change your mind about what?" Fanny asked innocently. Helen, who caught my drift, started to choke on her iced tea and Weasel leaped to his feet, pounding her gallantly on her back until she gestured for mercy.

"Well, we have to do something," Fanny said when no one answered her question. "You can't go like that." She waved at my current outfit. I was wearing a hot pink sweater topped with a black leather vest and a short, fringed matching miniskirt over tights and cowboy boots. It was a sort of a punk Patsy Cline homage. Nether Weasel nor Burly had complained.

"I guess not," I admitted, acknowledging to myself that the Duke campus was probably the largest area in the entire state certified cowboy boot-free. Then I had an idea. "I'll call my fashion consultant," I told them.

I had Marcus on the phone within minutes and he was all too happy to help. In fact, I found his laughter a little insulting.

"I don't find it all that funny," I said stiffly.

"You want to pass for twenty-one?" Marcus laughed even harder.

"I'll get back to you," I decided.

"No, no," he protested, "I have the perfect solution. Collegiate goth."

"Collegiate goth?"

"Sure. There's enough Duke students going that route so you won't stick out, and the pale foundation and black eye makeup will disguise your scars and all those wrinkles you're starting to get around your eyes because you refuse to follow a skin care regime like the one I've been desperately urging you to follow before it's too late."

"How tactful of you to put it that way," I said. "What the hell is collegiate goth?"

"It's a modified form of punk mixed with horror and a pinch of sci-fi," Marcus explained. "Toned down a bit, but with basic core elements and punk accouterments."

"I feel like I'm being dressed by Margaret Mead. Next you'll be poking into my mating rituals."

"Wouldn't that be a full-time job?" he said coolly. "I am sorry the look is not more original but, as you know, there is nothing new under the sun. Except for those fresh wrinkles of yours."

"You bitch," I said, but agreed to be his guinea pig later that evening. He, in turn, promised to stop by with some sample wardrobes and makeup tips.

"This should be good," Weasel proclaimed when I announced that I was going goth. "I can't wait to see it."

"Get out of here now," I warned him.

He just smiled and shook his head.

"Just don't pierce anything, dear," Fanny recommended.

Too late, I thought, but I smiled at her in reply. "Maybe just a tattoo or two," I promised.

By late evening, the case had been launched in style. The day's revelry had wound to a close, with Helen left looking happily exhausted and full of Fanny's chicken and pastry by bedtime.

Phone calls had been made and bribes elicited. My name was being placed on the computerized class registration file for Abnormal Psychology 152, giving me a chance to keep an eye on Brookhouse and, maybe, spot his next victim if he was culling them from his classes. Burly was close to finding the addresses of the past rape victims and cracking all the past and present class lists for Brookhouse. I'd examine them for possible matches.

More important, Marcus had arrived with his makeup kit, Clairol and wardrobe tips in tow. The zeal with which he dyed my hair platinum and cut it in a sort of modified dandelion do, made me suspect that Marcus considered me a living, breathing Barbie doll put here on the Earth for his sole entertainment. When he was done, I looked like a cross between early Deborah Harry and late Courtney Love, with a pinch of Elvira, Mistress of the Dark, thrown in.

"You want me to wear conservative gold earrings with this?" I asked dubiously, surveying one of the recommended outfits he had demanded I model: a loose black jumper worn over a tight silver T-shirt and torn black fishnets. At least I could wear my hiking boots with it.

"Trust me," Marcus said, not for the first time. "I know what makes those frat boys horny."

We locked eyes in the mirror. "That was not the purpose of this exercise," I reminded him.

"It makes me horny," Burly offered as he wheeled into the room.

"Really?" I took a second look at the ensemble. "Maybe it isn't so bad after all."

CHAPTER FOUR

Over the next week, our lives settled into a routine so well-ordered it seemed preordained. As so often happens with large groups of people, our lives centered on eating. The smell of sausage coaxed people from their beds in the mornings while the odor of popcorn marked their return. In between, we ate our way through Helen's pantry with Thanksgiving-like abandon. We devoured chicken and pastry, Calabash-style fried shrimp, turnip salad, stewed green beans, candied yams, Brunswick stew, chicken-fried steak and hush puppies galore. And that was just on Monday.

Burly and Fanny shared chef's honors, while Hugo made runs to the Food Lion down the road. I'd never lived in a group before, not exactly being the sorority type, and so I found myself, for the first time, caught up in the rhythm, the noise, the ebb and flow of human routine en masse. It was fascinating, as was the glimpse into the secret shadows of people I thought I knew.

Bobby D., to my great surprise, proved to be a meticulous dishwasher, treating the utensils of eating as lovingly as he treated the food. He'd wipe each plate carefully before placing it in the dishwasher, then don sterilized gloves to place the freshly washed china back on the shelves.

Helen let the activity swirl around her, sometimes part of it and sometimes lost in her own private Idaho. She would help out here and there, but spent much of her time huddled with Hugo. They were planning the layouts of her winter gardens so she would be able to see them from her windows.

Miranda, caught in her world of lost dreams, would descend the steps every morning in full makeup to lounge on the sofa and watch old movies. She sipped Fanny's loaded Mai Tais methodically through each scene, muttering endlessly about how she could have done a much better job. What a peculiar form of self-torture that was.

And me, well, I spent most mornings with Burly, dogging David Brookhouse through cyberspace, examining his career under an Internet microscope, hoping to find some sort of clue in his past to indicate whether he was a monster. The guy changed jobs a lot for an academic, but otherwise he seemed squeaky clean. I knew one reason he had been hired at Duke was that he was an enthusiastic writer of original articles on abnormal psychology, meaning he was managing quite effectively to ride the public's seemingly endless appetite for the criminal mind. This same fascination had probably saved him from getting the ax after his rape trial. Well, that and Duke's fear that he would turn around and sue the school if they dismissed him before his contract was up, especially since he had been found innocent.

In the afternoons, I attended my class with Brookhouse or staked out the homes of the rape victims who had remained in Durham. I could not afford to contact them outright, not with Marcus Dupree's cover at stake, but I told myself that if I could just get a look at their faces, I'd gain some clue to their character and know whether it was safe to approach them for a talk.

On the third day of watching, I realized that I was not alone in my scrutiny. Angel Ferrar, the detective in charge of the new task force, was apparently visiting each rape victim in turn. I watched him with envy, wishing for the power of his official status. As it was, I had to be content with an occasional glimpse of their faces through the windows. All of the women were white, and in their twenties or thirties. One had a jagged scar on her cheek.

Funny thing about those women, not many seemed to go out much. And none but Helen lived in a house. Apartments seemed safer, I guess.

None of them had responded to my phony sexual harassment flier. A special phone number that could not be traced back to Helen had been installed among one of her many lines. Fanny had offered to answer when I was not there, as we all believed a woman's voice would be more reassuring than a man's. We got some calls, but none of interest to the case. So far, I had determined that there was a custodian in the athletic department who stole the panties of the female basketball players while they showered, and that there was a professor in governmental policy following an eminent domain policy with his coeds. But no one had called in about Brookhouse or any of his colleagues.

Three times a week, I donned my goth attire and hightailed it over to campus to get a firsthand look at my quarry. Venturing onto the campus of Duke University was like migrating to another planet. Fall had been kind and the lawns were still lush, with marigolds and pansies blooming in tidy beds arranged around trees crowned with heavy foliage just beginning to turn color in the warm October air. No one seemed in a hurry. I could not imagine such a life. Students lounged on low stone walls, or sprawled across lawns, or lingered in noisy groups along the sidewalks, debating topics so unimportant to my reality that they seemed an exotic and forbidden luxury. I envied them their innocence and age. My knapsack held my .357 Colt Python. Theirs held books. They were seeking knowledge. I was seeking a killer. They could afford to argue long and loud about ideas. I was trying to repair a life.

My sole college experience until then had consisted of a year at the University of Miami, the year I met my ex-husband and left any other dreams I had behind. So it was impossible for me to feel as if I fit in. I entered Brookhouse's auditorium classroom each day feeling like an impostor, then listened to each word of his lectures as if he were offering up a confession.

I was pretty sure my age would not give me away; the makeup hid a lot of flaws. But my attitude surely set me apart. I was wary, uneasy and determined. The other students were, to a person, in that all-too-fleeting state of suspended animation known as college. They could afford to be bored and distracted. How badly I wanted to be them.

Was I being a complete idiot? What did I hope to gain by being there? All I had to go on was Helen's belief that her attacker had sounded and handled her like Brookhouse.

He certainly did not look like a rapist. Not that they come with warning stickers or anything.

David Brookhouse was a lanky, attractive man in his late thirties with short sandy hair and small gold-rimmed glasses. His face was benign and narrow—maybe even kindly-looking. He had a habit of blinking both eyes, like an owl. He frequently ran his fingers through his hair, leaving small furrows in their wake.

He dressed in attire befitting a professor at a prestigious university. His tweed jacket actually had leather patches at the elbow, while his pants were narrow-ribbed corduroy immaculately creased down the middle of each leg. Sometimes his voice would trail off as he sought to clarify a point, and his eyes would fix on a place far beyond the room's one row of windows. At those times, his face took on a sadly searching look, making it impossible not to at least sympathize with him.

It was easy to see why so many supporters had rallied to his side when Helen had accused him of rape.

On the other hand, whether or not he was a rapist, his was indisputably the face of a man who had no problem filing a multimillion dollar countersuit against a woman whose life and body had been destroyed. I reminded myself that I did not know him, not really. I only knew what he looked like on the outside.

Each day, I lingered behind in the hall after class, hoping to see who approached Brookhouse. I wanted to get an idea of how close he was to his students. This was not as easy as it sounds. I did not want to initiate direct contact with him, at least not yet. So I had to wait outside, peeking in the room every now and then, trying to keep all the students apart. At the end of each class, at least three or four would stay behind, probably to argue an assignment or grade.

On my third day of watching and listening, I decided that one particular brunette coed was definitely batting her eyelashes the good professor's way. She had lingered behind two class days in a row. How many college students are that conscientious about their work? I peered around the doorway, watching her sashay toward Brookhouse. She waited until the other students had left, then stepped toward him with a smile. She stood too close and leaned in too far. Something was going on between them.

I stared too long, however, and Brookhouse sensed my presence. He was like a hound dog that has caught the scent of his quarry on the wind. He lifted his head and glanced straight at me. Our eyes locked across the empty classroom. The base of my spine started to tingle. He was unnaturally aware. That alone made me suspicious.

The coed tugged at his sleeve, breaking our eye contact, but I remained in the doorway, wondering how I could explain my scrutiny.

I need not have worried. When he had dismissed the girl, he strode up the stairs of the auditorium and met me at the door.

"I don't remember seeing you before," he said in a pleasant voice that held no accent. But I knew he'd been born in Virginia, thanks to Burly's Internet prying.

"I recently changed my, um, style," I offered, hoping that Marcus's dandelion hairdo and my new platinum shade would serve as a plausible excuse.

He nodded. "I like the look. It's different." Just to make sure it was different enough for him, he let his eyes travel all the way down my body to my ankles and back up again. Double uh-oh. He was definitely a wolf in sheep's clothing.

"Are you enjoying the class?" he asked.

"It's fascinating," I admitted, though I kept the real reason for my fascination to myself.

"Wait until next week," he said. "We're going to talk about encopresis and autonepiophilia. You're going to love it, I promise you."

"Really?" I looked as eager and as stupid as possible. For me, this was a stretch, understand.

He accepted this witty response on my part and flashed me a huge smile. Then he whispered into my ear, "If it intrigues you, ask me about assignments for extra credit."

And with that, the horn dog sauntered off down the hall. I saw the brunette waiting for him at the corner of the hall. He glanced down at her dismissively, then walked by without speaking. She scurried after him.

It didn't take a trained expert in abnormal psychology to grasp that, whatever else David Brookhouse might be, he was the kind of person who didn't want what he could have. He only wanted the not-yet-attained.

I was still standing in the hallway, wondering if being a well-dressed sleazeball qualified Brookhouse as a rapist, when trouble reared its cute little head.

In this instance, the cute little head belonged to a kid who could not have been more than nineteen or twenty. He had been standing in the doorway of another classroom watching my exchange with Brookhouse. As the professor turned the corner, he advanced toward me, stopped a few feet away and stared. The boy had the prettiest face, very delicate, with a slender nose and deep brown eyes framed by thick eyelashes. But he had shaved his head on the sides, leaving a magenta-tinted Mohawk strip of hair right down the middle of his skull. His clothes were pure Berlin punk, but the overall effect was that of a kid dressed up for Halloween. That pretty face undermined all his efforts at toughness. Not even the brass rings piercing his right eyebrow helped. He still looked as if he were masquerading as a punk. Thank god his nose was bare of piercings. What do people with nose rings do during the cold season anyway?

"Why did you tell him you'd been in his class all year?" he asked me.

Oh shit. Already my cover was blown. "What do you mean?"

"If you'd been in our class all year, I would have noticed you by now." He stared at me with such undisguised sweetness, tinged with hope, that my gut started to churn. A mere babe in the woods. He did not belong in the picture that was rapidly developing in my mind.

"I've been here," I insisted. "You must not have noticed me."

"No way." He shook his head. "I would have noticed someone like you." He stared at my outfit in admiration. Marcus had done too good a job, it seemed.

"You must have been distracted by all those other girls," I said.

He looked disgusted. "They're so fake, they make me want to puke. This whole school is phony. Don't you think so?" He looked again at what I was wearing, as if bad taste in clothes validated my genuineness.

"Absolutely," I agreed, thinking of myself first and Brookhouse second. "It's like no one here is who they pretend to be."

"Exactly," he said, very seriously. He fell into step beside me. "So where have you been until today?"

"Cutting class," I said with a shrug. "I was down in Mexico with my boyfriend."

"You have a boyfriend?" He sounded disappointed.

"Ex-boyfriend," I lied. "We broke up down there. That's why I came back."

"Oh." He brightened up at that whopper. "Lucky we didn't have any papers while you were gone. But you did miss a test. That's a quarter of your grade."

I shrugged. What did I care? School was just so phony, I reminded myself, and you are supposed to be monumentally bored.

"You're not trying to suck up to him to improve your..." His voice trailed off.

"Listen," I said, grabbing the kid's arm. He wore so much leather, he squeaked like a saddle. "I wouldn't touch that guy if someone paid me."

He looked relieved. "Good, because he's a real sleaze. I've been watching him. He hits on someone new every week. Guys like that give guys a bad name."

I was touched by his sweetness—and by his knowledge about Brookhouse.

"What do you mean?" I asked.

"Well, he's always saying he needs a new lab assistant, but that's just an excuse to spend some time alone with the moron who applies for the job."

"And that would be one of the babes?" I guessed.

He nodded. "Guys never seem to get the job. Then, when he's done with them, he dumps them and some poor girl comes to class with red eyes for a while and he ignores her until she drops out and someone new takes her place."

"Whoa," I said. "You sound pretty sure about that."

"Like I said, I've been watching him," the boy admitted.

"What's your name?" I asked, curious. Anyone who hated Brookhouse couldn't be all bad.

"Luke. What's yours?"

"Casey," I said, grateful we were keeping it on a first-name basis. You had to show ID to gain admittance to some areas and a false identity would have been too much trouble. I was enrolled under my real name. Better to keep it simple. You can do that when you're an obscure female P.I. from another town.

"Where are you from?" Luke asked. "I'm from New Jersey. This place is like Mars to me."

I could only imagine. Northerners who moved to Durham always went into shock for the first six months, dazed that waitresses could move so slow or that the many "good mornings" raining down on their ears were not meant sarcastically. But I had no desire to create a fake background story with this kid. It would be just one more thing to remember, and remembering to be in my twenties was hard enough. "I'm from all over," I said mysteriously.

Bad move. He liked mysterious.

"Cool," he declared. "Like an army brat?"

Somehow, he had attached himself to me all the way down the sidewalk to the street. Was this kid going to ask to carry my books next?

"Sort of," I agreed. "Listen, I have to run. Nice meeting you."

"Want to go get some coffee sometime?" he blurted out. "We could sit and watch all the posers drink their Starbucks and talk about, I don't know, what we're doing stuck here surrounded by so much..." He searched for a word and failed, then simply shrugged.

"Sure," I said, wanting to kick my own ass once the word was out of my mouth. "We'll get coffee sometime."

Good grief, I should have just squelched the little bugger right then and there. But his big brown eyes were so sad. And he was such a baby. I was way too softhearted for my own good.

It was no big deal, I told myself. I'd just avoid him from here on out.

"See you, Casey!" he shouted after me and I could feel his eyes on my ass as I walked toward the distant parking lot.

Men. Boys. Sweet little punks packed into leather gear. What's a girl to do?

That night, when I returned to Helen's, I found we were relatively alone. Fanny had flown to Fort Worth for a few days to visit her daughter and Bobby was taking the opportunity to check out a couple of new topless bars that had opened up near Garner. He called it research. I called that horseshit. Worse, he'd taken Hugo with him.

"Is he out of his mind?" I asked Burly. "How could you let him do that? One too many beers and one of those good old boys could decide that Hugo is the beaner who stole his construction job out from underneath him."

This was a valid concern. In general, my part of North Carolina embraced the recent flood of Hispanic immigrants wholeheartedly. In fact, the local economy depended on them to fill the lower-paying jobs as well as the ones so difficult that no spoiled, fat-ass American wanted to attempt them—like nailing down melting asphalt shingles on a burning rooftop under the hot Carolina sun. Unfortunately, some of the jeeters around here were not interested in fostering Mexican-American relations. They'd consider kicking the shit out of Hugo with their work boots almost as much fun as putting a whooping on the local pederast.

"Aw, come on," Burly said. "Give the kid a break. He deserves some fun. He's been working hard. You should see what he did for me down by the pond. Besides, Weasel went with them."

"Weasel weighs one hundred and twenty pounds soaking wet."

"You'd be surprised how tough he is. Come here. Quit pouting. You're not the whole world's den mother." He pulled me onto his lap and snaked his hand underneath my black stretch T-shirt. "Is it true punk chicks always go braless?"

"Burly," I complained, "your hands are ice cold." He pulled them away, disappointed. And not a moment too soon as I realized we were not alone in the room. Helen was sitting quietly on a window bench, staring out at the dusk creeping over her front lawn, oblivious to us. Neither one of us had even noticed her, she was so still.

"Helen?" I said. She did not respond.

"How long has she been like that?" I asked.

Burly shrugged. "She's seemed a little distant all afternoon. I thought she was still in the kitchen."

"Helen?" I repeated, louder.

She turned to look at me, surprised to see me there. She touched the scar at her throat. "So you've seen him in action by now," she finally said. "You've seen him."

I nodded. "I even spoke to him today."

Her body seemed to draw into itself, collapsing as it shrank from the very thought of David Brookhouse. "Was he—" She stopped, then started over, the words rushing out. "Was he laughing? Did you hear his laugh?"

"No. And He seemed perfectly normal," I told her. "Though he is, without a doubt, a complete slimeball. Did you know about the lab assistant routine? Apparently, he uses the job as an audition for his girl-of-the-week."

She stared back out the window and shook her head. "When I was his TA, he didn't have anything to do with the lab assistant jobs. That was Lyman Carroll's project. Carroll had a contract with a Research Triangle Park firm. He was testing a new psychotropic drug for them. They were doing a control group study on volunteers and the lab assistants mostly got stuck with paperwork, witnessing volunteers taking the medication, conducting questionnaires on their emotional state. David didn't have anything to do with it. Is it the same study?"

"I don't know. But Brookhouse is in charge of some study now."

She turned to me, surprised. "Then Carroll must have screwed up, because he would never have invited David Brookhouse to be a part of it. They hate each other. They're the department's biggest rivals. Only one of them is likely to get tenure and after my... my trial, I thought it would be Lyman Carroll." She stared at the floor. "He was the only one in the whole department who ever called to ask how I was doing. And he only called me once. Right before the trial."

"Carroll called you?" I asked. That was interesting. Maybe he'd be an ally.

She nodded. "But if David has control of that study now... something must have happened."

"I'll check into it," I promised her. "How are you doing?"

"Me?" she sounded startled, as if the question was ridiculous. "I'm fine. Mother is upstairs resting. She does that a lot these days. It... helps. The house seems so quiet. I'm just..." Words failed her and she stared back out the window. "I'm just waiting for Hugo to get back."

My god, I thought, how we humans find our comfort when we need it. It was pathetic and moving at the same time. Pathetic because Helen Pugh's greatest friend in this dark time in her life appeared to be her Mexican gardener. Moving because that Mexican gardener had not only accepted the responsibility, but did so with compassion and pride.

"Come on," Burly whispered in my ear. "I want to show you something before it gets too dark. Outside."

"Will you be okay?" I asked Helen. "Burly and I are going to take a walk."

She nodded. "I'll be fine. So long as I'm here inside."

We left her sitting in the same position, staring out the window. Burly was being mysterious. I followed him as he wheeled down the front ramp. Within seconds, the weight of Helen's case had lifted from my shoulders and I felt gratefully free from the gloom that pervaded her house. It was a perfect October evening, the air was crisp, the sun a fiery ball in the sky as it headed toward sunset, the blue sky bleached to a pale aqua, the air smelling of distant wood fires and, from somewhere nearby, freshly cut grass. God, but it reminded me of home, of my grandfather's farm, of the infinite and well-earned quiet we used to enjoy after a hard day's work in the field.

"Where are we going?" I asked as Burly wheeled down a hard-packed path.

"You'll see," he promised.

The path led to a narrow road that snaked back between the trees. "Someone's been working on this road," I said, examining the newly graded surface.

"Hugo," Burly said. "He wanted me to be able to get down to the pond. He brought in a backhoe and smoothed it out, then ran over it about a hundred times in his truck."

"That Hugo's a good fellow," I decided.

"Just wait," Burly said.

The path led back into a patch of pine scrub forest that gave way to hardwood trees. The shaded darkness ended abruptly a few hundred feet down the road in a sudden clearing that was flooded with the liquid light of sunset.

"Oh, my god," I said.

I had expected a muddy pond rimmed by overgrown kudzu and dried cattails. Instead, a small lake glittered in the scarlet of the sun's last rays, one-third of its shore lined with pure white sand that curved gracefully in an unexpected crescent around the pristine waters. The beach was dotted with thriving banana palms. "How the hell did he do this?"

Burly laughed at my surprise. "He said it took thirty-two truckloads of sand and the banana palms are a special hybrid they've been developing over at N.C. State. That Hugo is no slouch. He knows his stuff. He's growing the damn things as part of an experiment over at State, so they gave them to him for free. Look at those suckers. There's freakin' bananas hanging off them."

Burly could go no closer, as there wasn't a wheelchair in the world built for sand. But I wandered across the fine-grained beach in wonder, touching the tiny bananas that dangled in clusters from the palm fronds.

"Why?" I asked. "This must be so much work."

"Helen likes the beach," Burly explained. "Hugo has this plan. He thinks if he can make the pond perfect, Helen might leave the house long enough to visit it."

"This is so weird," I admitted. "So weird and so wonderful and so..."

"Inspiring?" Burly suggested. He patted his lap. "Come here, darlin'. There's a reason I passed up that trip to the topless bars."

"Oh yeah?" I asked. "And that reason would be?"

"I can get my own private lap dances at home."

"You bet your ass you can," I promised, climbing aboard to prove my point. I settled in, facing him, the sun setting to our right. "This place seems a million miles away from the rest of the world, doesn't it?"

"Our little slice of paradise," Burly promised.

CHAPTER FIVE

I caught a break in the case early the next week. Monday morning, the hotline phone rang just as I was starting on a pile of homemade waffles courtesy of Burly. Fanny, who was in charge of the hotline, was still in Texas, so I hurried to answer it. No one returned my "hello," but I heard rapid breathing.

"You don't have to give me your name," I said into the silence. "Just tell me what happened. Are you calling about the sexual harassment flyer?"

"Yes." It was a woman, her voice faint.

"Have you been harassed by a professor at Duke?" I prompted.

"No."

"No? Then why are you—"

"I've been raped by one."

Before I could say anything more, the caller hung up.

"What was that about?" Burly asked when I returned to the kitchen.

"I don't know. She hung up before I could ask. But she says she was raped by a professor at Duke." I noticed that my plate was cleaner than a soul on All Saints' Day. "What happened to my waffles?"

Burly stared at the empty plate, dumbfounded.

"Bobby's not back, so someone else ate them," I accused him. The faintest of burps floated up from beneath the kitchen table. I lifted one corner of the tablecloth and peeked beneath it. Our dog Killer was stretched out lazily in the darkness, his long flanks heaving up and down with each happy breath. "I've located the suspect," I said.

As I probed his belly, Killer opened one lazy eye and regarded me with disinterest. I came bearing no food. What use was I to him? His stomach felt remarkably firm, but Helen had been slipping him tidbits for days. They were co-conspirators out to stuff the greedy little pig until he could no longer walk.

"I never saw him move," Burly said, astonished. "I swear, I turned my back for seconds. I didn't even know he could move that fast."

"It was him all right," I declared, wiping my fingers on a napkin. "The little bastard has sticky lips."

Killer sighed happily at this pronouncement, closed his eyes again and began to snore.

"It's a dog's life," I said, deciding to make do with the waffles left on Burly's plate. Luckily, with him being in a wheelchair and all, I was out the door before he could catch me.

I returned to the bedroom office and checked the notebook that listed the calls we had received on the hotline up until then. Fanny had logged each one in her flowery girls' school hand, the details meticulously recounted, no matter how ludicrous: "The caller said that her sociology professor was staring at her like she had no clothes on and it was making her uncomfortable," one entry read. Welcome to the real world, honey, I thought, and continued reading. There had been thirty-three calls in all, and over fifty hang-ups. No caller had yet mentioned rape. Had the woman called before? Was this the first time she'd found the courage to hang on?

She phoned again just before lunch.

"I called earlier," she whispered into the phone when I picked up the line.

"Yes," I said. "You did. Who raped you?"

"I can't tell you."

"Why not?"

"Because if he finds out that I know it was him, he'll kill me."

The simplicity of her statement chilled me to my toes.

"Was he wearing a disguise?" I asked. "Is that why he thinks he's safe?"

"Yes. A mask. But I could tell it was him. It... it smelled like him."

"You knew him, then?"

"Yes." She did not offer any details.

"When did this happen?"

"Two months ago."

Near the start of the semester, I calculated. Was she a student?

"Just tell me where it happened," I begged her. "So I can keep it from happening to someone else."

"In the basement of the psychopathology department."

She hung up.

A wave of adrenaline surged through me. It had to be connected to Helen's rape. It had to be. I sat on the edge of the bed, staring at the receiver. This was not a victim from the police department files. The details were too different. This was someone new.

"Same woman as before?" Burly asked. He had joined me and was rapidly punching in a code on his keyboard, trying to crack the Internet firewalls protecting a network sponsored by a small community college where David Brookhouse had once taught early in his career.

"Yes. She says she was raped in the basement of the psychopathology department."

Burly did not react as I had hoped. "Kind of convenient, don't you think?"

"What do you mean?"

"Would a rapist be so stupid as to rape in his own backyard?"

I thought about it. "Maybe it's not something he can control," I said. "Maybe it was part of the thrill for him. He was wearing a mask. So there he was, a couple feet away from his real life, yet completely concealed."

Burly shook his head. "Maybe. But I want to find out more about Brookhouse before I decide. He's skipped around a lot when it comes to jobs. I think that's kind of unusual for a professor. They usually stay put to try for tenure."

"Maybe he was moving on before the heat came down?" I suggested. "Can you dig up any info on sexual assaults in those towns?"

"With enough time I can," he said. "But I can't crack the rinky-dink network at this last place. Some student did a real job with the security on this one. Hope they gave him an A. It's gonna take me days to get through."

Days? I thought of the wait involved in cracking site after site. There was no way in hell I would be able to dredge up enough patience to sit through the painstaking process again and again. So I made a decision right then and there. And like a lot of my decisions, it was a hasty one. But the one thing I cannot abide in life is indecisiveness.

"Burly, all this waiting is driving me crazy. That woman calling the hotline is a sign. I'm going in the right direction and I need to push things a little. I need to get in even deeper over there."

His face was dark with worry. "I just hope you're not being set up, Casey. What are you going to do?"

"Apply for the lab assistant's job," I said. "So I can get closer to Brookhouse."

He stared at me for a long time, then returned to his computer screen. "You're as stubborn as a mule," was all he said.

Luke, the baby punk who followed me around like a lost puppy dog, knew what he was talking about when it came to Brookhouse's lab assistant routine. By mid-week, the brunette I had spotted flirting with Brookhouse was nowhere to be seen. The notice on the hall bulletin board advertising an open lab assistant position was back in place. I wondered why they ever bothered to take it down. I also wondered why the work-study folks didn't notice the revolving door of student employees that paraded through Brookhouse's world, but that question was answered when I saw a line on the bottom of the flyer explaining that the salary was paid out of a private grant every two weeks.

Luke caught me staring at the job posting—which was no surprise. He followed me everywhere but the ladies' room and even then I bolted the door just in case.

I was pretending not to notice.

He had been sitting next to me in class ever since we first spoke, alternating between staring at my legs, writing me notes about Brookhouse and drawing weirdly beautiful sketches in the margins of his notebook. He had a flair for drawing breasts, probably from long practice, and he had clearly been weaned on comic book art. One of his favorite motifs was a punkish female heroine with giant gozongas, platinum hair and a face that looked suspiciously like mine. Of course, Luke had thoughtfully airbrushed out all of my imperfections. God bless the dewy eyes of youth. But the figure on that babe... well, let's just say I'd have to sacrifice a whole rack of ribs to fit into the black rubber costumes he designed for his fantasy girl. It was kind of sweet, though. I'd had guys fall in love with my tits before, but no one had ever institutionalized them.

"You're not thinking about taking that job, are you?" he asked, nodding toward the job posting. "He'll put the moves on you if you do."

"I can handle him," I promised. "And I really need the money. My bastard of an ex-boyfriend left me with a big debt to some not very nice people."

Luke made a face. "Drugs are stupid."

"I couldn't agree more." So Nancy Reagan had made a difference after all. "But my ex is a believer and he ran up quite a tab before he took off."

"And he's left you holding the bag?"

"You got it." I shrugged. "I need the money and how hard could the lab assistant work be?"

"It's not the work that's hard," Luke said angrily, unaware that he had just made a very bad pun. "The guy is a sleaze." He reached into his jacket pocket and produced a small wad of tissue, then thrust it at me almost fiercely, as if warding off evil with a talisman. "Here. I made you a present."

Praying it was nothing that required piercing another part of my body, I unwrapped the gift. It was a thin cord of black leather, marked by intricate knots along its length. Small silver beads flanked each knot. It was beautiful and primitive at the same time, like something a Bedouin prince would give to his favorite whore. "It's great," I said. "Is it a bracelet?"

"Ankle bracelet," Luke explained. "I made it myself on Ninth Street. Want me to help you put it on?"

Without thinking, I handed him the cord. He knelt at my feet, like a knight paying homage, and carefully wound the bracelet around my ankle, tying it off with a matching knot. "This is for good luck," he explained. "The combination of leather and silver means something like the protection of friendship surrounds you. I forget exactly. The lady at the store explained it, but I was trying to get the knots right and wasn't really listening."

"What kind of knot is that?" I asked.

He shrugged. "I can't remember the name. My dad taught it to me once when he took me fishing. We only went that one time." He touched one of the silver beads. "I thought with you having that bad experience in Mexico with your ex and all, you might need some good luck." He ran a finger along the cord. "That looks beautiful against your skin."

I froze, staring down at his bent head, reminding myself that he was just a kid. His ears were pink and scrubbed. The magenta tips of his Mohawk only highlighted the wholesomeness of his blond buzz cut. His hair was growing in and looked soft and feathery, like duck's down. God, but he was still a baby.

His hand still lay against my leg, not moving, just resting gently on the curve of my ankle. "Wow," he said. "You sure have great feet."

This was a preposterous compliment by anyone's standards. My size nine clodhoppers, far from delicate, were firmly encased in clunky black shoes. But his declaration, while short on being suave, was uttered so sincerely that the touch of his fingers against my skin took flame, sending a small river of warmth up my leg. He felt my shiver and glanced up at me, his dark eyes large and solemn.

"I'm going to have to ask you to drop the foot and back away slowly," I said.

He was too young to get the joke.

Brookhouse was in his office, pecking in something on his computer keyboard. He turned the monitor away from my view when I knocked on his open door, but I got a glimpse of a screen heavy with text before he did. The "publish or perish" principle at work, I figured.

"Come on in," he said, sounding infinitely benign. He ran his hand through his hair, leaving little spikes in its wake. "You're in my intro class. We talked last week, right?"

"That's me," I admitted.

He nodded. "Have a seat. What can I do for you?"

My chair was way too deep for comfort. I sank in like I was being sucked into a feather bed, my legs flying into the air. Brookhouse stared at the leather and silver ankle bracelet as I rearranged my skirt and covered the essential parts. Would the bastard really stoop so low as to deliberately install a crotch-shot chair? Well, of course he would, I reminded myself. Those illicit peeks were probably a lot more fun than the plethora of blatant offerings he received from naive coeds.

"I'm here about the lab assistant job," I explained. "I need to pick up some extra money."

His sigh was preoccupied, weary. "That job is turning into a real pain in the ass." He glanced at me in apology for the minor profanity. I tried to look faintly shocked at this egregious affront to my delicate ears. "The turnover in the position has been horrendous and it's starting to affect my study results. I really need someone stable this time around."

I was going to suggest that not screwing his assistants might help with the turnover, but I had a feeling he had reached that conclusion on his own.

"You have a boyfriend?" he asked, picking up a letter opener and sighting down it like he was checking the barrel of a gun for accuracy.

"What's that got to do with it?"

He shrugged. "Girls with steady boyfriends are more apt to stay put. They don't cancel out at the last minute for a date with some new guy."

"I have a two-hundred-eighty-pound boyfriend who's a wrestler at Carolina," I lied. "He'd kill me if I even looked at anyone else." I smiled brightly at him. Hey, the guy liked a challenge. I was giving him one. "And he has a lot of away matches, so I need a job in part to give me something to do."

Brookhouse was staring at me with an intentness that made me uncomfortable. It was not sexual interest. It was suspicion. What had I said?

"How old are you?" he suddenly asked.

"Late twenties," I lied. "But my boyfriend doesn't know that. I dropped out for a while, then re-enrolled after I got my shit together."

"Perfect." He smiled and sat back in his chair. "Maybe an older student will be more reliable. Like an old car you can depend on."

Like an old car, I thought. That's me. Plenty of miles on my tread and in dire need of a lube job. "What's the story?" I asked.

Turns out the job was mainly interviewing students who were paid volunteers in a study sponsored by a Research Triangle pharmaceutical company. He couldn't tell me the name, but there were three likely possibilities, all well-funded, thanks to healthy corporate holding companies. Brookhouse was likely pulling down a nice fat grant for this study. No wonder he was starting to put his professional life ahead of his pecker. He'd lose a lot if the study got yanked from him.

"We're in phase two of the trials for a new drug similar to Prozac, but without the side effects or withdrawal problems," he explained. "Before we test it on subjects who are actually suffering from anxiety disorders or depression, we're testing it on healthy student volunteers. We're trying to determine that the drug causes no harm before we give it to individuals with impaired emotional states. Your job is to interview the volunteers each week about specific topics. The questions are designed to measure their emotional well-being. It's really very simple. You follow a multiple-choice questionnaire."

"All I have to do is interview these people every week?" I asked.

"That's right." He nodded. "But it's a blind study. Do you know what that means?"

"Everyone will be wearing sunglasses?" I suggested.

He ignored the joke. "It means you won't know the real names of the student volunteers. In addition, approximately one-third of the volunteers are taking a placebo, meaning it's just a sugar pill. I'm the only one who knows whether a subject is taking the real thing or a placebo."

"Because?" I prompted, wondering if the people with real emotional problems would have to make do with a placebo as well.

"It's a necessary step to measure what effect expectations and mental outlook have on the drug's benefits."

"Okay. And it pays fifteen dollars an hour?"

"That's right. And if you want to pick up a little more change, one of my colleagues is working on a different study still in the preliminary stages. He needs someone to check on the cages each day."

"Cages?" I asked, visions of a dungeon crossing my mind.

"Mice. Genetically bred lab mice. Cute white furry creatures."

"I can do cute and furry. I'll take both jobs if they're still open." That would give me a chance to drop in every day and keep an eye on Brookhouse.

"Great." He smiled. "See the receptionist in the department's main offices for the paperwork. She'll also have your paycheck every other Tuesday. Can you start this week?"

"Sure. I'm ready when you are." Oops, not what I really meant.

He didn't pick up on the cue. He really was minding his P's and Q's. "We interview the subjects every Monday afternoon. And you have to witness them taking their medication as part of the interview. That's one of the benefits of this drug. It's a weekly dose. No daily pills to remember."

"I can do that," I promised.

"Excellent." He stood and I was surprised at how tall he suddenly seemed. He towered over me. "What was your name again?"

"Casey," I said, sounding chipper and female and distracted. No need to highlight the last name. He did not ask for it.

"Good to have you aboard, Casey," he said, gripping my hand. His hand was cold and limp. I tried to pull away but he held me firmly in a too-close hand clasp. Then he stared into my eyes as he unconsciously ran his tongue over his bottom lip.

The breath went out of me in an instant.

His gaze was like diving headfirst toward the bottom of an empty well. I felt myself surrounded by darkness, caught in a void that seemed to pull all light and goodness from me, just sucked it clear out of my toes, emptied my heart, draining me of all feeling.

I pulled my hand away quickly, and looked toward the light of the open door.

Brookhouse did not seem to notice.

I hurried from his office, my heart pounding. I had felt that way only once before in my life, when I had stopped at an I-95 rest area late one night in the middle of nowhere in southern Virginia. A lone man had been standing on the concrete sidewalk outside the bathrooms, head down as he smoked a cigarette. There was not another soul in sight. The man was slender, no physical threat to me, but I automatically registered his appearance. He wore blue jeans and a matching denim jacket, with a baseball hat pulled low on his face. I gave him little consideration as I hurried by.

But once I was in my bathroom stall, a vague feeling of doom insinuated itself into my consciousness. The whisper grew, becoming a wave. I was suddenly overwhelmed by a complete feeling of darkness, a void, a black hole of being that I knew, with absolute certainty, had everything to do with the ordinary-looking man lurking outside the building, smoking a cigarette.

Without even considering an alternative, I locked the bathroom door from the inside, jimmied open a side window and wiggled my way out, leaving the building in the shadows of a heavily wooded area. I hurried to my car in silence, praying that someone else would pull into the rest area soon. The only vehicle in sight was a small camper. Oh, god, the man was driving a camper.

I was panting by the time I reached my car. As I slipped into the driver's seat, I slammed the door shut in my near-panic. The smoking man's head jerked up as I turned on my headlights. He glanced at the bathroom door, then back at me. Even in the blinding glare of my headlights, his eyes seemed to burn with darkness across the expanse of the sidewalk, boring into me. His surprise and anger were palpable. He held his cigarette in an outstretched hand and a wisp of smoke curled up from it in the dusty brightness of the headlights' glare, as if his smoldering anger had reached the burning point at his fingertips.

I burned rubber pulling out of the deserted parking lot, hit the fast lane of the highway and never looked back.

Six months later, I heard from a friend in the Durham Police Department that a serial killer was stalking victims at rest stops off I-95 in North Carolina and Virginia.

I was unable to give a description of what the man had looked like. But I could remember to this day what he had felt like. And David Brookhouse felt exactly the same way.

"What is it, babe?" Burly asked. We were sitting down by the pond later that night, in search of quiet. Helen's house had filled back up and she was once again playing cards with Fanny and Bobby D., with Killer curled at her feet. Her mother was back to grumbling in front of the television. Weasel had reconciled with his latest girlfriend and was racking up the overtime on his job, hoping to take her to Jamaica for a vacation. The pond was an oasis from all the human expectations and disappointments that filled Helen's house.

Hugo had started to cut back the banana palms for the winter, but was only a quarter of his way through the job. He'd given up for the night when we appeared, leaving us to our romantic sunset. I was sitting on Burly's lap near a grill that Hugo had built from an oil drum and some old oven racks. You could fit a whole pig inside that grill, which was probably what Hugo had in mind.

"There's something wrong with Brookhouse," I told Burly. "I can feel it."

Burly tightened his arms around my waist. "Forget about him. Look at the sun."

The setting sun was perfectly framed between two palms on the opposite side of the pond. It hovered, an immense scarlet ball that seemed to dance back and forth between the ponds, a private juggling act for our pleasure.

"This is so weird," I said. "The sand and the palm trees, it's like we're not even in North Carolina. We'll have to cookout down here one night. Look at that grill Hugo's built."

"And look how he intends to start it." Burly pointed at a metal can the size of a milking canister with a large hose attached to its lip. It was tucked beneath the grill.

"What the hell is that?"

"Bush burner," Burly explained. "Maintenance guys use them to burn down brush along the edge of the highway."

"You mean that sucker is a mini-flamethrower?" I asked.

Burly nodded. "That Hugo scares me sometimes," he said.

"Look, a dove." I pointed over the pond where a female mourning dove was winging her way across the flame-tinged water. The sunset gave her a pinkish glow. She seemed to radiate her own inner light as she coasted on the air currents, her movements graceful and unhurried.

"Uh-oh—trouble," Burly said. "There, to the west."

A hawk had soared into view, clearing the tree line in a heartbeat. The dove, unknowing, continued on her way—beautiful and clueless. Behind her, the hawk beat its massive wings in that deceptive, almost slow-motion way predators have as they time their approach and display their confidence. The hawk's sharp eyes fixed on the dove and never wavered as it moved into position above and behind her. I knew what was coming and wanted to cover my eyes.

"Relax," Burly said. "Hawks only eat land mammals, they're not fast enough to catch other birds."

"Someone forgot to tell the hawk that," I said. "I don't think I can look." I started to cover my eyes. But I then peeked anyway.

Few of us can resist the lure of violence, especially the random destruction of innocence by pure power.

The hawk never saw us, and never cared it was supposed to be too slow. Its complete concentration was on the dove. For an instant, the hawk seemed to freeze in mid-air, silhouetted against the setting sun. Then it struck, dropping from the sky with a terrifying beauty, wings folded upward, talons outstretched, sharp beak ready to slash. Like a dark angel bent on revenge, it descended in a free-fall of fury, hitting the dove within seconds, the impact exploding in a burst of feathers that floated down toward the pond's placid surface. Both birds tumbled, then the hawk tightened its grip and recovered, extending its wings for balance and gaining altitude with a few languid flaps. It regained speed and soared toward the far forest, the injured dove struggling only briefly before it grew still.

The whole thing had taken less than a minute.

"Jesus," Burly said. "She never even saw it coming."

I thought of Helen trapped in the house a few hundred yards away. "No, she never did."

Naturally, the lab assistant job required me to tramp daily into the very basement where my anonymous caller had been raped. Attempts to find out more about the incident went nowhere. Not even the administrative dragons in the department's office were willing to talk about it. They looked at me like I was crazy. Either the woman had not reported the attack or there was some serious cover-up in place. Neither alternative made me feel all that safe as I wandered through the winding and somewhat mazelike system of hallways and rooms that had resulted from a renovation of the basement area. The floors and walls were as pristine as a hospital's, with everything a bright white. But there were no windows. Anywhere. And the effect was claustrophobic enough to make me want to blow a hole through a wall or two. Ever since I had been privy to Helen's own brand of prison— seen her standing at the window, looking out on a world she could not join—my own freedom had been increasingly important to me. Enclosed places made me nervous. White walls or not.

The animal testing area made me the most nervous of all. They weren't barbecuing bunnies or foisting mascara infections on helpless puppies. But the walls of the room where I was to monitor the preliminary stage experiment were lined with cages of genetically bred laboratory mice, as were two free-floating counters that dissected the room. Mice, mice everywhere. They teemed and quivered in masses of white that hovered at the edge of my eyesight no matter where I looked, like amorphous ghosts wanting to break free. My job was to check the electronic room monitor, which meticulously recorded room temperature, humidity, light levels and air balance every fifteen minutes—recording all but the type of music piping in over the intercom (classical: the mice loved Vivaldi and scampered in time to its beat). I scoured the electronic readouts for blips in the artificial climate, alerted maintenance if something looked awry, checked the automatic feeding tubes to make sure the little suckers were getting fed, ambled through calling out "Bring out your dead!" every visit and duly noted all untimely demises of said mice, preserving each miniature corpse for further examination in a refrigerator in one corner of the room. A cat's paradise.

It was not my first career choice, but it enabled me to gain access to the basement on a daily basis. My goal: to ferret out the confidential files of David Brookhouse's drug trials, he'd said the testing was still in the healthy patient stage, but I had visions of schizophrenics lurking in the bushes to follow women home and I wanted to get a look at the names of the participants anyway. Just in case Brookhouse was not our man.

My third day down in Miceland, I still had not located the room with the drug trial paperwork. But I did run into Lyman Carroll, the professor who was Brookhouse's rival. He was the colleague conducting the separate experiments involving the mice. He was also the person who had been conducting the drug trial until Brookhouse grabbed it out from under him.

Lyman Carroll could not have been more different than David Brookhouse. He was average height, with rapidly thinning brown hair, glasses, a pudgy face and a rounded middle that made it plain he spent most of his time behind a desk. He also had a disconcerting gaze, which he had turned on me full force at the beginning of the week when I first introduced myself and explained I was interested in taking care of his many mice for him. He responded with a series of rapid-fire questions designed to determine whether I was an airhead or not—useless, I felt, since who can be an airhead and attend Duke University? But I went along with him and defined the terms "humidity" and "temperature" and "federal regulations" accurately enough to satisfy his curiosity. He hired me, dismissed me with a wave of his hand, and then returned to some paper he was working on at his computer.

At least he wasn't a total horn dog like Brookhouse, I thought. At first.

This opinion was revised dramatically on Thursday afternoon. I had just left the lab after tucking the mice into bed, when I noticed Lyman Carroll emerging from the men's room looking scrubbed and spiffy in a fresh pair of khakis and a neatly laundered shirt. He was squirting breath freshener into his mouth and smoothing what little hair he had back into place.

I smelled romance and dropped back, curious to know whether his tastes ran to coeds, as was the case with Brookhouse, or to men, for example, or maybe even to mice. I put nothing past anyone. I've seen it all.

Carroll's taste ran to grown women. I peeled away from him at the main entrance, and noticed a gaunt, plain-looking woman with short black hair waiting for him outside the psychology building. She had one of those faces that percolates a perpetual scowl, like a fourth grade teacher with gas, and her lips were turned down in a permanent frown that barely twitched when Carroll approached her. But then they exchanged a kiss that was hygienically unsound, and involved way too much tongue-swapping from an observer's standpoint. That kind of stuff always completely grosses me out. Unless it's me in the middle of it, of course. He slipped an arm around her and they started to stroll away when their tête–à–tête was spoiled by the arrival of none other than David Brookhouse. What unfolded was interesting indeed.

By then, I was standing in the bushes like a good P.I., peeking over the top of a healthy hedge. I had a gopher's-eye view of the entire incident. Brookhouse came out of the building with a blond coed on his arm. She looked young enough to be a freshman and certainly not old enough to know better. He froze when he saw the other couple at the bottom of the steps.

Lyman Carroll looked up at his colleague and turned his back abruptly. His lady friend was less discreet. Her face froze as she took in Brookhouse and the young girl. Brookhouse stopped in mid-stride to stare back at her. His eyes grew wide behind his glasses. He'd seen something I had missed, because he ducked just in time to avoid a large textbook that Carroll's girlfriend lobbed at his head. It sailed over Brookhouse and thudded against one of the main entrance doors, falling open. The pages fluttered in the late afternoon breeze.

"What's the matter, Lyman?" Brookhouse called out to his colleague. "Can't you control your girlfriend?"

"Bastard," the woman in question spit back at him. She reached down for her shoe—a sensible leather walking style capable of putting quite a dent in anyone's forehead—and Brookhouse wasted no time in surrendering the fight. He dragged his startled coed down the steps and dashed toward the parking lot before another missile was heaved his way.

The older woman glared after him for quite some time as Carroll waited patiently for her to recover. After a moment, she retrieved her book, checking the spine for permanent damage. It seemed she was only into crippling professors, not books. Then she rejoined Carroll and they walked more slowly down a path that passed directly in front of my hedge.

"I hate that bastard," the woman said. "What he's doing ought to be illegal. I should report him to the ethics committee."

"Don't start, Candace," Carroll said wearily. "They'll never believe you once they get a whiff of what happened between the two of you."

"I'm not letting him get away with it," she answered back angrily. "Maybe those stupid little coeds he screws will go away quietly, but not me."

She stepped up her pace, forcing Carroll to scurry after her like some overgrown quail.

And I, well, I crouched there amid the greenery wondering if maybe that lady might not be a very good person to talk to about David Brookhouse.

Bobby D. disagreed. "You can't risk it," he said later that night, after I had suggested we liven things up by interviewing the woman who had lobbed the book at Brookhouse.

We were gathered around the fireplace in Helen's living room. It was the first fire of the season, and everyone from Hugo down to Killer had been drawn to the hearth by its irresistible light and woodsy smell. Killer was snoring softly at Helen's feet, amid the buzz of voices. Only Helen's mother was missing: she had staggered upstairs earlier to sink into dreams of past glory, no doubt with thanks to Fanny's special Mai Tais.

"I'm not much closer to knowing him than when I first started out," I complained. "I have to push harder."

"She needs to talk to her," Helen agreed. "The woman's name is Candace Goodnight. She's a professor of anthropology. I knew her a little, but we stopped speaking when she..." Helen paused. "...when she became David's girlfriend just before his trial. She was there almost every day during the proceedings, sitting behind him. I know she knows the truth. Or senses it. If she hates him now and will talk, she could really help us out."

It was the first time Helen had spoken since Fanny's dinner of country-fried steak had been put before her earlier, and we all listened in respectful silence. I had been worried about Helen over the last few days. She'd seemed more withdrawn than usual. Not even Weasel could draw her out during his quick visits. Whatever enthusiasm she had dredged up at first had drained quickly away. I feared old demons were back to haunt her.

"Casey can't waltz up to this dame and ask her about Brookhouse without blowing her cover," Bobby explained. "It's too risky."

"You could go talk to her Bobby," I suggested. "Say some student's parents had hired you to investigate Brookhouse because of his relationship with their daughter."

Helen glanced at Bobby and looked quickly away. Bobby, while a sweetheart where it counted, still looked and dressed like a third-rate lounge lizard from the seventies, despite Fanny's attempts to bring him into a new decade. He was currently wearing a shimmery neon green shirt that clung to his massive chest like polyester skin. The top three buttons were undone and a large gold medallion nestled in the soft forest of his chest hair. A wide belt had been cinched so tight atop his navy flared trousers that Bobby's big belly was squeezed into a giant figure eight. And he wore white shoes to match the belt.

In other words, Bobby was not exactly the picture of academic respectability.

"It has to be Casey," Helen said softly. "Candace Goodnight will only talk to a woman. And Casey's the only one I trust."

If it had come from anyone else, Bobby would have been offended. But Helen so seldom asked for anything that a resigned silence followed her plea. A pine log snapped and popped in the fireplace. Burly, sensing the weight that Helen's confidence placed on my shoulders, reached for my hand and held it without speaking. I was overwhelmed with a sudden sense of family, a feeling of belonging so foreign to me that I blinked away unexpected tears.

People are so strange, I thought. And I am among them.

"She could always disguise herself," Weasel suggested. "Even Casey could look respectable if she tried."

Burly laughed and I punched him on the shoulder.

"William is right," Fanny agreed. She was the only one who called Weasel by his real name. "Your lovely friend Marcus can make you over. He seems to enjoy it so."

And so it was that, two days later, I found myself dressed like a Junior League supplicant and on my way to see one Candace Goodnight, professor of anthropology at Duke University. It was a Saturday afternoon and most of the Research Triangle was at one college football game or another. Marcus had made me over in front of the television while his boyfriend rooted on Carolina. Perhaps inspired by glimpses of the stadium crowd, Marcus had outdone himself. I was unrecognizable. A brunette wig tumbled to my shoulders. I was wearing a ridiculously starched khaki shirt and a pink button-down blouse with a bright green sweater tied around my neck. Plus I had these goofy quasi-loafer type shoes on my feet that felt like they were maybe one step above flip-flops. Marcus had wanted me to wear knee socks, but I'd put my foot down, especially when I saw the gleam in Burly's eyes when he heard this suggestion. I knew I'd never get out the front door with knee socks intact.

Casey Jones, preppie P.I.

Someone kill me now.

CHAPTER SIX

Burly had discovered her address easily on the Internet. I was surprised at where she lived. Candace Goodnight was either underpaid or cheap as hell, since she lived in a small brick house in a so-so neighborhood on the outskirts of a forgotten shopping strip just off of I-85. Most Duke professors could afford something a little more upscale.

I was in luck. The good professor was home. I discovered her on her hands and knees in a small backyard landscaped with perennials. When she saw me turning the corner of her house, she sat back and stared. I guess she thought my outfit was as dumb as I did.

"I don't see students over the weekend," she warned me.

"I'm not a student," I explained, flashing my fake P.I. license so quickly she never had time to read the name. "I'm a private investigator. I've been hired to look into an incident involving another professor at Duke. Someone you know."

"And that would be?" she asked, accepting the concept of a preppie P.I. without question. I guess as an anthropologist, she'd seen it all, too.

"David Brookhouse."

"Aaahhh." Her comment hung in the air between us. We stared at each other. "Do you always dress like that?" she asked. "Or are you undercover?"

I glanced down at my outfit. "This is sort of a... costume," I admitted.

"Thought so. You don't look like you feel at home in that get-up."

Okay, so she was avoiding the real subject. But her tone was friendly, and her gaze was frank, and I was starting to like her. Anyone who lobs a book at David Brookhouse can't be all bad.

"Does this mean you're willing to talk to me about Brookhouse?" I asked. "Everything you say is confidential. I won't reveal your name. Will you talk about him?"

She wiped her hands on the plain cotton sundress she was wearing. "Only if you promise to strip him of all respectability and send him to the gas chamber."

"I can try," I offered.

She smiled. "Want some ice tea?"

"Sure." I waited outside, since she didn't ask me to come in, and eventually located a lawn chair behind a gardenia bush and made myself comfortable. She returned with a couple of glasses of the South's favorite elixir and sat on the grass at my feet. Up close, she looked a lot better than she did at a distance. She was approaching fifty and fine lines radiated from the corners of her eyes, but her eyes sparkled with intelligence and she spoke with such animation that the sharpness of her features was transformed into elegance. Her mouth, while thin, was very expressive, alternating between a sardonic smile and quick frowns when the topic was David Brookhouse.

There was no need to prompt her. Once I laid out my cover story—that a young student had been sexually harassed by him and her parents had hired me to investigate—her tale of woe involving Brookhouse tumbled forth like a waterfall of condemnation. He was on her shit list, but big time.

"Don't you know about his trial?" she asked incredulously. "He was accused of rape. A brutal rape."

"Sure, I do," I said. "That's one reason why my client hired me. As you can imagine, they're not anxious to have a suspected rapist sniffing around their daughter."

"Well, that makes them about the only ones in this entire state to think he might be guilty," she said angrily.

I pretended to scrutinize her face. "Hey," I said. "I remember seeing some photos of press conferences during that trial. You were in some of them, weren't you? But you were on his side, right? Or am I thinking of someone else?"

She stared at her bare feet, the light gone from her eyes. "That was me," she admitted.

"So you thought he was innocent, too," I said.

"At the time."

"What made you change your mind?"

She stabbed the ground with a trowel, slicing a beetle in half. "He used me," she explained. "I was nothing more than a prop during his trial. A respectful fellow professor, one known for her feminist anthropological outlook, no less. He dropped me like a used condom when the trial was over."

"What?" I asked, appalled.

"I had just gotten a divorce when I met David," she explained. "I didn't know it at the time, but the police were already questioning him about that woman's rape when he first asked me out."

I didn't tell her that "that woman" was actually my client, but I felt a pang of guilt at concealing it.

"He was the perfect romantic," she said. "He brought me books I'd been looking for, rare volumes that must have taken him a long time to track down. And flowers and—" She stopped, mouth hard. "All that shit women fall for. And I fell for it, too. By the time he was charged and brought to trial, I was already hooked on him. God, I was an idiot."

She stared up at the clouds, no doubt wishing she could roll back the months as easily as the hands on a clock. Like we all do when a relationship turns sour.

"I was furious that he'd been accused like that," she said. "I knew Helen McInnes slightly, and he used what I knew about her to turn me against her. He painted her as a vindictive, dumped girlfriend, one who was insanely jealous of me. I'm sure she hates me now. But now I know she was right. It was him all along."

"How can you know that?"

She looked down, unable to meet my eyes. "There were times during the trial when... details were discussed. Of the attack, you know?"

I nodded and waited for her to continue. She was silent.

"What about those details?" I asked.

She did not answer.

"They excited him?" I guessed.

She nodded, ashamed. "At the time, I didn't pick up on it. Looking back, I realized that whenever the day's testimony had been especially graphic, David was really turned on. He had to have me. And because he was out on bail the whole time, he could have me."

Man, I wondered how many showers she'd taken since those days, hoping to wash the scum of David Brookhouse off her body.

"Did he ever say anything concrete that made you think he'd done it?"

She shook her head. "He was way too smart for that. In fact, I think he was feeding me lies the whole time. Lies about Helen. Lies about other people who might be suspects. He was hoping I might leak the information, that word would get out and someone else's reputation would be tainted."

"Did you leak any of the information he fed you?" I thought of the character assassination Helen Pugh had endured.

"No," she answered emphatically. "I kept it all to myself. I don't accuse people without proof. But in David's case, I now know what he's like and what he is capable of and I know that the thought of getting away with it is almost as good for him as the original attack."

God, if she wasn't a feminist before her experience, she'd have turned into a card-carrying one afterward.

"I'm a coward," she said suddenly. "I've never called Helen to apologize. And she never did anything to deserve any of this. Except to have been the only woman Brookhouse ever saw who walked away from their relationship first. That's probably what she's paying for."

"It's not too late," I reminded her. "Isn't he suing her for defamation of character? You could testify at her trial."

She shook her head. "Testify to what? Besides, I'm still a coward." She glanced at me. "My reputation barely survived that trial. The people who thought David was guilty thought I was crazy. My colleagues who thought he was innocent still believed I should have distanced myself from him. I'm lucky it didn't ruin my career. I can tell you it hurt it. My guest lecture requests have pretty much dried up. Word gets around."

"But that's over. Now you would be righting a wrong," I pointed out. "That would show great courage."

"That would be admitting that I was stupid enough to support a brutal rapist, a misogynist of the worst kind," she said angrily. "And I am supposed to be one of the leading feminist voices in anthropology. Think of it: expert on the societies where females held all the power becomes a helpless, gullible simpering fool just because some charming man brings her flowers. It would set me and probably other women in my field back about three generations. It's bad enough he was seeing so many other women at the same time I thought he was in love with me."

"You knew he saw other women?" I asked.

"I knew he'd seen other women right before me," she said. "I just didn't know he was banging one coed after another until the trial was over, until I had successfully played my part as dutiful girlfriend and let my reputation be sacrificed to protect someone who is, I am convinced, a predator of the highest order."

"You mean that?" I asked. "You really think Brookhouse was guilty?"

"I think David Brookhouse is a user. I think he has nothing but contempt for women. I think he is a liar and a rapist and a killer and the devil incarnate. He dropped me one week after he was found innocent. One week." Her laugh was bitter. "You'd think he'd have at least waited until the press coverage was over."

"When did you find out about the coeds?"

She took a gulp of ice tea. "Someone sent me an anonymous e-mail about a month after the trial. It said something like, 'Don't despair. You're better off without him. Did you know David Brookhouse was having sex with a string of students the whole time he was seeing you? You deserve better.'"

"So whoever sent the letter knew Brookhouse had broken up with you," I said, curious as to who it could be. "Even though you kept it quiet. And they knew he was sleeping with his students."

"Sure he knew," she said matter-of-factly. "The person who sent the letter works with Brookhouse. In fact, he's my new boyfriend. I answered that e-mail and we started corresponding. He's helped me get through a lot. He's not really my type, but I need someone to pay attention to me."

"You're seeing someone else in Brookhouse's department?" I asked, though of course I knew the answer full well.

She nodded. "Lyman Carroll. We have a lot in common." She gave me a wary smile. "We both hate David Brookhouse more than any other person on the face of the earth."

"Lyman Carroll?" I pretended to barely know the name. "Isn't he Brookhouse's rival?"

She nodded. "That's putting it mildly. Lyman hates him."

"Because Brookhouse stole some drug trial from him, right?" I asked, as if groping for the facts.

She nodded again. "They're testing some new drug for a firm in the Triangle. Lyman had the contract but someone leaked that the confidentiality of the study had been compromised. They took it away from Lyman and gave it to David instead. Lyman was devastated that his reputation had been called into question. He's accused David of lying to ruin his career and it's going through all the official channels right now. Once it's all over, only one of them will still be at Duke. I'm convinced of that."

"And you think it will be Lyman Carroll?" I asked.

"You would think that, wouldn't you? I mean, David was accused of rape. You would think Duke would jump on the chance to get rid of him for cause." She spit an ice cube out on the grass. "But I think it will be David who lands on his feet." She shook her head. "I hate that bastard. But he's slick and he's smart and even I have to admit that he's a hell of a better teacher than Lyman. Plus, he has so much more control. If it ends up in front of the ethics committee, David will keep his cool. Lyman will lose it. They'll go with David."

"You think Brookhouse is a better teacher than your own boyfriend?" I asked.

She shrugged. "Look, I go out with Lyman and he's nice enough. He doesn't have all that much on the ball, though. I'm just killing time."

And keeping up with what Brookhouse is doing, I thought. You can't hate someone that much unless you're still tied to them with every emotional string you've got.

"Besides, Lyman is never going to get tenure at Duke," she explained. "He's like a scared rabbit. He worries too much about what other people think. He's always afraid I'll make a scene or embarrass him. The guy just isn't in the same league with David. Believe me, David will win in the end."

Hoo boy, I thought. With a girlfriend like that, what does Lyman Carroll need with enemies?

"You know what I'd do if I were you?" she said suddenly.

I was startled, forgetting for a moment that she had no idea who I really was.

"What?" I asked.

"I'd tell your clients to pull their daughter out of Duke and send her far, far away. UC Berkeley sounds good. Somewhere where David Brookhouse can never set either his eyes or his hands on their daughter again."

She spit out another ice cube. It sailed across the lawn and landed in a freshly dug mound of black earth.

"If I had my way, he'd be dead," she added.

CHAPTER SEVEN

Helen cried when I told her that Candace Goodnight now believed she had been telling the truth about Brookhouse. But I didn't tell Helen that Candace had made it plain she would not testify at a civil trial. What good could her testimony have done Helen anyway, since she had only a gut feeling and no proof?

Which was the problem with the entire case: no proof and way too many gut feelings.

When Helen kept crying, I caught on that something else was the matter. She showed me a stack of letters that had come that week. Each one was postmarked Durham, each one was frightening in the extreme. "I will come at you when you sleep," one read. "Close your eyes and I will be standing over you." The rest were equally scary, designed to touch some psychological chord of terror in Helen. Whoever it was knew her well. The letter writer was looking for a way to worm inside her head. Brookhouse, I thought. Master of the mind, playing mind games. It had to be him.

"Why didn't you tell me these had started coming again?" I asked her, wondering about the timing. We'd had a break of several weeks with no letters. Why had they started again this week? Had Brookhouse been busy with his coeds? Or was it even him?

"I just wanted to ignore them," Helen said. "It's so stupid of me to be afraid when the house is full of other people."

Laughter floated in from the living room where Fanny and Bobby were playing cards with Burly. "You need to take these to the police," I urged her.

"No police," she said angrily.

I let the subject drop.

On Monday afternoon, I donned my student drag and showed up for class once again. Brookhouse spent the hour and a half filling the class in on sexual deviance. This topic perked most of the students right up. I'd never seen such enthusiastic note-taking before.

I'd love to report that Brookhouse's eyes glittered like a weasel's, or that he kept licking his lips while he talked about bondage, or that he revealed details of the campus rapes that only the attacker would know—but the truth was that he seemed a bit bored as he led us through a litany of strange obsessions, none of them pertinent to the case. One thing was for sure: Brookhouse knew his stuff. By the time he got done detailing the sundry ways humans satisfy their sexual drive, I was ready to join a nunnery.

I changed my mind about the nunnery when I emerged into the hallway and saw Luke waiting for me. For once, he had not parked himself beside me in class. At first I didn't recognize him. He had dyed his hair. Gone was the magenta Mohawk, replaced by jet black spikes. Even his eyebrows had been dyed. The transformation was amazing. He was suddenly very exotic-looking, he looked older, more manly—with a strong dose of unpredictability and brooding added in. Just my type. Except for the fact that he still looked twelve years old.

"Wow, you look different." I stared at his hair.

"You like it," he guessed, his attempt at looking fierce spoiled by what was indisputably a beautiful smile. His eyes dropped to my ankles. Satisfied I was still wearing his bracelet, tie gave me another smile. "You didn't take it off yet"

"They'll have to pry it off my cold, dead foot," I promised. "Where were you today?"

"Back of the room. I came in late. I had to do something first."

"Like dye your hair?" I teased him.

"Something like that. Want to go get coffee?"

Uh-oh, I thought. Too much like a date. "Another time, maybe. I'm heading to the Gardens for some down time." As much as I liked Luke, I had an hour and a half before I was scheduled to interview the drug trial participants and see how their weekends had gone. I planned to spend this free time in splendid solitude. The frat house chumminess at Helen's over the past few weeks was starting to chap my nerves. I'd seen Bobby padding down the hall in bright yellow pajamas earlier that day and the sight had unnerved me.

Unfortunately, Luke took my comment about down time as an invitation.

"Was today's lecture disgusting or what?" he asked, falling into step beside me. We walked along one of the many pathways that led to Duke Gardens.

"I don't know about disgusting," I teased him. "I sort of thought that part about shoe fetishes was interesting. I mean, I love a good shoe. The curve of the arch. The smell of leather. I can see how some people might get carried away."

"Really?"

He sounded so luridly hopeful, I had to laugh. I knew it was criminal to flirt with this child, but his brown eyes were impossible to resist. They stood out against his white skin and contrasting black hair with incredible clarity, big and innocent and full of devotion. It was the innocent part I needed to remember—my job was to make sure they stayed that way.

"So, what's your fetish?" I asked him, selecting a spot in the sun near a magnolia tree. Nothing like a good academic discussion about sex to take all the fun out of it. I sprawled on the grass and let the sun wash over my body. I'll say one thing for black: it soaks up the heat. Within minutes, I felt like a piece of bacon sizzling on the griddle. The Carolina fall can do that to you sometimes.

"Me?" Luke plopped his knapsack down and sat beside it. "I'm not old enough to have a fetish yet. I hardly know about—" He stopped, flustered.

"Plain sex?" I asked. "There is no such thing as plain sex," I lectured him. "All sex is exotic and unique, because it's something created at a particular time and in a particular pace. It's there, then it's gone, and you can never get that moment back again." Maybe if I sounded deeply philosophical about the topic of sex, he'd wander off and find someone his own age to play with.

"Really?" He started to say something, then stopped. "So far, all I've gotten is the plain kind," he finally admitted. "And only that because of my car."

"What is so appealing about your car that it draws babes in like a magnet and causes them to drop their drawers?"

"It's a BMW 323Ci," Luke explained. "A convertible. My dad bought it for me when I graduated from high school. He thinks it makes up for the fact that he wasn't there when I did."

"Does it make up for that?"

"No." His voice was soft. "But the girls that have put out in it have helped make up for it."

I laughed. I didn't realize he had that much of a sense of humor. But then I got carried away. "I have a Porsche myself," I said, instantly regretting the words. Another personal detail made public.

"Really?" he asked with overly enthusiastic interest. "I love Porsches." Clearly, he was in that stage of a crush where you search for even the smallest things in common with your beloved, as all hopeful lovers do. "What kind?"

"A bathtub Porsche."

He looked at me blankly and I explained. "It's a 1961 356 B. Bright red. They're very cool. They look a little like a very lot-looking bathtub on wheels."

"Can I see it?" he asked.

"Maybe one day." I yawned. The sun was making me sleepy. "Right now, I have an uncontrollable urge to nap. I have to interview some drug trial volunteers in about an hour. I need to be rested and on my toes, you know, to avoid Brookhouse's groping and advances."

I was only kidding, but Luke was instantly angry. "Has he already tried to put the moves on you?"

"No, no," I assured him. "I was kidding. He's been completely hands-off. I think he'll stay that way, too." I took a sweater from my knapsack and rolled it into a ball. It made the perfect pillow. Sleep was mere seconds away.

"I know why he stays away from you," Luke said, leaning against his knapsack so that his face was almost level to my shoulders. His newly dyed hair glowed in the sunlight with an iridescent blue sheen. "It's because you're not a pushover like the other girls. You probably scare him."

"Scare him?" I asked.

He nodded. "You seem really strong, like you won't take crap from anybody. I bet that makes Brookhouse nervous. I bet he's afraid of you."

I thought about it. The kid was partially right. I wasn't enough of a victim for Brookhouse's tastes, I realized. That was why he was so hands-off.

"Do I scare you?" I asked Luke. "Being an older woman and all."

He smiled and lay down in the grass next to me, his shoulder brushing against mine. "Sure, but I like it."

"Isn't that a form of sexual deviance?" I asked, my eyelids drooping. I yawned again. "And kindly move at least two more feet away. Thank you."

He rolled over guiltily and parked our knapsacks between us.

"I guess we'll have to wait and see," I remember him saying just before I drifted off to sleep. When he woke me just under an hour later, my face was red from the sun. What was that line from *Maggie May* about the morning sun really showing your age... ?

"Were you asleep, too?" I asked him.

He grinned and shook his head. "Naw, I was just lying here and guarding you while you slept."

"Guarding me?" I asked dubiously.

"Sure, from horny college guys. You know?"

"As opposed to you?"

He grinned again. "You sure are interesting to watch when you sleep. You must dream a lot. Your eyelids twitch and stuff."

"You were watching me sleep?" I asked slowly.

He nodded.

"You have got it bad," I chided him. "If you think watching me sleep is interesting, you need to get out more and play with someone your own age."

"Maybe that's my fetish," he decided. "Older women."

I shook my head and stretched, ready to go to work. "You'll have to find one older than me, then," I told him. "Because my fetish is older men." There. That was one obstacle he couldn't dance around.

He didn't say anything, just gave me a little salute as I walked away. The buckles on his leather jacket glittered in the sun. When I reached the street, I looked back and he was still watching. I waved. He waved back.

I walked back to the labs, shaking my head. I'd gotten a good look at his jeans before I'd doused his fire and, from the looks of them, a lot more than hope was springing eternal. But not even that promise would get him anywhere.

The weekly interview was a snap, as usual. A parade of bored students marched into my small basement office, answered a series of dumb questions in various degrees of monotone, then stared at some ambiguous photos and offered lame explanations about what the blobs represented. Finally, they sniffed at their weekly pills—and then swallowed them without ever seeming to care that they were acting as human guinea pigs for an unknown drug. I was no psychologist, and god knows I'm no scientist, but no one seemed to have been driven mad by the experimental drug yet. A couple of people reported anxiety and many of the guys found sexual content in a remarkable number of the test photographs—including one that depicted an exotic orchid in a flowerpot that was shaded by the shadow of a hand coming down over it—but if it isn't normal for college guys to obsess about sex, our educational system is in trouble. Some of the male volunteers were definitely tall enough to have been Helen's rapist, but I could not suspect them of rape based on height alone. Not unless they were in the NBA, of course.

When I was done with the last volunteer—there were approximately thirty in all—I carefully bundled the scoring sheets, stored the empty coded medication packets in a manila envelope and set out in search of Brookhouse so I could hand over the summary results.

I could not find him anywhere, but the papers in my hands gave me a great excuse to snoop high and low for the study files. I finally located a file cabinet in the corner of his office that I decided must house the drug trial information. It was hidden behind his door, had a large plant arranged in front of it and was conspicuously locked up not only drawer-to-drawer but with two large metal bands that sealed it vertically. Sheesh. There was no way I could break in without leaving very obvious traces of my intrusion, so I left it for another day. I wasn't sure what I was looking for anyway. I placed the results of that day's interviews in a stack on his desk, covered the papers with a magazine and pulled his door shut when I left.

The brunette coed he'd most recently dumped from his life was standing in the hallway watching me as I left.

"He's not here right now," I said, ignoring her cold stare.

"I know," she spit back in a nasty tone of voice, as if she was convinced I was screwing the almighty Brookhouse. "I've been watching his office."

Yikes, I thought as I passed her and her rather large pocketbook. It was big enough to hold a knife. Or a gun. Or a matching negligee and peignoir. Stalkers were iffy. You never knew what mood they might wake up in. And it sure looked like Brookhouse had a stalker. Ah well, it couldn't happen to a nicer guy.

"Have a nice day," I told her cheerfully.

She curled her lip at me in disdain, then pointedly turned her back and resumed her hallway vigil.

Now there was someone who could have benefited from an experimental drug.

CHAPTER EIGHT

It was already dark by the time I turned onto a back road that was a shortcut to Helen's house. My route led me through a remote subdivision with five-acre lots thick with hardwoods and Carolina pines. The night was still. Gray clouds covered the rising moon, making it seem as if time had been suspended just so the world could stop and breathe in the cool of an October night. I caught a glimpse of movement beside the shoulder of the road up ahead and slowed just in time to let a trio of deer bounce across the asphalt.

I stopped the car and rolled down the windows so I could listen to the evening's sounds. Crickets chirped, owls quarreled in the woods nearby, traffic hummed along the highway a quarter mile away. How could such a perfect world conceal the kind of human monster that would try to destroy Helen Pugh's life?

As I accelerated again, I heard the growl of a car engine behind me. Someone else making their way home. Someone intruding on my brief solitude.

The moment over, I sped toward Helen's, taking the curves a little too fast just so I could enjoy the rocking of my Porsche. Gradually I became aware that I was being followed. It was only apparent on the straightaways, when another set of headlights crested the hills behind me.

Paranoia is a natural state for me. I've been shot at and run off the road too many times to ignore the anxious voice that lives inside of me. So I pulled into a driveway and cut my lights, then ducked down in the seat. The car behind me sped past without even slowing down; it was some battered station wagon packed with people.

So much for my instincts.

I eased back onto the road and arrived at Helen's just in time to be pulled inside the house by a frantic Fanny.

"She's called again," Fanny said, steering me toward Burly's impromptu office. "Wait here. She's calling back at nine. I'll bring you a plate of food."

I didn't have to ask who was calling back. Fanny knew how desperately I wanted to talk to the woman who kept calling our hotline number. I waved at the living room of people and went straight to the back of the house. I sat on the edge of the bed and stared at the phone, waiting for it to ring—something I hadn't done since high school. It was still ten minutes to nine, but if she called early, I wanted to be ready. Maybe she would ask me to the prom.

Fanny bustled in with a plate heaped high with rice and pork chops smothered in cream gravy. I was just getting started on this cholesterol-laden feast when the phone rang. She was early.

"Hello," I said. "I was hoping you'd call back."

"The woman who answered earlier was so understanding. She seemed to know what I was going through."

"She's a good person," I told the caller. "She doesn't have a mean bone in her body."

"Unlike some people," the woman answered.

"Unlike many people," I said. There was a silence.

"I really need your help," I started to say.

"I can't stop thinking about what you said," she said simultaneously.

"What did I say?" I asked.

"About it happening to someone else."

"Does that mean you're ready to talk?"

"I think so." She was silent. "There's something else you should know."

I got a funny feeling in my stomach. "What?" I asked cautiously.

"I think he's been watching me," she said.

"He?"

"The man who raped me." She paused. "I thought I saw his car tonight. On my block. It was parked a few doors down from my house."

I got a bad feeling then. A real bad feeling. "Hang up and call the police," I ordered her.

"No," she said. "I'd have to report the rape if I did that. I can't do that."

"If he really is following you, you're in real danger. If this is the same man who is stalking a friend of mine, he grabs hold and doesn't let go. It's the watching he likes, the terror he creates in others. You could be badly hurt again."

"I'm not calling the police," she insisted. Her voice slurred and I realized she had been drinking. Liquid courage. "I saw what they did to that other woman who accused him."

That other woman who accused him. She had to be talking about Brookhouse. She had to. A lightning bolt of adrenaline ran through me. If she named him, I could go after him without fear of having the wrong man.

"We have to meet," I told her. "Now. I'll come over to your house. I won't tell anyone. Just let me know where you live."

"No," she said. "I don't want you to know who I am."

"Please," I begged her. "Please just trust me."

She was quiet for a moment, thinking it over. "Do you know where the Tobacco Trail crosses University Drive?" she finally asked.

"Yes, but it's not a great place to meet. Not enough street lights. It's dark. Too dangerous."

"I know it's dark. That's why I want you to meet me there."

"No," I said. "Too dangerous."

"Listen," she told me, her voice growing sharp. "I'll park on the road that leads to the Bulls Stadium. There are lots of lights there. I'll be able to tell if anyone is following me. Just meet me at the base of the bridge that goes over University Drive. I'll be there in half an hour."

That would barely leave me enough time to get there. "So soon?" I asked.

"I can't do it any other way." Her voice fell to a whisper. A television set blared in the background. "My husband will be home around eleven. I have to be back by then. My kids are in bed. They're old enough to leave alone for a while, but I have to make it quick."

"I'll be there," I promised, then hung up the phone. Food forgotten, I ran for the front door. I wanted to get to that side street before she did, not only so I could get a look at her license plate, but because I didn't trust her instincts. I wanted to make sure she wasn't being followed.

I caught a glimpse of startled faces as I stuck my head in the living room. "Back soon," I promised.

"Back?" Burly said. "I didn't even know you were home." He was sitting next to Helen, showing her his famous disappearing ace card trick.

"She's agreed to meet you?" Fanny called after me.

"Yes," I yelled back and took the front porch steps two at a time. This was the break I needed.

She never showed. I risked every stoplight and stop sign to get there early. But the woman never showed up. I waited in darkness at the base of an old railroad trestle that had been converted into a walking trail paved with a wide asphalt band. Traffic whizzed past on University Drive. Cars pulled into the Amoco station on the corner, radios blaring, the beat of heavy bass rattling their windows. A wino wandered past, stinking of urine, never knowing I was sniffing him from inches away.

I waited another hour. Still she did not come.

My bad feeling grew worse with every passing minute. By eleven, I could stand it no longer and walked down to the Amoco station to use the pay phone to call Helen's house. One of these days, I'd have to break down and get a cell phone. Hell, my brain was already pickled. Why not radiate it, too?

Fanny answered the phone like she had been sitting on it, waiting for it to hatch.

"It's me. She didn't show. Did she call back?" I asked.

"No," Fanny said. "But Marcus called. He was very upset. He said to tell you, 'It happened again.'"

"It happened again?" I repeated dumbly. Don't let it be her, I thought. Please don't let it be her. I exhaled heavily. "Did he say where he was?"

"He's working late," Fanny said. "They called him in."

"Ah, shit."

"Not her?"

"I don't know." I was silent, thinking. "Don't wait up for me."

"I'll pray," Fanny promised.

I thanked her and hung up, but even then I knew it was too late for prayer. Even prayers sent up from someone as pure-hearted as Fanny.

Marcus met me outside in the parking lot of the police station. "I've only got five minutes," he said. "They think I'm on a cigarette break."

"What happened?"

"Some woman got raped and murdered over by the soccer fields off Broad Street."

"A coed?" I said, and god help me I asked this almost hopefully. The woman who had called me said she had older children. She was no coed.

But Marcus shook his head. "Not a coed. I don't know a lot. Her car was forced off the road near the Farmer's Market, you know that dark corner near the railroad tracks?"

I nodded. I knew it. It was a wasteland at night. People cut through the area to reach downtown quickly when they were coming in from North Durham.

"No one heard anything because it's a commercial area," Marcus explained. "But she was run off the road and taken from her car there. The window was broken in on the driver's side."

I had a sudden vision of a frightened woman hiding behind an inch of window glass, desperately hoping the car locks might protect her, honking, watching in horror as the man who had been stalking her crashed through that glass as easily as opening the door.

"What did he do to her?" I asked.

Marcus shook his head. "You don't want to know, Casey."

"I have to know," I told him.

Something in my voice made him look up. "You're not connected to this, are you?"

"I hope not," I said truthfully. "But she may have been on her way to contact me. What was her name?"

He shook his head. "That I don't even know. Not yet."

"What did he do to her?"

But Marcus only shook his head again. "I can't tell you that, Casey. You know that. I don't know what they're keeping private and what they're making public. I just can't do it."

"Why are you at work right now?"

"I'm doing the computer search, looking for a match on the crime specifics."

"Nationally?" I asked.

He nodded. "There's nothing coming back so far that matches the details. But it's out there. I can feel it."

"Because all the others matched?" I guessed, although I wondered if he would find a match this time. Perhaps the murderer had had no time to plan this one. He'd had to stop her from meeting me at all costs.

He nodded. "It's got to be the same guy. Someone is messing with our heads."

"Do they still think it might be a police officer?"

Marcus shrugged. "I don't know what Detective Ferrar thinks. I only know he called me himself from the scene and got me out of bed and pulled me in to start searching."

"He called you personally. Why?"

"He trusts me," Marcus said, not without pride. Which was when I knew I'd never get any details out of him, not until he knew what it was safe to disclose.

"Thanks for calling me, at least," I said. "I appreciate it."

He turned to go, but hesitated. "Casey, what he did to this woman was really sick. I can't see a police officer doing it. I just can't. I don't know who it is, but whoever it is likes some really funky shit. You have to help us stop him. Do whatever it takes. We need a break and I don't care where it comes from."

"You're telling me to go down to the crime scene?" I asked.

He turned to look at me again. "I'm telling you that whoever this person is, he needs to be brought down. Now."

Jesus, I thought, as I headed toward the campus. What the hell was this guy doing to the women he raped? And had he done it to the woman coming to meet me?

The area around the soccer fields was blocked off. A ring of police cars, yellow tape and determined officers kept every looky-loo at bay, including me. I parked behind a pizza place on Main and hiked back, circling behind some woods until I was approaching the crime scene from the only direction not marked by a building or thoroughfare. There was still a line of officers blocking the way, but they were far from the eyes of their commanding officers and chances were good I would know a few of them.

I walked past the perimeter, head down, as if I were a coed hurrying back to my dorm at one o'clock in the morning. After skirting three checkpoints, I finally recognized Hugh Fitzpatrick, a New York City transplant who took a lot of ribbing from his Durham cohorts about how Hugh fits Patrick and Patrick fits Hugh. They called him Fitz. He was a good guy, a little rotund, maybe, and had lost too much of his hair for my tastes. But he was happy as hell to be patrolling the kinder, gentler streets of Durham instead of the mean streets of New York. He was also a bachelor, which may have accounted for why he was more susceptible to my charms than your average bear.

"Fitz," I hissed at him from the cover of a mulberry bush.

He looked around, confused.

"Over here. Behind the bushes. It's Casey."

He checked to see that no one was watching and joined me in the bushes. "Why the hell are you hiding in here?" he asked.

"I want to know what's going on and you guys seem pretty serious about keeping everyone out."

"It is serious, Casey," he said. He tugged on his belt and rearranged his belly above it. "The wife of some big shot in the public relations department got offed. The husband broke through the tape and made a big scene. It was pretty grim." He frowned. "Turns out the poor guy was driving home and saw the commotion, then cut through downtown and saw his wife's car wrecked and put two and two together and came racing back here and collapsed."

"Did he do it?" I asked.

Fitz shook his head. "He's been at some fundraising dinner in front of a hundred witnesses, or something like that."

"Did they have kids?" I asked.

He nodded. "A couple. Older, I think. High school. Maybe junior high. I could get Samson over here for you. He knows the family, says the victim was a real nice lady. Knew her from church. Why? You involved in this?"

"God, no," I lied. "What was her name?"

Fitz shrugged. "Let me get Samson for you."

"No, no, no," I assured him, but it was too late. He called Samson Jones over. Samson was a real by-the-book kind of guy who hated my guts and thought all private investigators should be shot on sight. He took one look at me and made his feelings plain.

"I should have known you'd be around. Wherever there's trouble, there's Casey."

"Nice to see you again, too, Sam," I told him. He was a good-looking guy, if you liked biceps and buzz cuts. But he was such a dick you couldn't help but hate him.

"What are you doing here?" he demanded.

"I was driving by and saw the commotion. I wondered what was going on."

"You can read about it in the papers like the rest of Durham. Time for you to get the hell out of here."

Fitz looked a bit taken aback by Samson's vehemence, but truth be told, it was Sam who was the better officer. It was just my bad karma I'd run into him.

"Is it related to the other attacks?" I asked, pushing my luck. Too far, as it turned out.

"You know," Samson said, looking me over, his cop instincts kicking in. "I think maybe you need to talk to Ferrar about this." He cupped his hands. "Hey, Ferrar, I got someone you better question personally," he bellowed across the field. His voice cut through the night like the mating call of a horny moose. About twenty people turned around to stare.

"Nice talking to you," I told them both as I slipped back into the woods.

Samson yelled after me halfheartedly, but I had no intention of stopping to meet Angel Ferrar. Not tonight. And not in this lifetime, preferably.

Halfway back to my car, I stepped across the street, lost in thought, wondering who the dead woman had been in David Brookhouse's life and how she had come to be in the basement of his department's building, to be raped in the first place. I didn't have to wonder how she had come to be murdered. I knew that. She had been murdered on her way to see me.

And now I had someone I wanted to see.

Although it was nearly one o'clock in the morning, it looked like Brookhouse had every light in his entire downstairs blazing. I parked at the curb and stared through his living room windows, making no pretense at hiding the car. I knew he couldn't see my face in the shadows, and I wanted him to know that someone was watching him. I needed him to know that someone knew what he had done, that no matter how respectable and upright and cultured he seemed, there was more than one person walking this earth who was on to him. He had killed a woman that night, I was sure of it. And I wanted him to know that someone knew.

It was stupid of me. I could easily have been recognized. I got out of the car and walked to the edge of his driveway for a better look. He was sitting on the sofa in his living room, watching television, the newspaper spread open on his lap. A cup of something hot sat on a table near his elbow. He had on a plaid bathrobe and seemed absorbed in the television program. In other words, he looked every bit as innocuous as your average husband after a hard day at the office.

He didn't fool me. He was a killer.

And I was a hothead. I selected a hefty chunk of granite that bordered a flower bed alongside his driveway. It was about the size of a softball and would do nicely. I gauged the distance between the living room window and my car. I'd have just enough time to get away clean.

My wind-up would have done Catfish Hunter proud. That rock was going a good ninety miles an hour by the time it hit his window, shattering the glass and setting off an unexpected alarm. Then the rock kept going, as if under rocket power. It sailed across the living room and damn if it didn't crash right through the television screen. Sparks and electrical smoke poured from it. I hit the ground running, heading for my car. Let him be afraid in his own home for a change.

I was so intent on getting away that I almost hit another car rounding the curve and heading toward me. It screeched to a halt a few feet away. I shrank back into the shadows, and started to accelerate around it. The driver turned to glare at me.

It was dark. The street light was too far away to illuminate much. But I could have sworn I recognized the face.

What had brought Lyman Carroll, embittered academic, to the street where his biggest rival lived?

I thought about it all the way home to Helen's house, where Fanny would be waiting up to hear the bad news. My informant was dead. David Brookhouse's facade remained intact, even if his window and television weren't. And we may all have been wasting our time on the wrong man.

I guess Lyman Carroll could have been passing by that particular house innocently. I guess he could even have lived down the block. And I also guess pigs will fly one day if this genetic engineering bullshit keeps up.

But I didn't think it was a coincidence.

Shit. What if we had the wrong man?

No one was asleep when I got back to Helen's, except for her mother who was draped on the couch in the sitting room and snoring so loudly it sounded like a shoe with a loose sole had been jammed into the mouth of a foghorn. Killer was sitting in the doorway staring at her comatose figure with undisguised interest. He was probably trying to determine her species in hopes she might be edible.

I returned to the living room and exchanged a glance with Fanny, who looked away innocently. She was still dosing Miranda with her special Mai Tais, and this no doubt accounted for the snores.

"Let's all meet around the kitchen table," Fanny decided for us all. "I made a sour cream pound cake and you can tell us what happened."

Bobby crushed my foot in his stampede to get the biggest piece of cake. Burly and Helen sat to my right while Fanny squeezed into a chair on my left. I thought about saying, "You may wonder why I've gathered you here tonight," but no one looked like they were in the mood for a joke. They all knew something bad had happened.

"What was it?" Helen asked, her hand unconsciously caressing her throat. "Did it happen to someone else?"

"Worse," I said. "A woman was killed. I don't know who it is, but she's married to a bigwig in public relations at Duke and had a couple of kids."

"Was she the one on her way to see you?" Fanny asked.

I nodded. "I think so."

Fanny started to cry. "She had such a lovely voice. She sounded so... sad every time she called."

Helen reached across the table for Fanny's hands. "She's not sad anymore," she told her. "And if he did to her what he did to me, then believe me, she's better off dead."

"Don't ever say that again," Burly said sharply. Helen turned to him, startled. The glance they exchanged was a private one meant only for those who had suffered horribly. I was an outsider in such things, I realized.

A silence fell after Burly's words. No one could think of a thing to say. Helen truly believed she was better off dead, I realized. I'd better keep a closer eye on her, maybe check her medicine cabinet and pill bottles. Anything was possible.

A cough from the doorway distracted us. Hugo stood anxiously at attention, still dressed in his gardener's uniform of jeans and a T-shirt. "What's wrong?" he asked, his eyes on Helen. "Why are the lights on so late?"

"Sit down, dear," Fanny insisted, drying her tears and busying herself in hostess mode. "I'll get you a piece of cake."

"Something bad has happened again," Hugo decided, making the sign of the cross and touching the gold crucifix that hung around his neck.

"Something bad has happened," I admitted. "And I don't even know if we have the right man after all."

Helen's head jerked up. She stared at me.

"I went by Brookhouse's place after I saw the crime scene," I explained. "He was there."

"That proves nothing," Bobby D. said. He was the skeptic among us.

"And then I saw Lyman Carroll outside his house." I explained who Carroll was to Bobby and Burly.

"It's not Lyman," Helen insisted. She touched the base of her throat. "The man who did this to me was David Brookhouse. I'll never believe anything else."

"I still have to look into Carroll," I explained. "Find out why he was there tonight."

"I can start looking into him," Burly promised. "I'll run a background check starting tomorrow."

I nodded my thanks and evaded Burly's eyes. I'd tell him about the rock through the window later.

"Whichever man it is," Hugo said, "we must take care of him as soon as we are sure." His eyes were bright. "This must not be allowed to happen to anyone else. Where I come from, they both would be dead. Just to be sure. We must stop him as soon as we know. Without waiting for the police." He glanced at Helen and looked away.

"I'm with Hugo," Burly announced defiantly. He knew I'd be pissed, even if half of me agreed with their sentiment.

"Me, too," Bobby grunted. "So long as no one gets caught."

Fanny was in the pantry, rummaging for napkins, or Bobby would never have dared say this out loud.

"Helen?" I asked. "I'd have to say, karmically speaking, that this is probably your call."

She didn't hesitate. "David could do this for the rest of his life," she said, pushing her plate of cake away. "He's too good. They'll never catch him." She stared at Hugo. "I already know who it is. As soon as the rest of you are convinced..." Her voice trailed off.

"What?" I asked. "What do you want us to do?"

"I want you to kill him," she said angrily. "I want you to kill him again and again and again."

It took me less than half an hour to screw up the next morning. I drove by my apartment to pick up some clothes and the moment I turned onto my street, I knew I was in trouble. An unmarked car was parked a few doors down from my building. Skeeter Thompson was behind the wheel. He's a scrawny redneck cop who got religion before he could jump my bones, and so thinks I'm a slut bound for hell. As I unlocked the front door, I saw him reach for his radio. He was calling in the cavalry.

So it was no surprise when my doorbell rang about twenty minutes later, just as I was stuffing a pink babydoll nightgown and a pair of black high heels into a duffel bag. Too bad I hadn't been modeling the outfit: Detective Angel Ferrar had come knocking.

Not that he looked in the mood for love. "I'm too busy to be polite," he said, brushing past me without waiting to be invited in. He sat down on my couch and stared at me. Huge brown eyes with long Latin lashes. Wasted on a man who was all business. "What were you doing at the crime scene last night? What's your relationship to this case?"

"I'm impressed you didn't send an underling to interview me," I stalled. I sat across from him in a chair that showed off my legs. Not that he was looking. The only thing he intended to pull out was his notebook. Which he did.

"I don't trust any of my team to interview you without being distracted," he explained. No smile. "This is too important to screw up."

His sincerity was contagious. I decided this was no time to yank his chain. "I'm working for a woman David Brookhouse was accused of raping," I explained. "Her name is Helen Pugh. Your department knows her as Helen McInnes. She hired me to look into his background. He's filed a civil suit against her. I'm trying to find out anything that might help her case. He's already raped her once. I'd like to stop him from doing it again in court."

Ferrar looked me over in silence. I was glad I had told him the truth. I had the uncomfortable feeling that this particular detective could not only see beneath my clothes, he had bored right down into my soul and was busily deciding if I was a piece of scum or on the side of the angels. I suddenly wanted him to understand that he was not the only one with honorable intentions on this case.

"She hasn't left her house in eleven months," I explained. "Her cleaning lady came here to my home, and begged me to help her. No one else cared. The system let her down big time. If I don't find a way to convince her that she's safe, she'll never leave her house again. I know it. I've seen the way she can't even walk in front of a window without wincing. That's the only reason I'm sticking my nose into your homicide investigation. I'm trying to help her."

"And you think her case is related to my investigation?"

I shrugged. "I certainly don't like to think that there's more than one rapist and murderer hanging around these parts. That's inconceivable. Maybe where you come from..."

He didn't appreciate the slur. "Where I come from, you wouldn't find a woman who was afraid to leave her own home being left alone to suffer for nearly a year without help from family or friends."

"Sorry," I mumbled, not knowing whether I had insulted Miami or Cuba. His accent was hard to pin down.

"Who told you about the crime scene last night?" he asked—and I suddenly understood that this was the reason that he was at my apartment. Ferrar was worried about leaks. With an unknown cop as a possible suspect, he could not afford to ignore it.

"No one told me," I lied. Convincingly, I might add. If you didn't look at him, it was easier. "I had been tailing David Brookhouse and saw the commotion as I was driving home."

He stared at me for a few seconds. I tried not to move, but his dark eyes were impossible to resist. I ended up nervously bouncing one leg over the other, feeling as unworthy as when I'd been caught passing notes in church as a kid.

"You can verify where David Brookhouse was earlier in the evening?" he asked.

Well, shit, talk about a conundrum. If I lied and said yes, Brookhouse was off the hook for last night's murder. If I told the truth...

What was I thinking? "Actually, no," I admitted. "I can't. I lost him. I drove back to his house hoping to find him, and he was there. But I can only vouch for his whereabouts after midnight."

Ferrar nodded and rose to go. "He's not a suspect anyway."

"He should be," I said. "There's something seriously wrong with that man."

"Do you know something I should know?" he countered—and I got the feeling that this man was going to back me into corners all morning, picking my brain clean, if I didn't end the conversation quick.

Although, in this case, I had nothing to give him. "How can you be so sure he's not a suspect?" I asked.

"He's got an alibi," Ferrar offered, taking pity on my obvious lack of progress. "One of the best kinds you can have."

"What?" I asked. "He was in church?"

"He was with someone who hates him," Ferrar explained. "Another professor. They were meeting about some common academic projects and the meeting went longer than they expected. The guy only admitted he'd been with Brookhouse reluctantly. I got the feeling he knew why I was asking and would have been happy to see Brookhouse hang for it."

"Who was it?" I asked. "Lyman Carroll?"

"I see you are making a little headway after all." Ferrar gave me the briefest of smiles. It was like the moon emerging from behind a mountain on a winter night, silver and bright and comforting. The road not taken opened up in front of me for a tantalizing second. Nice guy. Warm home. Quiet life. So he had a wife and kids, shined his shoes, kept his hair short and probably went to Mass three times a week. Ferrar was still quite a guy. If I was going to do a Dudley Doright, I'd do him and I'd do him right.

"That's all you're going to give me?" I complained. "One measly scrap of information?"

"I'm watching you," he answered, pausing at my front door to give me the once-over. He shook his head. "You know too many of my men for me to trust you to behave," he explained in an almost apologetic voice. "But that doesn't mean you aren't telling me the truth. Just watch yourself and stay out of my way. This needs to stop. None of us can afford for me to screw it up."

He left me standing in the middle of my living room, wondering what he would say if he knew I was posing as a student in Brookhouse's class. I also wondered how long it would take him to find out.

Luke wasn't in class the next afternoon and I found that I missed the little squirt. I sat there, pretending to take notes, studying Brookhouse as he moved from podium to window, wondering if he had killed the woman who had been on her way to see me. I imagined a brightness to his eyes not seen before. And I wondered why the hell I had seen Lyman Carroll, well after midnight, heading back to see Brookhouse again? Had he forgotten something? Maybe he'd wanted to share the news of the murder—they were both invested in Duke's reputation. What other reasons could there be?

When class was over, Brookhouse asked me to stay behind. I didn't like it. Maybe my immunity from his sleazy advances was coming to an end.

But, no. He was all business. Hurried business. This time his pressing engagement was a blond who lingered in the doorway, shooting hopeful glances his way.

"There's been a change in the protocol of the trial," he explained. "After much debate between myself, the administrator of the former trial and the drug company, we're going to ask you to interview subjects twice a week instead of just once. You'll get paid for it, of course. But everyone involved feels a need to monitor possible mood swings more closely."

The administrator of the first trial? That would be Lyman Carroll. And it would explain why they had been together the night before. "When did you decide this?" I asked.

It was a mistake to have pushed for more information. Brookhouse stared at me for just a moment too long before answering. "Last night," he said. "Why?"

Well, shit... why indeed? "I just wondered if it was something in my reports," I improvised. "Maybe I screwed up?"

He dismissed me with a wave. "Your reports are fine. Just follow instructions. I'm having a secretary call the subjects and let them know they have to report to the lab on Thursday nights for an interview as well."

"Okay," I said. Mine was not to reason why. Mine was but to do and die. Or, hopefully, not die.

I was back at Helen's by early evening, half-fearing that Ferrar had stopped by to question her. It turns out he had called, and she had told him not to bother. I guess he believed her, as Bobby D. confirmed no one had showed up all day. They'd spent the afternoon playing cards without incident.

All that changed after dinner. I was in the kitchen, helping Burly scrape the remains of chopped pork barbecue into a bowl for Killer, when the doorbell rang. Certain it was Detective Ferrar, I stayed put and prepared to dash out of sight, if need be. I did not want to be grilled by him again.

Fanny answered the door with her usual fluttering friendliness. "Helen," I heard her call into the living room. "A gentleman wishes to see you." She knew better than to let Brookhouse in the door, so who the hell could it be. Ferrar? No. Even Fanny could peg him for a cop and would know to alert me or Bobby.

My curiosity compromised my caution. I crept into the hall and peeked into the foyer. Professor Lyman Carroll waited on the doormat, holding a bouquet of flowers. Helen stood in the living room doorway, staring at him.

"Helen," he said.

Her left hand trembled at her side.

"I know you've been..." His voice faltered as he groped for a tactful way to word the disaster of her recent life. "...under the weather." This had to be the understatement of the year thus far.

"It's been a difficult time for me," Helen said. Her voice was soft, but held more strength than I had expected. "What are you doing here, Lyman? I haven't seen you in almost a year and a half."

Carroll extended the flowers toward Helen. "I brought you these," he explained. "Along with my apologies for not... standing up for you. For not being there when you were going through all that trouble. I was a lousy friend. I'm sorry."

"Why tonight?" she persisted. Helen was smarter than I'd given her credit for.

He stared at his feet. "Did you hear about that other woman?" he asked. "The one who got killed on east campus last night?"

Helen nodded. "It was on the news."

"I thought maybe it might have reminded you of what happened. I thought you might need some moral support or something."

"That's very thoughtful of you," Helen said, seconds before she was interrupted by her mother.

"Who is it, Helen?" Miranda trilled from the top of the stairs in her contralto actress voice. Her accent had turned inexplicably Deep South. "Do we have another gentleman caller?"

Oh, god. Miranda was so looped she thought she was in a Tennessee Williams play. This I did not want to miss. I took the back door out of the kitchen, waving away Burly's questioning look, then slithered through the bushes until I reached the edge of the front porch. If I hung off the railing backward, I could see into the living room. Bobby and Fanny waited at the card table, their heads turned toward the hallway. Tapping lightly on the glass, I attracted Fanny's attention. She trundled over to the window and peered out, her face lighting up when she saw me. I pantomimed opening the window.

She raised it a few inches then whispered, "What are you doing in the bushes, dear?"

"I need to see what's going on," I whispered back. "But I can't let that man see me. I work for him at the college."

"Oh," she said, three syllables worth. Her face brightened further at the thought of such intrigue. "Leave it to me."

I couldn't hang around—or off—the porch all evening. If I moved to one side, I would pretty much be hidden in a camellia bush. I found a plastic milk crate Hugo used to tote tools around in, upended it and dragged it into place. Standing on it, I peered into the living room and watched as Fanny swept into the hallway in a flurry of oohs and cooing. Nearly sixty years of hostessing in the South had imbued her with unstoppable authority. She shooed both Lyman Carroll and Helen into the living room, motioning for them to sit. Behind them, framed by the doorway, Miranda was in the middle of an excruciatingly dramatic grand entrance down the stairway. An entrance being ignored by one and all.

I now had a great view of the entire proceedings and would have been able to watch in peace, had Hugo not crept up behind me and put his hand on my arm. I jumped and bumped my head on a hanging plant that dangled from the eaves.

"Damn it," I whispered. "Don't do that."

"What are you doing?" he hissed back. "You trampled through my impatiens like an *elefante*."

"Sorry," I mumbled. What the hell was an *elefante?* If it was what it sounded like, I was going to trample him next. "This guy is up to no good."

"What guy?" he asked, trying to elbow me aside.

I elbowed him back. "If you want to see him, go inside and see for yourself."

He took my advice and headed for the front door, reaching it just as Miranda stepped off the last stair and started a sweeping arc into the living room, arm outstretched. She was wearing her purple caftan again and a cloche hat. Her unsteady gait told me she'd been hitting Fanny's special Mai Tais pretty dang hard all day. "How lovely to have visitors," she slurred.

I watched the scene unfold before me as if in slow motion, knowing what was about to happen before it actually did. Hugo flung open the front door. It flew forward on its hinges with brutal efficiency, slamming straight into Miranda's face. She dropped like a rock in a pond. No dramatic crumple, no anguished cry. She just keeled over like she'd been shot. As everyone stampeded toward her, I saw Burly edge up the hallway in his wheelchair. He took one look at the scene, then hastily backwheeled out of view, heading for sanctuary in the kitchen. He had decided, wisely, to stay out of it.

All I could see was a bunch of butts sticking up in the air as everyone clustered around Miranda. There was a general commotion and much useless suggesting of water, alcohol and nonexistent smelling salts. Finally Bobby settled the matter by hoisting Miranda aloft. He half-dragged, half-carried her to the couch and flung her onto it. When she landed in an artistic drape, I knew she was milking her injury for all it was worth.

"Oh, you're fine, Mother," Helen said with disgust, flopping into an armchair. She rolled her eyes. Miranda groaned and put a hand to her forehead, where a goose egg was starting to emerge beneath the pancake makeup. The door had won that round.

Fanny hurried out of the room with a promise to bring back ice and some of her special Mai Tais. Miranda yelped her gratitude with such overwrought anguish, it sounded as if someone had just stomped on a Chihuahua. That did it. Not only did I no longer object to Fanny spiking her drinks, I began to fantasize that she'd replace the Valium with some Mexican brown heroin. Uncut. Miranda was going to play this one to the hilt. She was gunning for an Oscar.

Lyman Carroll looked thoroughly confused, and who could blame him? The house was packed with strangers, Helen had been unwelcoming, and a gothic Blanche du Bois had descended down the staircase only to be soundly KOed by a terrified-looking Mexican yard boy. Hugo hovered in the doorway, looking stricken and confused.

"Lo siento, lo siento," he mumbled over and over, unable to meet Miranda's eyes.

The old bat gave Hugo a diva glare, but her heart was not in it. She was enjoying the drama too much.

Lyman Carroll perched on the edge of a folding chair, staring uncertainly at everyone staring back at him.

"Lie," I silently willed Helen. She picked up on my vibe.

"This is my aunt and uncle," she said smoothly. "The woman on the couch is my mother."

Miranda extended a languid hand, too plowed to notice Helen's lie, and pressed her other arm over her forehead. Camille meets Cruella De Vil.

The bouquet had been trampled in the melee. Hugo began to pick the flowers up off the floor, smoothing out stems and leaves. Petals covered the entrance rug. Not much was left, just a few crippled daisies and a dangling gladiola that had sustained such a severe crick in its stem it looked like the upper half of the flower was desperately trying to escape. Hugo looked the same way. He gathered the remaining blooms, mumbled something about a vase and fled.

I stood outside in the dark, shaking my head. Too many cooks. This soup had been spoiled and then some.

"What brings you here?" Miranda quavered as she tilted her head coquettishly at Carroll. She actually batted her eyelashes when she spoke, which was disconcerting since they were fake and trembled on the edges of her eyelids like a pair of tarantulas dancing.

"I was just checking in to see how Helen was doing," Carroll stammered. Clearly, he had never met Miranda before. He looked terrified of her.

No one knew what to do. Miranda stared at her daughter. Helen stared at the floor. Bobby D. stared at Lyman Carroll.

Thank god for Bobby. He took over. "What did you say your name was?" he thundered, sounding every inch like Big Daddy in *Cat on a Hot Tin Roof.* Miranda perked right up, sensing more drama. I knew Maggie the Cat would make her entrance at any moment.

"I worked with Helen at the university," Carroll explained defensively. "We were friends."

The "were" hung in the room. Fanny interrupted the silence by reentering with drinks all around. I could only hope that the one spiked with Valium did not go to the wrong person—not that there was anyone in that room who would have refused a sedative at that point. But Fanny finessed it well. She handed Miranda a drink, then thrust the tray at Carroll. Without hesitation, he took a pink concoction topped with a paper umbrella, as if being served such a drink were standard fare in your typical Southern home. He sipped at it tentatively, clamped his lips together afterward, then set the drink on the card table, where it languished.

"Lyman and I worked together at Duke," Helen explained to the room. A new silence fell. Not even Fanny knew what to say.

"What are you?" Bobby finally demanded of Lyman Carroll. "Some kind of a professor? Are you a graduate student? Janitor? Speak up, man."

His gruffness surprised me. Bobby had been so passive for the past few weeks, his heart problems subduing him greatly, that I was taken aback at this glimpse of his old feistiness. What was it in Lyman Carroll that had inspired him?

"I'm a professor," Carroll answered peevishly. "Helen was my graduate assistant at one time."

Until, I knew, she had left him to work for David Brookhouse. This unspoken information hovered between the two of them until Fanny broke the awkward silence.

"What brings you here tonight?" she chirped.

"Oh, we all know the answer to that one," Miranda interrupted in a husky drawl. She attempted a suggestive laugh, producing a chuckle that was creepy enough to turn a sailor on shore leave toward celibacy.

Carroll glanced at her, his eyes lingering on her sheer caftan. A tremor passed over his face. His eyes narrowed and he stared at his shoes.

Fanny, as always, rescued the situation. "It was lovely of you to stop by. Helen gets so few visitors."

Carroll surprised me. "That's because we're all cowards," he said, as he got to his feet. "I came tonight because I thought maybe with the other woman being killed you might need a friend. Or some company. But it looks like you're covered."

"Oh," Helen said, her voice faint. She shielded the scar on her throat with a hand. "I'm fine. But I am glad you stopped by."

"Have you thought about pursuing justice in other ways?" Carroll suddenly asked.

"What do you mean?" Helen said.

"Hiring someone to look into what happened to you on their own? That sort of thing. I wouldn't blame you if you did."

I knew then that Lyman Carroll's girlfriend, the anthropology professor, had told him that a private investigator had stopped by her house and talked to her about David Brookhouse. He had connected the P.I. with Helen, but had he figured out who I was or that I was posing as a student in his department? More than anything, I needed to stay out of his sight. I crouched down, unable to see into the window, barely able to hear their voices.

"I hadn't thought about that," Helen lied.

There was a silence. I imagined the anxious glances being exchanged across the room.

"What is going on?" Miranda suddenly demanded.

When no one answered her, Fanny changed the subject. "Come with me, dear," I heard her say to Miranda. "We'll make you another drink in the kitchen."

I heard a cry. I risked glancing through the window. Miranda had risen from the couch and was starting toward Lyman Carroll when she stopped, frozen, an arm outstretched toward him, falling slowly to the ground. I thought for a moment that Fanny had done it: she'd finally drugged Miranda over the edge. But no, it was that idiotic fake heart attack act again. As Carroll rushed to Miranda's side, she collapsed against him, rolling her eyes and clutching him for support.

"Call an ambulance," Carroll shouted, staring at the others.

No one moved. Hugo dashed in the doorway, took one look, and walked back out of the room again. Helen shook her head in disgust.

"What?" Carroll said. "Why will no one help her?"

"She's faking it," Bobby D. said gruffly. "Old gal has a screw loose."

"That's a lie!" Miranda shot back, scrambling to her feet. She flounced over to the couch and sat back down. "I am an actress. An actress acts."

"Yeah, well, if you ask me, this actress acts crazy," Bobby mumbled back.

Lyman Carroll stared at Helen, and then at her mother. He looked, at first, perplexed, and then... something more. Something I could not interpret.

"I have to go," he announced and, without waiting for anyone to accompany him, he fled out the front door. Who could blame him? I barely had time to dive into the bushes when he passed within a few feet of my hiding place, headed for his car.

I had expected him to be angry. Or frustrated. Or embarrassed.

I had not expected him to be laughing.

Before I could pump Helen for information on her past relationship with Lyman Carroll, the doorbell rang for the second time that evening. I wasted no time. I jumped into the hallway broom closet. If Carroll was returning and saw me, my entire case would be ruined and my undercover role would be blown. Preserving my insider's look at Brookhouse was worth a lot more than a mop handle perilously close to being a stick up my ass.

It was Luke, my lovesick friend from class. I heard his voice with such astonishment that I gasped, inhaling dirt from a dust mop dangling off the door in front of me. This triggered a sneezing fit. I fell out of the closet, desperate for fresh air, and came face to face with my punk suitor. Worse, Burly had wheeled into the hallway to see what the hell was going on now, and the rest of the house stood behind him, gaping. Who could blame them? It isn't every day a nineteen-year-old punk with spikes for hair shows up, yes, bearing flowers.

"What the hell is going on here tonight?" Bobby D. demanded. He snatched the flowers from an astonished Luke and marched away with them down the hall. "Better put these in water before they get trampled," he growled as Fanny scurried after him.

"What the hell is going on here tonight?" Burly echoed. He looked at Luke, then looked at me. I didn't like all the things I saw in his eyes: mainly, that he could see right through the expression on Luke's face. But the one thing I'll say about Burly—he minds his own business, not mine, even when my business may very well have an impact on him. He didn't wait for an answer, just wheeled away down the hall, his hunched shoulders saying everything. Helen trailed behind him, casting anxious glances over her shoulder, wondering, no doubt, who this kid was, how he had found her house—and why.

Only Miranda remained. "What's this?" she demanded, giving Luke the once-over. "Honey, you better think twice about getting involved with this one." She jerked a thumb my way. "She'll eat you for breakfast."

I interrupted her cackle with a retort calculated to blow her wrinkled old hide out of the water. May as well dispense with her presence pronto. "This one's mine," I told her. "And if you come near him with your horny old ass, I'll come after you with a shotgun." I grabbed Luke and kissed him hard on the lips. At first he froze, his lips clamped together, then he woke up to the opportunity before him and actually slipped me some tongue, the opportunistic little bastard. I pulled away and stared at Miranda.

"Do you mind?" I asked. "A little privacy would be nice."

"Well, I never," she huffed, staggering down the hall looking for someone who'd agree that I was an amoral slut. I was sure there were at least one or two people in the kitchen who would gladly agree.

"What are you doing here?" I demanded once we were alone. I grabbed Luke by the arm and pulled him inside the house, then slammed the door. What if Lyman Carroll was sitting in his car somewhere, watching the house? He might recognize Luke from the department and put him together with me.

I marched Luke into the living room and demanded he sit on the sofa. He sat. I pulled up a chair and faced him as if he were an interrogation suspect.

"Do you realize what you're doing? How did you get here?"

"I followed you," he said defensively. "And where'd that fat guy with my flowers go? I brought those for you, not him."

"Oh, I'll get the damn flowers," I assured him, perhaps not the most gracious speech of thanks I had ever made. "Tell me how you found me."

"I followed you home the other day," he said. "Don't get all excited. It was your fault."

"My fault?" I asked.

"You're the one who told me you had a bathtub Porsche. It was easy to spot. I just had to drive around campus until I found it. Then I waited until you got off work and followed you."

"Aren't you a little young to be a stalker?" I asked. "And don't think you're going to get away with that tonguing at the door."

"You're the one who started it," he shot back. "What are you so hot about, anyway?"

"Because—" I said, then stopped. "Because. That's all."

"Because you're a private investigator and this has something to do with Brookhouse, right? That's why you've been asking me all the questions about him."

"How did you know that?" I asked, alarmed.

Luke looked away, ashamed. "I went through your knapsack the afternoon you fell asleep. I found your license and stuff. And your gun."

"You went through my knapsack?"

"God," he said. "Don't get so upset. It was your fault."

"My fault again?" I asked incredulously.

"Yeah." This time, he was the indignant one. "Feeding me that stupid story about a boyfriend and drugs and dropping out and coming back and being in your twenties and all." He straightened his shoulders. "I may be young, but I'm not stupid. I knew you were at least thirty. And the rest of your story didn't make sense either." He had the decency to issue a disclaimer. "Not that you aren't really hot for someone who's over thirty," he added. "I still really want to, you know, maybe, go get coffee or something."

"I can't tell you how your offer brightens the evening of this decrepit, ancient old crone," I said sarcastically.

"You mean the old lady who just left?" he asked, missing the point. He shivered at the thought of Miranda. "She's scary."

"Forget it," I said. "Do you know what you've walked into the middle of?"

He shook his head. "But I want to help you. I do."

What choice did I have? He knew enough to blow the whole case. I had to tell him. With any luck, he'd help me out by keeping quiet about it.

Luke was triumphant at the thought Brookhouse might be a murderer and rapist. "I knew it," he said. "I told you he was a scumbag. That man has got to be brought down." He slammed one fist into his palm, making a smacking sound. Something he'd seen in a movie, I knew.

"Well, you are not going to be the one to bring him down," I explained. "No way. This is really serious. You know that gun you found?" He nodded. "I use that gun just about every Sunday. At a shooting range. So I can kill with it, if I have to. People shoot at me and I shoot back. I don't want you in the middle of anything. This isn't a game. I don't want you hurt."

"You think I'm too young to be of any help," he accused me.

"I think you're too inexperienced in things like this to be of any help, even if you want to be."

"You need me," he pointed out. "I'm on the inside, too. Please, I know I can help you."

We were interrupted by the arrival of Fanny. "Here we are!" she said brightly. She was carrying a tray piled high with homemade oatmeal cookies. "I knew you would want some of these, dear," she said. "And I brought us some nice milk, too."

Milk and cookies? Was this some sort of subtle slap in my face? I watched her carefully, but no, Fanny seemed sincerely engrossed in making sure Luke got his refreshments. No sarcastic subtext for her.

"Give me some of those," Bobby demanded as he strode into the room, a fresh deck of cards in hand. I guessed the right to privacy had a statute of limitations of approximately five minutes in this house. "And I don't want milk," he complained. "Christ. Is there some bourbon anywhere?"

Bourbon and cookies? God. He'd keel over by midnight.

One by one the rest of the household filtered in, drawn by their curiosity about the young boy who had arrived bearing flowers for me. But no one was rude enough to ask outright who he was or what he was doing at Helen's. Not even Burly, who wheeled his chair over by the fire and sat there, stabbing a burning log with the fireplace poker and sending sparks showering.

"What's your name, dear?" Fanny asked and, upon receiving it, proceeded to grill him about where he had come from, who his parents were, what he was studying, his dreams in life and everything short of what favorite position he enjoyed while having sex in that hot car of his. And here I thought I was good at wringing information from people. I was but an amateur compared to Fanny. Four daughters had apparently taught her how to squeeze a young man dry of every scrap of personal information. She learned that Luke was from New Jersey, that his father was CEO of some software company, that his mother was dead and a much younger model had taken her place—and that both his father and stepmother were now on an around-the-world cruise to celebrate their fifth wedding anniversary.

"Oh, dear," Fanny said. "You're all alone here at school. Didn't they help you move in?"

Luke looked at her like she was crazy. "I can move myself in just fine," he assured her. "I've been going away to school since I was eight."

"No." Fanny was appalled. "I wouldn't have dreamed of sending my Charles away until he was at least fourteen."

Luke shrugged. "I guess I was in the way."

"If you don't mind," I began as I stood and glared at everyone assembled in the room, "Luke and I are going out into the front yard to have a private conversation." This was getting a little too chummy for me. If I didn't nip this bonding in the bud, Luke would soon be sitting at the card table with the rest of the crew, sipping Mai Tais and getting in my way.

I grabbed Luke by his arm and dragged him out the front door before he could protest. Behind me, Burly was stabbing at the burning logs with such enthusiasm, I heard a crash as they tumbled to the hearth.

"Ouch," Luke complained when we reached the front porch. He pulled his arm free and rubbed it. "That hurts. Jesus, you're strong."

"You have no idea," I promised him. "Get in your car."

"What?"

"Get in the car. I don't want anyone who might be watching this house to see us together for any longer than he has to."

"Like who?" Luke asked. He sounded excited. "Who's watching the house? What's going on?"

"Nothing is going on," I said slowly as we settled down in the front seat of his BMW. Man, the kid was right. The car was like a rolling palace. The seats were covered in leather and if you pulled a lever, fell straight back. I know because I accidentally pulled the damn thing while looking for the seat adjustment and ended up flat, laid out like a Sunday buffet.

Luke took this as an invitation. Before I could stop him, he was on me like a fly on cow flop. He pressed his mouth on mine and this time he went straight for the tongue.

"Stop it," I demanded, struggling back to an upright position. "Are you out of your mind?"

"Well, if we can't work together, why can't we be together?" he asked. "I know you like me, Casey. I felt you really kissing me in there. We would be a great team."

I wiped my mouth with the back of my hand, and glared at him. "Forget about it, Luke." I should have been nicer, but I couldn't help it. I couldn't afford for him to get in the way. "I appreciate your help. I really do. But I don't date guys younger than my dirty laundry and I can't expose you to danger."

"I'm not afraid of danger," he protested.

I sighed. There was no way I was going to win this battle and I wasn't going to waste my time trying. I'd have to think of a way to throw him off the scent. But I needed more time to think.

"Look, I'll see you in class the day after tomorrow. We can talk afterward, go get that coffee you keep talking about. Maybe you can help me out after all."

"Really?" His eyes widened and he smiled. Man, it was a great smile. "I knew I could talk you into it."

"Who says you've talked me into it?" I asked, peeved. "I didn't say you could help. I said maybe you could."

"I meant I knew I could talk you into getting coffee with me. Admit it. You like me. A little."

He waited, head ducked, those long eyelashes of his resting against his cheeks. Damn. Like taking candy from a baby.

"I've got to go," I said firmly. "Don't say a word until we see each other again, you hear me?"

He followed my instructions to the T. Not a word passed his lips. Instead, the cheeky little bastard leaned over, put a hand on the back of my head, pulled me toward him and laid a kiss on me that I could feel clear down to my size nine toes. God help me, I kissed him back. And by the time I regained my sanity, it was too late. As I scrambled from the car to moral safety, he was grinning ear to ear.

"Don't ever try that again," I warned him as he backed down the driveway, still grinning.

141

I watched him drive away, too quickly. What nineteen-year-old in a BMW wouldn't floor it after a shot of testosterone? Was that what it had been like to be nineteen? God, but life must have been pretty damn hot back then. Too bad I couldn't remember.

The scene inside Helen's house was considerably cooler. I stuck my head in the living room. Fanny and Bobby were playing gin rummy. Helen was staring out of the window at the darkness, her face taut, as if she expected someone to come barreling out of the night at any moment to attack her.

Burly was in the hallway, on his way to bed. Whistling Mrs. Robinson. Off-key.

"A little tutoring on the side, Case?" he asked. I thought that he sounded more amused than peeved. Maybe.

"That kid's going to be a problem," I predicted.

"Not for me, he's not." The bastard was laughing as he wheeled away. God, but he knew how to get me. I couldn't tell what he really thought about it.

"Casey, get in here," Bobby ordered gruffly.

"Excuse me?" I asked. "And you are who? The King of England?"

Bobby slapped an ace of hearts down on the table and Fanny scooped it up. "I don't like that guy," he said, scowling at Fanny as she rearranged her cards with triumphant glee.

"He's just a kid. Relax," I said. "He wants to help with the case."

"Not him. The other guy. The snotty professor. Something's funny about him showing up here." He stared at the two of spades Fanny had discarded with disgust. Fanny giggled.

"He was just checking up on Helen," I said.

"I don't think so." Bobby nodded toward Helen. She was still staring out the window. "I think maybe you better talk to your client."

"Do you mind?" I said. "It's rude to talk about her like she's not here."

"She's not here," Bobby said. "That's my point."

He was right. Helen was a million miles away. I took her arm and pulled her back. "What's going on?" I asked her. "Why did Lyman Carroll show up here?"

She shook her head. "I don't know, but I've got a bad feeling about it." For a moment, I thought she might cry, but her composure held. It was as if she had made a deal with herself: in return for not functioning on a larger scale, for not being able to take a step out of her front door, she would prove her self-control on a smaller scale instead. She would not cry. At all.

After a moment of deep breathing, she began to tell me the whole story of Lyman Carroll. Not that there was much of a story. She had known all along that the drug trial had been pulled from him and given to Brookhouse. Partly because it had been her fault. She had been Carroll's graduate student at first. And she'd had a feeling he liked her, but he had never made any overtures. Together, they had set up the protocol for the first drug trial. He had been sloppy with it, she felt, unethical at times. He'd wanted to fudge the reports. Just a little, she said. Not change the results. But when people failed to show for their weekly interviews, he had not always included that information. Maybe he had even falsified a weekly interview or two. She had gone to Brookhouse with the information. Brookhouse had notified the drug company and taken over the trials. And Carroll had never forgiven Helen for it. Especially when she started seeing Brookhouse romantically. They rarely spoke after that and avoided each other. Carroll had never attended the rape trial.

"Then why did he come out here tonight?" I asked, though I suspected I knew: to find out if Helen had hired a private investigator to track Brookhouse. But why would he care if anyone was closing in on Brookhouse? So he could make his move and take over the drug testing again?

Helen shook her head. "I don't know. But it feels wrong. I don't think he's up to anything good."

"My point exactly," Bobby nearly bellowed. He threw his cards down on the table. Fanny glared at him. "Just because the doc says I've got to take it easy on my ticker, doesn't mean I'm brain dead," Bobby said. "There's something I don't like about that guy. He's a weaselly, pale little prick. With a stick up his stuffy professor's ass. I'd watch out for him if I were you."

Good old Bobby. I could always count on him for a cool, measured professional opinion.

CHAPTER NINE

Some men deal with rivals by erupting with jealousy and displaying their Neanderthal heritage. Others take the smart route. They smile. They shrug. Then they rip your clothes off and ravish you until morning.

Burly was one of the smart ones. The next morning, I rolled out of bed humming like a tuning fork on caroling day, then followed the scent of frying sausage to the kitchen. Bobby D. was ensconced at the table, shoveling in pancakes with one hand while lining up his heart pills with the other. No one else seemed to notice this irony. Fanny was on chef duty and wore a frilly pink apron that made her look like a giant bonbon. She greeted me with a plate full of hotcakes and a stack of sausages that ignited lust in Bobby's heart.

"How come she gets four pieces of sausage and I only get one?" he complained.

"I'm the one doing all the work," I explained with a smug smile.

Bobby grunted, annoyed that Fanny was keeping him in line, even marginally. "Where's Hot Wheels today?" he asked, using his favorite name for Burly.

"I wouldn't expect to see him before noon," I answered confidently. "Frankly, I'm surprised he survived the experience."

Bobby ignored this reference to my sex life. I think the very thought of it scares him. He stared at me intently instead.

"What?" I asked, moving my plate out of his reach. He was worse than Killer when it came to sausage.

"You need to pull out of that bullshit undercover poking around," he said bluntly. "I told you not to talk to the girlfriend of that professor. That guy showing up last night was the result.

145

Too many people know your face now. You're going to get made any day. You better get out before you have your own civil suit on your hands. Besides, Fanny is the one who got you in that class, and I won't have them tracking it back to her. I don't want her involved."

Fanny began to clean the counters with the misplaced energy of the guilty.

"No, Casey can't give up now." Helen stood in the doorway, her voice close to panic. How long had she been standing there listening?

She was dressed in her bathrobe, her hair still rumpled from sleep. "I know Casey is getting close," she said. "I could feel something off Lyman last night. I couldn't sleep. I think he's involved somehow. But I can't think how he could be."

"Then sit down," I ordered her, "and let's talk." I ignored Bobby's glare.

Over breakfast, I made her go through it all again—her relationship with Lyman Carroll, her complaints about the drug trial, her leaving to work with Brookhouse and their subsequent affair. Then, of course, I brought her back to the night she had been raped. By the time we reached this point, Bobby D. and Fanny had quietly moved into the living room, giving us more privacy.

"Could you be wrong?" I asked her. "Could the rapist have been Lyman Carroll?"

Her reaction was immediate. "No," she said, shaking her head. "Absolutely not. The man who attacked me was tall and thin. Lyman is almost fat. You've seen what he looks like. I would have—" She stopped and took a gulp of coffee. "I would have noticed if the man who raped me was that overweight."

"So how could he be involved with the attack on you?" I asked.

"I don't know. But I know the answer is in that department somewhere. And you're the only one who can help me. Promise me you won't give up now."

It was the first time she had shown any real appreciation for what I was doing for her. What could I do?

I agreed to hang in there. Despite Bobby's protests, I left in early afternoon to check on my furry lab friends. It was Thursday, but there had been no time to alert the study volunteers about the new interview night. My mission would focus solely on mice.

The days I did not have to interview drug trial volunteers, I still had to stop by Lab 14D and make sure the specially bred mice in Lyman Carroll's study were happy and well-fed—and not because they were nibbling each other's cute little heads off. All was well in Rodentville. A small population explosion in cage three had produced more pink morsels of mouse flesh, but Mom did not seem in the mood to sample her young—surely a good sign for the new tranquilizer being tested? All seemed normal.

I checked the read-outs on the room monitors. Temperature, humidity and light levels had behaved over the past twenty-four hours. This, apparently, was a big deal: if levels dropped below acceptable limits more than once within any fifteen-minute period, the feds would come busting down the door to free the mice, haul us away in chains and feed our carcasses to attendees of the next local PETA meeting. At least, that was the impression I got.

However, while little rodents were found in abundance that afternoon, the big rats escaped me. I saw neither David Brookhouse nor Lyman Carroll, though I did hear them arguing behind closed doors at one end of the basement hall. It was a room with a wall of one-way glass that was normally reserved for the videotaping of subjects in psychological studies. The room was supposed to be soundproof, but it was an old building and not even meticulous renovation had brought about that miracle. I hovered outside the door, ear pressed against metal, and could catch a little of what was being said.

Lyman Carroll was mad as hell at David Brookhouse. Best of all, the argument involved sex.

"Your behavior is endangering the grant," Carroll was yelling. "Can you not keep your hands to yourself for a few more months at least? We agreed. There is a time and place for everything. This study is not the place for you to indulge your obsessions."

"You're one to talk. And I'm not touching anyone in the study." Brookhouse sounded equally angry.

"No, you're just screwing every other coed who walks in the door. Word gets out, David. Word *is* out. It was bad enough after your trial. It was a miracle we kept the grant. We have a lot to lose here."

Unfortunately, Brookhouse calmed down during this speech, so his reply was difficult to hear. I only caught portions of it: "... my private business... nothing to do... innocent... if you hadn't walked a gray area to begin with..."

Walked a gray area? Okay, so they weren't professors of English.

I wanted to hear more, but a door banged shut in the stairwell and I could not afford to be caught with my ear to the proverbial keyhole.

As I drove back to Helen's, I thought about what I had overheard. At least Carroll and Brookhouse had not been discussing me. Or the existence of a private investigator on Brookhouse's tail. It meant Carroll was keeping that little tidbit to himself. But then he had a motive to keep it to himself—if Brookhouse fell, Carroll was in a position to take over a lot more than the drug trial.

"Do you think they know who you are?" Burly asked me the next night. We were down at the pond, waiting for the sun to set. I was perched on top of the picnic table and Burly was in his wheelchair beside me. We were holding hands as the sun inched toward the horizon. It was all very romantic—except that we were discussing whether my undercover role had been blown.

I shrugged. "I don't know. Maybe Carroll has figured out who I am. But I don't think that Brookhouse has me made. He'd never let me near him, or his study, if he knew who I really was. He'd have fired me or called me on it before now."

"Unless he's waiting for a time to get you alone," Burly mumbled.

I laughed. "Which one of us are you worried about? If I end up going one-on-one with Brookhouse, I'll snap his skinny ass in two."

I was going to illustrate my testosterone-inspired claim by karate-kicking a bunch of small green bananas off a nearby palm, but a distant buzzing stopped me. The sound grew louder. Like a plane taking off... but in the woods? That made no sense.

"Do you hear that?" I asked.

Burly heard it. And Burly knew it. "This is not good," he shouted, wheeling furiously toward the oil drum grill. "Are you armed?"

"God, no," I said. "Why?"

The answer swept into the clearing in an avalanche of deafening sound. Motorcycles. Choppers. Six or seven of them. All manned by refrigerator-sized human beings whose faces were obscured by helmets and goggles. They wore an assortment of leather and denim, cuffed, torn, their colors and emblems taped over with black masking tape so that I could not tell which club they were with.

There was no question why they were there. The moment they saw us, they started shooting us the bird, shouting insults and gunning their engines. They must have been waiting, and watching, when Burly and I headed down to the pond. Talk about sitting ducks. He was Donald and I was Daisy.

"Shit," Burly shouted. "Take this." He tossed me a long barbecue fork, then grabbed a grill brush and started swinging it as if testing a bat for weight.

I caught the fork and held it out in front of me like a sword. What the hell was I supposed to do with it? Stab some biker in the rump and see if he was done?

"Who are they?" I yelled at Burly over the din of engine whine. The bikes roared into the clearing and bore down on us. Burly positioned himself so that his back was protected by the large metal grill. I stood beside him, determined that no one was going to hurt him if I had my way.

"I can't tell who they are," he said. "But there must be someone I know in there." Burly had been a biker. A long time ago. In his pre-wheelchair lifetime.

"What do they want?" I wondered out loud.

"Us," Burly said.

He was right. The bikers reached us and dropped into a circle formation. The noise was incredible as they whirled around us, shouting, gunning their engines, drawing the circle tighter and tighter, cutting off escape. They were definitely trying to intimidate us, at the very least. A couple of rocks whizzed past, their names for us were getting ever more personal and a few of the guys started to take turns running their bikes in at us.

As their circle drew closer, they gouged up gravel from the clearing and sent dirt and sand spinning. Pebbles bounced off my exposed ankles like BB gun pellets.

"Assholes," I shouted at them. They probably took it as a compliment. "Is this about you?" I yelled to Burly.

"I don't think so. These guys are seriously pissed off. It's got to be you."

I didn't have time to ponder the implications of this remark. Because, apparently, Burly was right. It was about me.

"You bitch," the fat guy yelled as he swept by again. He must have been the leader. The others fell silent. He passed by again. "Go the hell home," he yelled.

"What do you want?" I screamed, holding out my fork.

"We want you to mind your own business," he shouted back on his next time around.

That rankled me. I don't like to feel intimidated. It tends to piss me off. I waited until he was coming at me again and tried to stab him in the arm. The fork slid off his thick leather jacket, but he skidded slightly before recovering. "Maybe you need training wheels," I yelled after him.

"Casey," Burly's voice cut through the commotion. "Get back here and shut up."

"No," I said. "They have no right to be here. This is our space. Cowards." I lashed out again with the fork.

Bad move. A couple of the riders reached into their pockets and produced objects that popped open in well-choreographed malice. Blades glinted in the sunset's glare.

"Shit," I told Burly. "They've got knives."

The men held the blades out as they passed, stabbing their arms forward, trying to draw first blood. One nicked me on the elbow. It stung like an insect, then started to throb. "I'm cut," I shouted, somewhat incredulously—then jumped back toward Burly as another arm lashed out at me.

"This is not good," Burly said. "I've got nothing on me." He'd gotten a new wheelchair, a stripped-down model made for rougher terrain. There was no console and hence no gun in the console.

Burly does not like to be unarmed. "What the hell are we supposed to do?" he yelled in frustration. "Spit at them?"

"The noise has to attract someone," I said, hoping it was true.

The bikers began to take organized turns darting at us with their bikes, thrusting the front wheels at my shins and pulling away at the last minute. They were laughing when they did it. Which really pissed me off. I was about to punch one in the face—helmet, goggles and all—when the sound of Burly's voice stopped me.

"I've got it," he yelled. He wheeled backward, reached under the grill and began dragging a canister toward him. There was a hose attachment at one end. "Get out of the way, Casey," he ordered me. "This thing's got some range on it."

I heard his tone of voice and obeyed. I scrambled to one side just as Burly pulled the bush burner onto his lap, aimed the hose toward the bikers, then adjusted the gas outtake dial. He pulled back a slide mechanism and fire whooshed from the nozzle in a seven-foot flame as big around as a man's arm. The biker darting in toward Burly took it in the face, screamed and pulled away to one side, dropping his bike in the dirt. Bike and rider slid sideways toward us, sending dirt and gravel spraying. The bike stopped, its wheels spinning wildly in the air. The rider cursed and scrambled from underneath the chopper, crabwalking away from Burly. He was wearing black cowboy boots with red inlaid tooling. I stared at those boots. If I ever saw them again, he was a dead man.

"Get him," Burly screamed. "Take it. Take it. Make them back off." He held the bush burner out and I grabbed it, tucking it to one side like an action hero toting a bazooka into the jungle. I ran at the bikers, chasing the fallen rider out toward the circle. The others swerved to avoid hitting him. The circle broke rank. I turned the outtake valve, and flames leaped out at them. If I swiveled the dial back and forth, the release action catapulted the flame forward in bursts, almost like fire balls, unpredictable and frightening, burning an arm here, catching the edge of a leg there, scorching a seat cover.

The bikers backed off. I pushed my luck further, stepping over the downed bike and rushing at them. The man on foot shouted to a buddy, who slowed. Before I could turn his ass into smoked pork butt, the runner jumped on the back of the second bike, tucked his arms around his companion and shouted, "Let's get the hell out of here."

"Good idea," I hollered back, running toward them.

"Gun," Burly screamed at me. "I saw a gun."

I heard the sharp pop of a handgun and was about to hit the deck, flamethrower and all, when a blast rocked the clearing, the boom audible even above the roar of bike engines. A shotgun. With some serious firing power behind it.

I threw myself to the ground. The bush burner's flame jerked to one side and settled on the downed motorcycle. A flannel shirt wound around the seat back caught fire and flames licked toward the gas tank. Oh, shit, it was going to blow.

"Get out of there," I screamed at Burly. He was only a few yards from the burning bike. If I had to, I'd carry him out. But Burly was quick. He didn't need my help. He tucked his head down and started pumping. His arms were a blur as he wheeled furiously to safety. The riders were in chaos. Who had fired the shotgun? Another boom echoed through the clearing. Who the hell was aiming at what?

"Who's firing back?" I yelled at Burly.

It didn't matter. The bikers had decided they were outarmed. They were heading straight for the narrow dirt road that led them out of the clearing and onto the gravel drive back to the highway. They were giving up.

Bobby D. stood in their way.

He was wearing a shiny blue sharkskin double-breasted suit that glittered in the coming sunset's light. His wraparound sunglasses made him look like a villain in a James Bond movie. So did the shotgun he held up to his chest. He had reloaded quickly and it was pointed straight at the lead rider's head.

"Let them go!" I screamed at Bobby. "Just let them go."

He cocked the shotgun with a savage pull to make clear it was ready for firing, then held it up in the air, pointed over the trees, and squeezed the trigger again. Another blast rent the air. The bikers panicked. They swarmed out of the clearing and roared down the road. Suddenly, one of the bikers swerved, his head jerking back. He crashed into the bushes, snapping limbs and spraying leaves, but emerged miraculously back onto the gravel a few yards down the road and sped unsteadily away.

Fanny stepped out from the side of the lane, a cast-iron frying pan in hand, her face lit up in triumph.

"I got one," she hooted as she waved the frying pan around like a club.

"Let them go," I yelled at her. "There are too many of them."

It was a moot point. The last of the bikers disappeared in a cloud of dust just as Hugo came running down the dirt path, his face frantic with worry.

Behind me, the gas tank on the smoldering bike blew. It wasn't like in the movies where a huge blast rocks the world and a mushroom cloud of flame shoots toward the sky. It sort of popped, not all that loud, either, and then long fingers of fire began to lick in a contoured arc around the crank case.

"Put it out," Burly screamed. "Put it out, put it out." He'd wheeled to safety, but that wasn't his concern. "We can find out who they are through the bike," he yelled in explanation.

I scrambled toward the bush burner and turned off the flame, then grabbed a white plastic bucket and began to run toward the pond.

Hugo was faster on the uptake. He whipped off his leather belt, looped it around the burning bike's handlebars and began to drag it toward the water. I hurried to help him. We pulled it over the sand and into a few feet of water. The metal sizzled as oil slicks bloomed on the pond's surface and black smoke choked my nostrils. We dragged it out further until the machine sank beneath the surface, bubbles marking the spot. I was waist-deep in bilge and smelled like a mechanic's wet dream. But most of the bike had escaped being scorched.

"Jesus Christ," Bobby D. complained, trudging through the heavy sand like Godzilla lumbering toward the ocean. "What was that all about?"

"Someone doesn't like what I'm doing right now," I said. "They think I should mind my own business. That's all I could find out."

"That's all we need to know," Bobby growled. "You're not going back to Duke. Period. That part of your plan is over."

Fanny was huffing and puffing behind him, her face deep red. "Did you see that, Robert?" she shouted. "I banged a man."

Well, I never thought I'd hear those words from Fanny's lips.

"Right in the face," she crowed. "With this!" She held the frying pan above her head in victory. I had to give her credit. It had probably taken both hands to swing that sucker. She must have at least broken his nose. I was impressed he'd been able to keep on riding.

"God," I said, making my way to shore and flopping down on the sand. "What the hell are bikers doing getting involved in this mess?"

"Drag it out," Burly ordered from the edge of the sand. "I want to see it."

Hugo waded back out into the pond, grabbed the handlebars and wrestled the bike across the beach. I helped him drag it toward Burly.

"That was a pretty good move there with the bush burner," I told him.

"Man, if I'd been able to move, they'd be dead now," he replied. He was as seriously steamed as the bike. He examined it carefully. "This is a Kawasaki. It's designed to look exactly like a Harley, but it's bush league." He ran a finger along the edge of the bar that held the front wheel in place. "Look at this," he said, pointing out a decal that had been slapped on the metal. It depicted silver-and-black crossed swords impaling a yellow heart.

"I think that's a tarot card," I said. "What riding club is that? Do you recognize the symbol?"

He shook his head. "No. But Weasel will."

"You should have let me shoot one," Bobby complained as he joined us, wheezing, to check out the bike. "I brought plenty of ammo."

"I'm gonna need you and your ammo," I assured him. "What I don't need is you behind bars."

"It's okay, Robert," Fanny consoled him. "I hit my man hard enough for both of us." And I had been naive enough to think that Fanny would be a good influence on Bobby. Instead, it was working the other way around. I'd have to be on my toes next time she was frying up sausage in case she got in the mood for a little target practice.

"Why would a bunch of bikers be involved with professors at Duke?" I wondered out loud.

"Hired," Burly said. "They're probably some loser outlaw band with bad-ass aspirations who hire themselves out to intimidate."

"Well, it worked," I admitted. "I'm intimidated."

Hugo was starting up the road at a run.

"What?" I yelled after him.

"We left Helen alone at the house," he called back.

"Oh, shit." He and I began to sprint toward the house.

She was safe. The bikers had passed her by. But she was in no way okay. We found her slumped in the hallway on the other side of the front door, crying inconsolably.

"I couldn't even get out the door," she was sobbing. "I couldn't even turn the handle." Her muffled voice broke and she cried even harder. "I wasn't any help at all. I'm no good to anyone. I may as well be dead."

I knelt beside her and put my arms around her shoulders. She laid her head against my chest. Her tears stained my shirt and seeped through the thin cotton. I could feel the dampness on my skin. "Ssshhh," I soothed her, rocking her back and forth.

Hugo knelt by her other side and gently placed a hand on one of her shoulders. He didn't say a word. He hardly moved. He just let his hand move with her as she rocked back and forth, lost in her shame.

I'd never heard Helen cry before. The sound pierced my heart. She seemed so utterly full of despair. I wondered if she had ever cried about what had happened to her until now. Her sobs seemed dredged up from some dark place deep inside her soul that she had never visited before.

I felt someone staring at us. Helen's mother stood at the top of the stairs, peering down. One half of her face was shrouded in shadows, the other half masked by a spreading bruise caused by her run-in with the front door. She stared at her daughter, her face familiar yet somehow unrecognizable, as if she were a creature conjured from the fringes of hell. She watched her daughter sobbing yet never moved. Instead, she seemed to drink in the sorrow with a rapacious detachment, as if storing it for use on the stage one day. Then she slowly turned her head away and, without a single word, walked back into the darkness of the second floor.

If it wasn't about her, I realized, Miranda just didn't care.

Bobby D. and I may bicker, pick, banter and ridicule each other, but we rarely fight. And we certainly never fight in front of other people. Professional solidarity being what it is and all.

That night, after Helen had been seen safely to bed, Bobby D. and I broke all of our rules—in a knock-down, drag-out argument that sent Burly and Fanny fleeing from the living room in search of peace. By the time we had waded through the mutual name-calling, physical threats and litany of past professional failures, even I was exhausted. But Bobby had not budged.

"No," he said. "Absolutely not. I'll fire your big white ass if you go back to Duke. Use your head, darlin'. You've been busted. That's what those bad dudes on bikes were all about."

"You can't fire me," I said defiantly. "Who would do all your work for you? Besides we're partners, remember? You can't fire a partner." He always liked to try and forget that single moment of largess in an otherwise stingy proprietorship career.

He made a sour face and rubbed his chin. I suspected what he was really pissed about was his sharkskin suit, which he had intended to wear out dancing with Fanny. Instead, it had been splattered with mud from choppers roaring past and would likely never recover. Then Fanny had proved too elated from her face-cracking pannery to want to go out dancing—as well as too dismayed by Helen's collapse to leave her.

Bobby stared down at his mottled pants legs morosely. "I was gonna get me the Texas Ranger Special at Hartman's tonight." He pouted. "There's nothing to eat in this damn house."

Right. There was enough food to supply a manned air force carrier to China and back. I ignored his attempts at changing the subject.

"I have to do something, Bobby," I explained. "I can't just leave Helen to deal with this alone. She's a good person. With the Wicked Witch of the West for a mother and no one else in the world to care."

He shifted uncomfortably and glanced toward the windows. Hugo was sitting in a rocking chair on the front porch, Bobby's shotgun across his lap.

"He can't hear us," I said. "Now that you've dropped the volume below buffalo bellowing." Bobby doesn't like anyone to observe his softer side, except Fanny, I suspected.

"I didn't say you had to give up the damn case," he grumbled. "I said you couldn't go back to Duke and pretend to be a student, which was a stretch in the first place, if you ask me."

"What do you propose to do then?" I asked. I jabbed a burning log and sparks showered out in a burst of color. Killer stretched lazily in his spot on the hearth, opened one eye, then fell back asleep. Unless the house was in full blaze, he'd take his chances.

"I've been thinking about it," Bobby admitted. "It's time to attack this creep outright. In public. Where it hurts."

I started to listen. One thing about Bobby: he can be maddening, self-absorbed and lazy. But he has been around for thirty years in all the right dark rooms and alleyways. He knows people. He knows how to push their buttons. I'd be a fool not to listen to his advice.

"I say that we convince Helen to file a countersuit against Brookhouse for the rape and attack," he suggested.

"Can she do that after the criminal court finding of innocent? Isn't that double jeopardy?"

Bobby shook his head. "Not in the eyes of the law. We get her to file in civil court. Very visibly. Then we put the pressure on. I can pull in some men. They can follow him everywhere he goes. You drop the undercover. Don't ask for trouble. Stay out of his way. It's better he never sees or recognizes you. But keep questioning the people he works with. Have Burly look into his past even more. And look into that other professor who came sniffing around here just as hard. Let's find out who's dirty and who isn't."

"You think it has to do with the drug trials?" I guessed.

Bobby nodded. "I think when you've got a pair of professors and a bunch of bad-ass bikers and a drug study in between, that drugs might be the link. What else could it be?"

"What do you think the cops are going to do if Helen files suit?" I asked.

Bobby grunted. "From what you say, Ferrar is smart. He'll probably stand back—he has his hands full anyway—and let us do all the work. Then he'll come in and ask to see what we've found out. He won't stop us, I can guarantee you that. He needs his manpower to look into other problems."

"So you don't think Helen's rape is related to everything else that's been happening?"

Bobby shrugged. "I sure as hell don't know. But we've got to start somewhere, and I think that means the drug trials."

"I need to get a list of the students in the trial," I said. "I could break into the department secretary's offices. She's supposed to be calling everyone in the study about the new interview night. She'd have a phone list, at least."

"Let Burly keep working on that through his computer," Bobby ordered me. "I don't want you going near that joint."

I kept silent. No sense starting a new argument. "What is Brookhouse going to think when I don't show up for class. Or work?"

"Use the kid," Bobby suggested gruffly.

"Luke?" I asked.

"The punk," he confirmed. "Did Brookhouse see the two of you hanging out together?"

I nodded.

"Tell the kid to feed him some story. You ran off with a boyfriend. Anything. Didn't you say he wanted to help?"

"Okay. I'll get on it." I thought about it. "What about a good lawyer for Helen? The one she has now is a defendant's lawyer. We need a pit bull."

"Fanny will take care of that. She knows the best lawyers in town. Meanwhile, we're staying put. I don't want those biker dudes coming back here with only Helen and that wetback around."

"Bobby," I complained.

"Sorry." He rolled his eyes. "That Mexicali guy."

"His name is Hugo. You're hopeless." I stared at him. His face was as worried as I had ever seen it. He looked like a giant bulldog in mourning. "How long have you been thinking this new plan through?"

"Since this afternoon," Bobby admitted. "And I'll tell you why: whoever we're after knows who we are and where we're living. But we don't have a goddamn clue who we're up against here. We are shooting at possums in the dark."

Fanny and Burly were up to something. I discovered them the next day making lists in the kitchen. They covered the pages when I entered the room. "What's going on?" I demanded as I headed for the coffee machine. I'm still waiting for those geniuses at Mr. Coffee to invent an intravenous drip model. I'll be the first to sign up.

"Thanksgiving," Burly explained.

I stopped, dumbfounded. Had the weeks really passed that quickly? What the hell was the date anyway? "Thanksgiving?" I repeated.

"Two weeks, Casey. We've been camped out here nearly a month."

God. I thought about it. Had time really gone by that fast? It had been like living in a foreign country. My old life in Raleigh seemed planets away. Bobby had been dealing with the forwarded phone calls. I'd only had to worry about Helen's case.

Wow, I thought. I had never lived with so many people for such a long period of time, at least not without guns being drawn.

"I can't believe it's that close," I admitted. "Why all the secrecy?" I tried to peer over Burly's shoulder at the notebook in front of him, but he folded his hands over the page. "Go away," he said. "We're planning the menu and Thanksgiving guest list. This house could use some cheering up."

"And so could Helen," Fanny chirped.

"Thanksgiving guest list?" I said. "What guests? This state ran the Indians out long ago."

"Maybe so." Burly smiled mysteriously. "But we plan to have a few surprise guests anyway."

I stared at them both. "I don't like surprises."

"You'll like this one," Burly predicted.

"It will be good for Helen," Fanny explained as she bustled around pouring cheese grits into a bowl for me and unearthing the bacon, which she had hidden from Bobby D. in a cupboard too low for him to ever bother with. "She needs more company."

"More than us?" I was incredulous. "Is there anyone left in the Western world not living here yet?" I'd had to wait a good fifteen minutes for the bathroom that morning. It was not a good way to start the day. Besides, crossing my legs and waiting has never been my style.

"Trust me," Burly said, nodding confidently. "You're gonna love it."

"Right," I said sarcastically, annoyed that someone had nabbed my favorite coffee cup—the one with bullethole decals on it that I'd brought from my apartment. Bobby was probably the culprit.

God, but I was getting tired of other people. It was going to be a very long weekend.

CHAPTER TEN

Tracking Luke down was easy. He had a phone in his name. The phone led me to a dorm room. By Sunday, I was parked outside it, waiting.

But of course, he wasn't there. I cruised around, searching for his car. No luck. The kid had a lot of nerve, maintaining a social life without me.

Thus, by Monday afternoon, I was reduced once again to crouching in the bushes outside the psych department building, like some academically inclined Peeping Tom.

He came ambling up a good two minutes after our class together was supposed to start. Clearly, punctuality was not his strong suit. Unaware that he was being watched, he looked much younger than when he was trying to swagger about. He was eating a Twinkie, for godsakes, as happily as a kid. Bits of white cream filling curved around the corners of his mouth like a pair of parentheses. He was wearing gray jeans and a maroon-and-black striped knit shirt that all the lead singers in rock bands wore these days. For Luke, it was a positively garish outfit.

"Pssst," I hissed at him through an opening in the bushes.

His face broke out in a huge smile. "Casey?" he whispered back, searching through the branches to see where I was hiding.

"Just get in here," I ordered him. I grabbed his sleeve and pulled. It stretched out preposterously, then he sort of boomeranged into the clearing where I was huddled. We crashed together and stayed together. A completely inappropriate turn of events.

"Hello there," he said and smiled. The icing still clung to the comers of his mouth.

"Get off me," I demanded, untangling myself from his arms. "You are way too young for me. Now that we both know who I am, let's just say I'm old enough to be your mother."

"My mother's dead," he offered.

"Oh, god, you're so romantic." I tried to push him away. "I mean it. Back off."

He took a step back and looked me up and down. Very slowly. I was dressed in my regular clothes again, black jeans and tight black T-shirt topped with an open denim shirt. "You look different," he said. "Like you could kick my ass."

"I could," I assured him. "So keep your hands to yourself."

"Cool." His voice dropped. He stared at my body. It was a strange feeling. Outside, the fall day was sunny and crisp. Inside the cluster of bushes, it was as artificially dark and hushed as a bedroom in the middle of the afternoon. The time when people cheat on their spouses. Suddenly, unbidden, a mini-fantasy of Luke and me thrashing around in the bushes while people walked a mere few feet away began to unroll in my mind.

I stared at him. He stared at me. The boy was watching the same mental channel that I was.

"We can't," I said.

"We could," he offered.

"We aren't."

"We should."

"Oh, Luke." Why did we have to get into this? He was so sweet. I didn't want to be mean. And, sure, I'd love a tumble in the bushes as much as the next unprincipled slut. But I'd spent the last few weeks slamming Brookhouse for taking advantage of kids too young to know the difference between lust and love. And I wasn't about to turn around and do the same damn thing with Luke. My heart had a thick covering of rawhide around it at this point in life, his was still very tender. And very breakable.

"I know what you're thinking," Luke said, staring at me with that head-ducked look that made his eyelashes seem even longer. Man, he was probably deadly with girls his own age.

"I doubt that," I said firmly.

"You think I'm too young to know what I'm doing. You think I'm not serious about my feelings for you, that it's all just a crush."

"It probably is, Luke," I tried to explain. "It takes a while to find your footing in things like love, and until you do, you can get hurt and be confused and trample on people without meaning to. I love the way you think of me, but I don't want to be someone who stomps on your heart, okay? I like you."

"I'm old enough to know how I feel," he protested. "If I'm old enough to be drafted and go fight for my country and maybe even be killed, then I'm damn sure old enough to know who I want to be with."

"This isn't a war," I pointed out, though, in truth, my private opinion was that the tricky dance of the heart that goes on between men and women was the oldest running war in the world.

Luke stared at me, using those huge puppy dog eyes to their full advantage. I felt like I'd just pulled out a newspaper and smacked him over the nose with it for no reason other than to be mean.

"Don't look at me like that," I said. "I have a boyfriend."

"That guy in the wheelchair?" Luke said. "He doesn't care about you."

"How can you possibly say that?" I countered. And even though my words were true—Luke had no way of knowing what Burly's feelings were for me—his assertion somehow carried an ominous warning. My heart cringed a little. What would make Luke say such a thing?

"Look, I saw the way he was staring at us when I came over to that house," Luke protested. "He was sitting in his wheelchair at the far end of the hall when you kissed me. And he didn't look like he cared a bit."

"Burly knows how to handle me," I explained, pissed I had not noticed Burly behind us when I'd pulled that kissing stunt in front of Helen's mother. "He knows not to hem me in."

"If you were mine, I'd never let anyone else get inside your head. You'd belong to me—and only me—and you would want it that way."

"Well, then, we have a difference of opinion right there," I said. "Because I don't belong to anyone. Not even to myself." I had no idea what I'd meant by that last remark, but it sounded good.

Luke thought so, too. He responded by grabbing me and kissing me hard on the mouth, trying to force his pure intentions on mine—with the use of good tongue work, apparently.

I couldn't help myself. The kid could kiss. I licked the icing from the corners of his mouth and that led to one thing, and then to another. Before I knew it, I was right in the middle of trying to kid myself that a little making out never hurt anyone when the unmistakable sound of a window being raised interrupted us.

"Hey! You kids can't do that in my bushes," an indignant voice called out.

I peered up and saw a black guy hanging out a second-story window. He had a bottle of cleaning fluid in one hand and was waving it at us like a club.

"Go do that nonsense in your dorm rooms," he ordered us, his face outraged: the portrait of a janitor on the warpath. "You trampled my pansies and don't you know the whole building can see you in there? You kids today got no shame. No sense of decorum."

The guy had a point: I realized we were on display for the entire second floor; the opening in the bushes formed a perfect stage for our shenanigans, at least for anyone sitting in the balcony area.

"Go," I said to Luke. "We'll solve this another day. Right now, I need your help. I need you to give Brookhouse a cover story to explain why I'm not interviewing the drug study subjects tonight."

"Only if you agree to meet me later," he insisted.

"Luke, that's blackmail." My voice was deadly, but one look at his face and I knew he would not budge. "Okay," I finally agreed. "Meet me at my apartment later tonight."

"What time?" he asked as he wrote down my address on his open palm with a ballpoint pen. His smile was spectacular—and triumphant.

"Late. Midnight." I didn't want to say more. "I have some things I need to do first."

"Midnight?" He sounded hopeful. Too hopeful.

"Only to talk," I said sternly, not sure who I was kidding more—me or him. "Only to talk."

"Do I have to come down and chase you away with my broom?" the janitor yelled at us from above.

Luke and I started to laugh.

"You'd better go," I said. "More classes start on the half hour." I told him what I needed for him to tell Brookhouse. All he had to do was say I had called him in the middle of the night on the way to Florida with my boyfriend and asked him to tell Brookhouse I wouldn't be back. I'd call later with an address where he could send my paycheck, I added, just to make the story sound more believable. Just in case.

"A boyfriend in Florida? That's easy," Luke said. "It's what you told me in the first place."

"I did?" The kid remembered a hell of a lot more about me than I did about him. But then, I was an ancient old crone of thirty-six and my memory was clearly failing me. "If Brookhouse knows who I am," I explained, "you could be in danger. So don't ever let on that you know anything else about me but the cover story."

"What else am I going to learn about you?" he asked hopefully.

"Don't get cocky on me," I warned him. "I can always change my mind."

"What if you can't get away?" He looked slightly panicked. "What are you doing until then?"

"I'll be there," I promised. "But late. Midnight, okay?"

He kissed me again, then poked his head out of the bushes and began walking toward the building. The janitor had reached the front steps and was pretending to shake out a mop. He had clearly seen Luke do his gopher act. He watched closely as Luke bounded up the steps like a colt who's approaching the starting gate of his first Preakness.

That janitor was no fool. He lingered on the steps, pretending to mop them, eyeing the bushes for what seemed like a good ten minutes before he finally gave up and went inside, leaving the coast clear for me to escape.

I had just enough time to stop by the anthropology department for a word with the ubiquitous Candle Goodnight, feminist professor. If she'd given me up and tattled on me to Lyman Carroll, I wanted to know it.

I waited outside her department building for a while without luck. Where the hell was she? I could have sworn she taught her sole afternoon class at this time.

I finally wandered inside, made my way through musty halls to a sleepy-looking office and was told she had the day off.

Clearly, I should have gone into academia.

I trudged back to my car, drove to her depressing brick house and knocked. No one answered the door.

I guess it was possible she had a life. Just because I didn't have a life outside of work didn't mean the whole world was as equally pathetic. Maybe she was having an early dinner out, doing her laundry, enjoying an afternoon delight with Lyman Carroll. Maybe she was even getting her nails done.

But her house looked so quiet and dark. No lights on inside. At all. Outside, the porch light glowed, as if someone had forgotten to turn it off that morning.

I had a very bad feeling about that porch light.

I should have gone back to Helen's, but that would have meant facing Burly and, even though I had no intention of sleeping with Luke, I still felt guilty about agreeing to meet him alone. Plus I would have had to face Bobby D., who would have instantly smelled something far worse on me: rebellion.

I was a coward and called instead. I learned that Helen was deep in conversation with a well-dressed lawyer not only willing, but anxious, to take on her civil countersuit. It seems this lawyer had a daughter in college at Duke and was not keen on her taking any psychology classes as long as David Brookhouse walked the campus. Plus, like many Durham lawyers, he had stopped by the rape trial and been outraged by what Brookhouse's Atlanta lawyer had gotten away with. He was genuinely anxious to repair a miscarriage of justice. It sounded good to me.

I also learned that Burly had not yet met with success in tracking down the biker club that had attempted to terrify us. The pierced heart logo may not have been the club's symbol after all, he explained, but Weasel was looking into it. He added that Weasel's current relationship was apparently going well: his new girlfriend had invited him to scrape the rust off her trailer and help her paint it. She had even offered to let Weasel pick the color. That's a sure sign of domestic bliss in some circles. As an aside, I learned that Hugo was still on the front porch, shotgun across his lap, and was thought to have slept there all night. I could only surmise he enjoyed watching his handiwork in the front yard grow—or was fulfilling some manly vow of his own to serve and protect Helen.

All this information I gleaned from Burly. I declined to talk to Bobby D. "I've got to go now," I hedged. "Some people have agreed to talk to me about Brookhouse. Some of his colleagues. I'll see you later on."

"Sure," Burly said. "Do you want us to save you some dinner?" That was his roundabout way of asking when I would be home.

"No," I said, feeling more than vaguely guilty. "I'll get something to eat on my own. I won't be back until really late."

Not wanting to contemplate the hidden meaning of that particular statement, I hung up quickly and checked my watch. Right about now, the drug trial volunteers would be showing up for their Monday evening appointments. I wondered who had been drafted to interview them. Would Brookhouse do it himself or drag Lyman Carroll back into the process?

From what I could tell, most of the drug trial volunteers were showing up for their interviews, staying about twenty minutes each before exiting with looks of relief. No one looked all that damn happy, I noted, and wondered if this was because they felt the new demand to report twice a week from now on was a real pain in the ass—or if this new happy drug was turning out to be not so happy after all.

I had opted to hide behind a large magnolia tree instead of in the bushes. After all, you can't go back to Paris again. Besides, it was getting dark early these days. November nights in Carolina are mean and stingy. They always seem to leap on you without warning—a far cry from the full harvest-mooned kindness of October. Worse, the temperature had dropped dramatically with the arrival of twilight, a reminder of the winter to come. I was as cold as shit, despite my jacket.

By the time eight o'clock rolled around, eighteen volunteers had reported for their interviews. Not a bad turnout. There were twelve more to go, unfortunately, and the warmth of my car was clear across campus. I could not afford for my Porsche to be spotted near the department, too many people had seen it. It was blocks away, parked near the hospital and Duke Gardens. In prime stalking territory, in fact, but that could not be helped. I was well-armed, just in case.

The building had pretty much emptied out by six o'clock, when the last of the clock-punching academic and office staff straggled out, anxious to get home and hunker down against the sudden cold. For the next few hours, more dedicated professors and grad students left sporadically. Lyman Carroll hurried out, alone, just before seven, his round face wearing the slightly perplexed look that gave him such a benign air. Head down, he had not noticed me behind the magnolia, but by then I was frozen stiff as a board so perhaps he thought I was part of the trunk. He seemed preoccupied, in a hurry and clearly worried.

So who was staying late to get the interviewing done? Brookhouse? An unlucky grad student? From past experience I knew a few obsessive graduate students would remain hard at work until close to eleven o'clock, when the building was officially locked. Whoever it was needed to leave—because I needed to break into the drug study files.

I got my answer about nine o'clock when, after a lull of more than half an hour without any new drug trial volunteers showing up, David Brookhouse emerged into the night air dressed in a designer trench coat. He surprised me by stopping to light a cigarette on the front steps of the building. I had not realized he indulged in anything stronger than a pipe. He stood on the top steps, illuminated by the glare of a recently installed security light, looking like an actor loath to leave the spotlight. He stared up at the beam as if it were the Holy Grail, dragging in lungful's of smoke, contemplating some unknown thought.

I didn't get it. Brookhouse looked like such a nice guy. He was handsome, accomplished and, apparently, completely empty inside. What did he really see when he looked in the mirror? Who was it that stared back at him and compelled him to plow through coeds while, possibly, committing far worse crimes against women? What secrets was that man carrying around in his soul? And what made him think he could get away with it forever?

Maybe because he was.

After another minute or so, he took one last drag, then ground the cigarette with a decisive twist of his foot. He danced lightly down the steps, happier than Fred Astaire leading into the grand finale. No inner worries for this man. Whatever his colleague Lyman Carroll was carrying around in his soul did not plague David Brookhouse. He was whistling as he passed by my hiding spot. As he reached the tree, I imagined that the cold night air grew even colder, that some sort of vacuum from inside him tugged at my guts, sucking me toward him. I wanted to say a prayer. Images of demons from long-forgotten Sunday school texts rose in my mind. But they never look like that in real life, do they? No horns, no hooves, no snouts, no fire-filled eyes. Instead, they always look just like you and me.

Why was Brookhouse so happy? Whatever professional facade he maintained was slowly crumbling around him, that was easy enough for any observer to see. His colleagues were warning him about his actions. He still had the past rape trial hanging over his head. He'd never get tenure at Duke, not with that stigma surrounding him. Yet here he was, perpetuating the issue with his mean-spirited civil suit against Helen. On a more practical level, I had supposedly fled to Florida with my boyfriend, leaving him with the scut work.

So why the hell was he so happy?

He disappeared down the brick walkway, the picture of academic respectability, a successful professor heading for a well-deserved armchair and maybe a little nighttime reading with a snifter of brandy by his side. I waited until he had turned the corner, then took off for my apartment. The coast was clear. It was time to put Plan B into action.

Lights were on in some of the other apartments of my building, and I was in no mood to answer questions about where I had been for the past few weeks. I crept quietly into my place and retrieved what I needed. First up was a warmer outfit. I unearthed my thermal underwear and put it on beneath my black jeans and black tee-shirt. We're talking functional, not stylish. Long underwear is not sexy, it never has been, I am convinced, not even in pioneer times. For one thing, it always looks slightly dingy, even when it is new. For another, those little thermal pockets scream retained sweat. But I wasn't heading out on a date. I was heading out to break the law.

I had recently started storing my burglar tools in a metal chest hidden beneath the floorboard in my closet, next to my Colt Python. Call me paranoid. I've had my place tossed enough times to have long since reconciled what I was willing to lose with that which could not easily be replaced. I've also learned the hard way not to carry my gun and tools on me unless absolutely necessary. My conspicuously red Porsche invites traffic stops by Durham's finest. My gun is illegal. Hell, I'm illegal. Best not to take chances.

Tonight I needed all the help I could get. I checked the Colt to make sure it was loaded, put it in the outer pocket of my knapsack, then located everything else I would need.

Remembering the glass on the office doors, I added a roll of masking tape at the last minute.

Just before eleven, I was back on watch behind my magnolia tree, waiting for the final grad students to be shooed home. They left right on schedule, pale figures hunched against the cold, heads down, anxious for a sliver of real life before their academic grind began again in the morning. What happens to people like that when they finally graduate? I wondered. Do they disappear into libraries across America? Or finally get suntans and blend in with the rest of us?

At last it was showtime.

I was contemplating scooting inside the front door before anyone could lock it when the janitor I had seen earlier in the afternoon poked his head out into the night. He looked pretty happy, as he should. By my calculations, he was earning time and half by now. Like Brookhouse, he emerged to stand on the front steps and enjoy a cigarette. He took his time about it, too, unbothered by the cold or the dark. When he was done, he carefully stubbed out the butt, then pocketed it. He even leaned over to retrieve the butt that Brookhouse had left behind. The front steps once again immaculate, the man disappeared back inside the front door. Stopping, I was sure, to bolt it.

I'd have to find another way in.

It was a race against routine. I ducked into the shadows along the side of the building and reached a side door just as it slammed shut. I could hear the click-click of bolts being drawn and tested. Double damn. I scurried around the building to the other side, where it was dark and masked from the view of passersby. A back entrance was hidden by a row of Dumpsters. This time I beat the old coot to it, I was sure of it. But would I have time to get inside before he locked the safety bolts? I scrambled down a few concrete steps onto a dark entrance well. Looking around at the shadows surrounding me, I got to work. I knew these doors led into the basement hallway.

The basement where the hotline caller had been raped.

It was locked, of course, with a half-assed spring lock, but it would only take me a minute or two to slip it. I had my jamb card ready in my back pocket, and worked the metal carefully between the double doors until the lock sprang back. I was inside and heading for the shelter of a lab doorway when I heard the clang of the stairwell door. Damn. For an old man, he was fast.

A pair of soft drink machines had been placed in a spare alcove. I had just enough time to squeeze behind one of them, concealed by the dark, when the janitor came whistling by. This was one man who enjoyed his job. He pulled a heavy ring of keys from a drooping back pocket and double-locked the back door, testing it twice to make sure the deadbolts held. They held all right. Fort Knox had nothing on that set of doors.

It occurred to me that, if this was how all the doors locked, I had no way to get back outside again. God, spending the night in a psych lab basement with a bunch of scurrying mice was not my idea of fun.

I held my breath as the janitor passed me, but he seemed fixated on his work ahead. More doors to lock, no doubt. More ways to trap me inside.

The minute he headed back upstairs, I hightailed it out of my hiding spot and followed. He had at least two or three more exits to secure, I was sure. And I needed to use that time to get my ass to the second floor where the psychopathology department offices were located. The old man's footsteps echoed on the steps above me as I waited, holding the stairwell door open, mindful of the noise it could make. As soon as I heard him push through the doors to the first floor, I hauled my ass up the stairs as fast as possible.

The second floor was as dark as a mausoleum. And, like all college buildings, it smelled faintly of dust. Like a tomb. Combine that with all the skeletons rattling around in the closets around here and, well, you had a real uplifting theme going. It was creepy. Very creepy. It was also impossible not to think about the nut jobs Brookhouse discussed in his class all day—the sociopaths, the sexual deviants, the men who fantasized about sex with sheep or liked to spy on their sisters. Their ghosts seemed to linger in the hallways, watching. This was where they lived in perpetuity, I realized. This was where their fame flourished.

I shook it off and headed down the hallway toward the main offices. The locked doors were no match for my skills. I was inside and at the receptionist's desk within minutes. She was Brookhouse's designated lackey, the secretary who always got stuck doing favors for him without any additional pay, I was sure. It took a good ten minutes to rifle through her desk drawers. I found the usual paperwork, stamps and office supplies, a box of incontinence pads—what was she, forty-five at most? Yikes, was this what the future held for me?—plus a bottle of gin, maybe that was the source of her bladder problem, and, bingo, a fuzzy photograph of the secretary posing with David Brookhouse at some Christmas party. Brookhouse was wearing a red-and-white Santa hat that drooped over his right eye. I'm sure it had seemed like a good idea at the time. The photo looked worn and well-caressed. God, how pathetic. I hated these glimpses into people's souls. No wonder she did so many favors for him. I pocketed the photo and kept going. No phone number lists for anyone. Not even the department faculty. And especially not the drug study volunteers.

I'd have to break into his office.

If I'd paid more attention to the janitor's routine, I'd at least have had a decent idea of where he cleaned at night. But, in the grand tradition of the human caste system, I had never even noticed him before that day. He could be sneaking up on me at any moment. I didn't like that feeling at all.

Brookhouse had an office at the far end of the second-floor hallway. I held my breath and moved slowly toward it, pausing every few steps to listen. A faint clanging echoed up from the first floor. A metal pail, perhaps? Was he mopping the foyer? That would give me a little more time upstairs.

Dang. Brookhouse had no easy spring lock on his office door. The bastard had a deadbolt in place. It's awful how untrusting some people are. I ended up having to tape the glass on his door window and tap out a hole big enough to put my hand through. It broke with a crack of my flashlight handle but the shards held, clinging to the adhesive. I peeled away an opening and carefully worked a hand inside. If the bolt required a key on both sides, I was sunk. But no, it clicked open with a twist of my wrist.

I was inside.

Of course, I still had the metal-encased file cabinet to conquer. This was not something that could be done in the dark.

I propped my flashlight up on a pile of books and aimed it at the file cabinet. Light patterns danced across the wall behind the metal case, and the fronds of the office's oversized plant swayed every time I brushed past it, casting a shadow that looked like a giant hand quivering toward me. Nothing like an overactive imagination to calm the mind.

God, but I hated paranoid people. Brookhouse had some nerve. I'd have to pry the heavy metal bands encircling the file cabinet apart enough to get the drawer open before I even thought about picking the drawer lock. Fortunately, I had watched Brookhouse retrieve the drug trial information pretty closely and I at least knew that I was aiming for the middle drawer. I took a crowbar from my knapsack and jimmied it in place, between the metal band and the lower drawer. I knew the thin walls of the file cabinet would buckle first, and I did not want to inadvertently jam the second drawer shut. I balanced the crowbar, lifted my right leg up, placed my foot against the rod and started to push as hard as I could, my back pressed against a wall for leverage. After a moment, the pressure started to buckle the lower half of the file cabinet, bending it inward and changing the angle of the entire case enough to give me a few inches' clearance between the middle drawer and the heavy metal bands. I positioned the crowbar a little bit higher and repeated my technique. This time, the bottom of the middle drawer crumpled in a few inches. I hoped to god it would still open. I switched sides and applied pressure to the other metal band. By then, the file cabinet looked like it had been hit by a truck. But I had a good chance at prying the middle drawer open at least six or seven inches. It might be enough to pull out the files I needed.

The drawer lock was easy to pick. Soon, I had my hand inside. I was able to reach back about halfway before my arm got stuck in the narrow opening. Damn, I thought, not quite far enough—until I realized I could simply empty the front of the drawer first, then slide the back hanging files forward to where I could reach them. I did this as quickly as possible, using a ruler from his desk to fish the heavy back files forward. At last I had what I needed. I wrestled the folder out of the narrow opening.

Oh, yeah, this was it: pay dirt. Names and phone numbers of drug trial volunteers results of interviews, correspondence between Brookhouse and the drug company. It was all there. Now I could start running a cross-match against the women who were attacked and see if they could all be connected somehow, though I knew it would not be that easy.

I stuffed the folder in my knapsack, repacked my tools and headed out the shattered office door. There would be no covering of my tracks tonight. I'd declared open war. But at least I was wearing gloves. And I didn't think the Durham PD would give a probable rapist much support in tracking down whoever had burgled his office. Except for the reaming I'd get from Bobby D., I'd be okay. And I would simply remind Bobby that it had been his idea, not mine, to put on the pressure. The fact that I had gotten away with it would make all the difference.

Except that I didn't get away with it. At all.

As I headed out the door, knapsack on my back, I nearly collided with the janitor. I was surprised. He wasn't. He had been lying in wait for me.

"Step back, miss," he said in a deep voice so filled with authority I automatically obeyed. "Stand against the opposite wall where I can see you. I want at least six feet between us while we talk. And don't move your hands until I tell you to."

Jesus. He knew the rap better than a cop. And he wasn't as old as he had looked from far away. He flicked on a hallway light and I could see that he was actually only around fifty. He was built like a farmhand, with biceps that bulged beneath his blue tee-shirt and a neck the size of a sequoia stump. His complexion was so dark I could hardly see his features—he had stepped back into the shadows, leaving me exposed in the light. But I could see enough to know he wasn't smiling. I could also see that he held a metal rod of some kind in one hand, with a casual readiness that made me very sure he knew how to use it.

"Who are you?" he asked.

"I'm a private investigator. I have some ID in my pocket."

"And you just broke into that office?"

"That's right." Hell, what else could I say? He'd caught me with my hand in the cookie jar.

"That's the office for the tall guy, right? The fellow with those elbow patches on his jackets?"

"That's right," I said again. "His name is David Brookhouse."

"He's the professor got accused of rape, am I right?"

I wished I knew where this was going. "You're right." My voice came out a little clearer than before, at least it no longer sounded like a squeaky toy was lodged in my throat.

"Rape of that woman named Miss McInnes?"

"She's the one. She goes by the name of Pugh now. Her husband left her. You knew her?"

He nodded. "I knew her. She was a nice lady. But one day, she just sort of disappeared. Mid-term."

"She's not able to leave her house these days," I explained. "She's too afraid."

"Understandable," the man answered. "He got off."

"He did indeed. In more ways than one."

"Why?" he asked.

"Why what?"

"Why are you breaking into his office?" He waited, casually thumping the metal rod against a palm, a gesture that inspired anything but casualness in me.

I wondered whether to tell him the truth. This seemed like a damn good time to be straight up about it. "He's filed a lawsuit against Helen Pugh. I'm trying to find out if he might be guilty after all."

"He raped Miss Pugh. And now he's dragging her back to court?" the janitor asked, displaying no ambivalence about whether he thought Brookhouse was guilty.

"That's right." Now was not the time to initiate a discussion about legal guilt vs. innocence.

"After all she went through?" he asked.

"Yes."

"I see him in the hallways a lot, you know."

"I can imagine. I can imagine most people don't notice you when you're around."

He didn't say anything. The guy didn't give a damn about my political correctness. He was too busy thinking the situation over.

"Did you find what you were looking for?" he asked.

"I don't know. Maybe. I got some papers out of a drawer he seems to keep locked pretty securely."

The janitor took a step forward to get a better look at me. "I've seen you around here, right?"

I nodded. "That's right. I was... I was posing as a student for a little while."

He pointed a finger at me. "I remember now. You were hanging out with that young fellow who's trying so hard to look tough."

Aw. Luke deserved better than that. "He's a good guy," I felt compelled to say. "Young. But a good guy."

"He put the moves on you, too?" he asked me.

"Who? The young kid?" Had he recognized us in the bushes after all? I flushed.

"No." He shifted impatiently at my stupidity. "The elbow-patch fellow."

"Brookhouse?" There was a reason why the janitor refused to learn his name, I realized. He hated the guy, pure and simple. "No. He never put the moves on me." I hesitated. "I'm not his type. I think he was a little afraid to. Or something."

The guy laughed. It was not a happy sound. "He would be. He always picks the mousy little girls. His kind always does. Someone little to make him feel big."

We stood in silence for a moment and I was about to say something smart ass like, "Well, it was nice chatting with you"— thus ruining our rapport—when he saved me from myself.

"I expect you're anxious to get home," he said.

"That I am." I resisted the urge to embellish.

"Follow me."

I followed.

We made our way down the stairs to the first floor, where he headed for the front door. The foyer smelled like pine disinfectant, a sharp, artificial odor that tickled my nostrils and made me want to sneeze. How could he breathe it all night? Our footsteps echoed against the marble floor.

Halfway there, he stopped and turned to face me. Why was this guy crowding me? I stared over his shoulder at the front door. Freedom beckoned. If he would just get out of the way.

"You didn't see me tonight," he said.

"Deal. And you didn't see me."

I could smell his sweat in the darkness. "Just for my own personal information," he said, "how did you get in?"

"One of the basement doors. Just before you bolted it."

"I thought I heard something down there." He scratched his head. "I got to learn to follow my instincts more."

"I think you do just fine." But his mention of the basement reminded me. I grabbed his forearm. Muscles leaped beneath my touch. He was built like a tank.

"About that basement," I began. His muscles stiffened and I removed my hand from his arm.

"What about it?"

Uh-oh. "Did you... did you ever know about anything bad happening down there?" I asked. I was thinking about the woman who had called the hotline, the one who said she had been raped in the basement. I wondered if she had been telling the whole truth.

A silence lengthened between us. Outside, a horn honked.

Inside, a clock ticked on a nearby wall. My stomach growled. I was hungry.

He waited so long to answer, I knew he had seen something. A prickle of excitement crept up the back of my neck. "You saw her, didn't you?" I guessed. "You saw a woman who had been raped?"

He still took a moment to think it over before answering. "I promised her I would never tell no one. She wanted it that way."

"I think she's dead," I said.

I could feel his dismay.

"I'm sorry. I thought you knew. I think she was the lady who got killed a couple nights ago. Did you know her well?"

He shook his head. "I saw her here a few times. I think she had something to do with the office. You know. Alumni or fundraising or something."

"Her husband works for the university."

He was silent for a moment. "So, there you have it. It's why she wanted me to keep it quiet. She didn't want her husband to know."

"Did you find her?" I asked. "Were you the one?"

"I found her. I found her lying on the floor downstairs." His voice was indefinably sad, as if he had seen many terrible things in his life and finding a broken woman on the floor of a basement was just one more of them. "She was tore up pretty bad. She was propped against one of the soda pop machines down there."

A chill ran through me. He'd found her in the exact same spot where I had chosen to hide.

"Whoever done it ripped off her clothes. Down here. You know?" He indicated the area below his waist. "She still had on her blouse."

"She was badly hurt?" I asked.

"Seemed that way to me. There was blood. In the wrong places." He hesitated, then went on. "Blood on her legs, you know? And on her head."

"Did she say who did it to her?"

"She didn't say nothing to me. Except to beg me not to tell anyone," he explained. His voice broke. "The second I found her, she grabbed my shirt and started in on begging me not to tell anyone. That was all she would say. Even after I promised I'd keep quiet, she kept on begging me, like she didn't believe I'd keep my word. He knew she'd be that way, too."

"Who knew?"

"The man who did that to her," he said. "He could have killed her just as easily as leave her there. From what I saw that he did to her body, he could kill in a heartbeat. But he wanted her to live. He wanted her to know that he had done it. Because he knew she wouldn't tell. He knew she'd beg whoever found her not to say a word. That's my opinion, anyway. I've been around people like that. I know what they're like."

I felt a little sick to my stomach. "What did you do with her?"

"She wouldn't let me call the police, but I had to do something. I used to be a medic and I knew she was hurt bad. So I carried her over to the hospital."

"You carried her?" I asked, incredulous. "It's eight blocks away."

"I don't have a car," he explained. "I couldn't take her on the bus, now could I? Or leave her here. So I carried her to the emergency room. To the front desk."

"Jesus," I said. "What next?"

"I put her down in a chair by the counter. She was crying by then. And then I ran like hell. Right out the doors. And back here. Where I kept on working."

He didn't have to tell me why he had run. I was pretty sure he had a record. Why else would a man of his intelligence be swabbing floors? And I knew what it was like to have a record following you around. And while I didn't know what it was like to be a black man, I could guess at part of it. At least enough to know that toting around a raped white woman was taking a big risk.

"You're a good man," I said.

"Sometimes. I've done bad things in my life. Real bad things."

"Well, you did a good thing tonight."

We walked to the front door together. He unlocked it without a word. As I started to leave, he gripped my arm. His fingers were like iron clamps. "You have to hit me over the head first," he said.

"What?" I was inches away from him and could see the sheen of sweat coating his face. Honest sweat. He'd been working hard all night, with no one even there to see it. He was probably the only one in the entire fucking department who worked for work's sake, who wasn't jockeying, plotting, moving up the ladder or moving on to greener pastures.

"You got to hit me over the head," he repeated. He held up the metal rod in his hand—it was a piece of rebar. "With this."

"I can't do that." I was appalled.

"I'll lose my job," he explained.

"Oh, Jesus." I shook my head. "How hard?"

"Hard enough to make a bruise," he said. "I'll fake the rest."

"Oh, god. How hard is that?" I held the rebar in my hand. Now I felt more than a little sick to my stomach.

"About as hard as you'd swing an ax when the split is already started and you just want to finish off the log," he explained.

"How did you know I'd understand that?"

"You're a farm girl. I can tell."

I hoisted the bar and resisted the urge to shut my eyes. If I missed, I could do real damage.

"Where?" I asked, poised to strike.

"Near the front. To the side of the temporal lobe. Less chance of permanent damage that way."

"How do you know that?"

"Miss, I'm a janitor. I'm not a moron. I can read."

"It's your head," I said. And swung.

It made a soft thwack, like I'd just thumped a melon with a nightstick. He crumpled to the floor.

"Oh, goddamn," I said, crouching over him. "I've killed you."

"Not yet," he replied, holding his hands to his head. "But you must be a hell of a wood splitter. It's a good cut. It'll do. Now get on out of here."

I pushed through the front door and took off down the steps at top speed. I'd had enough action for one night.

Which reminded me. Luke was waiting at my apartment to talk to me. I ran even faster.

CHAPTER ELEVEN

My car was gone. I could not believe it. Unwilling to park as far away as I had earlier—after all, everyone had gone home and I was in no danger of being seen—I'd left it hidden behind a payloader in a parking lot under construction a block away. Where the hell was it? I examined the patterns of tracks that vehicles had left in the heavy red dirt. I was no Sherlock Holmes, god knows, but it appeared that my beloved car had been towed.

Someone had called it in, I was sure. A campus cop would never have noticed it on his regular rounds.

I checked my watch. I would have to wait until morning to track it down. It had been dragged in ignominy from campus before—and I knew the rap on getting it back. They busted your balls every step of the way. And I'd need a phone and cold hard cash to begin the ransom procedures.

Screw it. I had better things to do. And only fifteen minutes to get home, shower and dress before Luke arrived for our little chat.

I started hightailing it through campus, pissed that on this, the coldest night of the year so far, I was hiking more miles than a bunch of Swiss tourists hitting the Alps.

The campus was deserted, as only an early cold night in the South can cause. No one was prepared for the chill. No one wanted to face it. Winter was coming. Let's all huddle indoors. Except for that schmucky blond broad racing against the wind in the middle of campus. Must be some fool Northerner from New England who doesn't know any better.

Must be me.

A car passed by, in a hurry. I could see the lights of Duke Medical Center through the bare trees. It is a massive complex, with acres of buildings filled with floors and floors of the dying and desperate. Sometimes it made me sad to think of so many faces, pressed against their hospital-issued pillows, suffering, hoping, despairing inside the granite and brick structures that looked so much like prisons. People came from all over the world to seek miracles at Duke. It was the Lourdes of modern medical science. And so many, I was sure, returned home, disappointed, to die.

I heard a car approaching behind me, fast. Too fast. I turned, but it was already gone. It had swung quickly into a side street and disappeared down a hill. A compact, maybe. Glowing taillights. That was it.

I was jumpier than a cat on a hot griddle.

Duke is a well-lit campus. In spots. Some sections are not meant for cross-country treks. I'd need to cut through three dark areas or I'd add another half hour to my already way too long walk. One of the worst sections was just ahead: a thick patch of fir trees that could easily obscure anyone hiding inside. I wasn't stupid. I knew there was a rapist/murderer on the prowl. I knew I was getting close to him. I knew he could well have been the one who called my car in and had it towed.

I knew he could be behind me right now.

The thought made me stop in my tracks. Maybe I should have found a pay phone and called Burley or Bobby D. for a lift. But then they'd each find out what I was up to.

And then I would not be able to meet Luke and settle things once and for all.

See what happens when you start to lie? The lies just grow and grow and grow, eventually weaving a spider web that will surely trap you.

God, I was being morbid tonight

I jogged through the pine forest, shoving the overhanging branches aside. Sharp Douglas fir needles pricked my face. The softer pines brushed against my skin, an eerie caress that inspired me to run faster.

I emerged on the other side, panting but safe, two blocks closer to the bright lights of downtown Durham where my cozy apartment waited.

I still had at least two miles to go. I followed a winding sidewalk around a section of buildings, then cut across the campus in front of Duke Chapel. Its single spire rose in silent glory into the night sky. I stopped and stared, transfixed. The cold air was thin and the stars blazed through, bright pinpoints of fire scattered behind the slender shadow of the chapel's cross. It looked like a Christmas card of Bethlehem. Peace on earth.

I wished.

I rested, staring at the beauty of the chapel, my head bent as I gulped in the cool air, my hands resting on my knees. A couple of cars passed by a block away, cruising around a traffic circle that whirls cars off its axis like a pinwheel during the daylight hours, sending visitors and students in all directions. It was the heart of west campus. I had a long damn way to go.

I was near Duke Gardens, I realized, and very near where Helen had been attacked a year and a half ago.

The lawn felt soft beneath my feet, soggy from recent rain, and the open expanse of grass stretching before me was crisscrossed with shadows from nearby trees.

I thought I saw one of the shadows move.

Maybe the wind? It had picked up again. I noticed clouds on the edge of the horizon, moving toward the stars. A storm rolling in? The air smelled tangy, probably the first fire of the season for someone. How I longed to be back at Helen's, poking a log and watching the sparks swirl.

This is what happens when you lie. I should have told Bobby what I was doing. I should have told Burly about meeting Luke.

Someone was watching me. I could feel it. If I stood very still, I could hear something hovering on the edges of my consciousness. An engine slowing? The faint squeal of car brakes? A medevac helicopter approaching Duke Medical Center? What was it? I waited, then walked some more.

There it was again. I held my breath.

Someone was watching me.

I checked the darkness behind me. What had been the outline of two streetlights melded into one. Had someone stepped out of view? I narrowed my eyes, trying to see through the darkness. Bushes quivered near the street lamp. A person waiting? The autumn wind?

I needed to reach a busier section of the campus—and quick. It was getting close to midnight. I was going to be late. Would Luke wait? Most lights were out in the buildings and dorms that dominated the distant skyline. Even the hospital complex loomed darkly like a slumbering giant, the main parking structure rising above the trees like a behemoth venturing out at night to feed.

Maybe I should just turn back, I thought, and make a run for the hospital. I eased the Colt out of my knapsack and held it ready. A car door slammed in the distance. I upped my pace.

I reached the other side of the open lawn and considered my options. I could make a run for it through the middle of Duke Gardens and save myself a mile of trudging around it. After all, I was armed. And prepared for an assault, so the element of surprise would be gone.

I wasn't that much of an idiot. I decided not to take the chance. Instead, I followed a sidewalk that curved around one end of the Gardens, then arched in a stone bridge over a shallow pool that gleamed in the moonlight. The stars reflected off its surface with aching clarity. This part of the garden was home to some of the largest magnolias in the South, but I gave them a wide berth. No shadows for me tonight, thank you. Not with the clouds racing toward the moon. It would be dark enough, soon enough. I needed to get the hell home.

Footsteps approached on the path behind me.

I whirled. No one was there. The footsteps had stopped. I waited, then started down the sidewalk.

Footsteps. Again.

I slipped into the cover of the nearest magnolia, hiding beneath the canopy of an overhanging limb still thick with flat leaves as wide as a dinner plate. Last season's leaves crunched beneath my feet. I froze, not breathing. The sound could give me away. Footsteps approached.

In a moment, Luke came hurrying down the sidewalk. He was looking to the right, then to the left, an odd expression on his face. He had his knapsack slung over one shoulder.

I started to call out, but something stopped me.

What was he doing here? How had he found me?

Luke was a sophomore. He'd been at Duke nearly a year and a half.

The same time frame as the attacks.

He was tall and lanky.

Rougher, privileged information now rose to the edges of my consciousness. I felt sick to my stomach. Had our episode in the bushes been a... tryout for this? What had I been thinking? More to the point, what had Luke been thinking while it was going on? What scenario had been running through his head?

I realized I didn't know him at all. There was so much I didn't know about him. And what I did know hit me with a sudden and terrifying new impact.

He was majoring in psychopathology and often near the department. He hated Brookhouse—and constantly pointed a finger at him.

He had followed me home to Helen's house, insinuated himself into my case.

But most of all—why was he following me now?

He stopped and peered into the darkness of Duke Gardens, searching the shadows. He ran a hand through his spiky hair. I was close enough to see that he was chewing on his lower lip.

"Casey?" he finally called out, his voice sounding panicked, yet hushed.

Guaranteed to get me to respond.

The sound of his hushed voice made my skin crawl. Why was he being so quiet?

"Casey," he called out again, the whisper floating over a hollow that lay between two small hills. "It's me. Are you in there? I saw you come this way. I've got my car. I can give you a lift. It's not safe for you to be walking."

Yeah. Right. Not safe at all. Better just to climb into the front seat of your car like some pathetic older woman blinded by your phony devotion.

"Where are you?" he said, his voice rising. "I got to your apartment early and followed you back here. What's going on?"

Like I was going to tell him anything. I didn't want to shoot him. I didn't want to confront him. I just wanted to go home and think about it. Without him.

He wasn't that much of a kid, I realized. He could have played me for a fool. Oh, man. I'd been a fool not to see it. And a fool to believe his reasons for wanting to stick close to me. Love? What a joke. What woman doesn't want to hear that she's not too old? That she's beautiful? That a young man wants her? What a fucking idiot I'd been.

If I returned to the sidewalk, he'd see me.

I slipped into a night-shrouded patch of azalea bushes instead, then headed for the heart of Duke Gardens. As long as I knew where Luke was, and he did not know where I was, I was safe. I kept my gun ready.

The azaleas gave way to a series of stone-terraced flower beds that were thick with marigolds, day lilies and patches of winter cabbage. These layered gardens were beautiful throughout the year. They would also expose me to Luke's sight. I followed a hedge to the lower path of the garden instead, sticking close to the tree line as I made my way around a koi pond and past a stand of Japanese cherry maples. I could hear a body moving through the bushes behind me, someone in a hurry, someone not bothering to cover their tracks.

No one else was in sight. Normally, at least a few lovers would be huddled in the shadows, stealing some privacy away from their shared dorm rooms. But publicity over the recent attacks and warnings posted by a women's organization had pretty much brought night traffic through the Gardens to a halt.

Which meant it was just me and my shadow.

A few feet from the main pond that links the regular gardens with the Japanese section, my pursuer made his move. As I was cutting across a pile of boulders clustered beside a small beach, someone dropped to the ground behind me from the top of the highest rock. I heard the thud of shoes hitting granite, but a stiff palm chopped my gun from my hand before I could react. My knapsack tumbled to the ground. A hood of thick cloth was slipped over my head from behind. Someone grabbed my arms, twisting them backward. A rope tightened around my neck.

How did Luke get here before me?

All I had left to fight back with were my thunder thighs. I used them.

I lifted my right leg in a high kick position then drove it backward, visualizing a steel rod pistoning at full force. I hit a shin. A man screamed in pain. Hands let go and I started to pull the hood from my head. But even stronger hands stopped me. Yet the man was still screaming. Were there two of them?

"Let me go, Luke," I screeched. "I know it's you."

The attacker laughed. It was a sound I had never heard before. High-pitched. Almost a giggle. But frayed along the edges. Out of control.

Just like Helen had heard.

That single thought inspired a surge of panic-driven power. I threw myself forward and knocked someone over my fallen knapsack. We tumbled down together; I heard a thud as his head hit rock. I rolled free, pulled the hood from my head, scrambled in the darkness for my gun and knapsack, then scooped them up and ran. Like hell.

Behind me, I heard cursing. Someone had recovered. A body was crashing through the bushes toward me, coming up on me from behind. I scrambled and slid over a series of slippery rocks arrayed along a shallow edge of the pond. If I could just reach dry land again, I could haul ass out of there. I knew the edge of the pond was lined with a series of short overlapping docks that were arrayed on different levels, creating walkways for humans and shelter for ducks. If I could get to them, I'd be able to move quickly above the muddy ground and put distance between me and my attackers.

Someone crashed through the bushes ahead of me. How had he gotten in front of me so fast?

There was nowhere to go but into the pond. But I had to protect my knapsack. It held the data I had pulled from the drug trial files and it was all I had, all I had in the world, to go on right then. If I survived, it might give me a clue to who was after me and why.

Where could I stash it?

I slammed into a redwood bench that had been built overlooking the pond. I almost fell, but recovered in time to slide my knapsack under the seat, against one set of legs where it would be partially hidden by a shrub's overhang. Then I headed for the water where the crisscrossing dock pathways intersected with land. I steadied myself along the side of the lowest pier as I waded into the pond. The top of the dock barely came to my waist. I moved faster as the crashing sounds grew louder.

Thank god the pond was warmer than the night air; it had yet to catch up with the cold front. I felt my way along the edge of the dock, sinking deeper and deeper into the water, my gun held carefully above its surface. The warm liquid seeped through my jeans and mounted to my waist. Mud sucked at my feet. I reached a corner where the first dock was overlapped by a slightly higher dock. Footsteps thudded along the planks of a nearby walkway, heading toward me. I hid my gun in a dark corner where the piers came together, then backpedaled into the pond, sinking quietly until only my head showed above the surface. It was a windy night. Tiny waves rippled the surface under a cool breeze. I shivered and sank lower, grateful for the warmth of the pond. The mud was soft beneath my feet, the bottom littered with rocks and clumps of vegetation. But the footing was secure and I slid silently through the darkness, easing myself away from the shore.

"Do you see her?" a voice asked. A man. He was too far away to hear clearly.

"No, but I heard something," a different man answered. "She came this way."

There were two of them. Neither one sounded like Luke. It confused me.

"Over here," the first man suggested. The footsteps moved away from me, then stopped abruptly. "I heard something," he said. "Check the edges of the pond. She may be in the water."

I did not wait to hear more. I took a deep breath and slipped beneath the surface. A calm had overtaken me. They were the hunters. I was the hunted. But I knew just where I was going. The spring before, there had been a modern dance performance in the pond. Not along the edges of it. In it. Workmen had built a series of underwater platforms near the middle of the pond. Dancers had balanced on the platforms as they performed, creating the illusion of skimming across the water's surface. It had been standing-room-only three nights in a row, and I remembered reading at the end of a glowing review for the performance that the platforms were being left in place as a sort of multilevel amusement park for the Gardens' many ducks.

If I could find one of the platforms, I'd be far enough out into the pond to avoid detection, but I would not have to tread indefinitely. The water reached just above my mouth at the deepest part and I had to kick to stay afloat. Worse, my fleece jacket had grown soggy and leaden—how did sheep do it?—and I peeled it off, pissed that I was throwing away a hundred dollars' worth of outerwear. At least my gun wasn't in the pocket. I needed to get back to my gun, and dry land eventually, but I couldn't afford to approach that part of the shore until the men chasing me were gone.

I could barely see their figures as they raced along the water's edge, pushing aside bushes, scanning the pond, hoping for a break in the accumulating cloud cover. One man was tall, the other chubby and of average height. I could see no other details.

Shit. I bumped my shin on one of the dance platforms. But at least I had found the right spot. I ran my hands along the wood surface. It was about two feet beneath the water. If I lay prone on the platform, my head tilted back slightly, I could balance in place beneath the pond, with only my eye and nose above water, like an alligator waiting for prey. I slid into place. They'd never find me this far out. I'd wait here all night if I had to.

Oh, no. The ducks. I could not believe it. More than men were after me. At first I heard only a few tentative quacks. Then the sound grew louder. Other quacks joined in, until a chorus of multi-toned squawkings filled the night air. The cacophony was heading straight for me.

The ducks had detected an interloper.

Duke Gardens was home to dozens of tame ducks, grown plump and lazy on bread scattered by humans. They responded to the presence of people by besieging them for food. Two dozen of the noisy bastards had now roused themselves from slumber on the far side of the pond and were expecting me to dole out a midnight snack.

They were moving rapidly across the pond toward me in a tidy V-shaped formation, quacking their excitement. I wanted to strangle every one of the feathery little traitors. They reached me en masse, surrounding me, squawking and honking—great, a few geese had joined the mob.

"Get lost," I hissed, pushing one particularly ballsy specimen aside. The duck turned, quacked its outrage and re-approached.

Ouch. One of them nipped my cheek with a beak. Visions of Alfred Hitchcock movies flashed through my mind. Jesus, this was a nightmare.

The ducks surrounded me, quacking even louder when I failed to come across with the goods.

"Over there!" one of the men on shore shouted. "Follow the ducks."

It was time to bail.

I slid beneath the surface again, swimming quickly, holding my breath in the brackish water. I moved away from the figures on shore, back toward where I had hidden my gun.

The ducks moved with me. Like a squadron of tattletales, they quacked their way behind me, their sharp cries cutting through the stillness of the night, as effective as an air raid siren.

When this was over, I was visiting a Chinese restaurant and gorging on Peking duck until I dropped. If I ever got the chance.

At least the two men had been lured to the far shore. That bought me some time. I reached the shoreline near the docks and retrieved my gun, then felt my way through a thick patch of cattails that gave way to daylilies scattered among round stones. My clothes were soaked, slowing me down. The smooth ovals of rock that looked so serene in the daylight only caused me to slip and repeatedly bang my ankles. I'd never make it to safety in time.

Then I heard my name.

"Casey!" a voice called out. "Where are you?"

It was Luke. Was he one of the men? Was he with the men? Was he trying to help me?

"Don't come near me," I commanded him. "I have a gun."

"It's me," he answered. "Why are you hiding? Listen you're in danger. I know who it is—"

A blast rocked the air. Dirt and stone exploded in my face. Another shot boomed and a shower of pebbles rained into the pond. Someone was firing straight at me. I dropped to my knees on the rocks, ignoring the pain, steadied my gun and fired right at where the blasts were coming from.

The sound of my Colt was more like a pop compared to what they had. I was outarmed for sure. But the men had not expected to be fired back on. I heard cursing and wild scrambling sounds among the rocks. Then shouting and the sounds of running. My ears rang from the two earlier blasts. Who was it? I couldn't tell. Their voices sounded muffled as the two men argued; they were running away at the same time. "Why did you fire?" one shouted. "Are you insane? She's got a gun."

"Let's go," a second voice commanded. "It's too late now."

More pushing and scrambling. Figures scurried up the slope toward the path that led out of the Gardens.

One of them was tall and lanky. Maybe Luke? And who else?

Should I shoot? How could I explain shooting a man in the back to the cops?

How could I even explain the gun in my hand? It was illegal. Worse, how long until the cops arrived in response to the noise? Detective Ferrar would be on my ass like a cat on cream. I needed to get the hell out of there.

I peered through the darkness. The figures had disappeared. Gravel crunched beneath their feet as they ran up the path toward the parking lot. On the run.

I tripped and fell over a patch of ragged roots, banging my elbow. The gun flew from my hand and splashed into the pond. As I grabbed for it, my hand brushed against a leg. I scrambled backward over the rocks. No one approached me. I moved forward and touched the leg again. It did not move. As my eyes adjusted to the dark shadows, I began to make out a body splayed face up across a carved boulder, the head lolling off the opposite side. All I could see was the lower half of the torso and two legs dangling off the stone like inanimate objects. I froze. Two people running away toward the road? Then who was here with me?

I rose to my knees. My palms were bleeding. The figure lay still, unmoving.

I'd hit someone. Who was it?

I scrambled to my feet and approached cautiously. Still, the figure did not move. I leaned over it, poking an arm. It flopped to one side. Was he dead? As I worked my way around to the other side of the boulder, the moon broke through the racing cloud cover. For a few brief seconds, a sliver of light fell across the pond and the surface sparkled, then the light moved toward the boulder and illuminated the body for a single instant before darkness once again shrouded the scene.

But I had seen his face. I had hit Luke.

He lay sprawled across the huge rock, face up, his head dangling over the edge. I cradled his head in my hands and eased it back up on the boulder, then scrambled up the incline until I was crouched beside him. His leather jacket was flung open to each side, the T-shirt beneath it exposed to the night air. A dark stain spread across his chest like spilled red wine. I looked down at my hands. They were soaked with his blood. The rock was soaked with his blood. The night seemed soaked with his blood.

Oh my god. What if I had killed him?

I began to scream for help at the top of my lungs. I screamed and shouted bloody murder, almost wrenching the tissue from my throat. I knew I could not leave him, but I had to get help. Someone would hear me, someone had to.

Frantically gathering his leather jacket around his torso, I pulled it tight, trying to trap the blood inside. Where had he been hit? A lung? The heart? Blood oozed from the wound, washing over me.

Oh, Jesus. What if I had killed him?

He was unresponsive. I had to get him to the hospital quick.

Where was help? I screamed again, begging for someone to hear.

I could not wait any longer.

I eased him into my arms, took a deep breath and lifted, almost buckling beneath his weight. I willed myself to be stronger. I made myself dig in. He lifted. I turned, slipped, regained my balance, scrambled down the slope that led from the boulders to the shore below, then plunged along the curving path that bordered the pond. To the left, the hospital loomed at the top of the hill, hallway lights glowing dimly through narrow windows. Someone could help him there.

I did not think I would make it. I screamed as I ran, cradling him in my arms. I was screaming for help over and over, begging for someone to hear me. Begging for Luke to hang in there.

Halfway to the hill that led to the street above, someone finally heard my cries. "What the hell is going on down there?" a voice shouted from the pathway above.

A man. God, please make him a friend. God, please send me an angel.

"He's been hit," I screamed back. "My friend's been shot. He's hit and he's bleeding and I think he may be dying."

"Stay there," the voice commanded. "Don't move him any further."

I sank to my knees. I'd carried Luke out of the mud and the cattails, halfway across the Gardens. I couldn't move anymore.

"Lay him down on the grass gently," the same strong voice told me as it drew closer. I collapsed under Luke's weight, sinking to the grass, unable to speak or breathe.

"Let go!" the voice ordered me. I realized I was still gripping Luke tightly to my chest. Strong arms pried my hands away. Luke rolled forward, flopping on his back in the moonlight.

"Jesus Christ," the man said. "He's just a kid."

I lost it. He was just a kid. What was he doing involved in all this? Had he been following me? Was he the one? Was I just paranoid? Had he been trying to help me? What had he called out just before he was shot?

Oh god, what if I never got the chance to find out the truth?

"I've got a pulse," the man said. I could finally see his face. It was plain and narrow. He, too, was young.

"Pull yourself together," he snapped at me. "I can't leave him. Stand up."

I scrambled to my feet.

"See that building at the top of the hill?" His voice was sharp.

"I know it, I know it," I babbled. "It's the hospital."

"It's not the right building, but they'll send help. Go in the back door. The one near the Dumpsters. Go straight up the hill and look for some white vans. Run as fast as you can. Faster than you can. Understand? Tell them to bring plasma. Tell them it's a gunshot wound to the back, probable shotgun from a distance. Exit wound in the front. But off-center. Damage to the lung area. Can you remember that?" He was shouting in my face, but I could barely hear him against the roaring that had started in my ears.

"Yes, yes," I promised. "I can remember that."

"Go. Now." He bent over Luke as I turned and ran, the cold wind lifting the moisture from my exposed skin. The feeling was somehow comforting. I was alive. I could do it. I could run faster. And what had the man said back there. What did I need to remember?

As I scrambled up the hill, slipping on piles of loose pine needles, it came to me: Luke had been hit from behind. With a shotgun, the man had said.

Not my gun. Not me.

Someone else had shot him.

He had been there to protect me.

It felt as if my lungs would explode. I made myself keep going.

I reached the winding asphalt road that led to the medical center, searching frantically for a parking lot filled with white vans. There. To my left. Like ghosts lined up in the darkness. I scrambled toward them, banged my shin on a bumper, fell, got back up and found the back door to the building. It was open. I burst through it and collided with a woman who was pushing a trash container on wheels. She screamed and threw herself back against the wall.

"Emergency," I shouted. "Emergency. There's a boy shot in Duke Gardens."

They flooded the area within minutes. Ambulances. Crews of medical technicians with stretchers. Campus cops. The Durham police would not be far behind.

I stood on the top of the hill, guarded by a pair of campus cops, watching the medics run to Luke's aid. The man who had waited beside him rose to his feet and started shouting orders. God had sent me a doctor on his way home. Or, at least, an intern who had stayed late at the hospital.

A squad car pulled up on the sidewalk nearby. Doors slammed behind me. Two Durham cops approached. They looked serious. Thank god. It was Hugh Fitzpatrick, the roly-poly bachelor cop who was appallingly easy to wrap around my little finger. I'd need to do some serious wrapping tonight.

"What's going on, Casey?" Fitz asked, staring at the pool of liquid spreading across the sidewalk from my feet. His eyes widened. "Is that blood?"

"A friend of mine got shot as we were walking through the Gardens."

He stared at my clothes. "Are you soaked? Is that water?"

"We were near the docks when it happened. I was scared. I fell into the pond. Then I picked him up and tried to run. The blood is his. I'm okay." My words tumbled out in a nervous rush. The wind picked up and I shivered. Fitz stood beside me, staring down at the medical team working below.

"What the hell were you doing walking around in Duke Gardens at night?" he asked. "Especially with all that's going on?"

"I think I better talk to Detective Ferrar," I said between chattering teeth.

"I think maybe you better," he agreed.

"Can I change first?" I begged him. "Please, please, please. Give me a ride home. I'll give you my clothes, I'll put them in a plastic bag for you. You can watch me undress. I just need to put on something dry. And come back here and check on Luke. That's my... that's my ..." Words failed me for a moment. Then I started to sob. Like some dumb girl. "That's my friend down there," I finally choked out. I began to cry even harder.

"Jesus," Fitz begged me. "Don't cry, Casey. Sure, I'll take you home. Let me just clear it past Ferrar first. No problem. I'll radio Ferrar on the way. Come on." He patted my shoulders in helpless sympathy. "It'll be okay. Your friend's got the best doctors in the country a few yards away. Come on, pull it together." He sounded worse than I did. "Christ, Casey, I never thought I'd see you cry."

"Don't tell anyone," I said through my tears. "And make your partner swear the same."

"Sure, sure. Anything. Just come on, kid. We'll get you some dry clothes."

"Geeze, Casey," Bobby grumbled. "I don't know whether to strangle you or hug you." He plopped down beside me in an empty plastic chair. It shook beneath his weight.

"For godsakes, don't hug me," I said. "For one thing, I smell like pond scum."

"There's a joke in there," he said, clumsily patting my leg. "But I'm not going to touch it."

We were sitting in an empty examining room. Ferrar had let me change clothes under the watchful eye of a female officer, making me feel like a suspect. I felt like even more of one when he refused my request to shower. "Not yet," he had commanded via radio.

That "not yet" worried me.

The doctor had come in half an hour earlier, looked me over, pronounced me healthy as a horse, painted half my hide in expensive iodine gunk, then warned me that the police were waiting to question me. I was all theirs.

I was really worried by then. But sometimes fate helps. My palm and fingers were now coated in Betadine. A residue test would be unreliable. If it came to that.

Luke was in an operating room with a team of trauma surgeons working to save him. He'd taken a shotgun blast in the back. It had hit him off-center and been fired from a distance, thank god. His right lung was damaged but not destroyed. Still, he was in grave danger and had lost a lot of blood. No one would tell me whether they thought he was going to live or die.

And no one could find his parents.

"Where's Fanny?" I asked, suddenly longing for her maternal comfort.

"She's talking with the cops," Bobby said glumly.

"The cops? What did Fanny do?"

"She's just trying to help them find the kid's parents. She's the only one who seems to remember his father's name and where he works. They're also trying to get through to the Duke registrar. Casey, what the hell was he doing in—"

"I don't want to talk about it right now," I interrupted.

"What the hell were you doing in the—"

"I'll tell you later," I said as Detective Ferrar entered the examining room.

"Need a lawyer?" Bobby asked, rising to his feet. He automatically averts his face from all cops. I wondered, as I always did, where that habit of his had come from. I knew so little about Bobby's past.

"Not yet," I said hopefully.

Ferrar stared at me.

"But I might later."

Bobby squeezed out past Ferrar with an anxious glance and trundled down the hospital hallway toward the waiting room.

"Friend of yours?" Ferrar asked. He turned Bobby's chair around and sat in it backward, resting his arms on the plastic back and staring at me intently.

"My partner," I explained. I could not meet his eyes.

"Better tell me what happened."

I told him. As best I could. I left out the breaking and entering part. In fact, I sort of skipped over the entire episode at the psychopathology department. But that was all I left out. Naturally, he noticed what I had not said more than what I did say.

"What were you doing on campus?" he asked.

"I was following Brookhouse," I improvised.

"Who's the kid?"

"Someone in one of Brookhouse's classes," I explained. "He was helping me out by keeping an eye on Brookhouse."

"He might die," Ferrar interrupted. "He might die because of you."

"Not because of me," I shot back. Now it was my turn to be angry. Yes, it was partially my fault. And no, I would never forgive myself. But I was in charge of my conscience, not this man. I did not then, nor had I ever, needed help accepting moral responsibility for what I did. My grandfather had taught me better than that. And I damn sure didn't need Ferrar's help in feeling bad about what happened to Luke. "I'm not the one who shot him."

"Then who did?" Ferrar asked. I could tell he believed me, which made me wonder if they had found the shotgun.

"Look," I explained. "I wish I knew. I swear I would help you if I did. I was just walking through campus after some surveillance."

"Pretty stupid," he remarked. "Did you have a sign on your back that said 'Rape me'?"

I glared at him. "I had no choice. Someone had my car towed and I couldn't find a phone."

He made a note on his pad. "We'll take care of following that up," he said. "You are to back off. Understand?"

I nodded. "Luke started following me," I explained again. "I freaked out. I thought he might be... the one."

"That's why you cut through the Gardens?"

"I didn't have much choice. But someone else was following me. Two men. Luke was just trying to warn me. I think he got shot trying to protect me." I stared down at the tiled floor. The cleaning crew had missed a few drops of blood that led from the edge of the examining table to Ferrar's chair. Someone else's mistake, I thought. And what a small one compared to mine.

Ferrar ran a hand through his hair. "This is so bad," he said in a low voice. "So very bad. If this kid dies... I don't know what I'm going to do. This town has really had enough of whoever this is. And so have I. He could have been my kid. He is someone's kid."

I didn't know what to say back.

"Can you give me anything else at all that might help?" he said. "Voices? Height? Anything? How close did you get to them?"

I went back and told him again about the struggle near the rocks. I tried to remember everything. I closed my eyes and visualized. He asked me all sorts of questions. What had the men smelled like? Where had their hands wrapped around me? When I kicked back, where had I hit the man in the leg? Did I recognize the awful laugh?

By the time it was over, I had given him almost everything I had, except for my burglary of the drug trial papers. He had given me nothing. I had no clue if he considered Brookhouse a suspect in Luke's attack or not. Nor did I know if he intended to follow-up on the idea. By then, I didn't care. I just wanted to go home.

I nearly burst into tears again when Ferrar finally let me go and I saw that both Fanny and Bobby were still waiting for me in the anteroom. Morose clusters of the injured waited around them, faces averted from one another, hands wrapped around injured fingers, clutching swollen ankles, pressing head wounds. Everyone looked drunk at this hour of the night. Everyone probably was drunk at this hour of the night. Emergency rooms are like that.

"Where's Burly?" I asked, both scared and disappointed he wasn't there.

"He was afraid to leave Helen alone with her mother," Bobby explained. "He's still at the house with her. Hugo is out rounding up some of his friends to start a twenty-four-hour watch. We all think he's coming after Helen next."

"Good thinking," I said. But I didn't believe him about why Burly wasn't here. Burly would figure it out, I was sure. He would know I was involved with Luke on some level. I would have to face him about it sooner or later. "Can we go back there now?" I asked. "I need to talk to Burly."

Fanny looked up for the first time. Her face was streaked with tears. "I can't leave him," she said, sniffing into a lace-trimmed handkerchief. "He has no one. He's such a boy, and he's lying up there on that operating room table all alone. His parents are in the middle of an ocean somewhere. No one they can reach right now even remembers what cruise line. I can't leave him. He has no one."

As she began to cry harder, Bobby patted her back gently. He didn't know what else to do.

"Then we'll all wait here together," I decided. I looked at my watch. "It'll be daylight in a couple of hours anyway."

The sun was just starting to streak the sky with golden wisps when medics brought in the janitor from the psychopathology building. I recognized him by his clothing. His head was swathed in a huge bandage that was way bigger than I had expected. I hadn't hit him that damn hard.

"What happened?" I asked, rising to my feet. I couldn't stop myself. I had to get a closer look. No way I had hit him hard enough to keep him unconscious all night. No way.

"You know this man?" one of the medics asked. She exchanged a glance with her partner.

I crept closer to the gurney. "Yes. He's the janitor at the psychopathology building on campus. He's a really nice man. What happened to him?"

"Someone bashed his head in, that's what happened to him."

I felt sick. "What do you mean?"

"A student found him in the foyer about twenty minutes ago. Someone smashed his head in," the first medic explained impatiently. She waved me aside. "Unless you know his name or family, please get out of the way."

I watched in horror as they wheeled him through a set of double doors into the treatment area.

"What is it?" Bobby asked. He had wandered over, sensing that something was up.

"Oh, Bobby," I said. "This is even worse than I thought."

By early morning, Luke was out of surgery and in a recovery room. I knew foot traffic would start across the Gardens soon. I had to get my gun and knapsack while I could. "I'll be back," I said. "Give me the keys to your car."

Bobby handed them over without comment. He was methodically feeding Fanny peanut butter crackers from a vending machine. She was praying for Luke in between bites.

Suddenly, just being around her made me feel like pond scum in addition to smelling like it. I hurried out into a cold morning. Everything looked so different in the daylight, so benign and clean and impossibly safe. Had Luke really been shot so close to this place of haven?

Yellow police tape blocked off parts of the Gardens, but the area where my knapsack was hidden was still accessible. God knew where my gun was. If they had searched the whole Gardens or dragged the pond, I was sunk. It was tough for me to replace guns. I had a felony conviction and had to buy them on the black market from the kind of person I usually spent my time trying to bring down.

I stopped, thinking of what I had been about to do. Ten hours ago, I had almost killed a friend with my gun. Now I was hurrying to find it—so that I could shoot it at someone else.

I thought of Luke's blood pouring from his chest, the smell of it on my hands, the sounds of his breath gurgling in his chest.

Maybe I wouldn't replace my gun after all.

I watched as a cluster of students headed toward the taped-off area. I hurried to catch up with them, then fell into step right behind them, as close as I dared. We passed a cop guarding the scene. He looked familiar, but I couldn't dredge up the name. I turned my head away. He didn't seem to notice me, just waved us away from the edge of the tape. He was watching a brunette coed in a tight sweater instead.

As the students chatted and speculated about whatever latest horror had hit the campus, I matched them stride for stride. Just one of the gang. We neared the network of docks and I began searching for the cluster of rocks where my gun had slipped from my hand. No footprints. It was probably still there in the shallows. The damn ducks saw us coming and came squawking over. Where was my gun when I really needed it? I wanted to strangle some of the loudest birds for betraying me last night and I searched the flock for anyone looking particularly self-satisfied. But the ducks turned and left when they saw we had no bread. I took a quick peek into the shallows: no gun was visible. God, what if someone else had already discovered it? Someone besides the police?

That didn't make me feel too good, either.

I hurried to rejoin the group of students. They passed the bench where I had hidden my knapsack and I sat down as if to rest. The students walked on, and the cop was eyeing a new cluster of the curious. The sun shone brightly overhead, taking the chill from the November air.

Seeing me on the beach, the goddamn ducks started quacking their way toward me yet again, ready to harass me for food as if they had never seen me before. These were not genius ducks, that was for sure.

I fished around with my left leg, located my knapsack and gently dragged it to my side. I'd forget my gun for now. Waiting until a new group of students passed by, I stood and shouldered the knapsack, joining the kids in a final trip out of the Gardens. Maybe I'd never go back. The beauty seemed spoiled forever.

By noon, even Fanny was dozing off in the antiseptic waiting room. My knapsack was safely stashed in Bobby D.'s trunk, the illicit gains of my breaking and entering the night before still intact. My stomach felt sour from too much black coffee. And Bobby was snoring so loudly that the nurses at the reception desk were starting to glare.

I elbowed him awake.

"Knock it off," I said. "The paint is peeling from the walls."

"Any news?" he asked gruffly, flaring his nostrils. "Maybe I ought to get me some of those sleep strips."

"Maybe you ought to lose two hundred pounds?"

It was a much nastier remark than I was apt to make. Something inside me felt coiled, mean and ready to strike. Guilt looking for a victim. Bobby understood. He ignored my remark.

A doctor approached us, staring at Fanny. Sensing his gaze, she opened her eyes, looked flustered, and automatically patted a few of her curls back in place.

"Mrs. Broadhurst?" the doctor said tentatively. He was the epitome of distinguished medical achievement, tall and trim with silver hair and expensive metal-rimmed glasses. "I thought I recognized you."

It was more likely he recognized her pocketbook. Fanny had pretty much built a goodly portion of the medical center with donations from her family trust.

"What are you doing here?" he asked in a professionally concerned voice. He glanced around the waiting room as if it were a bus station in Calcutta.

Fanny explained that a young man of her acquaintance had been shot and his parents could not be found and it was sad and blah, blah, blah. She sowed the seeds. The doctor provided the sunshine.

He trotted off, anxious to help protect future donations.

Twenty minutes later, we heard the news.

It was not good. But it could have been worse.

Luke was alive. He was in a coma. He had been moved into the critical care unit and if Fanny wished to wait, considering the special circumstances, she might be able to see him in a few hours.

Fanny cared to wait. She had taken to calling him "that poor Yankee boy," as if we were sitting around following the massacre at Bull Run, praying for someone else's child to pull through just in case, up North in the land of the infidels, another mother was doing the same for our son.

"That poor Yankee boy," Fanny muttered. "His parents just taking off like that."

"Jesus," I said, in no mood to be tactful. "How much money do you have anyway? These people are practically genuflecting in front of you."

Fanny did not smile. "Money is of absolutely no use in situations like this, Casey," she scolded me. "Not really. We can see him because of my money. He'll get good care because of my money. But my money is not going to help him pull out of his coma. If I were you, I'd join me in prayer."

It was the closest she had ever come to a rebuke. I joined her in prayer. All I could remember was a bunch of dire entreaties ingrained into me by snake-handling aunts and alcoholic uncles who delighted in the gibberish of speaking in tongues. Frankly it had all started to sound like gibberish long before I was ten. But somehow a few prayers had stuck. I dredged them up and prayed.

A couple of very long hours later, a nurse led us upstairs. Luke's room was unguarded, but a nurse stood watch inside.

Luke looked so young. He lay against the pillow, unconscious, his face crisscrossed with tubes that snaked from his nostrils and throat, then led in labyrinthine paths to machines that hummed and blipped around him. A sterile tent protected his chest. Only his hands looked human. One dangled over the edge of his bed. I touched it. The screens on the metal boxes surrounding him did not waver. Luke was a long way away.

"Can I hold his hand?" I asked the nurse.

She stared at me for a moment. I must have looked a mess, even with a change of clothes. But she nodded.

I held his hand and stroked his fingers while Bobby waited in the doorway and Fanny prayed some more. The steady beep-beep of his monitors set the rhythm for Fanny's gentle murmurings. I caught "this poor Yankee boy" a few times, but other than that Fanny was pretty private about her prayers. What she had to say was between her and God.

Luke did not move; no twitch, no sighs. He seemed more dead than alive, kept in a semi-human state by these cold and mysterious machines. The spark that was him was gone.

"Will he come out of it?" I finally dared ask.

The nurse looked up from the magazine she had been reading. "We don't know," she said. "I'm sorry."

What else was there for her to say?

What had Luke been trying to tell me in the Gardens? Who had he been trying to protect me from?

"If he does ever come out of it," I said, needing to know more, "will he be able to tell us what happened?"

The nurse stared at me again, as if she knew damn well what had happened. "Chances are very small that he will be able to remember anything for a significant period of time before the attack," she explained. "It's a side effect of trauma."

"For how long before the attack?" I asked.

She shrugged, "There is no way of telling. For most people, it's a matter of at least twelve to twenty-four hours. Often longer. We won't know until—and if—he wakes up."

Twelve to twenty-four hours? That would mean he would not remember what had happened in the gardens... or our near tumble in the bushes... or the fact that I had not believed him when the time came. There was a good chance he would not remember that I had run away, convinced he was a killer.

We left the room a few minutes later, shooed out by the private nurse. I didn't have to ask who was paying for her services. Fanny is generous to a fault, especially in times of crisis.

Detective Ferrar was waiting for us in the hallway. He wore crisply ironed khakis and a black polo shirt. His face gleamed with a fresh shave. He, at least, had gone home to revive, delivered back into the world with some of its horror mitigated by the love of his family. I envied him far more than the clean clothes he wore.

"He's in a coma," I said. "He can't tell you a thing. He probably won't even be able to remember anything once he wakes up."

"I'm not here for him," Ferrar said, taking my arm. "I'm here for you."

I looked back at Bobby. He nodded and turned toward the critical care unit's special waiting room, where phones sat on every coffee table: lifelines to the healthy, instruments of tragedy. And a way to call my lawyer.

"She doesn't need a lawyer," Ferrar said, waving Bobby away. "I just want to ask her about someone."

We rode in silence down two floors, sharing the elevator with a priest handsome enough to convert me on sight. Ferrar seemed to know the priest, they nodded their greetings. But Ferrar would not even look at me. And he didn't bother to explain where we were going. I didn't like it. One bit.

"In here," he said as we entered a private room.

Of course. My new friend. The janitor. He looked weak. But his eyes were bright and his mouth curled up to let me know he was awake and well.

"You're okay," I said, relief flooding through me.

"I'm okay," the janitor assured me. His voice was raspy; a tube had probably been forced down his throat. "They had to relieve some swelling on my brain, that's all." I started to ask him a question, but a warning look in his eyes stopped me. "I have been explaining to this gentleman here," he said, "that you did come to see me, that you questioned me about that professor, and that maybe you got a better look than I did at whoever hit me over the head like this."

I glanced at Ferrar, then back at the janitor. What did he want me to say?

"We have a witness who saw you leaving the building," Ferrar interrupted gruffly. "So we know why you were on campus. It seems you left that little part of your episode out."

"There was no harm in her questioning me," the janitor said gruffly. "She was just doing her job. I had a right to speak to her if I wanted to." The janitor stared at me. "Miss, did you know that right after we spoke, I discovered that professor's office all tore up and such?"

"You're kidding?" I managed to say.

"Nope. Must have been the same man as hit me."

I finally got it. Someone else had been in the building, right behind me. Bad luck for the janitor. Good luck for me. The second intruder could take the rap for the burglary.

"I didn't tell you I had questioned him because you told me to back off," I explained to Ferrar. "I didn't want you to know I was still investigating Brookhouse. Sorry."

The detective waved away my apology. "I don't care about that. What I want to know is if you saw anyone at all who might have followed you into the building and done this to this man."

I stared at the janitor's bandages. Had I caused all that damage?

The janitor was sharp enough to read my look correctly. "Someone hit me from behind," he explained to me quickly. "They found a baseball bat nearby, my blood all over it. My tissue, too. Bits of my brain probably. They practically drove a hole in my head right here." He touched a spot toward the back of his head and winced. "Must have taken a second swing, cause I also got me a smaller wound right here." He touched his forehead where I had taken my best shot. That was when I understood more. Whoever had come up behind me had tried to do this poor man in with a baseball bat.

"I'm sorry," I said. "I didn't see anyone. And I think I would have noticed if I was being followed. Like I said, I was paranoid when I found out my car was missing."

I stepped up to the janitor's bedside. "Are you going to be okay?" I asked. "Do you have family?"

He nodded. "My sister is on her way down from the mountains. My boy is coming up from Atlanta." He didn't mention a wife. I didn't ask. The world was a complicated place these days.

"Are you sure there's nothing you need? Anyone I could notify?"

He thought about it and smiled. "Well, I do have me a close cousin. Name of Jim. Jim Beam. Smooth fellow."

"Tall?" I asked.

"Big as they come."

"He'll be here by nightfall," I promised. I'd buy him a gallon jug of Jim Beam every week for the next year, if that was what he wanted.

"Did you know my friend got hurt?" I told the janitor as I turned to go. "The kid with the punk look? He got shot. Real bad."

"I'm sorry to hear that," he replied. "But you know what else?"

"What?" I asked.

"I think you best be watching your own back right now."

I nodded, touched his hand and left. He had a good point. A very good point.

"You're not much help with anything," Ferrar said as we walked down the hallway. He sounded angry at me again.

"I'm sorry. I can't make up details just to suit you." This blatant lie fled my lips with convincing outrage. "Why is it so important? You think the same person who hit the janitor chased me and shot Luke, don't you?"

Ferrar didn't even bother to answer. Of course he did. How many maniacs were running loose in Durham?

A good question, I realized. How many indeed?

CHAPTER TWELVE

By the time I got back to Helen's house, I was too tired to care whether Burly was mad at me. By the time I woke up—a good sixteen hours later—Luke was still in a coma and Burly was squirreled away in the bedroom office, lost in cyberspace.

"What's with Burly?" I asked Bobby as I wandered into the kitchen, still clad in the pink nightie and matching gown that had failed to catch Burly's attention a few moments before. "Why's he locked away like that?"

Bobby was eating a stale muffin as if it were dog shit—a form of pouting brought on by Fanny choosing to spend her waking hours at the hospital by Luke's side instead of cooking for her man. Luke's parents were still MIA.

Helen was sitting beside Bobby at the table, staring at an untouched cup of tea. She answered my question when Bobby ignored it. "Burly says he's on to something," she offered, not sounding enthusiastic about the prospect.

"What does that mean?" Was it possible that instead of being angry at me, Burly was pouring his energy into helping me?

Helen shrugged. "He won't say. He just said he cracked some firewall last night and found out something interesting. He's following up now."

I poured a cup of coffee, not believing my luck. At least Burly was still on my side. He was not giving up.

"I don't want you to go near that campus," Bobby ordered me. He knew my expressions well and could tell I had been plotting. "Ferrar read me the riot act. He's gonna pull my license if you keep it up."

What he did not say in front of Helen was that if Ferrar went fishing for P.I. licenses, he'd soon discover that I didn't have one. I got the message anyway.

"I'm not planning to go near the campus," I promised as I rummaged through the cupboards. God, there was nothing to eat in the house but Cap'n Crunch, Hugo's favorite American delicacy. When was the last time Hugo had gone to the grocery store, anyway? That was his main task in our carefully balanced community, by his own preference. He loved wallowing in the bounty of an American grocery store and always overbought. If it's possible to overbuy food with Bobby D. around.

"Where's Hugo?" I asked.

"Hugo's out front," Bobby grunted. "With a whole pack of Frito Banditos."

"You ought to consider a career in the diplomatic corps," I suggested. He stared at me blankly, muffin crumbs tumbling from his mouth.

"Where's your mother this morning?" I asked Helen.

"In bed. She says she's not feeling well."

Probably Valium withdrawal, I thought. What with Fanny not being around to mix up her special Mai Tais.

"I think it's the black eye and bruises on her face," Helen explained. "She hates for anyone to see her looking less than perfect."

Less than a perfect what? I wondered. She looked, dressed and acted like the Wicked Witch of the West as far as I was concerned. But at least she was staying away from the rest of us. Saved me throwing a bucket of water on her.

I wandered out to the front porch, coffee cup in hand, spoiling for a fight to take away the crawlies creeping through me at the thought of what I had helped do to Luke.

Bobby had not been kidding about a "pack." Hugo sat in a rocking chair facing the narrow highway that wound past the house. Two other thin Mexican guys balanced on the railing beside him, while one stocky, bullet-headed fellow blocked my way down the front steps. Between him and Burly's wheelchair ramp, there was barely enough room for my fabled refrigerator butt.

"What gives?" I asked, wiggling into a spot next to Bullet Head. He glanced at me, then moved as far away as the ramp would allow him, going so far as to perch on it rather than sit next to me. Maybe I should have showered again when I first woke up.

"These are my friends," Hugo explained. "We're waiting for the bad man to come after Helen. And then we will get him."

Or bad men. I surveyed her new protectors. The two fellows on the porch railing looked like brothers. Or at least they shared the same bad hairdresser, obviously someone who had watched too many Air Supply videos in the 1980s. Both men wore their hair long in that peculiar fashion where the top is feathered tightly against the head like a helmet, but a mane is left to dangle down the back like some sort of mutated coonskin cap. People from Charlotte call it a "mullet" because it looks like a giant fish has died on the wearer's head. People from the rest of the state call it a "charlotte" because so many rednecks from the Queen City favor it. These guys were from Tijuana, however, as their round faces, broad noses and wide lips testified. They had small raisin-like eyes. Eyes that were checking me out even more thoroughly than I was checking them out. Perhaps it was time to slip out of something a little more comfortable and into something a little less revealing? Did they even have pink night slips with matching fur-trimmed robes south of the border?

Only in bordellos, I suddenly realized.

Bullet Head could read my mind. I caught him trying to sneak a peek at my fur trim. And I am not talking about my robe. "Just pretend I'm your sister," I suggested to him sternly.

He looked away, offended. "If you were my sister," he informed me, "I would not let you sit on a porch in that outfit."

"Welcome to America." I raised my coffee cup in a toast. He hid a smile. Bullet Head was also a Pineapple Face, with deeply pitted skin and black hair that stuck up in inky spikes. At least his hairdresser had moved on to a Sid Vicious phase.

"It takes all four of you to guard one house?" I asked the men.

"My friends and I do not mess around," Hugo announced with satisfaction. "Let this coward come after us and we will show him how real men deal with scum like him." The men shifted proudly, touching their waists. That was when I realized that the bulges in their britches were not due to Mother Nature's bounty but mankind's folly. They were packing. And how. Especially Hugo.

"Is that Bobby's favorite shotgun?" I asked. It was a double-barrel .12 gauge that could cut a man in two from close range. Bobby had been insane to lend it to Hugo.

Hugo didn't think so. He held the shotgun across his lap as he rocked, making him look like some old-timey mountain man waiting for a dagnabbit varmint to wander across his property so he could blow it to smithereens.

"Mr. Dodd trusts me with it," Hugo said. Great. Someone who actually gave Bobby D. some respect. More of that and Bobby's ego would swell to the size of his gut.

"We have everything under control." This was from Bullet Head.

I took the hint. I stood up, giving Bullet Head a taste of my pink fur. Right in the kisser. A small piece of fluff clung to his lips as I moved on. That's what he got for licking them when I was around. "Think I'll check on Burly," I announced.

"He was up all night," Hugo told me. "He is hot on the trail. He is a good man. Mr. Nash is a genius."

Burly merited last-name status, too? It looked like everyone's star was hanging high in Hugo's heaven at the moment. Except mine, probably.

I was right. "How is that boy who got shot doing?" Hugo asked, his mouth grim.

"He's not awake yet," I explained as I hesitated at the front door. The men shook their heads sadly. "His *madre*," one of them muttered. The others nodded sadly.

His *madre* indeed.

I spent a couple of hours going through the files I had stolen from Brookhouse's office. There was a lot of correspondence between Brookhouse and the drug company funding the study, including a flurry of kiss-ass letters from the department assuring the company that all was well, no corners were being cut. Others announced that Brookhouse was taking over the study for Carroll due to changing schedules, etc. Damage control. Keep that funding in-house.

I was astonished to see that there was no mention of Brookhouse's rape trial in the file. Was it possible no one in the drug company had caught on to it? Or cared? I knew that particular firm was ultimately owned by a German conglomerate. Maybe the news had never made its way over the Atlantic. Or, more likely, the negotiations that had gone on over the trial, and Brookhouse's character, had been conducted unofficially—to avoid legal problems—and Brookhouse had separated that paperwork from the drug study data.

There was no list of volunteer names to guide me. What I had thought was a directory of the volunteers was actually a list of names in code. The participants of the study remained a mystery—except for their phone numbers on the list the department receptionist used when she called and informed the volunteers of the new Thursday night interview requirement. The names of the subjects had been blacked out with a Magic Marker. Only their phone numbers were left visible, along with whether they were male or female, their ages and an identifying number. Another row, I knew, indicated what sort of treatment each person had been receiving: the actual drug, a placebo and, it seemed, some sort of third comparison option. It was also in code and I could not decipher it.

Nothing else in the file was of much use. Weekly reports had been supplied to the drug company. They all sounded pretty much the same: no major changes in mental ability, the moods of the volunteers were holding steady, the drug did not appear to cause any discernible side effects, things were looking good, oh, happy day, start spending those big profits now.

That was pushing it, I knew. There were times when I had interviewed the drug study volunteers and more than one of them had reported headaches, feelings of hopelessness and a decreased ability to deal with frustration. It had not happened often, but it had happened.

None of this had made its way into the reports to the drug company as far as I could tell. Which meant Brookhouse had fudged the data, or at least reported a far rosier picture of results than the strict truth merited. On the other hand, I had no idea what was statistically significant in such cases. Perhaps that sort of data was put on hold, accumulated with other weekly data, and examined in more thorough quarterly reports? I looked through the file carefully and found other reports. None spoke of potential complications.

What did it mean? Maybe Burly would know.

I knocked on the bedroom office door. "It's me," I said.

"Come on in." He sounded distracted. I knew the tone well. He was in the middle of tracing back elusive bits of data, jumping from Web site to Web site, cross-correlating, backtracking screens, opening new sites, and trying to keep all the connections straight. He didn't need any interruptions.

"Keep going," I said. "I have a list of phone numbers. Can you get the names for me?"

"Sure. Put it on the table." He didn't even look up.

I put the list down and left. After all, a genius was at work.

In the early afternoon, Fanny called from the hospital to say that the police had located Luke's parents. As soon as they got close enough to shore to be picked up by helicopter, they were on their way to Duke. Fanny would keep vigil in the meantime. I promised to stop by that evening with food and moral support. "Bobby, too," I added, seeing his look.

"Why do you keep staring at me that way?" I asked Bobby after I hung up.

"I'm not. It's your conscience," he said with maddening certainty. He and Helen were playing rummy in a halfhearted way. Helen kept glancing out the window. Maybe she was afraid of Bullet Head. I know I was.

"Time to talk," Burly announced from the doorway. God, but he kept his wheels well-greased. I never, but never, heard him coming. He wheeled into the living room with a stack of printouts on his lap. "I think we've got them."

"Them?" I asked, exchanging a glance with Helen.

"Them," Burly said. "Everybody gather round."

"We're going to make this a group activity?" I asked.

"Damn right we are," Bobby said. "When my partner starts lying to me, I start paying closer attention."

I ignored that little comment. I had to.

"We need Helen to stay," Burly explained. "I have some questions for her."

"Okay, fine." I could deal with it. "What's going on?"

"You remember that junior college where Brookhouse worked for a couple of years in the early nineties?"

I nodded. "You were having trouble hacking into their system."

"I got in. Brookhouse was there all right. In fact, he got fired."

"Oh, yeah?" This was interesting. Duke would never willingly hire anyone who was fired elsewhere for cause, I was sure.

Burly nodded. "But I don't think it's on the official records, because when I track down his resume after that, it says he left to pursue research opportunities elsewhere."

"He got fired for falsifying study results?" I guessed.

Burly shrugged. "That I couldn't tell. Not all the records from that time period are computerized. I was able to pull up a couple of letters exchanged between some provosts discussing what they called 'the situation,' but no more than that. All I know is that it was sensitive and they were afraid of a lawsuit. So when they fired him, they agreed to keep it quiet."

A lovely and quite common habit of modern employers. Fire some deadbeat and do all you can to make him someone else's problem. I knew this because many companies paid me to find out the real dirt on prospective high-level hires.

"So he could have been let go for boffing coeds," I said. "That's sensitive."

"Yes," Burly agreed. "But that's not the most interesting part of what I found out. As I was checking the class schedules to see what he had taught there, I noticed another name. That other professor who came to see Helen the other night."

"Lyman Carroll?" Helen asked.

Burly nodded. "His name was listed as a short-term lecturer in the psychology department. He taught for eight weeks while someone else was on medical leave."

"So what?" I said. "They've been hating each other for longer than we thought. Big deal."

"It's a big deal if they hid the fact that they knew each other," Burly explained.

"They did hide it," Helen interrupted. "They definitely hid it. I was there when they supposedly met for the first time at a faculty tea. It was right after Brookhouse was hired. They hated each other on sight. Everyone talked about it. They shook hands, glared at each other and stalked off. I even remember talking to Lyman about it. I asked if he knew Brookhouse and what was the story? He told me that he didn't know him, that he just hated his type. He called him something like a pencil-dicked, academic leech with an ego as big as the campus."

"Not bad," I said in admiration. "That's probably pretty accurate. Though I didn't realize that leeches had dicks. But is it really significant?" I wasn't following Burly's point.

"Yes, it is," Burly said. "I traced Lyman's background. He and Brookhouse grew up together in a little town just over the Virginia border near South Hills. Brookhouse went away to a private high school, so the overlap doesn't show on their official records. But I know that town. There's no way they could both grow up there and not know each other. In other words, they've known each other a long time and they've gone out of their way to hide it."

"No one at Duke knows that, I promise you." Helen looked at me. "Don't you see? They've been pretending to hate each other, to be rivals."

I got it. "That way they could cover for each other and no one would suspect it. Why would anyone lie to help someone they supposedly hated?"

"I told you that guy was a prick," Bobby D. added. "Man brings flowers and thinks a woman can't see through it. I knew he was a phony son-of-a-bitch."

"But it's still not proof they've done anything wrong," I explained. "Except maybe been sloppy with their credentials and the drug study." I told them about the weekly reports and how they seemed to be leaving out negative information.

"Those kinds of problems should be reported as they occur," Helen said. "In fact, that's why the study was yanked from Lyman and given to Brookhouse in the first place. The whole point of having Duke test the drug instead of an in-house study, is to create objectivity."

"So Brookhouse looked like a hero instead of another lying scum bag when he took over the study," Bobby said. "I bet they're working together and siphoning off the grant money somehow. It's always the money."

"But that doesn't tie them into the campus attacks." I was disappointed. I wanted to nail Brookhouse for Helen's rape, one way or the other.

"It might tie them into it," Burly said. "It sounds crazy, but take a look at these." He started distributing printouts. Mine showed a list of professional publications, the kind academics live and die by. Long names. Technical terms. Obscure publications. My eyes crossed within seconds. But Helen was poring over her copy avidly.

"I need your eyes," Burly explained to us. "I went to all the colleges where either Carroll or Brookhouse have worked over the past twenty years, at least the ones I could get into. Plus I searched the Net for their names together and separately. A lot of academic and medical publications are now online and have uploaded their archives to make it easier for people to use their material when doing research or writing term papers. Then, I downloaded a list of the official publications both men claimed to have authored by the time they got to Duke. These guys are obsessive about listing their work."

"They have to be," Helen said. "It's supposed to be evidence they do original work. It's the only reason why they were hired at Duke in the first place. Both of them moved around a lot, but they've really pioneered some new theories and Duke was getting a little worried about their reputation in that regard." Whenever

Helen spoke about academic matters, she had a confidence lacking in all other areas of her life. It was her world and she was good at it. I hoped she would get back to it one day.

"Okay," I said. "I'm with you on their publications. But so what?"

"The lists don't match," Burly explained. "They change over time. Both men started dropping off titles, I think. But there are too many papers listed for me to keep them straight. I need your help comparing them."

Mine was not to reason why. Mine was but to do or die. I humored Burly and dutifully checked my lists against the titles he called out, marking down the names of any that were missing.

By the time we were done, I understood where he was going. Brookhouse had several papers missing in his recent credits, including one dropped from his curriculum vitae in the early nineties that was called "Sexual Predators: A Study in Diversity." Not exactly the kind of diversity America needed. But earlier descriptions of the paper positioned it as a major breakthrough study. Why drop it from his professional credentials before he came to Duke?

Carroll's omissions were equally telling: "Trauma and Memory Loss: A Protective Mechanism?" plus one obscure short paper penned early in his career that was goofily entitled: "Social Habits of the Anti-Social: A Biker Gang in America." It took me three seconds to make the connection. Judging from the publication date, the men who had attacked us had been zooming around on their choppers for close to twenty years. No wonder their reflexes were rusty.

Both men had also dropped off a few arcane publications, but they did not seem connected to the case.

"That's it," Burly said. "I knew there was a reason the lists didn't match."

"You think Carroll met the biker gang who attacked us while researching his paper?" I asked.

Burly nodded. "I do. And I think if I give Weasel the town where Carroll and Brookhouse grew up and he puts his biker buddies on it, we'll find out that those guys are coming over the border from Virginia."

"I warned them to close that border down years ago," I said. No one laughed.

Helen was trembling.

"What?" I put my hand on her arm, steadying her.

"That paper of Brookhouse's," she said. "The one about sexual predators. Can you get a copy of it?"

Burly shook his head. "I couldn't find one on the Web or in the college networks. Why?"

"I know what's in it," she whispered.

"What do you mean?" I asked.

"One of the problems they had during my trial was tying him into the other rapes because the details were so different."

It hit me. "He was staging them to match old crimes. Crimes he had studied for his paper. Ferrar was right when he said they were being staged. He was just wrong when he thought it was someone who had access to police files."

Bobby grunted. "This guy is sick. That's what I'd call organized."

"It's what the FBI would call 'highly organized'," I said. "And I think Lyman Carroll was helping him."

"But why attack women so methodically?" Burly asked. "I thought people like that were following horrible impulses they couldn't control."

"Some are doing it on impulse," I said. "Others plan. And stalk. That's where they get their satisfaction." No wonder Brookhouse had lectured so authoritatively on the minds of men like that. He was one of them.

"Why those women?" Helen asked, then stopped, realizing what she was saying. "Why choose me? What did I ever do to them?"

"It's connected to the memory loss study Carroll did," I realized. "It must be. When I asked the nurse about what Luke would remember when he came out of his coma, she said Luke would not be able to recall anything for at least a day before the attack." I looked at the others. They stared back.

"Don't you see?" I said. "Suppose all of the women attacked were connected to the drug study, or maybe to Brookhouse and Carroll personally. Like a girlfriend or some coed they were boffing." I thought of Candace Goodnight, the anthropology professor. Carroll's recent girlfriend. Was she still missing? I wondered. God, which crime had been imitated with her in the starring role? And was one of them losing control? Brookhouse? Never. Maybe Carroll.

"Keep going," Bobby said. "We're listening."

"Maybe these women all found out something that could jeopardize the study in some way. It's possible they didn't even know they had that knowledge. Destroying them through a brutal attack and rape would be a good way to make sure they had worse things to worry about than the study. They'd drop out of school, quit their jobs, leave town or whatever."

"Why not just off them?" Bobby asked.

"Bobby, that's so... pedantic." He looked at me blankly. "Not to mention, they have killed two women. And they did a fine job of almost killing Helen." I glared at him. He got the point.

"Sorry if I was insensitive," he mumbled halfheartedly.

"Killing everyone would have the cops on them and their study in a heartbeat," I explained. "Not even Brookhouse's outraged refusal to release the list of volunteers would hold up in a case like that. But women get attacked on campus all the time. A college is a sexual predator's paradise. It would take the cops a lot longer to make the connection. They might never make it, in fact."

"But why have no men been attacked?" Bobby asked. "You'd think some men in this new drug trial might blow the whistle, if there were problems."

"Not if the side effects of the new drug only affect women," I guessed. "As for the people outside the study who might threaten them, who would that be? A secretary. That would be a woman for sure. A girlfriend. Or some lackey with inside information, also sure to be female. Those two men surround themselves with women. That's why all their victims are female. They're the only ones in a position to know what's going on."

"You're all missing the point," Helen interrupted bitterly. "Raping women is fun for them. Think of the power it gives them over our lives. Over my life."

"She's right, you know," I told the others. "They're also doing it for the power it gives them. They get a rush out of it. And it's a way to protect the study at the same time." Bobby looked skeptical. "Think about it, Bobby. That's why they went into this field in the first place, all this shit about deviance and crimes and craziness. Because it excites them. And then they found each other, kindred spirits. Maybe they've been working together for years."

"I can still check on that," Burly offered. "I can trace sex crimes in all the areas where they've lived. I just haven't been able to get around to it yet."

I nodded. "Which brings up a big point: who's going to tell Ferrar about this?"

They all looked away.

"Fine, I'll do it," I volunteered. "God knows I need the brownie points." This time they all looked at me. In silence that I could read all too easily.

"No way," I said firmly. "We cannot keep this information from the cops. What if they do it to someone else?" I stared at Helen. "If we try to handle this ourselves and they victimize someone else in the meantime, you'll never forgive yourself."

"So let's take care of it quickly," Burly suggested.

"Bobby?" I turned to my heretofore law-abiding boss. He shrugged. "I can't believe you're going along with this. If Brookhouse turns up murdered—and let me be the one to say the word, because we are talking about killing another human being—his blood will be on our hands."

"Those guys are not human beings," Burly interrupted. Bobby grunted his agreement.

"Regardless, the first person Ferrar is going to look to for it is me."

"We'll make sure you're far away when it happens," Bobby said. "Leave it to us."

"Bobby, I've never seen you like this."

He wouldn't answer me. But he wouldn't look away, either. He clearly felt justified in his conviction.

"This is a bad idea," I warned them. "You think you can live with yourselves afterward, but don't count on it." I thought of how I had felt when I thought I'd been the one to shoot Luke. "Killing another person is a big responsibility. It's going to weigh on all of you. Even you." I looked at Helen. "Even when you have the best reason of all of us to want it done. Helen, it's not as easy to live with as you think. It makes you just like them. A killer. Is that what you want?"

"Casey," Burly said. "It's not like the system has worked so far. Look at Helen. Look what that skell Brookhouse did to her. And he not only walked away, now he's about to make her life miserable again by dragging her name through the mud at a civil trial. That's balls. That's scary. And that's more than enough for me. I think he needs to be brought down. And his friend, too."

I tried to reason with Helen. "What about your countersuit?" I said. "Suing Brookhouse in civil court might buy us some time. Let's just let your lawyer know what we found out. Get his advice. What's his plan?"

It was Burly who answered for her. "He's filing the countersuit next week. Right before Thanksgiving, so that it makes the papers before the holiday. But Brookhouse won't have time to respond before the courts close for the long weekend."

"Then let's leave it to the lawyers about what to take to the police. This information could blow the case out of the water." I needed to be more careful in my choice of words, I realized, given the level of blood lust running through this crowd.

"Not good enough," Burly said. "We don't have enough evidence for the courts. I say we take care of it ourselves."

"Me, too. We damn sure have enough evidence for me," Bobby butted in.

"Bobby, if Fanny heard you say that, she would be appalled."

Wee doggies. He blew a fuse at that one.

"I don't want Fanny to hear a single word about this, you understand?" His tone was deadly. "There are some things that people like Fanny never need to know, and it's a kindness to protect them from it. Fanny doesn't understand that people like this exist. And I don't want those two scumbags in her world or her head or her prayers in any way. Keep her out of it."

"Okay, okay. But this is still a bad idea. Let's get the evidence instead."

"What evidence?" Burly asked. "There is none. They're too good. They've studied the best, don't you get it?"

"What about the names of the drug trial participants?" I asked. "If we can find some or all of the rape victims among them, or connect them in some way, then Ferrar can't ignore that. That's evidence and then some."

"I've got about half of the names for you," Burly said, pushing another printout my way. "I can get most of the rest tomorrow. Right now I need some sleep."

"Then let's see if we get any hits on this half list first," I suggested. "Before we do anything we might regret."

The room was silent.

"I guess this has been decided without me." No one would meet my eyes. "One suggestion." I nodded toward the window where the Mexican Posse was keeping watch. "Let's keep those guys out of it, understand? They've got enough problems as it is. I doubt even one of them has a green card. Don't drag anyone else into this."

"Seems to me I told you the same thing," Bobby pointed out. "And look where the kid is right now. In a hospital bed."

A silence fell over the group. My mind flashed back to the image of Luke bleeding out on a boulder in the moonlight. "Thanks for reminding me, Bobby."

"Let's talk about something else for a while," Burly said, playing the peacemaker. "I do have some good news for you."

"It better be real good," I told him.

"It is. The mystery guest for Thanksgiving?"

"Yes?" I waited.

"I invited your grandfather. He's coming up from Florida."

I stared at Burly. "You talked to my grandfather?"

Burly nodded. "Sure. He has a telephone. Big deal. I called him. We talked."

"You talked to my grandfather without telling me?"

Burly shrugged. "I've been waiting for you to introduce me to your family for a long time now, Casey. I just decided it was time."

"That's nice," I said sarcastically, ignoring the fact that now more than ever was the time when I needed to make it plain to Burly that he was my boyfriend and that he did matter to me. "And what did the two of you talk about?"

"You." Burly sounded genuinely perplexed. "What else?"

I didn't know whether to kill Burly or thank him. If my grandfather came up, I would have someone on my side. He'd never condone taking justice into our own hands like what the others had planned. He was honest to a fault. That's why he was so poor. And that was what had made it so hard to face him after I got out of prison. The law was the law in my grandfather's eyes.

"Fine," I said, playing it cool. "Invite whoever you like. The more turkeys here for Thanksgiving the merrier."

"What's up her ass?" I heard Bobby ask as I stalked away to my room. That Bobby D. He has such a way with words.

I had a bad feeling about it all. I had taken on the case because I felt sorry for Helen. She seemed like a broken person, unable to function, as crippled as a dove with two broken wings. And now she was coming back to life—but only because a lust for revenge had consumed her. I couldn't blame her. But it made me feel as if I had never really known her. In fact, it made me feel as if no one was who they seemed to be.

Yeah, I could do with Brookhouse being dead. But it doesn't feel good to have blood on your hands, either literally or figuratively, and I had no desire to be god. Nor did I want someone I loved—like Burly—spending his years in prison. Detective Ferrar was good and he was determined. He'd find out who killed Brookhouse. Or never stop trying. Which was worse.

And then there was the matter of not really knowing what exactly Brookhouse had done. Or where Lyman Carroll fit in. We didn't really know. You can't go around killing people based on supposition.

Or could you?

As Bobby and I left to check on Luke, Burly and Helen were getting ready to go through the boxes of materials that some kind soul in the psychopathology department had packed away for her after the attack. She had not gone near them since that day, she said, preferring to let that part of her life fade off into the past. But on the theory that the attack had been motivated, in part, by some nugget of information she had stumbled on about Brookhouse and Carroll, she had dragged the materials into the living room. With Burly's help, she was ready to confront the reminders of how she had once had a life outside the walls of her home.

"What are we looking for?" she said as Bobby and I headed for the front door. Burly had wheeled into the kitchen to make her a cup of tea.

"Anything that Brookhouse or Carroll would be anxious to have you forget," I explained, leaving her more confused than before.

Bobby and I squeezed out past the ever-growing crowd of macho men guarding Helen's front porch. Word had gotten out and two younger boys had joined Hugo's posse. Fortunately, based on close scrutiny by *moi*, they seemed to be packing nothing more deadly than your average-sized six-inch shooter. Trust me. I can take the true measure of a man at twenty paces.

No one said a word as we walked past. Hugo was asleep in his chair and two of his compadres were snoring happily on the porch floor, resting up for their chance to prove they were real men.

"Is it just me," Bobby asked, "or is that bunch multiplying like rabbits?"

"We'll know at dinnertime," I predicted.

I retrieved my car from the impound lot with little fanfare and no luck finding out who, if anyone, had called it in to be towed away in the first place. Ferrar had gotten there before me, it was obvious. The girl who took my money—cash on the barrelhead—refused to talk.

Ferrar. The very name made my conscience turn over and groan.

How could I not tell him what was going on? But if I did tell him about our theory, and he put cops on Brookhouse and Carroll to watch them, I would be inviting them to witness the people I loved most in the world commit a crime.

What's a girl to do?

I had the printouts of their academic publications and half the drug study participants on me in case I decided on an answer.

Luke was still in a coma, visiting some other netherworld. I offered to sit with him while Fanny went home and took a nap. She did not want to accept my offer, but a little coaxing did the trick. She was really far too old and far too plump to be spending days and nights in a hospital chair. Besides, Luke's parents were rumored to be arriving by the next morning and she wanted to be there to support them when they first saw him. I didn't bother to tell her that Luke's stepmother probably wouldn't give a rat's ass. Maybe Fanny's sympathy would shame her into showing more compassion.

Bobby left to escort Fanny back to her home in North Raleigh—an abode she seldom frequented.

I stayed by Luke's side—just me, my shadow, the nurse—and my conscience. They had removed the tubes in his nose and you could see more of his face. It was pink with pumped-in oxygen, as rosy as a little boy who has fallen asleep flush from the bathtub. Those beautiful eyelashes of his fluttered at times, or so I imagined. I wondered if it was a good sign.

Burly arrived around midnight. I was surprised to see him and said so.

"Hey, if anyone can tell this kid what to expect in the months ahead, it's me," Burly pointed out as he wheeled into the room. "Besides, Helen wanted me to come. And I wanted to tell him to hang in there if he was awake." He gave the night nurse a dazzling smile and she melted as they always do—handsome, appreciative and in a wheelchair? Burly was an irresistible magnet for the ladies in white, who so often found their devotion to the afflicted sorely tested by bad manners, bad attitudes and bad bodies. Burly had none of these. Burly had style.

He did a wheelie, showing off for the nurse. She blushed and went back to her book. "What's the word?" he asked.

I shook my head. "No word."

"He's alive," Burly offered. "And that's a start."

I was glad that Burly was there. I hoped he had arrived not just for Luke, but also for me. It was hard to say. All of his attention was on Luke.

As Burly launched into a long and technical discussion with the nurse about Luke's chances for recovery and what he would have to go through when and if he came out of his coma, I tuned them out and contented myself with watching Luke breathe. The rhythm was reassuring, whether aided by machine or not. After a while my mind settled down, thoughts began flowing in and out; ideas, worries and eventually conclusions.

I had to let Ferrar know. And I thought I knew a way how.

"God, girl, you drive a hard bargain. Where I come from, they call it blackmail." Marcus waved the air with languid fingers, sending clouds of smoke spiraling toward the ceiling of the men's room. He had not been the least surprised to discover me there at nine o'clock in the morning. He'd just rolled his eyes, opened the stall door and invited me in.

"Isn't it obvious to everyone in this entire building that you are sneaking smokes in here?" I asked him, coughing as I inhaled smoke from his obnoxiously long and slender brand of cigarette. He'd have used a diamond-encrusted cigarette holder if he thought the boys in blue would let him get away with it. Marcus is one of those smokers who is into the ritual, who savors the moments of suspended thought as the cigarette is extracted, lit and waved about. The cigarette is but a prop.

"Honey, they're just grateful I'm not smoking pot in here," Marcus explained after a moment of silence in which I do believe he was actually giving my question serious thought. He licked the tip of a finger and reshaped his right eyebrow. "They like to keep me happy because no one can work that keyboard like I can. I have magic fingers."

"So will you work it and go through the files of all rape and assault victims in Durham over the past two years?" I said. "I want you to correlate the data against the names on the drug trial printouts and see if you get any matches. I didn't recognize the names of any rape victims whose cases I studied, but maybe the connections are more subtle."

"What are you looking for?" Marcus asked.

"I think this new drug testing study connects everyone somehow. But I don't quite know how. It would be too obvious to start raping or killing drug study volunteers one by one. But maybe the victims are connected in other ways. Maybe they know the study volunteers. Or worked with Brookhouse in some way. I know there's a link somewhere."

A thought came to me. "You did tell me about all the attacks, didn't you?"

Marcus looked away. The bastard. There were more that he'd held back. "I can't let you touch those files again," he said. "For one thing, they are a lot thicker than they were before Ferrar took over the case. That man is seriously driven. And whatever this burning information is you are hoping to trade in return for these rape files, well, you had better—and I advise you this seriously—go to Ferrar with your info just as soon as you can get there. This is maybe the worst thing ever to happen in this town. And this happens to be my town. If you can live with being a party to standing in the way of maybe stopping it, that's between you and god. But you aren't my friend anymore if you do."

"Marcus." We stared at each other.

"You've met one of the victims," he reminded me. "I've met them all. And, in some cases, their families. I want this case solved for them. Period."

"Meaning I don't?" I asked him, hurt.

"Meaning Ferrar is the one who deserves to solve this case and get the credit. Not you. You don't know how hard he has worked on it."

"Then I'll trade you," I offered. "I'll put you on Brookhouse's trail in exchange for cross-matching these study volunteer names. And I'll go first."

"Hand over the names," Marcus demanded. I gave him the printouts and he thumbed through them. "Where did you get these?" he asked.

"I can't tell you."

He glanced at me sharply and continued to read. He had moved on to the list of publications authored by Lyman Carroll or David Brookhouse. His eyebrows danced as he read the circled titles. He understood their significance right away. "I've got to get my hands on that paper," he murmured.

We froze as footsteps approached the outer bathroom door. Someone paused but then walked on. What a world we live in when people are in too damn much of a hurry to stop and pee.

"Deal on a modified trade, then," Marcus said when it was safe to talk again.

I told him about Brookhouse and Carroll, the drug study and their past connections. "If you check the towns they taught in together, I bet you'll find more assaults. And I just know this drug study is the key to the attacks at Duke."

"I'll take it from here," Marcus said, folding the printouts and slipping them into the back pocket of his designer jeans.

"But you'll tell me if any of the drug study names start coming up in relationship to any cases, right?"

"If it doesn't jeopardize the investigation, I will."

"Marcus—" I started to complain, but he cut me off.

"Don't you go Marcusing me," he said with confidence. "You knew when you approached me that I was not going to stand for anything less than telling Ferrar all. That's why you're here. So I can take the information and be the one to do it and your conscience is clear." He held a hand up to stop me when I started to protest. "No, don't say anything else. I don't want to hear any more about what you and your friends are planning. But you check your phone messages carefully over the next few days, you hear?"

"I hear," I said.

"Timing is everything, Miss Casey. I'll let you know what you need to know, when you need to know it."

Relief swept over me. It was the right thing to do. I knew it was. If Ferrar could take our information and nail Brookhouse, and maybe even Carroll, too, the civil suit against Helen would have to be withdrawn, the murders of that poor mother and the coed could be solved, Luke's would-be assassin could be punished—and I would sleep better at night.

Voices approached the men's room; it sounded like two cops arguing. I heard my name and instantly froze.

"What's she got to do with it?" one of the cops asked as they pushed their way inside the bathroom. Marcus shoved my butt with his shoulder until I was wedged against the wall, balancing on the rim of the toilet. He stood at attention, facing the door, a warning finger on his lips.

"No one really knows what she's been into. She's done half the guys in the department, so Ferrar doesn't trust anyone to handle her right."

"No shit?" the other guy asked hopefully. "Half the guys?"

Dream on. From what I could see of his credentials, he was not qualified for a goodnight kiss. And I didn't even know the other guy, the one who was such an authority on me.

"That's what I heard," the first guy said confidently. "I know I'm one of them."

Oh, yeah? I definitely did not recognize the rear view. But why should I?

"She pretty hot?" the second one asked.

Marcus, the bastard, was silently laughing. His shoulders shook and he had a fist jammed in his mouth.

"Oh, yeah," the first one said. "She's hot all right." Hmmm... maybe he wasn't so bad after all. "If you like 'em kind of big and trashy-looking. I know I do." He started humming *Bad Girls*. Off-key, I might add.

"Big and trashy?" The second guy sounded interested. "Sounds sweet to me."

"Better take your vitamins first." They laughed. How nice someone thought they were hilarious. If only each other.

They zipped up and began messing with their thinning hair in the mirror. "I'd definitely keep a wide berth until Ferrar is done with her," the first guy counseled. "He's looking for her now. Turns out there was a photo of the last victim in the clothes Casey had on the night that kid got shot. So she was snooping into something. Ferrar is royally pissed off about it. I told him to try Another Thyme and maybe Sammy's. She likes to hang out at both places."

Oh, thanks a lot, Mark, you turncoat, I thought—suddenly remembering his name. I did know the first guy after all. He'd just beefed up a lot. I rued the day I had ever dated that traitor. If I recalled correctly, he damn well ought to know what bars I hung out at. He had tracked me for months trying to get me into bed—and left me underwhelmed once we got there. Now he was helping Ferrar find me.

What the hell did he mean there had been a photo of the victim on me? I remembered the snapshot I'd found in the receptionist's desk. I'd put it in my back pocket. But it had showed Brookhouse and the secretary. Had she been the victim? No way. It was some bigwig's wife, I remembered, someone who had to do with fundraising.

By then, Marcus had stopped laughing and was glaring at me. I shrugged, letting him know I had no idea what they were talking about.

The two men moved on to standard chatter about the coming basketball season. One of them was for Duke, the other rooted for Carolina. So, naturally, their collegiate pissing match lasted well beyond the real pissing match. It seemed like hours until they got the hell out and left us alone again.

"You told me everything, huh?" Marcus demanded.

"I have no idea what photograph they're talking about."

"Well, I suggest you go right to Ferrar and find out," Marcus ordered me. "Or else, you'll be getting no phone messages from me."

That Marcus. Sometimes I think his mom raised him a little too thoroughly in the ways of her church. I took his advice anyway. I walked into the lion's den willingly, all eyes upon me.

It was one of those moments when the room is filled with sound, then suddenly everyone clams up at once, making the object of their attention feel like a pariah. You could have heard a gun cock in that room. Fortunately, I did not.

"Where's Ferrar?" I asked a female detective I'd done a favor for once, a favor involving her insane, steroid-saturated ex-boyfriend, also a cop, who had no business drinking and aiming at the same time. He now lived out-of-state, where he planned to stay. At least until the statute of limitations on his transgressions, discovered by *moi*, were up. He'd be away a long time.

"Conference room three," she told me, one eyebrow raised high. "Better wear a bulletproof jacket."

Ferrar was huddled over a cluttered table with at least six other detectives. Once again the room froze when I entered. Maybe today was a good day to attend as many soirees as possible. I seemed to be knocking them dead.

Before Ferrar could get the words "Will you excuse us?" out of his mouth, the room had emptied. It was down to me and him.

"Sit," he said.

I sat, hoping he would ask me to roll over as my next trick.

"You see this?" he said, pointing to a photograph encased in a plastic bag. One corner of the image was stained with Luke's blood. It showed the department secretary standing happily beside a Santa-capped David Brookhouse at some long-gone Christmas party

"I see it," I admitted.

"Where did it come from?" he asked.

"Why does it matter?" I countered.

He tapped the eraser of a pencil on a figure in the background. "It matters because that woman is now a dead woman."

I had not noticed her the night I stole the photograph. "Oh." I was stunned. She knew David Brookhouse. Or, at least, had attended a party with him.

"Oh, indeed." Ferrar waited.

I examined the photo from across the table. A group of two or three people were laughing and toasting behind the couple in the foreground. An older woman with carefully styled blond hair stood to the left of Brookhouse, talking to an unseen person. She had money and good looks if this photo was telling the truth. What she no longer had was a life.

"That's a coincidence," I said. "I had no idea she was in the photo." I either had to lie or admit I had broken into the department's offices. Naturally, I lied. "My client, Helen Pugh, took this photo one Christmas at a department party," I said. "I was using it when I went around and questioned people about David Brookhouse. I showed it to the janitor the night he got attacked."

Ferrar nodded. "Thank you. You can go now."

"That's it?" I was confused.

"That's it," he said. "Except that I need your client to come in and talk to me."

"Helen can't come in. She's not able. She's not even able to leave her house."

"Then I need for her to agree to talk to me," he said. "You do the convincing."

"I'll try."

"Tell the others to come back in."

He turned his back to me and started reading a file. That stung. I was lower than scum in his book, not even worthy of more than a moment of his attention.

The other detectives filed back in without looking at me. I had a feeling I was going to have a hard time getting any cooperation out of the Durham Police Department once this case was done.

Marcus watched me as I slunk my way through the department, anxious to reclaim my freedom. I did not dare give him a signal, as my friendship with him was a carefully guarded secret. The fact that Ferrar was letting me leave would have to be evidence enough that I was still free to roam at will. As scary as that seemed to more than a few people.

I arrived back at the hospital a few minutes after Luke's parents arrived. They were huddled in his room with Fanny, conferring in low whispers. Bobby D. and Burly were waiting in the hallway. I had barely said hello before Luke's father joined us.

"You must be the woman who saved Luke's life."

I stared at the older version of Luke standing in front of me. He was tanned and dressed in expensive sports clothes, dripping a tasteful gold watch and subdued men's jewelry. His voice was a carefully cultivated businessman's dream. And he smelled like Fort Knox.

"I don't know if you could say I saved his life," I said. And let's not go there, I silently prayed.

"The doctors say you carried him out of the park. Yelled for help. They say it may have saved his life."

"The paramedics and a doctor walking past saved his life," I told him. "I'm just a friend of your son's. I only did what anyone else would have done."

He ignored my protests. "Thank you," he said, taking my hands and squeezing them. "The doctors say he's going to recover."

"They do?" I stared at Bobby D. and Burly for confirmation. They both nodded, smiling.

I smiled back.

A thirty-something blond came out of Luke's hospital room, adjusting the hem of her linen dress. I stared at her. At first glance, she appeared young, blond, thin and bored with all of her bucks. But her pinched face and narrowed eyes told me all four attributes were a stretch. She had to work at being the trophy wife. Hard.

"Who's this?" the woman demanded, looking me over and pegging me in a millisecond. Her female radar was on overdrive. She instantly calculated that I was bigger, bulkier and much poorer than she was. But I was single. And that made me a threat.

"This is Luke's friend," the father explained. "The woman who saved him."

"Oh." She appeared unimpressed. "I thought you'd be younger. His age." She turned her back on me. "I'm starving, honey. What do you think they serve to eat in this godforsaken place? Stewed possum?"

"Dirt," I told her. "Jethro will be out at any moment with a heaping big bowl for you."

"What?" She stared at me, her lower lip protruding in what I suspected was a much-used pout.

"Down here, we sit around and share buckets of dirt when we're not inside banging our brothers," I explained.

"Why don't we go inside and see how Luke is doing?" Burly suggested. He gripped my elbow and dragged me away from Luke's stepmother, running over my foot in the process.

"That was not going to help things," Burly told me.

"She doesn't give a shit," I said angrily, shaking off his touch and stepping up to Luke's bedside. The nurse made no comment. She probably agreed with me. Nothing worse than a trophy wife who thinks she's slumming it. It would have been my pleasure to put her fancy ass in a hospital bed down the hall from Luke's. The first thing of hers I'd bust would be that lower lip.

I watched Luke breathe for a few moments, then held his hand and wondered how the doctors had figured out he would recover. The boxes and monitors seemed as mysterious as ever, yet clearly one of them had spit out happy news.

What would he be like when he came back from wherever he had been? And would he remember me? "Where are you, my friend?" I asked him out loud.

Luke squeezed my hand.

"He squeezed my hand!" I yelled. The nurse put down her book and stood.

"He squeezed my hand," I insisted. "He did." I leaned over him. "Luke, can you hear me. It's Casey. I'm right here. Squeeze my hand if you can hear me."

I felt it: his fingers tightened around mine.

"He squeezed my hand again." I bounced on my toes in excitement.

"Please clear the room," the nurse asked crisply. She pushed the call button. "Wait outside."

The small group was still assembled in the hallway, debating where to go eat. Fanny was reciting a litany of fine restaurants in Durham, North Carolina—none of which served dirt.

"He's coming out of it," I told them.

Luke's father turned to me and I saw a hundred years drop from his worry-lined face. He smiled. I smiled back. His smile looked just like Luke's.

"Are we going to go eat or not?" the stepmother demanded. "I'm hungry."

Even Bobby D. turned away in disgust.

Helen was as relieved as the rest of us to learn that Luke was going to be okay. I think she saw everything that had happened as connected to her, maybe even caused by her. She'd had enough of the unhappiness and she wanted it to end.

We celebrated Luke's good fortune and Fanny's return from the hospital with an early dinner of fried chicken, creamed corn and okra. We let Fanny cook, naturally. She made homemade biscuits that melted on your tongue. Even Miranda stumbled down from her upstairs lair to partake, her bruises layered so thickly with makeup that it looked as if her face was melting.

The guys on the front porch refused to come inside, but they sure as hell accepted plates heaped high with food. I must admit that they looked a lot less mean when they smiled.

As we ate, Helen and I discussed what she had found in the boxes she and Burly had searched. It wasn't much help.

"I think I was working on a grant proposal the day I was attacked," she said. "I can't really remember much, but that was one of my jobs. I was supposed to be an expert in writing grant proposals."

"Do you remember which proposal you were working on?"

She shook her head. "I know there was some pressure at that time for Carroll and Brookhouse to pool their ideas into one study since they overlapped. I could make some calls and find out. But, obviously, the idea was never followed up on, or we would know about it."

"Did you find any papers about that particular grant in your storage boxes?" I asked.

She shook her head.

"Someone took them," I decided. "It all comes back to that department. I know it does."

No one at the table argued with me on that one.

I spent the weekend before Thanksgiving calling the hospital to check on Luke's progress. Now that he was out of his coma, his nonfamily visitor list had been cut to zero. His father never left his side, according to the private nurse. The stepmother was not to be found, the nurse added—and she sounded relieved. The nurse also promised to ask the doctor when it was okay for Luke to have other visitors, but she thought it would be at least a few more days.

I also spent the weekend listening to endless discussions about the menu for Thanksgiving dinner. How hard can that be? So long as there's gravy and mashed potatoes, who gives a shit about the rest? I finally started leaving the room every time the topic came up, particularly when the debate veered to coconut custard vs. pecan pie. I mean, for godsakes, just serve both. There is something unseemly with the world's preoccupation with food. Or maybe I just found it inefficient. If your mouth is going to be flapping about food, it ought to be because you're shoveling something substantial into it.

No one seemed to know when my grandfather would arrive and he wasn't answering his phone. If I knew him, he'd show up just as the turkey was being carved. Then leave once his plate was clean.

Marcus and his partner were being invited to dinner, likewise a few trusted people who had helped us out with prior cases. Weasel Walters, Burly's friend, would be there, along with his latest girlfriend.

We weren't so different from the Pilgrims and Indians, I decided. We were gathering together everyone we could find on

Thanksgiving Day and hoping to create a sense of belonging in that coming together. But, like the original celebrants, everyone had the same vague fear that it would never work and the day would be a disaster.

Marcus did not call about the case. For four long days, I sweated out whether he had brought my information to Ferrar's attention. On Monday morning, I had an inkling that Marcus had indeed presented our evidence to the detective: an insider's newspaper column on college politics in the Triangle reported a rumor that two unnamed Duke University professors had been suspended over the weekend, albeit with pay, while the feds and local police department investigated them for allegations of malfeasance and misappropriation of funds.

Who else could it be but our friends Brookhouse and Carroll?

Was Ferrar really looking into them—or was this a pressure tactic, much like the lawsuit we planned to file, a move made in the hopes that Brookhouse would be spooked into doing something stupid so Ferrar could catch him at it?

Marcus finally contacted me late Monday afternoon. Helen's new lawyer had just left her house with a promise that he was filing and announcing the counter lawsuit against Brookhouse in the morning. I called my apartment to retrieve my phone messages and found terse instructions to phone Marcus at once.

"Finally!" I complained when I got him on the line.

"It's going down," he whispered. I could hardly hear him, he was keeping his voice so low.

"I can't do this," I told him. "I've been waiting to hear from you for four days and I can't sit on the end of the line guessing what the hell you're talking about. Find a pay phone and call me at Helen's."

He did just that. What he had to tell me gave me the proof I needed to be absolutely certain that David Brookhouse was guilty as shit—in Helen's rape, in the recent murder, in the entire string of assaults. It didn't nail Lyman Carroll's coffin down quite so thoroughly, but it did make me believe he was helping Brookhouse. Why, I could not fathom.

What Marcus told me was this: he had taken my information on Brookhouse and pretended to have uncovered it himself through clever cyber-sleuthing. That was okay by me. Anything to help Marcus out. Ferrar had not considered the prior connection between Brookhouse and Carroll significant, nor had he so much as twitched an eyebrow at our theory about the ties between Carroll and the motorcycle gang. He probably thought we were making up that whole part. But Ferrar had immediately escorted Marcus back to his computer screen when told that Brookhouse had authored a paper years ago on sexual predators and their techniques. Marcus had obtained this study over the weekend, thanks to an alert librarian at North Carolina Central University, who had unearthed a paper copy filed away years ago. Marcus had checked the details in this paper with the specifics from various crime scenes. Yes. All the actual crimes committed in Durham against women—all the rapes and assaults with baffling and varied M.O.'s—matched the incidents described in Brookhouse's paper. The scary part was that he still had plenty of crimes left to imitate. Even Ferrar had immediately figured out that it could not possibly have been a coincidence, even if it was not conclusive evidence for a court of law. Ferrar had actually turned white when he realized the connection, according to Marcus. Well, "even whiter" were his exact words.

I knew I'd get a phone call from Ferrar soon.

After that, Marcus had told Ferrar that he had run a computer check of some of the names of people participating in Brookhouse's drug study against the files of the open investigations. Ferrar asked where the names had come from in the first place and Marcus lied, saying they arrived in an envelope addressed to the department as a whole and it had been routed to him.

The results of Marcus's search: one of the rape victims in a case Marcus had withheld from me because Ferrar had been reviewing the paper file had indeed been a volunteer in the study. Two other rape victims had been roommates of different participants in the study—roommates whose names appeared in the official files because detectives had interviewed them as part of the rape investigations. One other victim had worked in the psychopathology department at one time, then left for another school shortly before she was raped. Four hits. With half the list of volunteers to go. That was no coincidence, either, not in my eyes or in Ferrar's.

Detectives had been sent out to talk to the victims again, Marcus reported, this time focusing their questions on any connection the victims might have to the drug trial. Marcus did not yet know what had happened during those interviews. Some of the women had moved out of state. I didn't blame them.

But Marcus did know that Ferrar had started publicly investigating both men as a pressure tactic, triggering their suspension from Duke. Lyman Carroll was thought to be an ancillary character, at best, by most of the detectives working the case. Marcus was not so sure Carroll was that innocent, but now that he had given them a new direction to go in, the investigative team had taken to ignoring Marcus again. After all, he was only a clerk.

A clerk who knew every move they made. As promised, Marcus reported that Ferrar had assigned detectives to watch Brookhouse around the clock. This was an easy assignment. Since his suspension from the university, Brookhouse was apparently holed up in his home and going nowhere. Or at least not going anywhere without someone secretly following.

I thought this news would make me feel better. It didn't. Lyman Carroll was still free. And if Brookhouse found out about the surveillance, he'd never make a move. We'd never catch him.

But the cops might catch someone else. Like one of my friends trying to kill Brookhouse.

"There's one more thing, Casey," Marcus reported. "Neither Brookhouse nor Carroll has a head wound. And you said one of the men who attacked you in the Gardens fell and hit his head on the rocks."

"He did," I insisted. "At least, I thought that's what I heard."

Marcus promised to call back with any more news.

I thanked him, hung up and marched into the living room. We were back to a wait-and-see mode. Burly, Bobby and Fanny were playing cards with Helen. Hugo and his friends were still guarding the front porch, though a couple of the guys were snoring in one of the spare bedrooms. Even Miranda was back to her perch on the couch in the television room, sipping Mai Tais, watching old movies and attacking Deborah Kerr's hairstyle. What else was there to do but continue to live life as normally as our abnormal commune would let us?

"Marcus called," I told them. "The cops are watching Brookhouse. Both men have been suspended from Duke and are holed up at their homes."

The news made Helen and Fanny happy. They saw it as a sign that, finally, the police were taking Brookhouse seriously as a suspect. The news did not make Burly and Bobby happy. The look they exchanged told me that something had been planned. Something that was now to be called off.

Burly wheeled away to make a phone call. I took his place at cards. Bobby would not meet my eyes.

I had done the right thing, I told myself as I discarded the queen of hearts. I had done the right thing.

CHAPTER THIRTEEN

The day before Thanksgiving, the state's major newspapers all carried front-page stories announcing that Helen Pugh had filed a counter civil suit against Professor David Brookhouse of Duke University for emotional distress, loss of income and several other charges. On a slow news day, Brookhouse's affiliation with Duke, Helen's decision to take her side of the story public and the history between the two of them all conspired to make the story major news. I was pretty sure the television anchors would be reporting on it by evening as well.

I grabbed one of the morning newspapers off the kitchen table and retreated to my bedroom to read in solitude. Burly had been up before me and had already scanned the news. When he saw me heading back to bed with the paper, he quickly wheeled out of the room. It didn't take me long to figure out why.

Helen's lawyer had a different aim from the rest of us: his goal was to force Brookhouse to drop his original civil suit. He had leaked a judicious amount of false and real evidence to the press, hoping to put the pressure on for that to happen. There was new evidence, the papers reported, that linked Brookhouse to the original attack on Helen—as well as other assaults over the past two years. Helen's memory had recovered with time, the articles implied, and other witnesses had come forward with supporting evidence, prompting the countersuit. Reference was made to an "inside source" who reported that a recent assault in the Durham area had yielded an eyewitness who was prepared to testify against David Brookhouse on Helen's behalf.

Whose idea had that factoid been? I knew it wasn't true. And it seemed dangerous. It might push Brookhouse to leave his home on a witness hunt, but it would also place someone in danger.

With a start, I realized that this someone was probably me. Who else could it be? The woman from last week was dead. Luke was incommunicado in a hospital bed.

That left me.

Burly and Bobby had planned to use me as bait. Jesus. And when I disagreed with their plan to take out Brookhouse, they'd simply gone ahead without me—and fed the lawyer false info.

Only now, Ferrar's surveillance was going to interfere with their plan to take Brookhouse down. But Brookhouse didn't know that. What would he do when he read about a possible new witness?

The article ended with Helen's lawyer saying that his client welcomed the opportunity to return to court. No one mentioned that Helen was still too terrified to stand on her own front porch, much less leave the house for a courtroom.

Wow. If Brookhouse didn't back down or get arrested for the other assaults first, this was going to be an even bigger deal than the first trial. The papers were milking it more than a farmer who was down to one cow. No way Brookhouse was going to hold on to his job or the drug study now. The stench was too much.

I savored his probable panic. I pictured him in his living room, enraged, holding it in, that perfect, well-mannered facade of his masking what had to be a volcano of frustration and indignation at the thought of anyone even dreaming they could get the best of him.

I knew something had to give.

I paged through the rest of the *Durham Herald* and was amazed to see that Luke's stepmother had been busy inserting herself into the social news while her husband held vigil at his son's bed. She was shown at a benefit luncheon hosted by a prominent local family, looking ultra-concerned for the fate of a coastal island that was being threatened by developers. Had the developers been home-grown, no one would have cared, but they'd had the audacity to carpetbag it down from Maryland, and so the local gentry were up in arms.

Where was this woman's concern for Luke? And how come people like her never got shot, raped or ruined?

For the millionth time that month, it occurred to me that life wasn't fair.

"Casey," Burly demanded as he wheeled into the room. "We need you to cast the deciding vote."

I put the newspaper down and stared at him. "About what?" I asked, wondering when I would bring up the topic of me as Brookhouse bait.

"Do we put those gross synthetic French fried onion ring things on top of the green bean casserole or not? Bobby says yes and I say hell no."

I threw the paper at him, but he ducked.

The worst that could happen finally did. It began that night at dusk, when the rest of Durham was at home contemplating the lazy holiday stretching before them. The main phone line rang at Helen's house, startling us all. When Fanny answered it, she listened for a moment, her eyes widening, then handed it to me.

The man on the end of the line first confirmed that it was me, then announced that he was a nurse's aide on Luke's floor. "I thought you might want to know this," he said. "Even though the cops told us not to say a word to anyone about it." He told me that a man wearing a black ski mask had attacked Luke in his hospital room while his father was out having dinner. Luke's private nurse had been hit over the head with a blunt object, the caller explained, and had pulled a table over with her when she fell. Luke, now conscious, had screamed and pressed a call button. An orderly heard the commotion and investigated. He, too, had been injured, his hand cut by a knife—but not before he scared the intruder away.

And now Luke was calling for me.

"He sounds pretty hysterical," my caller confided. "I don't think he's going to calm down until he gets a chance to see you."

Fanny, Bobby and I all rode to the hospital together. I did not trust myself to drive. We left Burly behind with Helen—along with the growing crowd of armed Mexicans planted on Helen's front porch.

We reached the hospital just as darkness fell. Ferrar had gotten there before me. He was angry again. He was always angry, it seemed, and usually with me. An armed officer was guarding Luke's door. Talk about closing the barn door after the horses have escaped. Ferrar would not let me in the room.

"No one goes inside," he explained simply. He was holding a copy of that morning's *News & Observer*. Great. He'd probably assumed that I had been the one to feed Helen's lawyer the fake witness evidence. My fault again, of course.

"I didn't have anything to do with that," I said, pointing to the newspaper.

"No one goes inside," Ferrar repeated. He glanced at the armed guard, who nodded. "And you're going nowhere but downtown with me. We're having another one of our special talks."

"But Luke's asking for me," I protested. "Maybe he remembers something."

"That kid hasn't been asking for anyone," Ferrar snapped back. "The breathing tube was ripped from his mouth and he went into cardiac arrest. He hasn't said a word to anyone and we're lucky he's still alive."

"That's not true—" I started to argue. Then I stopped and thought about it.

Oh, Jesus god, what an idiot I had been.

"Give me your car keys," I demanded of Bobby. He and Fanny were huddled with a couple of officers, suggesting restaurants where Luke's father might be.

"What?" Bobby asked, slow on the uptake.

"Give me your car keys."

"Hey," he protested. "Every time I lend you my car, you end up—"

I reached into his pants pocket and grabbed them for myself.

"What the hell do you—" Bobby yelled after me, but it was too late. I was already sprinting down the hall.

"Send someone out to Helen's house," I shouted at Ferrar as I ran past. "He's going for her, I know he is." Bobby would have to fill him in on the rest. I had to get back to the farmhouse quick. Forget the elevator. I took the stairs. Voices and shouting and chaos echoed behind me.

Bobby always drove land boats—huge American-made luxury vehicles that looked like hearses and had engines the size of small houses. His current car was no exception. I floored that sucker as I rocketed toward Helen's house. There was only one reason that anyone would have bothered to draw me away from Helen's. I had to get back to her fast.

Despite breaking every traffic law on the books, I arrived at Helen's house too late.

Later, Hugo and Burly told me what happened: A few moments after I drove away with Bobby and Fanny in response to the call about Luke—just as the dusk was deepening into twilight—the men on Helen's front porch heard a drone in the distance, a persistent whine that grew louder and louder. By the time they realized it was the sound of a dozen motorcycle engines, the bikers were on them. They roared up the narrow blacktop in a disciplined formation, curved into Helen's front yard, ripping over the flower beds and gouging deep lines in the lawn. They circled past the porch, staying to the edges of the lengthening shadows, shouting curses and taunting the men on the porch. Then they wheeled away again, heading back in the direction from which they had come—straight to nowhere but open countryside. The final man in the line of bikers had slowed, pulled out a gun and taken aim at Helen's front windows, firing four shots in rapid succession. Before Hugo and his friends could react or return fire, he gunned his engine and was gone.

Their reaction was unanimous. Men poured off the porch like locusts descending on a wheat field. They ran, shouting for their cars, shaking their fists, spewing curses in Spanish, firing their guns into the air and even taking a few useless potshots after the rapidly disappearing motorcycle gang. By the time Burly had wheeled to the front door to investigate, Hugo and his friends were pulling out of the driveway, piled into a convoy of clunkers and beaten-down sedans not seen since the sequel to *Mad Max*. Men were hanging out of windows, aiming guns at nothing, honking their horns, screaming threats of murder. No one stopped to think. Like hounds that have seen a rabbit flash past, the men kicked into overdrive and chased.

Perplexed, Burly wheeled out onto the porch, looking for bodies. He had heard the shots and the shattering of glass. He was amazed to find no one injured.

Then he heard more glass breaking in the back of the house and realized what was happening. He headed toward Helen's bedroom—where he had warned her to stay—stopping only to retrieve his handgun from a drawer in the front hallway. He remembered seeing Miranda hovering on the steps above him, her hands clutching her bathrobe tightly around her neck, her face a terrified mask.

"Call the cops," Burly shouted at her, not realizing that all the telephone lines had been cut minutes before. He wheeled furiously toward Helen's bedroom, bumped the door open with his chair, gun in his lap, ready to shoot if he had to. A man dressed in black, a ski mask hiding his face, was bent over Helen, pinning her to the bed. He had something in his hand, a knife, or maybe a syringe, Burly thought. Behind them, the cool November air poured through Helen's shattered bedroom window. Burly shouted at the man to step back and raised the gun to shoot.

He was hit from behind. Someone knocked him hard over the head and light pinwheeled before his eyes. His vision blurred. The second man grabbed his gun and yanked it away, pulling a hood over Burly's head and trying to drag him from the wheelchair. Burly fought back, biting and struggling, but his useless lower body weighed him down and his hands were held fast by someone with a strong grip. The man pulled harder, ripping out Burly's catheter tube in the process. Burly hit his head on the armrest on the way down and thought he passed out for a few seconds. When he came to, he was being dragged down the hall toward another bedroom. Astonishingly enough, Killer appeared, roused from his perpetual slumber at last. Burly could hear him growling at the intruder, could feel the brush of air as the basset darted past, nipping at the man's heels. But then the man kicked out, there was a thud, and Killer squealed piteously. Burly cried out to Killer to run, not knowing if the dog would understand. He did. Killer's toenails scrambled against the hardwood floor as he ran from the hallway, seeking refuge beneath a chair or bed.

The man started dragging Burly again, then hoisted him over the threshold of a bedroom and flopped him down inside, rolling him over and over like a sack of sand until he was wedged against the bed. When the man tightened the hood around his neck, Burly thought he was trying to strangle him and tried to fight back, only to realize his hands had been bound behind his back at some point, maybe when he had passed out. The man laughed when Burly tried to butt him with his head, the only part of his body he could control. Then he let go of Burly. Burly slumped to the floor. He heard footsteps, a door slamming, the click of the lock—and knew he was alone.

As he worked frantically to undo the cords around his wrists, he listened carefully to the sounds outside the locked door.

The bikers and men chasing them were long gone, but Burly could hear more than one person crashing through the bushes beside the house, probably two people, he decided. They were cursing and hurrying, bumping against the siding, maybe dragging something. Then he heard footsteps slapping against the asphalt of the driveway, one loud thump and more cursing. This was followed by a single set of running footsteps. A few moments later, a car drove up near the house, then stopped with its engine idling. There were more dragging sounds and car doors slammed. Then the engine gunned and the car sped away.

They had taken Helen.

By the time I arrived, Burly had managed to untie his wrist cords and remove the hood from his head. He had crawled across the bedroom, dragged himself up on top of an overturned chair, unlocked the door and was halfway down the hall, trying to reach a telephone when I burst through the front door.

"Where is she?" I yelled.

"I don't know," he said. "They took her."

It was all I had to hear.

"Where is she?" I screamed at Miranda. The old woman was huddled on the stairs leading to the second floor, eyes wide, a zombie of selfishness.

"Took who?" she stammered. "Who are you talking about?"

I wanted to shoot her dead right then and there. Instead, I tried all the telephone lines. They were dead. I threw the phones against the wall and ran toward the front porch, nearly tripping over Killer, who lay whimpering in the hall. I examined his fat, tubular body. He was okay, thank god.

"He's scared to death," I said, feeling his shivers. "See what you can do to calm him."

I couldn't afford to stay. I had to go after Helen. I was almost to Bobby's car when I thought of Burly inside, crawling on his belly toward his wheelchair, fueled by thoughts of revenge. I changed my mind and ran back inside.

"Where are they?" I asked him.

"Where are what?"

"Your car keys." I didn't want him following me or trying to track down Carroll or Brookhouse on his own. He'd kill someone and be locked away forever.

"I'm not telling you," he said. "Get away from me." His colostomy bag had leaked out all over his pants and he smelled like a Bowery bum. He hated for me to see him like that, but that wasn't why he was mad. He knew why I wanted those keys.

"You can't take them," he said, trying to swat me away.

"I can and I am." I patted down his pants. His pockets were empty.

"I have a right to fight back," he yelled as I dashed into our bedroom and checked the bedside table. There they were, next to his shaving kit. I scooped up the keychain, pocketed it and ran.

"You bitch!" Burly screamed after me. "You need my help."

"Stay here," I shouted back. "When the cops get here, tell them what happened. Tell them that I think they must be taking her to Lyman Carroll's house since Brookhouse is being watched." But not watched well enough, I thought. Not if two men had carried Helen away. "You have to be here to tell them, Burly. I can't trust her to remember."

We both knew I meant Miranda. Burly didn't like it. He wanted to follow me. He wanted to take both men out.

I couldn't let him take the chance. I didn't want Burly to be anywhere near them. I had to make sure he stayed behind.

And now I had to find Helen.

Halfway to Lyman Carroll's house, I realized I had no gun. It was lying in the mud on the bottom of a pond in Duke Gardens. I had no idea what I would do when I found them. I had to stall, had to find a way to deflect them until the cops arrived.

Carroll's house was dark. I screeched to a halt in front of the curb, hopped out of my car and raced to the edge of the house, examining every window, even checking what I could see of the basement from the outside. No signs of life at all. And there were no cars anywhere near the house.

They hadn't taken Helen here. And they could not have been at Brookhouse's. Where else would they take her? If they had a special place, there was no way I would ever find it. But then, none of their victims to date had mentioned being taken anywhere.

Think, I told myself. Take a deep breath and think. I sat behind the wheel of my Porsche. What had Brookhouse once said in class? Something like: the key to understanding a troubled mind was to be able to get inside it, to follow the twisted logic of a twisted mind. I tried to put myself in Brookhouse's shoes. Why had they taken Helen? Because of the countersuit, because she had caused them to be suspended from their jobs, because they believed she was starting to remember something that might hurt them, because she had taken away all their power?

They would return to where they felt most powerful. That was when I got it. They had taken her back to campus. It made sense. It was the night before a holiday. The building would be empty. And I knew the interview rooms in the basement were soundproof. That was where they would take her.

How could I let Ferrar know? All I could find was an old parking ticket I had failed to pay and a tube of lipstick that had fallen out of my knapsack. I scrawled a message in red on the back of the ticket, TELL DET. FERRAR THEY'VE TAKEN HER TO THE PSYCHOPATHY BUILDING. I prayed it was true with every word I wrote. Then I used a wad of old chewing gum to stick it to Lyman Carroll's front door. God, but I hoped the responding officers would notice. If they even believed Burly and bothered to send someone here.

The front porch light in the house next door to Carroll's blinked on just as I turned away from the front door. An old man stuck his head out into the night and stared at me.

"Call the cops!" I yelled at him. "Tell them to get out here right away. Tell them a murder's about to take place."

The old man's mouth fell open. I knew he would be able to remember nothing more than what I had just told him. He was in information overload.

"See that note," I yelled, pointing at it. "Just make sure the cops read it."

None of it made sense to the old man. But he'd call the cops, I knew. He was an upstanding citizen. And, god willing, one of the cops would call Ferrar.

The campus was deserted. Every building seemed locked up and dark. Only the International House on Anderson Drive showed a spark of life—here were the non-Americans immune to the holiday of mass gluttony sweeping the land. I sped past it, looking at the lights longingly. I knew the psychopathology building would be as dark as the others.

I was walking into the unknown, unarmed. And I had no choice but to do it.

Worse, I did not know why they had taken Helen. To kill her and silence her as a witness? Perhaps worse, not to kill her, but to maim her further, thus silencing all other possible witnesses? Or had they taken her as bait for me? Was I the one they were ultimately after?

No matter. I had to go to Helen. I had given my word.

I didn't see a single person as I pulled into the parking lot of the building. Dim lights glowed through some of the basement windows—security lights? I doubted a cleaning crew or the injured janitor's replacement would be here the night before Thanksgiving. Maybe Brookhouse and Carroll?

It was a definite maybe that they were there: a dark blue van was parked by the back door. And it had rental plates. I peeked into the back window of the vehicle. The seats had been removed from the rear. There was a bedspread heaped in the center of the floor—the bedspread from Helen's room.

They had probably gotten in the bolted door by using their keys—keys the administration had failed to confiscate when they were suspended—then loaded Helen into the building through the basement. Chances were good she was still unconscious.

Surprise did not matter. Only speed. I grabbed my tire jack from its storage compartment in the hood space. All the basement windows were blocked with security wire and I didn't have time to pry my way inside. I chose the fastest way instead. I drove my Porsche onto the sidewalk, over landscaped flower beds and through the bushes until I was parked directly beneath a first-floor window. I climbed onto the roof of the car and began swinging the crowbar as if I were driving in the winning run. Glass shattered; wood splintered. I kept swinging. It took me a good two minutes to smash an opening large enough for me to crawl through and I still cut my leg in the process. I dropped down into the middle of a darkened first-floor classroom. Its door was double-locked from the outside and I had to smash the glass to get into the hallway.

By then, I'd made enough commotion to alert a passed-out frat pledge to my presence. Footsteps running up the hallway toward me told me that Brookhouse and Carroll knew I had arrived. Instead of fleeing from the approaching footsteps, I ran toward them, then stepped into a side corridor at the last possible moment and pressed myself against the wall. Lyman Carroll ran past me, his chubby body moving with surprising grace. It was dark, but my eyes had adjusted. I could see that he was carrying a gun, either his or the gun he had taken away from Burly.

Burly's gun? Was that part of the plan? Was I being set up to make it look like I had killed Helen?

No, that was too weird. The whole thing was too complicated if you started getting that crazy. I needed to focus. The one thing I had to do was find Helen. Everything else would follow from that.

With only the tire jack for a weapon, I darted down the hallway, heading for the stairwell doors. I could hear Carroll behind me, his shoes crunching the shattered glass into shards as he reached the classroom where I had gained entry.

I slipped through the fire door and fled to the basement. I knew they had to have taken her there. I opened the door slowly, holding my breath. It groaned as loudly as ever. God, had no one ever heard of WD-40 in the maintenance department? Light from the two vending machines cast a yellowish glow along the corridor. It was empty. I darted into the hallway, dashing from room to room, stepping inside each threshold and peering into the small square windows that opened onto the various labs. The soundproof interview rooms were on the far end of the floor, but I needed to make sure the other rooms were empty first.

I had just glanced into the lab containing the rows and rows of white mice in cages when I heard the stairwell door open. Lyman Carroll had followed me back downstairs. I tried the door to the mouse lab. It was unlocked. I slipped inside, closing the door softly behind me. Hundreds of mice—sensing a human presence—began to scurry about in their cages. Their movements woke up still more mice. Ingrained behavior kicked in. The natives were restless. Some thought food was coming. Others eagerly awaited the arrival of their happy drug. The scrambling and rustling grew louder. They were about as subtle as the damn ducks.

Carroll was coming down the hall toward me. I could hear him opening doors, checking rooms, slamming doors shut again. All of the labs had been unlocked and I had a bad feeling about why: they were setting a trap for me.

His footsteps neared the room next door. A doorknob rattled and a moment later, his footsteps approached the room I was in. I ducked behind one of the counters just as the door of the lab opened. Carroll had turned the lights on in the basement hall and his round body was silhouetted against the background glare. He leaned inside, listened, heard the scrambling of the mice, hesitated, started to leave—then changed his mind and stepped inside. A moment later, the fluorescent lights blazed on, casting a greenish glow over gleaming metal counters and the white tile floor, sending the mice into frantic action.

Carroll took another step inside. I sank down on the floor and leaned against the counter behind me, planning my escape. If he stepped to the right and went down that line of cages, I might be able to slip around the central counter—it ran through the middle of the room like an island—and be out the front door before he could fire. If I could keep him chasing me until the police arrived, Helen and I would have a chance.

If the police ever arrived.

Carroll stepped to the right and I moved quickly. Too quickly. I slipped, and the tire jack clanged against the metal counter wall. The sound vibrations sent the mice into chaos.

"Get up," Carroll demanded. "I know you're in here."

"Screw you," I called out, still crouched below the counter. At least I had several metal walls between me and his gun.

"You can't get away," he said in a calm voice.

"Screw you," I told him again.

"You did a good job but it's over." His voice was a parody of soothing encouragement. "David and I are impressed. But this is the end of the line. Please do not mistake my innocuous appearance as a sign of weakness. I assure you it is a deliberate and deceptive disguise. I could drill a bullet hole through your right eye with my eyes closed. I am very good at what I do."

"Bullshit," I called out. "You're telling me that you're a pathetic, tubby nobody by choice? You're nothing but a limp dick coward who can only overpower women smaller than you, women frightened out of their minds, women who have never had to fight back before. You can't take me down. I could kick your fat ass with both hands tied behind my back."

"You might get the chance to prove that," he said—then laughed. That I did not like. He sounded too confident. "Stand up slowly, hands over your head, and I promise I won't shoot."

Above me, a row of empty beakers stood arrayed in descending size. I grabbed two of the biggest and lobbed them at Carroll. The containers sailed across the room and shattered against the wall behind him. The mice began to squeak, a chorus of frightened pips that grew in volume when Carroll started to laugh. And I'd thought Brookhouse had a creepy giggle: Carroll sounded as if someone were simultaneously tickling him and twisting his nuts. No wonder the mice were freaked out.

"Where's Helen?" I shouted.

"Helen's a little tied up right now," he told me.

"That's very funny. Where did you hear that one? While sitting home alone on a Friday night watching shitty TV movies and dreaming about how you're so much stronger than those poor women you tie up and drug? Because that's the only way you can get it up and we both know it. And the only way a woman would stand still long enough to let you get near her. What did you do with that poor woman you were dating, anyway? What's her name? Candace? She was only screwing you to get close to Brookhouse again, you know. She said she had to close her eyes and pretend it was someone else to get through the sex."

That made him mad. But only for an instant. Not long enough to do me any good. He swept a counter with his arm, sending books and jars and pens flying across the floor.

"You are nothing but a balding, big-gutted putz," I told him. "It's pathetic. You're a cliché. You and all the other tiny-dick rapists."

I was inching my way toward the door, hoping to get him mad enough to squeeze off a wild shot, at which point I was ready to run like hell.

"Nice try," he said, his voice calmer. "But I wrote the textbook on people like me," he explained. "And I'm not going to fall for your goading. I win. You lose. There isn't much more to say about it."

"I lose what?" I asked. I had crawled halfway to the door, but I still had a good fifteen feet left to go. Above me, the mice had reached frenzy status. They were swarming from side to side in their cages, panicked, confused, giving in to the fight-or-flight reflex.

Sort of like me.

"You lose everything," Carroll announced. "Stand up and let's get it over with."

"You can't possibly get away with this," I stalled. "Believe me, the cops know everything. I told them all of it. Including all about you."

He laughed again. With intimidating confidence. "My dear, when we are done with you, you will wish it was all over. And yes, I've known who you are since Candace said a female P.I. came by. I knew you were too old to be enrolled here as a regular student. I've been playing you for weeks."

"First of all..." I promised him, eyeing the teeming cage above me. Maybe I could...? No, that was ridiculous. "You're not laying a finger on me. If you think you're getting near me without the fight of your life, you're wrong. I'm not scared of you. I'm not intimidated by you."

"Really?" he asked. "Then why are you hiding behind that counter?"

I lunged upward, grabbed the closest mouse cage, opened the door and started flinging mice. I tossed them two and three at a time over the counter at the fucker, hoping to confuse him long enough to buy some free time.

It confused him all right. He started shooting.

I crabwalked down the aisle, knocking cages off the counter, opening doors, releasing at first dozens and then what seemed like hundreds of mice into the room. Some of the cages bent open on impact as they crashed to the floor, others I stopped to unlatch. The more the merrier, I decided. The harder time he would have getting to me.

White mice flooded the floor. They scurried everywhere, including up my pants and into my lap and on my shoulders and into my hair. I grabbed them and flung them at Carroll, moving closer and closer to the door.

Carroll squeezed out another shot, but then he slipped on a horde of running mice and went down, his upper body falling hard. He landed behind me, his torso sprawled at the far end of my row. Mice swarmed over him and he tried to scramble free, brushing them away so he could clear a spot and stand.

I heaved myself up on my knees in a sprinter's stance and dashed for the lab door. It opened just as I reached it, slamming into me with full force. I bounced back against the counter, hitting my stomach dead on. It knocked the wind out of me. I doubled over, heaving for breath.

Brookhouse took me from behind. He grabbed my hands and twisted them behind me, securing them with a pair of handcuffs. "I've got her," he told Carroll. "Get the fuck up off the floor." Mice scurried toward us, around us, over our feet. "What a mess," Brookhouse said mildly, kicking a flattened mouse with the toe of his shoe. "This is so typical of you, Lyman."

Carroll didn't like that. He pulled himself aloft and waved his gun at me. "We're not done with her until I've had a private word with her."

"No," Brookhouse announced firmly. "There's no time for that." He was dressed in black slacks, a matching turtleneck sweater and a gleaming pair of ebony loafers. The gentleman rapist. A dapper killer. And that made him a better man, apparently, than the fat slob dressed in a rumpled sweatsuit who was drooling on me from a few feet away. What a great pair of guys.

"We don't have time for your recreational pursuits," Brookhouse lectured Carroll. "And I find your lack of control rather troubling. Helen is arranged in the other room. Help me get this one in there. Everything is ready to go."

"I told the cops about everything," I lied. "There's nothing you can do to get out of this."

"Of course there is," Brookhouse said mildly. "We're going to burn everything. The records, the rooms, the drug samples. Plus you and Helen, did I mention that? And now, thanks to Lyman's bumbling, I fear we are going to have to hurry." He smiled at Carroll, who did not smile back. "In case you had not noticed, gunshots are loud."

"Does he always talk to you like this?" I asked Carroll. Brookhouse wrenched my arms upward in reply and I screamed.

"Not so tough now," he said, smiling. "Keep your gun on her," he ordered Carroll. "Do nothing unless I tell you to."

Carroll opened his mouth to argue, then shut up and moved closer until he was directly in front of me. He pressed his stomach against me and reached his hand under my shirt. His fingers were cold and stubby as he snaked his hand under my bra. He grabbed a handful of breast and squeezed painfully hard, pinching my nipple between his thumb and forefinger at the same time.

I kicked him in the balls so hard he dropped to his knees, grunting like the pig he was.

"I warned you," I said. "You're going to have to kill me before you touch me like that again."

Brookhouse was laughing. He was also poking a gun into the small of my back. "Don't do that again," he suggested in an almost pleasant voice.

Two guns. And, despite my bravado, what Carroll had done to me had scared me. His touch had triggered some primordial fear deep inside me. It made him stronger than me somehow, the fact that he had been able to rob me so easily of my physical privacy like that. I had faced guns. And assholes bigger than him. But he wanted to take something from me that was only mine to give, and just the thought of being violated like that compromised my will to fight. It made me feel inherently weaker. It made me lose my focus. Fears flashed through my mind: there were two of them. They could hold me down. Tie me up. Look what they had done to Helen. Unwillingly, scenes played in my mind: Carroll, naked, breathing above me, Brookhouse watching with a dispassionate gaze. I could almost feel his hot breath on my face, his weight on my body.

I had to get beyond it. I couldn't let the threat of being raped rob me of my power. I had to stay angry enough to fight back.

"Get up, you little limp-dicked coward," I spat at Carroll. I was putting on a good face, but my knees had turned to jelly.

Carroll struggled to his feet, one hand still holding his crotch. He slapped me across the face with his gun hand, metal hitting bone. I felt a tooth crack. And maybe my jawbone, too.

"That's enough," Brookhouse commanded. This time he sounded serious. "Move it," he ordered, poking me in the back with his gun. He glanced at Carroll. "Follow me and don't touch her again until I say it's okay."

Brookhouse opened the door to the lab and prodded me with his gun. I marched out into the hallway, followed by Brookhouse. Carroll and several hundred scurrying mice brought up the rear.

The smell of rodent fear was overpowering: urine and... something else. I glanced down. My pants were dry. I wasn't that damn scared. Yet. But still...

Then I saw it. A long dark line that ran along the basement corridor, snaking across floors and into rooms, splashed against the wall. It had an acrid odor.

They really were going to burn it all down. With me and Helen inside.

"This way," Brookhouse said, pushing me toward the sound-proof interview rooms. "A friend of yours is waiting."

Where the hell were the cops?

Helen was in one of the interview rooms, either unconscious or dead. She was splayed in a chair that had been pushed up to a table. Stacks of files and papers surrounded her. She had been arranged so her head slumped forward. It was resting on a stack of documents.

"It won't work," I told them, knowing they were somehow setting Helen up to take the fall for their dirty drug study. "She hasn't gone outside her house in almost a year. Thanks to you. No one will ever believe she had anything to do with this."

"Don't be an idiot," Brookhouse told me. "We study the gullibility of people for a living. Our story is believable for one simple reason: we are willing to sacrifice our careers. People will believe us when we tell them you were trying to blackmail us about the drug study. Because we'll admit to sanitizing the results. We'll say Helen remembered our improprieties and convinced you to help her blackmail us. That she was here with you, going through the evidence, hoping to milk us for more. Any evidence that escapes the fire will support our charges. We may lose our jobs but, believe me, we'll walk on everything else."

Ah yes, the principle of believable sleaziness. It worked all the time. Politicians built entire careers based on admitting to lesser charges—and slipping past with the real crimes.

Brookhouse shoved me into a chair. Carroll began tying my feet to the legs with thick hemp rope that cut into my ankles. The metal handcuffs had started to dig into my wrists. Somehow, the pain helped ground me.

I realized with some surprise that I wanted to get inside Brookhouse's head almost more than I wanted to live. I had hated him every minute of every day for over a month and I was not about to go down without a fight.

"They'll catch you," I told him, forcing myself to smile. "You will never be able to walk down a street again without being watched. Every breath you take. Every move you make, they'll be watching you." I hummed a few bars of my favorite Sting song. Neither one of them looked like they appreciated my talents. Or my seeming nonchalance.

"You'll live in a prison," I predicted. "It may be the outside world, but it will still be a very big prison."

"Really?" Brookhouse sounded like he was making chitchat at a party. "Then why am I walking around free right now?" he asked. "After all, the police are watching my house, aren't they?"

Asshole. How was he walking around right now? The bastard was going to make me say it.

"How did you ditch the cops?" I asked, reluctantly.

He shrugged. "I didn't have to. I was never there."

"Never there?" I was confused.

He laughed, pleased at his own intelligence. "When the police come out of the shadows and knock on my front door, it will be answered by a very perplexed and very innocent grad student who has been housesitting on my behalf for the past week, frantically trying to finish his dissertation. Meanwhile, I have been staying with Lyman and admiring his uniquely decorated abode." He enjoyed my discomfort. "Don't look so surprised. I told you before: I know people and how they think. It's my job. I knew enough not to go home after I was suspended from the university. The police have simply been watching the wrong man. That's what they get for making assumptions. We academics may all look alike to outsiders, but the first thing we learn is never to assume too much."

"Which of you brilliant academics took the fall on the rocks and cracked their noggin?" I demanded.

His smile faded. "That would be me, of course. Unlike Lyman, I have the hair to hide the wound."

"That's too bad," I said, trying to be as cheerful as he had been, though I don't think I fooled him. "I hope it hurts. A lot."

His eyes flickered. "It didn't hurt as much as that gunshot wound your little friend suffered, though, did it?"

"His name is Luke," I told him. "And he'll be able to help put you away."

"With an unreliable memory like that?" Brookhouse asked, sounding shocked. "Tsk. Tsk. Think of what a good lawyer would do to him on the stand."

"You're gonna stink so bad by tomorrow morning, there won't be a lawyer on this planet who will even get near you, not for any amount of money."

"And that shows how very little you understand about the human mind," Brookhouse answered calmly. He sat on the edge of a desk and gazed at me almost fondly. "I offer a lawyer something better than money: notoriety. Fame. Headlines."

I hated to admit it, but the asshole was right.

"This was a trap, wasn't it?" I asked. "You brought Helen here just to get me here."

"Right," Brookhouse said happily. "And it worked."

I stared at him, willing my hatred to become a palpable force. He held my gaze.

"I've seen through you since the very beginning," I said. "You never fooled me. Not for five seconds."

"What a coincidence," he returned. "I've seen through you from the start as well."

Carroll, who had been nervously circling me, as if surveying me for a good spot to bite, chose that moment to reintroduce his ego into the equation. "No you didn't, David," he protested. "I'm the one who figured out who and what she was after Candace told me a female P.I. was asking questions about you."

"But don't you see, Lyman?" Brookhouse suggested pleasantly. "I'm the one who told you to get close to Candace in the first place." He smiled at me again. "A neat trick, wasn't it? I get Lyman to keep an eye on Candace for me, to make sure she doesn't start spreading vicious rumors that might hurt me. Scorned women are very prone to such habits, I've found. And, in return, Lyman gets laid. Something he doesn't seem to be able to do without my help."

God, what a jerk. He couldn't even be nice to his killing partner. "Where is Candace Goodnight?" I asked. "What did you do to her?"

"Me?" Brookhouse looked offended. "I didn't kill her, thank you. That would be Lyman's department."

"You're worse than him," I told Brookhouse, nodding toward Carroll. "You see yourself as better than him, but you're even worse. You're a poser. You're a nobody who came from nothing and all the expensive clothes and good haircuts in the world can't hide the fact that you're trash. How did your parents pay for your private high school anyway? Or was it a scholarship? I bet you studied all night, every night, praying you could escape where you came from."

That got to him. He hit me. Hard. He slapped me across the face with such force that my head snapped back. And you know what? It felt good. I had cracked his facade and wormed my way into that crack. And he hadn't liked it one bit.

"They'll find you out," I predicted. "Soon everyone will know what you really are, no matter what you do to me."

"The police and the good people of this town don't care about you," he said quietly. "They only care that all this nastiness goes away quickly, so that everyone can pretend this is a sleepy, pleasant Southern town again. And as soon as the attacks stop or they find a scapegoat—that would not be me, by the way—they'll get on with their lives, grateful that their perfect world has been restored."

I knew then what he was up to. "He's going to pin it on you," I told Carroll. "He's going to make sure you die in the fire, and he'll say you did it all."

Carroll looked alarmed; the thought had never occurred to him. But Brookhouse moved quickly to repair the damage.

"Don't worry, Lyman," he said soothingly. "We're in this together. They'll never get anyone for the attacks, everyone will be too relieved when they stop to care, and this young lady here will take the blame for Helen's death. And her own death, of course."

"How do you plan to explain the fire?" I asked. "The bogeyman did it?"

"No, PSNC. As in the gas company. All that accelerant scattered along the halls will go up in smoke. It will be indistinguishable chemically from the explosion caused when the gas furnace blows. Details count."

"And my being tied up and handcuffed will go unnoticed, too?" I asked. If only Helen was awake, maybe we could work something out. She was too far away from me to be able to rouse her. Whatever they had drugged her with was strong. Or she was already...

"We're going to set you free before the blast," Brookhouse promised. "We just have to strangle you first." With that, he slipped a black hood over my face and tied it around my neck. Panic set in. I began to struggle, jerking my body, lifting the chair, rocking it as hard as I could, doing anything to escape.

Brookhouse started to laugh, that creepy chuckle of his that made my skin crawl.

It was the last sound I ever heard him make.

The room erupted in thunder and glass. The one-way observation wall blew out from the force of an explosion triggered on the other side. Glass and metal flew past, Brookhouse fell on top of me, then slid off to the floor behind me. Carroll screamed and whirled around, I know because he trampled my bound feet in the process. That was when I recognized the smell filling the room. Gunpowder. I pitched myself forward instantly, toward the floor, sending Carroll tumbling away from me. The chair fell over just as a series of quick, loud pops rocked the room. A handgun.

I heard a thud as Carroll hit the ground. I could see nothing, could hardly breathe inside the hood. Someone burst in the door.

"Help us," I croaked, as I heard my chair being set back upright.

Hands grabbed me and hoisted me back on the chair. But then the person brushed past me, moving toward where I thought Carroll lay on the ground. I heard clicks and rustlings. The process was repeated behind me, where Brookhouse had been shot.

"Who are you?" I called out. "Bobby? Is that you?"

Silence.

I heard my unseen rescuer walk past me, heading toward the table where Helen lay slumped over the papers. Why? I wondered. Chairs scraped. I heard heavy breathing, then a grunt. Footsteps re-approached, then paused behind me.

"Let me go," I pleaded.

"No."

That one word was loud, deep, abrupt—and disguised. I froze.

"Wait." The same deep voice, all inflection removed. Who was it?

I waited.

The footsteps continued toward the door, something heavy swung past, thumping me in the back. Helen's feet? Was she slung over his back? I heard the door open and shut again. Who was taking Helen? And why?

I waited some more, listening as the footsteps lumbered down the hall. The back door to the basement was unbolted with a clang, metal hit metal. The sound echoed down the hall. Then I heard another clang as the steel exit bar was depressed. Someone had pushed their way outside. The basement door stayed open. I could hear car doors opening and slamming. A powerful engine roared to life—a truck, or maybe a van? The engine idled for only a moment, then another door slammed and the vehicle pulled away. Within seconds, I could hear it no more.

What in god's name had just happened?

I began to struggle against the handcuffs binding me, though I knew it was no use. I then tried to wriggle my feet free somehow, but the cord only cut into my ankles more. I stopped, discouraged. That was when I heard the sirens. It sounded like hundreds of them, all converging on the building. Within a minute, cars were screeching to a halt, orders were shouted, doors slammed.

"I'm in here!" I screamed. The goddamn hood would not come untied. I needed a knife. I couldn't breathe. "In here!" I screamed again. "Help me! Help me!"

Voices, footsteps, shouting, chaos. It all flooded into the room at one time. Someone whistled. Someone barked to stay back. Someone swore as they stepped on a mouse. Hands reached out to help me.

"Unlock them," a voice ordered. I knew that voice. Ferrar. Oh god, I had never been happier to hear that voice.

"Don't move," a woman ordered me. I froze again. Gentle hands fumbled with the handcuffs and suddenly I was free. "Let me," the same voice ordered, and I waited while she cut the rope around my neck. The cord binding the hood fell to the ground. I tore off the hood. I was staring straight into Ferrar's face.

"What the fuck just happened?" he asked me. It was the first curse word I had heard him utter.

He was staring down at the floor. I followed his gaze. Lyman Carroll sprawled, dead, in front of me, two bullet holes neatly drilled in the center of his forehead. He lay on his side, obscuring all but the barrel of a shotgun cradled in his arms. I looked back up at Ferrar, shaking my head. I had no idea who had killed him. He pointed over my shoulder.

The female officer had freed my feet from the rope. I twisted around in the chair, looking behind me.

David Brookhouse lay on the floor, his arms flung to each side. The center of his chest was missing. It had been blown completely away. His right hand gripped a small gray gun. It was not the gun he had been holding before. And it was not Burly's gun, either. Whose?

I turned back to Carroll. What the hell was he doing with a shotgun?

"What happened?" Ferrar asked again.

"I have no idea," I said. I think my utterly confounded expression convinced him. "I have no idea at all."

CHAPTER FOURTEEN

The official story dominated the headlines well beyond the holiday weekend: Brookhouse and Carroll had killed each other in a dispute about the tainted drug study. The world seemed to believe it. But I know that no one at Helen's house did. We spent the weekend reading the newspapers, arguing over the menu for our canceled and now rescheduled Thanksgiving dinner—and debating how and when the cops might come to haul me away.

Several days after the shootings, evidence was uncovered that linked Brookhouse to the rapes. Despite his vast expertise about the criminal mind, as he liked to put it, Brookhouse had been unable to resist the lure of keeping trophies from each rape. There were Polaroid's of him in action discovered in a safe in his house, including photos that were undeniably of Helen. She had been right. David Brookhouse had raped her—and written her threatening letters as well as made the harassing phone calls. The letters had been lovingly stored on the hard drive of his home computer, while long-distance records showed a pattern of Brookhouse phoning Helen's house. She was his obsession, it seemed, once she became the first woman in his life ever to break off with him first. His outrage over this insult had made him uncharacteristically careless about covering his tracks. And there were more Polaroid's of her than of anyone else.

"Excuse me," I said when Marcus gave me this news. "But hasn't anyone thought to ask who exactly took the Polaroid's of Brookhouse raping women?"

Marcus sighed. "You aren't going to like what's about to happen," he predicted. And I didn't.

269

Within days, the official story of the showdown in the psychopathology basement had conveniently morphed into a tale in which Lyman Carroll played the part of hero. This myth was strengthened when the true records of the drug study were discovered in one of Brookhouse's home files. The actual data confirmed what more and more people had come to suspect: there was no way that particular drug was going any further forward in testing. It caused harm to healthy subjects. The company pulled the plug. And the press discovered that both Brookhouse and Carroll had owned a partial interest in the drug venture from the start, even though they were supposedly studying the drug's effects objectively.

This bit of news raised eyebrows. Within a few more days, Duke had announced a new policy: no staff member was allowed to hold a financial interest in any venture undergoing testing or scrutiny by any department of the university. Objectivity must be preserved, it seemed. Or, at least, the illusion of it.

About this same time, the rumors of Lyman Carroll as hero conveniently intensified. He had confronted Brookhouse about the study, people whispered, then it had escalated into an argument involving charges of murder and rape. Brookhouse had fired a gun at Carroll and, with his last dying breath, Carroll had blown Brookhouse away with a shotgun.

This was preposterous nonsense not fit for a B movie. But I had to learn to live with it. People need heroes in this world. They don't need more criminals. So sometimes we create heroes out of the bad guys. Lyman Carroll rode in on this tide. The schmuck in life became the savior in death.

It galled me, but what could I say? Especially when I figured out that this was a fiction Duke University encouraged. Its reputation required it.

Very few people knew the truth: that Lyman Carroll had been an accomplice to it all and, most probably, the one who had started to spiral out of control, killing the coed as well as the woman who had been on her way to see me.

I knew Lyman Carroll was guilty. My friends knew he was guilty. And Detective Angel Ferrar damn sure knew: he uncovered videos, journals that recounted the attacks in loving detail, more Polaroid's of each rape and murder, plus mementos like scarves, panties, jewelry and locks of hair neatly stored in hidden cabinets built into Carroll's basement. This evidence proved his presence at the scene of each and every crime. He had been at the rapes to record them for posterity on Brookhouse's behalf; he had been at the murders, solo it seemed, for his own gratification or when the necessity of silencing witnesses had demanded it.

Eventually, Lyman Carroll made more of a mark in his field than he ever got the chance to realize, when it was generally decided by the experts brought into the case by Ferrar that Carroll suffered from a psychosis not yet detailed in the textbooks he prized so highly: Carroll had been Boswell to Brookhouse's Johnson. While David Brookhouse had undeniably been the perpetrator of the rapes as a way of exerting his control and protecting the drug study, Carroll had been his biographer, meticulously chronicling each action the two men took. Apparently, Carroll had taken peculiar pleasure in recording it all in exhaustive detail. Every scrap of evidence was carefully preserved, so the two men could review their crimes over and over, reliving their roles as player and spectator. Psychopathic Peeping Toms. How mankind has evolved.

The only crime unmentioned in Carroll's journals was what happened to Candace Goodnight. She was declared officially missing and merited three inches in the local newspaper before being relegated to the old news column.

If the truth about Carroll was a closely guarded secret successfully kept from the press, even fewer people knew I'd had anything to do with the bloody scene in the basement of the psychopathology building. And absolutely no one knew who the hell had saved my ass, including me.

It made no sense. Especially since Helen had been returned home without harm. She was discovered, sleeping, back in her own bed. Burly swore he had not seen how it happened.

"I was stuck in the van," he explained when I called him from the police station where Ferrar was holding me for questioning. I was frantic about Helen's whereabouts. "I don't know who brought her back or why," Burly said. "But she's back in bed, asleep."

"What are you talking about?" I demanded. "How did you get stuck in your van?"

"I remembered I had a car phone in the van and that the back doors were unlocked," he said. "I didn't want to wait for the sheriff to come to tell him where you had gone, so I wheeled out to the van and got the back doors opened and crawled through to the front seat and called him. He sent the Durham cops to Lyman Carroll's house."

At Carroll's house, the Durham cops had found a pair of uniformed cops already on the scene who had been summoned by the crazy old coot next door, some nut who was babbling about race cars and trucks and old men waving shotguns. No one, including me, knew what the hell he was talking about beyond the race car, which had to be my Porsche. Together, this band of merry uniformed men had discovered and deciphered the lipsticked note on the front door of Carroll's house. Someone had finally called Ferrar and he had responded immediately, although too late, arriving most decidedly after the nick of time.

So who was the hero?

"You're telling me you got stuck on the floor of your van for over an hour?" I asked Burly after he related his stranded story.

"Yes," Burly insisted. "Killer bumped into my wheelchair and it rolled down the driveway incline. It was a comedy of errors. Hugo found me when he came back from his wild goose chase."

"Why didn't you call someone for help?" I asked.

"Call who?" Burly countered. "All the lines to Helen's house had been cut and I knew someone would be home soon."

"Where's Killer right now?" I demanded.

"You care more about the dog than me?" Burly asked, incredulous.

"I care about the dog," I answered. "And I don't believe you. Something's going on."

"Excuse me for being paralyzed," he shot back. "I got stuck, okay? Let it drop."

"Don't pull that 'poor me' crap," I told him. "I know you had something to do with this."

"Have it your way," Burly said abruptly. "Killer is sleeping on the bed next to Helen, by the way." Then he hung up on me.

It was nice to know he cared.

I filed his story away for future reference and went to tell Ferrar that Helen had been found safe and sound at home.

He looked as startled as I was at the news.

As it turned out, the drugs Brookhouse and Carroll had given Helen protected her from the entire episode. She remembered nothing at all. This was a fair trade-off, I thought, given the horrors she was already sentenced to remember.

I wasn't much more help than Helen when it came to who had really killed Carroll and Brookhouse. I told Ferrar everything I knew, every nuance and detail—except my suspicions about Burly, of course. But I could not help Ferrar with the identity of the mystery man wielding a shotgun.

I'm not sure he believed me. I'm also not sure he cared. I think we were both just relieved that I was out as a suspect: I had been bound and handcuffed when he found me, so there was no way I had fired either one of those guns. My hands were tested for powder residue anyway and came back clean. So Ferrar gave me a walk. I gave him an IOU. I know he'll call it in one day.

In the end, I think I was the only one who really cared who had killed the two men. And, to be truthful, I only cared for my own personal reasons, reasons that had nothing to do with the loss of two lives such as theirs.

By the end of the week after their deaths, Ferrar had determined that all of the rape and murder victims were connected, albeit unknowingly, to Brookhouse's drug protocol in some way. Two had been in the study and complained of episodic violent tendencies. One was a roommate of a drug study volunteer. She had noticed a change in her roommate and approached Brookhouse with her concerns when the roommate denied there was a problem. One of the other victims had been a girlfriend of a boy in the study. She, too, had tried to tell Brookhouse that her loved one had changed and, worse, refused to acknowledge that a problem existed. A few other victims had inadvertently uncovered potentially damaging evidence through their jobs as lab assistants or administrative help. The woman who had been on her way to see me, it was thought and never proved, had perhaps learned too much in the course of an old-fashioned extramarital affair with Brookhouse, an affair that went bad. She had been killed by one or both men to keep her from telling me what she knew. Ferrar also discovered that the murdered coed, whose parents I had watched stagger into the Durham Police Department what seemed like a lifetime ago, had spurned Carroll's advances, according to a girlfriend of the victim. This, it was thought, had triggered her killing by an increasingly out-of-control Lyman Carroll.

As for Helen, no one would ever know whether Brookhouse had raped her in anger over being dumped or whether she had stumbled on information that might harm the drug study. I am sure that the exact reason was immaterial to Helen. At this point, only the lingering damage really mattered.

In short, all of the wounded and dead had been deemed disposable by Brookhouse and Carroll, then nominated for participation in their own sick study of the destruction of the human spirit.

The next big crime is always just around the corner. It didn't take long for everyone but me to get on with their lives. Within days after the deaths of the two professors, the newspapers had moved on to other headlines, Ferrar had moved on to a new case—but I was still stuck in the same old rut wondering, "Who the hell had come to my rescue?"

I don't like being beholden to anyone. But someone had saved my life, and Helen's, too, then ended the lives of two killers with the efficiency of an experienced hunter—and gotten away with it all.

Who was it? Not Burly. At least not alone. Unless a genuine miracle had occurred, there was no way it was his footsteps I had heard moving through that interview room the night Carroll and Brookhouse had been killed.

It could not have been Bobby D. who came to my rescue, either. He had spent several anxious hours at the hospital with Fanny, sans car and any hard information, wondering what the hell was going on.

It took me a while to discover the truth.

Our Thanksgiving Day dinner had been rescheduled, seeing as how I was in the pokey being questioned by Ferrar, Helen was too groggy to get out of bed, Fanny refused to leave Luke's bedside, where she was keeping fresh vigil with his father, and Burly was no longer speaking to me. Only Bobby D. seemed in the mood to celebrate the strange turn of events with a massive meal, and when is Bobby ever not in the mood for a massive meal? But it was just as well we canceled the dinner: in the midst of the madness, as it turned out, my grandfather phoned and left a message on Helen's voice mail system. On Thanksgiving Day, when I had recovered sufficiently to wonder where the hell he was, Burly checked the voice mail system and reported back that my grandfather had phoned the night before to say he could not come, the irrigation system was on the fritz. It was a bad time to leave his crops. I was disappointed when Burly relayed the news. But I knew I'd see my grandfather one day soon.

Over time, we slowly returned to our regular lives. Fanny went back to her North Raleigh home with a newfound appreciation of solitude. Bobby and I headed back to our office in Raleigh, ready to track down the landlady and demand repairs on our still-soggy quarters. We finally found her in Myrtle Beach, overdosing on bingo and romancing some over-the-hill Romeo whose urgings shamed her into returning with us to take care of the mess. Only Burly and Killer stayed behind with Helen. We all agreed that suddenly being left alone with her mother was too abrupt, given Helen's fragile state, and Burly's schedule could accommodate the extra days.

"This way I can keep making plans for Thanksgiving Day dinner," Burly said.

I was just glad he had started speaking to me again, though he was still very pissed at me for taking his car keys and doubting his story. I was pretty sure he'd stay pissed for a long time to come.

The delayed dinner had been set for a Sunday afternoon two weeks after Thanksgiving. Luke could not come, he was still in the hospital. But he had survived the second attack on his life and would recover. The doctor even said that if he worked hard, he could be back to school by the next fall semester. He was young, he was healthy, he would recuperate with six to nine months of physical therapy.

He would also, in all probability, never remember much of that night in Duke Gardens or of the afternoon before it—including the time he and I had spent in our spot among the bushes, discussing love, liberty and the pursuit of happiness.

I was sad he did not remember how close I had come to giving in to his entreaties. I was not sad enough to remind him. We lived in different worlds, not to mention different eras. But he did remember that I was his friend, and that he'd had a crush on me. It was sweet. And it would have to be enough. His father made plans to move him back to New Jersey as soon as he was able to travel. Luke would be out of my life, it seemed, sometime after Christmas. But he'd always be in my thoughts.

Luke was not the only no-show at our rescheduled Thanksgiving dinner. Weasel Walters and his new trailer-trash girlfriend called in their regrets. They were going down to South Carolina to get married instead. We all wished them well and said a few silent prayers that they'd not pop up on the Jerry Springer Show by this time next year.

The rest of the motley crew promised to arrive in full force on the designated day. Helen was going to serve as hostess. She had been fine once the effects of the sedatives she'd been given wore off. But the doctor who came to check her out—perhaps the only man left in the state who made house calls—would not take no for an answer when he suggested she speak to a therapist about her agoraphobia. With Brookhouse dead, it seemed like the right time. She made the phone call, and then another one.

By the day of the delayed Thanksgiving dinner, Helen was, at least, two phone calls closer to leaving her house eventually. It was a start.

That Sunday afternoon, Marcus arrived for the dinner with his boyfriend, Robert—a civil engineer given to buzzed haircuts and attire so incredibly clean-cut he looked perpetually fresh from the Marines. Which, once upon a time, he had been. They carried in a vat of cherry cobbler prepared by Marcus's mother—who was no doubt thanking me in her own special way for the promotion her son had received a few days before. They also offered a basket of corn sticks that made my mouth water. Boy, how my grandfather would have gone for those.

One of our guests of honor showed close on the heels of Marcus—the janitor who had helped me escape the night I broke into Brookhouse's office. He had been discharged from the hospital a few days after the attack on his skull and had, indeed, proved to be a remarkably hard-headed fellow. And well-labeled. His name, it turned out, was Richard Moore Tuff. They sure didn't come more tough than that man.

I was planning to have a little fireside chat with Mr. Tuff once the after-dinner rituals began.

Hugo and his friends had also been invited to the dinner. Only a handful of the fellows took us up on our offer. The others were too shamed at the failure of their machismo to show. Hugo was humiliated at having been so easily deceived—the bikers were never found and may never be—but he perked up considerably when Burly enlisted his help in deep-frying turkeys for the festivities.

Together, they returned to the clearing by the pond and filled a large metal drum with fresh peanut oil. This was heated over a fire to bubbling levels, then one by one, ten-pound turkeys were drenched in flour and dropped into the drum, where they sizzled and fried to juicy perfection, the skin turning crispier than any I had ever encountered and the inner meat more tender than an

Elvis love song. Bobby D. staked his claim to one entire turkey as his portion. I agreed to give him half and suggested he indulge his gluttony on the seven pies we had saved for dessert instead. Fanny had been busy in Helen's kitchen all day long, baking and mashing and stirring and, most of all, adding butter to anything and anyone who stood still long enough for her to slather it on. Maybe we could get a group rate on a cardiac unit at Duke when dinner was done.

By the time early evening rolled around, we were famished and primed for a feast the likes of which even that well-used farmhouse had never seen. We pulled two tables end-to-end in the enormous kitchen so that everyone could be seated together. We made Helen sit at one end of the table, and endured Miranda's insistence that she grace the other end as "the matriarch." This was not the word that most of us would have chosen to call Helen's mother, if given a choice, but we agreed graciously, despite the fact that this meant we all had to stare at her ghastly stage makeup and the low-cut red evening gown she had deemed fitting for the occasion. I think her get-up confused the Mexican contingency, who were having trouble sorting out whether it was a Thanksgiving or Halloween celebration they were attending.

Within seconds, no one cared what Miranda was wearing. For a very good reason: few of us had ever encountered a deep-fried turkey before. It made Thanksgiving dinner a whole new ballgame. My jaw ached from where I'd been whacked during the showdown with Carroll and Brookhouse, but sometimes you just have to swallow the pain and reach down where champions are born. I ignored the throbbing and ate. And ate. And ate.

We chewed with astonished satisfaction. God bless grease. And god bless this great part of the country that still dunks its foods in it whenever possible.

"Did you know that seventy-two percent of all sewage blockages caused by lard occur in the South?" Marcus's boyfriend Robert announced as we munched.

Talk about your conversation starters. And stoppers.

Burly burst out laughing. It was a sound I had not heard from him lately. Bobby nodded sagely, then wiped his greasy fingers on the tablecloth as a sort of coda to the remark. Fanny delicately slathered more butter on her biscuit, while Marcus beamed at his boyfriend as if he had just announced the cure for cancer.

"That's interesting," I managed to say.

Miranda had a different reaction. She stood suddenly, eyes wide, mouth open in mute appeal, arms outstretched.

"For godsakes, Mother. Not now," Helen snapped.

Jesus, I thought. What a ham. Lay down on a platter and we'll serve you up.

The Mexican guys, who had never seen her schtick before, were staring at her, eyes wide, looking frightened. Hugo reassured them rapidly in Spanish.

Miranda turned a peculiar shade of red and started clutching at her right side.

Bobby pointed a turkey leg at her like a baton. "No one is in the mood for your fruity shenanigans," he said.

Miranda dropped to the floor.

"For godsakes, Mother," Helen complained. "Get up. We've all seen this act a hundred times before."

Miranda stayed down.

"Maybe she's really..." Fanny began, rising from her seat, her face pink with alarm.

"I doubt it," Helen said, determinedly plowing through her mashed potatoes.

Killer disagreed.

He ambled over to Miranda, sniffed her body—and then began to howl.

The hair on the back of my neck stood on end. I had never heard such a sound from that dog before. It was an eerie wailing that held and wavered in mournful salute. And it was enough to convince Burly that something was truly wrong.

"Does anyone know CPR?" he asked.

Marcus's boyfriend Robert leaped to his feet, rushed to the end of the table and hoisted Miranda aloft. She slumped like a giant marionette in his arms. He wrapped his arms around her, placed a fist over her diaphragm, and began to pump.

"She might be choking," he yelled as he thrust his fist into her again and again, her body jumping with each squeeze.

I didn't know how to tell him, but she was as limp as defrosted lettuce and her gaze was as vacant as an empty parking lot. My take: the lady was well beyond choking.

I looked around the table, my eyes locking on Fanny's. Thankfully, she shook her head no. Fanny had not been slipping Miranda too many Valiums.

"Oh, my god," Helen said, rising to her feet. "I think she really is having a heart attack."

"I'm not giving up," Robert assured her. He flopped Miranda forward, over the back of her chair, and began to thump her on the back. On the third blow, Miranda's hair popped off her head and flew onto her plate with a plop. The synthetic tendrils splayed out against the mashed potatoes like the arms of a hairy octopus. She was almost completely bald beneath her wig. Bald and dead.

"Stop," Helen commanded him. "It's not that she's choking. Let her down."

Robert laid her gently on the floor, placing Miranda's head reverently on the edge of the hooked rug as a pillow. The old lady's eyes fluttered, flew open, then rolled back in her head. She did not move anymore.

Richard, the janitor, took over. It turned out he had been a medic in Vietnam.

"She's dead," he said, checking all her pulse points. "Looks like a massive stroke to me. There was nothing anyone could have done. I'm sorry, miss." He directed this last remark to Helen.

Helen was still staring, a napkin clutched in her hand. "I thought she was joking," she said to us, sounding neither unhappy nor angry. Just... surprised.

"So did I," I confessed. "So did everyone."

We stood in a circle, looking down at the body.

"We better call it in," Marcus finally said. "Leave it to me."

"What should the rest of us do?" Hugo asked. His friends looked as if they had been mildly electrocuted. Were all American holiday dinners like this?

"I guess we may as well keep eating," I said. "I mean no disrespect to Miranda, of course. Or to you, Helen." I turned to her and waited for her response.

She was staring down at the body that had been her mother, disbelieving, confused and, I suspected, relieved somewhere down deep in her heart.

Bobby D. was blithely whistling *Ding Dong, the Witch is Dead*, driven by a subconscious impulse and without even noticing what he was doing. A poke in the ribs from Fanny silenced him.

"What?" Helen asked, looking up. "Of course, keep eating. I'll handle it."

And so we ate. What else could we do? People live and people die. The living must keep eating. We plowed through the turkey and were starting in on third round helpings when the paramedics arrived. It was a formality, they had been warned in advance, and they were there merely to convey the body to a funeral home. Marcus had already taken care of finding the name of one nearby.

"Come sit back down and eat, Miss Pugh," Marcus insisted, gently pushing Helen back to her place. "Your momma is not going to come back to us if you sit down and finish a piece of pie, but it might help you."

Good god, I hope that old bat's not coming back if we eat pie, I thought as I shoveled a second helping of banana cream into my craw. With Bobby D. around to pack in whole pies, we'd soon find ourselves in a remake of the remake of *Night of the Living Dead*.

After dinner, we sat around the fire, digesting, groaning, bragging about how much we had eaten, offering phony condolences on Miranda's death and rehashing her spectacular final exit. Once we had exhausted these topics, I steered the conversation to what was really on our minds—a replay of my adventures the night Helen had been kidnapped and a discussion about what Ferrar would do in the weeks ahead to get to the bottom of the mystery of who had killed Brookhouse and Carroll.

My money, of course, was on Richard Moore Tuff.

The janitor was not buying it, and he wasn't exactly subtle about it.

"Why is everybody looking at me?" he demanded when I got to the part of the by-now familiar story in which I recount how my rescuer blasted through the observation glass with a shotgun and nailed Brookhouse dead center, so to speak.

"You all don't think I did it," he said, outraged. "Oh, no. Don't be pinning that on me."

I nodded soothingly. It was okay, I signaled him. He was among friends. He didn't have to say a word. We would never tell.

"Don't you be nodding at me," Richard protested strenuously. "I am not shining anyone on. Yes, I am glad those men are dead. No, it was not me who did it. I was not even there. I was still at home on medical leave."

"You could have come back to the building," I said. "You had the keys."

"Who the hell needed keys, girl?" he protested. "What with you breaking all the windows in."

"Well, if it wasn't you, then who was it?"

"I suspect we are never going to know," Bobby D. predicted, with just a little too much satisfaction for my tastes. "Justice was served. That's all that counts. Case closed."

No, it wasn't closed. Not in my book, at least. My curiosity counted, too.

Late that night, we all bundled up in our hats and scarves, ready to trundle out to our cars, sated and ready for sleep. Burly offered to wheel me out to my Porsche, something he had not done in several weeks.

"How about you, buddy?" I said to Killer.

Killer stayed firmly at Helen's feet.

"Uh, Casey," Burly said. "I think maybe Killer may be staying here permanently."

I looked at my dog. My dog looked at me. His basset expression had never looked more mournful. He flopped down at Helen's feet, cast me a baleful look, and whined.

"*Et tu*, Brutus?" I asked him.

He barked his reply. Helen smiled at him.

What could I do? "Take him," I said, with a wave. I gladly gave him away, to tell you the truth. What good is a dog who isn't loyal? I mean, isn't that the point of having one? Besides, with all the tidbits Helen had been sneaking him, Killer's gas had reached epic proportions. A pipeline straight from his ass to a refinery in Texas couldn't handle the overload. I'd let Helen figure out that little habit of Killer's on her own. But most of all, she needed his company.

"Aren't you going to miss Killer?" I asked Burly, after we had watched the others drive away down the country road. The night was so clear that the sky seemed dusted with stars. The air had a winter bite to it. "You're more used to him than I am."

"Actually, Casey," Burly said, looking up at the stars, "I'm staying here with him."

"What?" I didn't get what he meant.

"I'm staying here with Helen and Killer."

"For godsakes," I said. "How much longer does she need bodyguarding? Brookhouse is dead."

"No, Casey," he said in a firmer voice. "I'm staying with Helen. I'm moving in."

"You're moving in with Helen?" I was starting to get the picture. So was my stomach. My Thanksgiving dinner began to churn. He wasn't... was he?

Burly looked at me, and without apology, I have to admit. I sort of admired him for that. "Yes, I'm moving in with Helen."

"And you and me?" I asked. "We're over?"

"In my sense of the word, yes," he said. "I'm not like you in that regard. You can have a million boyfriends and they probably all mean something to you. Me? I just want one person. One person who needs me."

"I need you," I said, and my voice came out much smaller than I expected.

"No you don't, Casey," Burly answered, shaking his head. "You don't need anyone. Or, at least, you think you don't need anyone. And that's what counts."

I let the silence lie between us while I thought that over. "Why didn't you say something before?" I finally asked.

"Like what? No one can tell you anything. It wouldn't have done any good."

I heard his voice as if it came from a distance. I was remembering all the little signs I had seen but not registered: his speaking up for Helen, the glances, his not caring about my flirting with Luke—what a joke to think he might be jealous; he had probably been relieved. It had been balm to his guilty conscience.

"I don't know what to say," I admitted. "It doesn't sound like I have much choice."

"I'm sorry," Burly offered.

"But why?"

The question just sort of slipped out.

"Look," he said, "why do these things ever happen? You and I tried and that's good enough." His voice was kind. Too kind. I felt a couple of tears coming on and was determined that he not see them. I pretended to wipe my nose and rubbed them away.

"There must be a reason," I insisted. "I know you love me."

"But you don't need me," Burly explained. "Helen does. How many women need, truly need, a man stuck in a wheelchair like me? I'm her knight in shining armor. That's what she calls me. My wheelchair is my armor. I'm her knight. We have a lot in common. We're both bound... bound to other people and to certain places."

"And I'm not?" I asked.

He actually laughed. "Casey, you are not bound to anyone or anything. You make me feel free. You make me feel like my life extends way beyond this chair. But Helen makes me feel like it's okay to be me. I don't know how else to explain it."

"Geeze," I said, letting out a long breath. "First the dog, then you."

"I'm sorry," he said again.

"Does Hugo know about this?" I tried to make a joke. It was a bad one. If Hugo really was in love with Helen, it was nothing to joke about. He'd be feeling as bad as me.

"I talked to Hugo," Burly said.

Before you talked to me, a voice inside me noted.

"He's cool. He always knew he was way too young for her, anyway. He knew she'd never even think of returning his feelings."

Touché, I thought. My thing with Luke had bothered him after all.

"I'm sorry," he said again, when I did not answer.

"So am I," I admitted as I opened my car door. I was afraid he would keep apologizing and I didn't want to hear more.

I hopped in my car and drove home.

A little over a week later, Detective Ferrar showed up on my doorstep early one morning, before I left for work. I was back to punching the time clock at our offices in Raleigh, back to being single, back to tailing cheating spouses and tracking down sons who had run off with granny's money. I was bored already. But not bored enough to welcome Ferrar's appearance as a positive development.

"It's you," I managed to say. Not my most enthusiastic of greetings.

"Is that any way to show a stranger how Southern hospitality works?" Ferrar asked. Then he actually smiled.

"Sorry." I opened the door. "Come in. Watch your step. A clothes bomb seems to have exploded in my living room. I can't guarantee you a seat."

"Actually, I was hoping you might come with me." This time his smile did not seem quite so friendly.

I groaned. "Again? Listen, I told you everything I know. I was completely straight with you. I really don't see how—" I stopped, suddenly aware that I was whining, a trait I loathe in other people.

"I'm done questioning you," he said. "This is for something else."

"Something else? I know nothing else that could possibly be of use." I noticed that he had dark circles under his eyes. "You working another case?"

He nodded. "Caught it last night. There's plenty of work for me here, I'm afraid. Even with Brookhouse gone."

"And Carroll, too," I added. "Why does everyone keep forgetting him?"

"Americans have gotten spoiled by movies and television," he said. "They like their villains to be just as tall, dark and handsome as their heroes. Carroll didn't make the cut. His time in the sun faded quickly."

"Speak for yourself," I told him, then grabbed my coat and followed. I could not afford to make an enemy out of the Durham Police Department, not in my line of work. Besides, I owed him.

"Where are we going?" I asked when I spotted the patrol car waiting for us.

"Downtown," he said.

I looked up at him. "You said you were through—"

"I just want you to look at something. Tell me if you recognize it."

On the way, Ferrar told me they had made a little more progress putting the pieces of the puzzle together. Phone records showed that a call had been placed to Helen's house from Lyman Carroll's the night the two men were killed, and we both agreed it was one of them posing as a hospital aide, luring me away from the farmhouse long enough for them to snatch Helen. And it had been Brookhouse who'd called my car in to have it towed the night they shot Luke in Duke Gardens. Hearing this, I was forced to acknowledge that the two men might have been watching me watch them the entire night I thought I was alone. And Luke, I figured, had come to my apartment early to wait for our midnight meeting. He'd seen me come home for my breaking-and-entering tools, then followed me back to campus and spotted the two men following me.

I didn't offer this theory to Ferrar, either. And when I asked him if Candace Goodnight had been found yet, he just shook his head no. I offered the hope that maybe she had fled the country and was living with some primitive civilization, fearful Brookhouse might come after her. Ferrar looked at me like I was daft.

After that, we rode in silence to police headquarters and Ferrar took me up to his tiny office. It was barely big enough for a desk, two chairs and a file drawer—but it had a door and walls that actually went all the way up to the ceiling, and that was an increasing luxury in all offices these days.

"Wait here," he told me. "I'll be back in a minute."

I waited, looking around his office. There was a photo of Ferrar with a drop-dead gorgeous Latina and two small children. His wife looked younger than him by at least ten years. She had long black hair, huge dark eyes, a round face and flawless skin. The kids were perfectly matched: one pretty little girl with a pixie face and a taller boy with somber eyes and freckles sprinkled across his nose. Both had dark hair and looked like their mother, although, if you picked up the photo and looked closer, you could definitely see traces of Ferrar's high cheekbones lurking beneath their baby fat.

"My family," Ferrar explained as he reentered his office. He held a plastic evidence envelope and a long leather bag. A shotgun case.

"Your family is beautiful," I said obediently as I carefully restored the photo to its place of honor. "Do you get to see them much?"

"I make sure that I do," he answered, touching his wife's face with the tip of a finger. She was his good luck talisman, his antidote against the hate he saw in all its dying color each day, I realized. I envied them their contentment.

"Take a look at this," Ferrar said, taking a handgun from an evidence bag. "Ever see this before?"

"If you're asking me if I have ever seen a Colt Python, the answer is yes," I admitted. "But this one? Not to my knowledge."

This last remark was a patent lie. I had seen that particular gun plenty of times, though not when I was searching the bottom of the pond at Duke Gardens for it. Chalk one up for the good guys. They had found my gun. I'd need a new one eventually. Maybe. If I ever decided to carry one again. I still washed my hands ten times a day, imagining Luke's blood on them.

"Okay," Ferrar said, seemingly unconcerned. "It's this I'm most interested in." He placed the leather shotgun case on his desk.

"What's that?" I asked.

"This is the key to the entire puzzle," Ferrar said. I knew instantly what puzzle he meant. He unzipped the case and removed a shotgun from inside it. He laid the gun across his desk, facing me, the handle displayed so that I could easily inspect the intricate carving of flowers that decorated an ivory inlay panel placed in the center of the triangular stock. The part that had been hidden by Carroll's body in death.

I was stunned to see it. The buzzing of a thousand bees started in my ears. I turned away so he could not see my face.

"It's the shotgun we found on Carroll," Ferrar explained. He paused. "Recognize it?"

I shook my head. I knew he was staring at me, but I couldn't stop myself from tracing the lilies carved into the ivory. I remembered them so well from my days as a young girl, playing on my grandfather's porch. He would carefully unload the shotgun, double-checking it for safety, then let me play with it for the afternoon. I'd pretend to be a hunter, or Davy Crockett, or Daniel Boone, or anyone who was allowed to lift the long barrel to eye level and sight. I had loved my grandfather's shotgun.

And now it was gone forever, thanks to me.

"Do you know that gun?" Ferrar asked.

I shook my head. "No. But it's a beautiful piece. An Ithaca. From the thirties, it looks like. Will it ever be put up for auction?"

"No way. This case will stay open. Forever, if it has to. And this shotgun will stay with it, as evidence."

It all made sense to me now. My grandfather was supposed to come up for Thanksgiving; Burly must have told him everything when they first talked by phone. And whether or not my grandfather had been part of the plan to kill Brookhouse and Carroll from the start or simply arrived at the right time, he had showed up at Helen's the night before Thanksgiving, right after I had been there and found her missing. Burly had ridden with my grandfather as they chased after me, first to Carroll's house where my grandfather had found the note and been glimpsed by the neighbor, and later on to the psychopathology building. Only when they'd had a good enough head start had Burly really called the cops and sent them to Carroll's house.

But my grandfather would never break the law.

Unless my life was in danger, I realized. And it had been. Plus, he had heard Brookhouse and Carroll laughing about their deeds while I sat bound and gagged, the men bragging of how they would get away with it all.

That would be enough, I knew; that would be enough to cause my grandfather to kill.

I could have asked Helen's mother if my grandfather had been to the farmhouse—but Miranda was dead. Only Burly knew. And I had a feeling he would never tell.

My mind refused to let it alone. Would my grandfather have killed two men like that? To save me: yes. Could he have done it? Without a doubt. He could shoot through a plate of glass and bring a man down with his eyes closed. He could do it confidently, even with me standing right beside the victim. And he'd have been strong enough to carry Helen to safety.

But why take Helen back to the house and not to a hospital?

I knew the answer to that one, too. I remembered once, when I was a girl of about twelve, finding an injured fawn. It was lying on the edge of a clearing with one of its legs dangling at an odd angle from the knee. I picked it up and carried it home, begging my grandfather to help. He knelt beside the creature, stroking its body to calm it, examining the broken leg. He was shaking his head the entire time, half at the probability the fawn would never survive, and half at the naive optimism of a twelve-year-old girl.

"Creatures of the forest belong in the forest," he explained to me. "I can bind the leg to help the fawn walk again. But we can't keep him here with us, or he'll never fit in with his own kind again. He belongs in the woods. It's cruel to take living things away from where they feel safe. Do you understand what I mean?"

I had nodded my solemn assent; I'd have agreed to anything as long as my grandfather helped the deer. He whittled two splints to fit the tiny leg and bound them in place with strips of an old pillowcase until the leg was sturdy and well-protected.

"He'll have to learn how to stand back up on his feet all by himself," he warned me. "There's only so much you can do for other creatures. We all have things we have to learn to do on our own. Standing up for ourselves is one of them."

He had gathered the fawn in his arms. It didn't struggle like it had when I carried it; my grandfather always had a calming effect on animals. We marched through the woods, back to the clearing where I had first found the poor thing. We placed him carefully near the boulder where I had discovered him. That was probably where he tumbled and injured his leg in the first place. I petted the creature while my grandfather carefully inspected the woods around us. The fawn had fur as soft as velvet, though fleas scurried across the brown pelt.

"The mother is nearby," my grandfather announced, indicating a patch of fallen leaves that had been flattened by a body lying in slumber. "The best thing to do is leave the fawn here. We've brought it back home. That's enough."

And so we left the deer in the woods. I never saw it again. I often wondered if it had survived. I think that maybe it did.

I like to imagine it did.

"What are you thinking about?" Ferrar asked, interrupting my memories. "You recognize the shotgun, don't you?"

"No," I said firmly, shaking my head. "It's just a beautifully made weapon is all. Look at the care someone has put into it. The handle has been sanded and oiled, the barrel's immaculate. Someone must have loved it very much."

"I know two guys who probably wouldn't appreciate its beauty. If they were still alive, that is."

I stared at Ferrar. "You really think this world would be a better place if Carroll and Brookhouse were still alive?"

He shook his head. "No. But I do think the world would be a better place if people would just let the system do what it's supposed to do. More often than not, it works."

I shook my head. I couldn't agree. I didn't believe in playing god, but I also knew it wasn't true that the system usually came through. Not anymore, it didn't. If the system worked the way it was supposed to, I'd know it. Because I'd be out of business.

"What?" Ferrar asked me. "What are you thinking?"

"I was just thinking that what goes around, comes around," I said. "But that, sometimes, it's good to help it along a little."

# # #

ABOUT THE AUTHOR

Katy Munger is the author of fourteen novels, writing under her real name as well as her pseudonyms, Chaz McGee and Gallagher Gray. She was born in Honolulu, Hawaii, raised in North Carolina, lived for a number of years in New York City and now calls North Carolina home. She is a former book reviewer for *The Washington Post*, a co-founder of Thalia Press and an original author of Thalia Press Author's Co-op, which seeks to connect established writers with new e-book audiences. All of her work is also available in e-book format. You can learn more about the author and her work at www.katymunger.com.

CPSIA information can be obtained at www.ICGtesting.com
Printed in the USA
LVOW11s1214181113

361770LV00001B/88/P